# THE BLOOD YEARS

## ALSO BY ELANA K. ARNOLD

*Damsel*

*Red Hood*

*What Girls Are Made Of*

*Infandous*

# THE
# BLOOD
# YEARS

ELANA K. ARNOLD

BALZER + BRAY
*An Imprint of* HarperCollins*Publishers*

Balzer + Bray is an imprint of HarperCollins Publishers.

The Blood Years
Copyright © 2023 by Elana K. Arnold
For information address HarperCollins Children's Books, a division of Harper-
Collins Publishers, 195 Broadway, New York, NY 10007.
www.epicreads.com

Library of Congress Cataloging-in-Publication Data
[TK]
Library of Congress Control Number:
ISBN 978-0-06-299085-3

Typography by Jenna Stempel-Lobell
23 24 25 26 27  LBC  5 4 3 2 1

First Edition

For my grandmother, Frieda Kuczynski (née Teitler).
I've done my best to bear witness, with love.

# TABLE OF CONTENTS

# FOREWORD

My nana was my benefactress in every way: she sang me to sleep and read me bedtime stories; she financed horseback riding lessons; she filled my bedroom at her house with secondhand Barbie dolls and all the books I could read; she brought me gilded bowls of sweating grapes as I read those books on the living room floor.

Nana had an interesting accent. Instead of "three," she said "tree," finding "th" to be an impossible sound, a fact I found both hilarious and endlessly charming. She spoke beautiful English as well as German, Romanian, French, Russian, Yiddish, and a little bit of Polish.

Her closets were full of garage-sale clothes and boxes of photographs, and her bookshelves were packed with titles of every kind—poetry and mystery novels and philosophy, thrillers and psychology and *Everything You Want to Know About Sex: But Were Afraid to Ask* and *Mein Kampf.* Nana wanted to know and understand everything, the beautiful and the terrible.

I always knew that both of my grandparents had survived the Holocaust—my grandfather, in Poland, and my grandmother, in Romania. They met and married after the war. I learned about concentration camps in school, and when I asked my nana if she'd been imprisoned, she said, "Not exactly." What I didn't understand for many years was that the experience of Jews (and Roma and disabled and gay people) in Romania during World War II was different from the stories made popular in American literature, media, and history books. There were no concentrations camps in Romania—but that absolutely didn't mean that there was no Holocaust.

It wasn't until after I published my first novel that Nana filled in some of the gaps in the war stories I'd heard. Hearing what she finally shared, I understood why. When I was young, she'd edited out the worst of things to spare me from them. Near the end of her life, she trusted me with much more of it—though I'll bet, knowing her, that even then she held back some of her most painful remembrances as an act of love. And she hoped that someday I could use her experiences in a book. "Just name the character Frederieke," she told me. "I've always liked that name."

*The Blood Years* is the story of my nana's teenage years in Czernowitz, Romania, before and during World War II. It's my attempt to do with my nana's gift of stories what I try to do with all my work—to transform pain into art, to embrace ambiguity, and to find beauty even in the ugliest of moments.


With love,

Elana K. Arnold

# A BRIEF HISTORY OF CZERNOWITZ

1778–1918: Czernowitz is part of the Austro-Hungarian Empire and a relative bastion of safety and tolerance for Jews, who make up close to 40 percent of its population.

1918: With the end of World War I, the Austro-Hungarian Empire is broken and Czernowitz comes under Romanian rule (and is renamed Cernăuți, though its Jewish residents cling to its former name and all it symbolized).

1927: The Iron Guard political party of Romania is formed. Purposefully antisemitic, the group promotes the idea that Jews, along with atheists, homosexuals, and others, are undermining society.

December 1937: The antisemitic Goga-Cuza cabinet is formed in Romania, advocating for an alliance with the Third Reich.

January 22, 1938: Jews lose status as citizens.

September 1, 1939: World War II begins; Romania declares neutrality.

3

May 1940: Romania joins the Axis.

September 1940: Soviet troops occupy the city and hold it for a year, renaming it Chernovtsy.

1941: Romania enters World War II, on the Germans' side and against the Soviet Union; Romanian troops, along with Nazi soldiers, occupy Czernowitz as the Soviets flee.

August 23, 1944: Romania switches allegiances to align with the Allies and the Soviets and declares war on Germany; Czernowitz is re-occupied by the Soviet Army.

# PART I
# ASTRA AND HER LOVER

Fall 1939–Spring 1940

# ONE

## PIGEONS AND PROMISES

When we were very young, Astra and I made a pact.

I was six; Astra, not quite ten. It was a sultry, miserable summer day. Father was missing—again—and Mama was in bed—still. Whenever Father disappeared, Mama disappeared, too. Not physically, but in every way that mattered.

Though it was nearly dusk, I was still wearing the nightgown I'd woken up in. I'd been wearing it for three days, as there was no one to make me change out of it. I remember how it stuck to my back like a second skin. Astra skulked around the kitchen, looking for something to eat.

"Come on," she finally said, taking the last of the jam from the icebox, the last of the bread from the breadbox, and heading to the stairwell.

I followed her, all the way to the roof of our apartment building. It was quiet up there. Still hot, but with a whisper of breeze, a promise that things would be better, soon, if we waited. We squatted side by side and took turns dipping hunks of bread into the jam jar. Down below and all around was Czernowitz. Our city. I saw people moving about, horses pulling wagons, the occasional automobile. The colorful hats the ladies wore were just small scraps of color from up here. Far away was the green metal cap of the train station, as pretty as any of the ladies' hats.

Father was out there, somewhere.

"Do you think he's coming back?" I asked.

Astra shrugged. "He always does."

Yes, I wanted to say, but he'd never been gone *this* long. Long enough for the kitchen to grow entirely bare. Long enough for Mama to forget she had daughters.

On the roof, pigeons landed, hopeful and hungry.

"It's so *stupid*," Astra said, "how men come and go, and women have to just sit around and wait for them." She pointed at me with her scrap of bread, its tip bloodred with jam. "Listen, Rieke," she said. "Do me a favor, will you? Never, ever fall in love. It'll just make a mess of things."

I didn't really know what that meant—to fall in love. It didn't sound like something you did or didn't do on purpose. Not like climbing, or jumping; those were things you chose, things you did. *Falling*, in my experience, was something that just happened, whether you liked it or not. I raised my shoulders, dropped them.

Astra turned to the city. "I'll tell you one thing, Rieke—*I'll* never fall in love. And I'm never getting married. You can count on that."

I believed her. My sister was the sort of person who did the things she said she was going to do. She'd said she was going to be the youngest girl in her dance studio to go up en pointe, and she had been, when she turned nine. She'd said she was going to read every book in the city library, and she was working on it, devouring three or four books each week. If Astra said she wasn't going to get married, then that was that. It was good news to me; it meant that no one would come between us. That I could keep her, always.

Around us, the pigeons grew thicker, bobbing their heads and begging. I tore them a strip of bread.

"If you feed them, they'll only want more," Astra said, watching me. "There are too many of them, and they're too hungry. You'll never satisfy them all, so you might as well keep the bread and satisfy yourself."

It was good advice. I nibbled at my piece of bread, avoided eye contact with the pigeons. Ultimately, though, I couldn't resist. When I thought Astra wasn't looking, I tossed them the last of my bread. Four or five of them descended upon it, beating their wings and racing to eat it up. Of course, Astra saw.

Sometimes my sister was cold with me, as far away as Father and Mama. Sometimes she was mean as a snake, calling me names and pinching me. I never knew who Astra would be, on any given day, at any given moment. But sometimes—like this time, when she tore her remaining bread into two pieces and offered me one—Astra was the person who took care of me. Who was there, when everything else had gone wrong.

Ignoring the pigeons, I shoved her bread gift into my mouth. "I'm never getting married, either," I promised. "I'll never fall in love." And then we got up, and we stomped our feet at the pigeons and waved our arms and yelled, and all of them, the great gray mass of them, startled and hopped and took flight, and Astra threw her arm around my shoulders and we laughed, loud as kings.

I was thinking about pigeons when Father returned the very next day. He even brought gifts: a bracelet for Mama, earrings for Astra, and a golden locket for me.

Mama got out of bed. Her face, which had been slack for days, burst open like a shining star. She kissed his cheeks, his eyes, his mouth, she smoothed his mustache and brushed back the curl that fell across his brow, and she begged him not to leave again.

He said what he always said: "Stupid woman. Of course, I came back. I always come back, don't I?" He made no mention of the bare cabinets, our dirty faces, the fact that we'd resorted to using newspaper for toilet tissue.

Behind them, Astra looked at me as if to say: *See what I mean?* And though I didn't, not really, I nodded.

This is what I did know: it was *them*—Father and Mama—and *us*—Astra and me.

Of course, Father disappeared again, not a week later and without leaving us a penny. Mama disappeared into her bed again, the food ran out again, and this time, Astra went to a neighbor's door and asked them to call Mama's father. Our opa.

When he arrived, Opa was dressed just as he always was, in spite of the heat: wool trousers and a long jacket, a tall hat which he drew off to reveal his salt-and-pepper hair, his neat round skullcap. Here he was, to save us.

"My girl, my girl," he said. He hung up his hat and swung me into his arms. He carried me through our apartment—bare cupboards; the empty, mildewing icebox; dishes, forgotten, days old and beginning to mold, stacked in the kitchen sink.

He peered into our parents' bedroom and shook his head at Mama, curled in a ball on Father's side of the bed.

Then we went into the room Astra and I shared. He put me down and went to my sister, who sat waiting on her bed with a book. He kissed her head and then said, "Girls, pack your things. A suitcase each for now, I'll return for the rest tomorrow. Come now, be quick about it and we'll be home in time for supper."

10

*Supper*—my mouth flooded with saliva. I practically ran to the bureau to gather my clothes; Astra did, too.

Opa went to Mama. The walls were thin, and we heard:

"Anna, enough with this. You and the girls will come home with me. Get up. Pack a suitcase. Enough is enough."

Voice muffled, as if her face was turned into a pillow: "I need some money, only, to tide us over until Alfred comes home."

Astra and I froze, fists full of clothing.

I squeezed shut my eyes and silently begged, *Please*.

Please, I meant, please let us go to Opa's apartment, where it was warm, where we didn't have to tiptoe past Mama's closed door, where his hired girl, Milka, would fix us something delicious.

"Nonsense." That one word set Astra and me back in motion. "You, I suppose, are a grown woman, Anna, and I can't make you come with me, but I won't leave the girls here. Half-starved, unwashed . . . you should be ashamed."

There was a long pause, a silence, and Astra and I shared a glance.

Finally, Mama spoke, and this time her voice was clear and rang like a bell. "You don't know what it's like. You don't know what it means to have a husband who disappears, who gambles away our grocery money, who whores around, who—"

"Enough! He was a louse when you married him, and he's a louse, still. Now, pack a bag, and make it quick. Your daughters are hungry, and I'll see them fed before dark."

And then Opa's shoes pounding across the wooden floorboards, a firm *click* as he closed Mama's bedroom door.

A moment later, his head peeked into our room, and when he spoke, his tone was gentle. "Are you chickens almost ready?"

When we left the flat ten minutes later, it was alongside Mama, whose eyes were puffy and red, but who had combed her hair.

That night, after a good dinner and a good bath—Astra washed my hair for me—she and I were tucked into bed. It was incredible, I thought, how quickly things could change. How we could go from unwashed and hungry to clean and full, just with Opa's knock on our door . . . just with Astra deciding to make it happen.

They were the two I could count on. Astra, and Opa.

I heard the even, deep breaths that meant Astra had fallen to sleep. I saw Opa's shadow as he looked in to make sure we were safe and sound. I pulled the blanket up to my chin, and whispered my promise, again: "I won't fall in love. I won't ever get married. And," I added, whispering even more quietly, just to myself, "I'm never leaving Opa's apartment—never, ever again."

And why am I remembering this now, today? It's because of how Astra comes into dance class—late—and because of the look she has upon her face. I can't place the expression, but I know I've seen it, somewhere, before.

I'm in the dressing room with the other girls. Penny Meyers is mooning over herself in the mirror, like usual. Didi Liebermann is trying to interest Connie Schneider in some piece of gossip, and Connie's nodding as if she's listening while stitching up a hole in her tunic. Ruth is helping one of the younger girls untangle a hair ribbon. Esther Glassman, my closest friend, is nose-deep in one of her film magazines, oblivious to everything. Then, Astra rushes in, pink-cheeked from the cold. She's unstringing her scarf and unbuttoning her coat as she crosses to her spot nearest to the mirror with the good lights—even though she's late, none of the other girls has thought about taking it. She throws her coat carelessly onto the bench, steps on the backs of her shoes, one and then the other, kicking them out of the way as she yanks down her woolens and starts shimmying into her black practice tunic.

One of her plain brown Oxfords lands upright, half under the dressing table. But the other falls on its side; I can see its insole, smooth and bright from wear. My fingers twitch with the impulse to pick it up and set it beside the other, to tuck them safely side by side.

But instead, I ask, "Where were you? I waited as long as I could."

Four days a week—Monday, Tuesday, Thursday, and Friday—I wait out front of school for Astra, whose classes run longer than mine, and then we walk together to Madame Lucia's studio. When it's very cold, which it will be soon as it's already the beginning of November, I wait in the vestibule, but I prefer to stand outside. Today, Friday, I waited close to an hour, stomping my feet and blowing on my hands to keep them warm, until my watch told me I had no more time to spare. Then I rushed here, alone. Maybe Astra had gone home sick, I told myself, even though it was unlikely. Of the two of us, I'm the one who catches each cold, who has an earache every year at Purim.

"Get my buttons, will you?" Astra turns her back to me, lifts her dark curtain of hair. I smell the sweet rose of her shampoo as I slip the pearlescent buttons from their catches, each a little noose.

It's then I notice that she's not wearing her school uniform. When we left this morning, Astra had been in her brown woolen school jumper and white cotton blouse, identical to mine. "What are you wearing? When did you change?"

"Never mind, just hurry! You're going to make me late."

"*I'm* going to make *you* late?"

She ignores me. "Ruth," she says. "Do you have an extra hairnet?"

13

Ruth always has enough to share and is always glad to do so. She takes one from the side pocket of her bag and sets it on the counter.

"Thanks," Astra says, just as I free the final button. She lets her blouse fall forward and yanks down her skirt. The tunic goes up over her shoulders, and now we're dressed the same, though the tunics certainly fit us differently. Astra will be seventeen in June; she's grown four inches in the last year, and she's filling out in other ways, too.

"Where were you?" Ruth winds her own chestnut hair into a bun at the nape of her neck, ensnares it in a net.

Astra grins, slyly.

*"No,"* says Ruth.

Astra doesn't answer. She smiles to her reflection as she arranges her hair, catches my gaze in the mirror, and then leans into Ruth to whisper something. Ruth gasps, clasps her hand across her mouth, laughs.

From the studio, I hear Conrad warming up on the piano, the gentle waves of the scales our cue to get out to the floor. Even though Astra arrived late, she's somehow the first through the door, soft slippers on her feet, pointe shoes tied together by their ribbons and tossed across her shoulder. Several of the other girls have taken to mimicking her, carrying their pointe shoes this way, too. I won't do it. I put mine toe-to-heel and wrap the ribbons around them tightly, binding them together.

I'm one of the last girls to go through to the studio. Just as I'm about to push open the door, I see Esther, still in her street clothes, hunched over the magazine in the corner. "Esther," I say, "you're going to get in so much trouble!"

She looks up as if I've shocked her into consciousness. Her glasses have slipped down to the very tip of her nose; through the lenses, her eyes are magnified into huge, gold-flecked discs. They are exactly the same color as

14

her brother's, though Conrad's aren't trapped behind lenses.

"Oh!" She stumbles up, closes her magazine, and fumbles for the zipper on her skirt. "Madame Lucia is going to murder me."

"I'll tell her you're almost ready, but hurry."

She nods and sets her glasses on the bench, fumbles blindly for her tunic. I shake my head and go through to the studio.

Madame Lucia isn't here yet, so there's a chance Esther still might avoid her wrath. Conrad's head comes up when he hears me entering. He looks at me questioningly, clearly wondering where his sister is. I shake my head, raise my shoulders slightly. Conrad doesn't need any further explanation; he knows what a featherhead Esther is.

Astra has her left leg up on the barre and she's folded completely in half, like a billfold snapped shut. There's no space at all between her chest and her thigh; her arm is stretched to her foot, gorgeously pointed and turned out just so, even in this casual stretch. Ruth is Astra's mirror twin, her right leg up on the same barre, folded just as flat. Their faces are tilted toward each other, and they share secrets as they stretch. They remind me of a postcard I once saw, a picture of two birds—flamingos, they were called. Long necks, long legs, ludicrously pink.

There's that look on Astra's face, again. Suddenly I'm a child on the roof. If she's a graceful flamingo, I am a pigeon, begging for scraps. The answer to my earlier question, about where I've seen her expression before, scratches at my brain. I can feel that it's about to come to me when suddenly—*bang, bang, bang!* Madame Lucia's stick against the hardwood floor.

She's beside Conrad at the piano, ash-blond hair raked into its customary bun, thin lips pressed tight, body held with rigid grace, chin up, always up. She's parting her lips to speak when Esther rushes in, stumbling

15

over her feet as she hastens to the barre. Madame Lucia presses closed her eyes. Her nostrils flare as she takes a deep, slow breath, as if to control herself. She practically vibrates with annoyance.

At the head of her stick, her fingers clench white, then relax. She opens her eyes and lets out the breath. Points the stick at Conrad. "Begin," she orders, and so we do.

Then, for an hour at the barre, there's no time to think. Only to move. Conrad sets the tempo for our shared work, Madame Lucia's stick becomes our metronome.

One thing I love about dance is that the only thing that separates us is ability. We all wear the same black tunics; we all do the same movements, newest student through most experienced. Here, it doesn't matter who's Jewish and who's not, the way it does outside of these walls. In school, for instance—when I was younger and attended public school, the teachers did their best to make girls like Esther and me feel that we didn't belong among the Christian girls. If I failed at something, it was proof I was a waste of a seat. If I excelled, I was being sly and a show-off.

Now, we aren't even allowed in public schools anymore.

As my cold, tight muscles warm and loosen, I can't help but steal glances at my sister. The rest of us go through the exercises, some of us well, like Ruth, others, like Esther, haltingly. But Astra—she floats. Even just at barre work, even in the simplest plié, Astra can't help but perform. Each movement of her arm seems to say: *Look. Here I am. You're welcome.*

She drives me absolutely mad. But oh, how proud I am to be her sister.

It's when we're changing from slippers into pointe shoes for floor work that it hits me, where I've seen that look on Astra's face. It was the same as on *Mama's* face, when Father came home, and kissed her.

16

# TWO

## THE WAY THINGS ARE

Before we moved in with Opa, Astra was the one person I could count on. She ran hot and cold, sure, but that didn't mean she didn't love me. After Opa rescued us from our dank apartment, I had two people I could trust. At home, Opa made sure there was food on the table and that we went to bed on time, whether or not Mama was having one of her headaches, whether or not she joined us to eat or to help us get ready for bed. And everywhere else, there was Astra. At school, when Didi Liebermann made me cry by teasing me about how Father had abandoned us, Astra cut her down in front of everyone by saying, "We might not know *where* our father is, but at least we know *who* he is." That shut Didi up.

On the street, if a boy looks at me in a way Astra doesn't like, she'll screw up her beautiful face into an ugly mask and spit in his direction.

She might be hard on me from time to time, but that's just the way Astra is. Sometimes, she gets jealous if my attention goes away from her. Once, when I was about ten years old, I started to get really into pressing flowers. It was neat to me, the way you could preserve them, and for a little while it was all I talked about—the interesting specimen I'd found at the entrance to the Volksgarten, a sort of bluebell I'd never seen before; the variety of posies that were planted in front of our school. Three times a day I checked on the delicate blossoms I'd sandwiched between newsprint and tucked into the heaviest book I could find (other than Opa's Bible, which he suggested maybe we should leave just to God). I worried about fungus over dinner, chatted on the way to school about how I might display the flowers once they were dry—until one morning when I went to see how things were progressing, only to find the book stripped of the flowers and returned to the shelf. The newsprint, crumpled, was shoved carelessly into the rubbish bin; the flowers were torn.

I was upset, of course. The flowers were something I cared about. But Astra made it up to me; after the incident with the flowers, she started taking more of an interest in my dancing, giving me tips after class and helping me with extra calisthenics on the weekends, holding my feet as I did sit-ups on our bedroom floor. A few dried flowers in exchange for an extra measure of my sister's attention was a good trade, in my opinion, even if I did quietly mourn the loss of my hobby.

Opa likes to say that everything is cyclical, and I've seen that to be true with Astra; she might spin away, off to other interests or other friends, but she always spins back in, to me. Is it *fair* that Astra can have her separate interests and secrets, but I cannot? No, of course it isn't. But it's the way things are with Astra and, for better or worse, she's my favorite person in the world.

I try to keep all of this in mind as I get dressed after dance class. Astra's waiting for me just inside the door to the street; I've dressed as fast as I could, but one of my stockings eluded me. I found it, finally, shoved in the pocket of my coat. She's impatient, foot tapping, as if I didn't spend an

18

hour of my afternoon waiting for *her* to appear after school.

"*There* you are." She opens the door and gestures, the grand sweep of her arm implying that I'm the lollygagger and she's just my humble servant. I could say something smart, but then we're on the street, walking side by side; she slips her arm into the crook of mine, our steps fall into sync, and I'm glad I didn't.

Dance class ends early on Fridays because even though Madame Lucia isn't Jewish, about a third of her students are. It's late fall, and though it's only ten minutes past four o'clock, the sun will be gone within the hour. Astra and I go together up the Herrengasse, toward home. Next door to the dance studio is the milliner's shop, and Miss Rosen is just coming out to lock up for the evening. She'll wait for Madame Lucia to join her and then the two of them will go home to the apartment they rent together as housemates.

She nods to us. "Good evening, girls," she says, and we respond, together, "Good evening."

Today she's wearing a thick fur cap, the first time she's donned it this year. It means the cold weather is here to stay, and that soon there will be snow. You can set the seasons by Miss Rosen's choice of hat, and everyone knows it. Her window display is shadowed now, but I can make out the shapes of disembodied mannequin heads, turned this way and that, each with its own hat, all crafted by Miss Rosen's clever hands.

The peanut vendor is on the corner with his cart, and maybe by way of apologizing to me, Astra pulls out a coin to buy us some. He takes a square paper from his stack, rolls its end to make a cone, and fills a metal scoop with hot, fragrant peanuts, pouring them expertly into the cone, not one peanut lost. He hands it to Astra and she thanks him in Ruthenian. As soon as he's pocketed the coin, he begins to close his cart for the day; he's

19

got a way to travel to get home to his village, and though he looks smart in his tall black boots, his white linen shirt, and colorful, embroidered vest, he really should have brought a warmer coat.

The peanuts are delicious—so hot that I have to hold them loose in my mouth for a moment before I can bite them open, salty and just a bit sweet.

This walk is almost as familiar to me as the route from our shared bedroom to Opa's kitchen, so many times have I walked it. When I was eight and Opa first signed me up for dance, Astra hadn't been happy about it—dance was *hers*, she complained. It stung, that she didn't want me there. "Anyway, there's no point in her joining *now*," she argued. "She's too old to be any good."

Still, Opa signed me up, and now, five years later, this walk home is my favorite part of the day, because even as Astra and I have gotten busier with school and dance and friends, this walk has remained just the two of us, together. Our arms are still linked; I tighten my elbow to squeeze her arm, and she squeezes mine in return.

I toss another handful of peanuts into my mouth. They taste just the same as peanuts have always tasted, even though the street we bought them on looks a little different lately. A few months ago, Germany and the Soviets signed a nonaggression pact—basically agreeing to stay out of each other's way, I guess. And then on the first of September—just two weeks before I turned thirteen—Hitler invaded our neighbor Poland. Great Britain and France declared war on Germany in retaliation, and some Jewish families here in town have decided that they want to move away.

Back and forth—it's like a dance, a scary one. Things get two steps worse and then one step better. There was an awful time a couple of years ago when two politicians, Octavian Goga and Alexandru Cuza, took over the government and promised to solve "the Jewish problem." That phrase sends a cold shiver up my spine every time I hear it. A lot of people were hurt, and restrictions were put into place having to do with citizenship and what sorts of jobs Jews were allowed to have; that was when Astra and I had to change from public school to private because Jewish kids weren't allowed anymore. But then, too, what Opa says about cycles seemed to be true. After just a couple of months, Goga and Cuza were forced to step down. Not everything went back to normal—all the restrictions stayed in place—but at least things stopped getting worse, unlike in Germany. We've heard about how they're incarcerating and deporting their Jewish residents and the terrible looting and destruction of Jewish-owned businesses, synagogues, even graveyards. Lots of people in Czernowitz say we should count ourselves lucky that we live here, where things are mostly normal.

And Opa insists that things will settle again, the way they always have before. "You girls just concentrate on your studies and dance and leave politics to the adults," he tells us. Mostly I'm glad to obey. If Opa says things will be all right, I believe him. He's the wisest person I know, after all.

Some of the shops on the Herrengasse have recently closed: the fishmonger's storefront is vacant and so is the cobbler's shop, three doors down. Their blacked-out windows are like teeth missing from a smile. Still, the delicatessen, the butcher, the dairy shop are all where they should be, windows loaded with delights, and so I shake more peanuts into my mouth and concentrate on what's in front of me rather than what's gone away, the way Opa is always telling me to do.

Astra's earlier expression returns unbidden to my mind. I want to ask her about it, and about why she wasn't at school this afternoon. Where she'd gone. Who she'd been with.

I *want* to ask, but also I sort of *don't* want to. Because I don't think I'll like the answers.

Wherever she was—whatever she was doing—has put my sister in a high mood; she walks quickly, and she whistles as we go, and though she bought the peanuts for us to share, she only eats a few, her mind elsewhere.

Just on this simple walk home from dance, you can see the city's complex layers, if you know how to look . . . and how to listen. As long as a Romanian officer isn't present to overhear, we call the city by her maiden name, Czernowitz, rather than Cernăuţi, the name Romanians thrust upon her when they took her from Austria after the Great War. The street signs are in Romanian, but everyone I know still uses the German names. Ruthenian must be spoken to the vendors who come into the city to sell fruits and vegetables or to work in domestic service. You hear Ukrainian, here and there; German in the homes of those of us with Austrian roots, Jews and Christians alike; Hebrew in the synagogue when Opa drags us along for the high holidays; and, in Jewish-owned shops, Yiddish.

Ours is a great and varied city, known far and wide as "Little Vienna" because of all the universities, the emphasis on arts and culture. Outside the city limits, in the countryside and in other, less-educated towns, it's true that there's antisemitic violence, coming and going like waves lapping the shore. It's terrible, but it's the way things have always been, and Opa says that for a Jew, there's no better place in Eastern Europe than Czernowitz. Still, over the past few years, the people who've left have one thing in common: they're all Jewish.

We arrive to our building and, like always, I feel a rush of fondness for it. It's nothing fancy, in fact it looks just about the same as most of the apartment buildings: four stories tall, made of large gray blocks, a small front staircase, five steps up to the door. But of course, it's not the building

22

I'm so fond of; it's what's inside.

On the second floor—our floor—we nearly crash into Mr. Oppenheim as he comes out of his apartment, holding a sack of rubbish.

"Good evening." Astra nods at Mr. Oppenheim, who nods in reply, his tight black mustache twitching. He's a small man who's dwarfed by his expansive wife—a shelf of a bosom, mouth wide as a trout's. The bag he carries stinks of fish, and I know why. Mrs. Oppenheim treats her cat, an overweight Persian named Mitzi, as if it is her human child. Maybe that's ungenerous of me to even think, but then, I'm still bitter over the fact that Opa's Turkish rug lives in their apartment rather than ours. Mrs. Oppenheim always coveted the rug, so when Opa's jewelry and repair business began to dry up when Goga and Cuza took power, her offer to buy it didn't feel like much of a favor. I picture our rug on their floor—its vibrant swirls of reds and blues covered in cat hair, that awful thing sharpening its claws on the thick, soft wool.

At our door, I touch the mezuzah out of habit and affection rather than a sense of devotion, and then we're inside. I was hoping the lights would be on, the fire built up, maybe even dinner on the table—the way things can be when Mama has had a good day—but instead we cross the threshold to find the front room as dark as the stairwell.

Opa will be home any minute, and he can't come home to shadows. I switch on a table lamp and ask Astra, "Do you want to start dinner or deal with Mama?"

Maybe she doesn't hear me, lost in her thoughts as she seems to be, because rather than going to the kitchen or Mama's room, Astra heads straight to the bathroom and closes the door behind her. *Maybe* she didn't hear . . . but more likely, she's just ignoring me.

I groan, let my bag thump to the floor. Still cold, I leave on my coat,

23

but I unbutton it. In the kitchen I start the kettle so at least there will be something hot for Opa to drink. The front door opens just as the kettle begins to scream.

I know exactly how long it will take Opa to get from the entryway to the kitchen: he'll kiss his fingers and touch the mezuzah; he'll take off his hat; he'll unbutton his coat, pull his glasses from his face, and wipe them on the edge of his vest. Glasses back on, he'll pat all the pockets of his coat, the way he always does. I love the routine of it, the predictability. Astra says it's boring, how much I like things to stay the same. Opa says it's because things were so unsettled when I was young that I like them so settled now, and that Astra shouldn't tease me about it. But teasing me is one of Astra's greatest joys in life.

Right on cue, I hear Opa: "Okay," he says. "Okay."

And then the coat will come off, to be hung on its hook in the front closet, right next to where I'll hang mine. And then—yes, here he comes to join me in the kitchen, just as I'm pouring boiling water into the teapot, a loaf of challah tucked under his arm.

"My girl," he says. He sets the bread on the table and pushes loose hair from my cheek, his palm rough and warm.

"Hi, Opa."

Droplets glisten in his long beard, like diamonds; the weather is starting. He wipes his hand down his beard, and the droplets disappear. "The women?" he asks.

I tip my head at the hallway, the closed doors. This is one thing I wish *would* change: my mother and her headaches, her depression. "Should I start dinner? We have eggs, some peppers . . . I could make an omelet."

"Better not." Opa picks up the cup of tea to warm his hands. "I'll get together some herring and cold cuts for supper. You see if you can rouse

24

your mother to make the Sabbath."

Even if dinner preparation required me to go to the sea and dive for the herring myself, I would gladly trade tasks, but I don't argue.

"Mama." I tap gently at her door.

No response.

*"Mama."* Louder, and I rap this time with my knuckles.

Still nothing.

Pushing open the door, I step inside.

She sits at the vanity, brushing her hair.

Before her are hairpins, lined up like soldiers. She keeps careful count of them these days, as they've become increasingly difficult to replace. Two large, four small. She wears her housecoat; her feet, tucked beneath the vanity, are slippered.

In the mirror, her eyes meet mine. "What is it?"

"We're back."

She nods and picks up the two large hairpins, places them between her teeth.

"Are you hungry?"

Instead of answering, she brushes her hair and collects it in one hand, sets aside the brush, and twists the hair tightly at the nape of her neck, forming a tail. Then she winds the hair in a loop, clockwise (always clockwise), and fastens it first on one side, then the other, with the two large pins. Her hands shake, just a little. A headache, again, or the pills she takes for them?

I try again. "How are you feeling, Mama? Did you have a good day?"

One by one, she takes up each of the remaining hairpins and spears her bun into place. When the last pin is placed, she swivels on the low chair to face me.

25

"Mrs. Fischer stopped by this afternoon."

The Fischers, like the Oppenheims, are among our building's Jewish families. About half of the residents are Jewish; the others are Christian, a mix of Romanians and people from other places. We know everyone in the building, more or less, at least by name even if we don't know the particulars. There are sixteen units in the building, four per floor; most of the residents lived here long before Astra, Mama, and I moved in, but the Fischers are new. They arrived just last year, coming from Bucharest when Mr. Fischer got a job teaching mathematics at the university. Mrs. Fischer is a painter; I've seen some of her work when I've watched their little daughter Sophie from time to time. I like it quite a bit. The way she uses the paint, so thick and saturated, almost as if she's sculpting on the canvas.

But from the tone of Mama's voice, I don't think Mrs. Fischer's visit was about art, or to see if I'm available to watch Sophie again. "Is everything okay?"

"She wanted to let me know—not that she wants to get Astra *in trouble*, she said—but she thought I should be told that she saw Astra late this morning, when she should have been in school. She was in the market. With a *man*."

Unlike some of the residents—Mrs. Oppenheim, especially—Mrs. Fischer isn't a gossip. If she felt the need to tell Mama, she must have had a reason. "What man?"

"That's what *I'm* asking *you*," Mama answers.

"*I* don't know who she was with. Maybe Mrs. Fischer saw someone else, someone who just looked like Astra."

"Pph," says Mama, and she's right—no one looks like Astra. My sister is beautiful, with her slim body and long neck, her soft lips and hooded eyes. But it's not really her features that set her apart. It's something else—something you can't *see*, but rather, something you *feel*, some quality that would make it inconceivable to mistake another girl for her. There is only one Astra Teitler.

"I'm disappointed, Frederieke. You know you're supposed to keep an eye on her."

It's backwards—for the little sister to have to watch her older sibling. But it's the way things work, with us. It's why I was born, after all—to watch my sister.

The story is family lore: Astra and her rages.

"Something is wrong with this child," Mama had told the doctor. "If I am not watching her every minute—every *second*—she grows enraged. Look." She'd sat Astra on the examination table and turned her back on her.

"Mama!" cried Astra. And then she yelled: "Ma-*ma*!" She rolled over onto her stomach and hung her legs off the edge of the table, dangling high above the hard tile floor. The nurse rushed to grab her before she fell, getting a tiny fist in her face for the trouble. When the nurse set Astra on her feet, she ran to Mama, grabbed the edge of her dress in both hands, and screamed as if someone was pulling her flesh from her bones. "Ma-*ma*!"

Nothing would stop her screams until Mama turned to her, put her gaze fully on Astra's face.

The doctor had the nurse remove Astra, kicking and screaming, from the examination room. Then he said, "My lady, my only advice is that you must have another child."

"Another? How could I possibly manage *two* children? I cannot be enough for the one I have already."

"Have another child, and soon," the doctor ordered. "Pray it's a girl and raise her up to be a companion to this one. If you don't, Astra will be the death of you."

I was born not ten months later.

"Find out what your sister is up to," Mama says, now. And then she lays her hand on top of mine.

I am a bird again, anxious and hungry. "Okay," I promise. "I will."

"Anna," calls Opa from the kitchen, "come and make the Sabbath! Girls, hurry up or you'll miss it."

Mama gets up, pats my shoulder.

Before she leaves the room, I ask, "Did Mrs. Fischer say who the man was? The man with Astra?"

"Marcel Goldmann," she says, raising her shoulders in a way that tells me the name means nothing to her.

When she's gone, I flop onto her soft, cushioned chair, still warm.

Marcel Goldmann. I catalogue the boys we know—school is all girls, of course, and so is dance, except for Conrad, so I don't know that many boys, and none of them is named Marcel. And anyway, Mrs. Fischer said *man*, not boy. That word, I feel, makes a very big difference.

There is one Goldmann I remember, but I don't know his first name. A doctor who came to our school a couple of months ago to give a talk about nutrition. All the older girls tittered about how handsome he was . . . but no, it couldn't be him. He was old. In his thirties, surely.

I pick up Mama's brush—heavy, bristled with horsehair. I look at my reflection, my mousy brown braids, which I'd pinned up for dance and let down again, after. Wanting to stall, I consider redoing my hair, maybe into something a little more grown-up—though I *feel* older than thirteen, I certainly don't *look* it, and the braids don't help—but instead I set down the brush and go to knock at the bathroom door.

"Beat it, Rieke."

"I have to pee," I lie.

"Use the sink in the kitchen."

"Opa's in there." When she still doesn't come to the door, I add, "And Mama. It's time to light the candles."

Another moment of silence, then the sound of the bolt sliding free. I let myself in and close the lid to the toilet before sitting down.

It's cold in here; Astra has the window cracked open, a lit cigarette perched on its sill—a thread of smoke, the threat of winter. She stands before the mirror. She's taken her hair out of its ballet bun, and now she's piling it atop her head, looking at it this way and that before finally she settles on a chignon—just like Mama. But I know better than to point *that* out.

Instead, I say, "Mrs. Fischer saw you at the market today. She came by and told Mama."

"Shit." Astra puts her hands on the edge of the sink.

"She said you were with someone."

"Hmm." Her fingernail taps the porcelain.

Not a confession, but not a denial, either. She picks up an eyeliner, pulls on her lower lid to apply a thin dark line of kohl. My stomach twists with unease.

"Are you . . . going out tonight?"

"Mm-hmm."

"To see the man again?"

"What man?" Astra says, teasing. She switches to the other eye.

I try to keep my voice light, to disguise my concern—Astra thinks I'm too anxious, too serious about things. "If you go out, I'll have to go, too, you know."

"She'll make you follow me like a limp rat's tail, is that it?"

29

It sounds mean, for Astra to call me a rat tail, but I hear the lilt in her voice that lets me know she's joking. That's just how Astra is—she says mean things, but she's not mean, really.

So I joke back. "I prefer to think of myself as more of a fluffy squirrel's tail."

"Slinking and trailing. You're no squirrel tail."

"Well, if I'm a rat tail, that makes you a rat." I grab up her red lipstick and smear some across my mouth.

"Rats are smart and fast, and they survive." She assesses my lips before tearing off a square of toilet paper and taking my chin in her hand. "With or without their tails." Expertly, she draws the paper across the bow of my lip, cleaning up the line. I sit perfectly still. "You're really getting beautiful, rat tail," she tells me. When she releases my face, I feel a rush of loss.

She crumples the square of toilet paper and puts it in the trash bin before picking up the lipstick. "You ruined the tip." But that doesn't stop her from applying it.

"Girls!" calls Opa. "I can't hold the sunset for you!"

I stand, try another tactic. "Maybe we should stay in. It's dreadfully cold out there."

"It's dreadfully cold out there." A perfect imitation of my inflection, followed by a wink. She takes one more drag of her cigarette, sucking it back to the nub, the sharp hiss of its burn a tiny, mean little noise. She stubs it out and flicks it from the window, then breezes past me.

Of course, I follow.

She plops down at the table, and I do, too, next to Opa, who looks glad to have us all together. Though the only one of us who's truly religious is Opa, we at least do the bare bones of the Sabbath—the candles, the wine—whenever we can. It makes him happy. I know he likes to keep to his faith, but it's something else, too; it's the routine of it. That's one of the many things Opa and I have in common, our love of routine. Our desire for things to stay the same.

He gestures to Mama, and she stands, strikes a match. The candlesticks belonged to Opa's mother; they're tall, made of brass that Opa polishes himself each week. Mama lights the candles, then drops the match into the tray where it burns out as she brings the light to her face, covers her eyes, says the blessing. Opa closes his eyes, too. Astra grabs my wrist, glances at my watch. She taps her foot, impatient. When Mama opens her eyes and sits back down, Astra doesn't waste a moment, bolting her food. I eat quickly, too, trying to keep up.

The second her plate is clean, Astra touches her lips with her napkin, being careful not to smudge her lipstick. "I've got to meet some friends for just a bit." All sugar, she rounds the table where Mama and Opa sit. She drops a kiss in the air near Mama's uplifted cheek and goes around to Opa, playfully snatching off his skullcap and planting a kiss square atop the bald patch on his head, leaving a red print. When Mama points it out, he laughs and scrubs it with a napkin.

Astra uses his distraction to slip her hand into the pocket of his vest, which hangs on the back of his chair. She fishes out his paltry fold of bills, peels two from the top, and returns the rest. Mama sees but says nothing. Astra's one arched eyebrow dares me to rat her out, but of course I don't.

"You should stay in." Opa sets down the napkin, puts his skullcap back upon his head. "It's cold, and dark already, and no good comes from gallivanting around."

I've begun rebuttoning my coat but stop, hoping against hope that Astra will listen to reason and change her mind.

"We won't be *gallivanting*," says Astra. "Who gallivants? Is that really a thing people do?"

"You know what I mean to say," says Opa, which of course Astra does. She is incredibly good at this—twisting what she hears into something else, tangling it all up until the other person loses hold of it.

"Oh, Opa. You worry too much. I'm not going far, and look, I won't even be alone. We'll keep an eye on each other." She throws her arm over my shoulders in a show of sisterly unity.

I shrug her off and fasten the top two buttons of my coat. In the front closet I find a scarf, wind it around my throat. There's a knit cap in the closet, too, which I pull down over my ears.

"Be careful, you'll muss your hair." Astra pulls off the cap, smooths the hair around my temple, arranges the cap more artfully. "There," she says.

As she opens the door, Opa pleads, "Be safe," and Mama calls, "Be home early," just as Astra says, "Don't wait up."

# THREE

## CAFÉ EUROPA

I follow Astra through the apartment door and close it gently. When I turn to the hallway, she's already disappeared around the corner.

Across the road, Jeremy Applebaum and his mother are entering their building. Mrs. Applebaum is a widow, and she terrifies me. She hates everything and everyone except songbirds and her son. There are rumors that she feeds poisoned fish to neighborhood cats if she catches them stalking the birds. She nods to us, curtly, and Jeremy raises his hand in greeting. "Hi, Astra," he calls.

Astra ignores them both.

I nod and wave. "Hi, Jeremy," I call, though he hasn't spoken to me—and then hurry to keep up.

I don't know where we're going, but I'm feeling too stubborn to ask. I walk as quickly as I can, but unlike earlier when our steps fell naturally into sync, now we're walking offbeat with each other, and Astra stays one step ahead all the way to her destination.

Café Europa.

Suddenly, I'm a little girl again, and it's the first night that Father did not come home.

Mama bundled us into coats and pulled us out of the apartment, onto the street, and from one of his haunts to the next, demanding, "Have you seen my Alfred? Where is Alfred? Have you seen my husband?"

Some of the men made eyes at Mama, and some of them seemed sorry for her, but all of them had the same answer, or some variation of it—they'd seen him, but not in a day, or a week, or a month, or, with the last man, in several hours.

"Where did he go when he left?" Mama demanded of the last man, the bartender of this place—Café Europa. Bruno.

"I don't know where he went, lady," Bruno had said, wiping the wooden bar with a red rag, "but I know he didn't leave alone."

Mama's face had collapsed. Bruno had turned away.

Tonight, I'm not a child following at my mother's skirts. But still, I am following—Astra this time, who nods curtly to a man holding open the door for us. "Come on, rat tail," she calls with a quick grin, and then she crosses the threshold. Panting with exertion and sweating despite the cold, I'm frozen in the doorway, staring in.

"Well?" The man is still holding the door. "In or out?"

I swallow, step inside.

The room is thick with smoke and sound. A jazz band plays loudly, big and brassy. All the musicians are Black—unusual for Czernowitz. They're probably from the United States. If Esther were here, she'd be wide-eyed. To her, anyone from America might as well be one of her beloved movie stars.

A waitress circulates, depositing drinks. She drops two martinis at a table nearby—Mama's favorite drink, she loves the olive—and with a start

I recognize who she's serving: Madame Lucia and Miss Rosen. It's strange to see our dance teacher in street clothes; she's wearing a neat dark skirt and a coat that shows the tight nip of her waist. She and Miss Rosen clink their glasses before taking a sip.

"Astra, look who's here," I whisper, but she ignores me, busy scanning the room.

We take a few steps into the café and find ourselves near a table of three men, each with a stein of beer. They're talking about the war, and Germany's invasion of Poland.

"We'll be next," one of them predicts, grimly.

Another shakes his head. "We're neutral."

"We still have the Iron Guard," says the third, so drunk as to slur his words.

Astra hears him, too; she looks at me and rolls her eyes as if to say, *What an idiot.*

I know what she means; if this man were a Jew, he wouldn't be bragging about the Iron Guard. What good is a military that only cares about some of the people it's supposed to defend?

"If only that goddamned bomb had hit its mark," says the first man—the soberest of the three. They're talking about last week's assassination attempt against Adolf Hitler. Lots of people were killed, but Hitler wasn't even scratched. "If Germany can take Poland that easily, we don't stand a chance—if Hitler wants us, he'll take us."

At home, Opa never talks about the war. For a second I'm tempted to stand quietly and listen, but then Astra's gaze lands, at the bar. She's found him—Marcel Goldmann. The doctor from the nutrition lecture.

*Really?* I want to say to Astra. *This guy?* I don't see what's special about him, what's worth all the trouble of sneaking around and coming out in the cold. He's just—a man. Nothing, compared to my sister.

And maybe I'd say something, except I feel the way Astra goes stiff when the brunette sitting next to him leans in close and puts her hand on his back.

I recognize her, actually. She's the waitress at a patisserie where Astra and I sometimes stop on our way home from dance. Her name's Colette; she always wears a little golden cross on a chain around her neck. Another woman leans in, this one a redhead I've never seen before. She laughs at something Marcel says and reaches across him, grazing his arm with her enormous bosom as she receives a drink from the bartender—Bruno, the same man that Mama cried to, all those years ago. Apparently, there's a competition between the two women, and somehow this ordinary-looking man is the prize.

They're grown-ups involved in something that has no room for me and Astra. Surely my sister will see that. But when I turn to her, it's to find her white with rage, squaring up and straightening the same way she does before a performance when she prepares to take her mark. And even though I don't understand what Astra is doing here or what she sees in this man, I can't help but admire how she parts the crowd as she crosses the café.

She's taller than all the women and most of the men, including Marcel. Completely ignoring Colette and the redhead, Astra unbuttons her coat and shrugs it off. Then she offers her long-fingered hand to Marcel. He grins as he takes it, and the two of them go to the makeshift dance floor where the mob of bodies shifts to welcome them. Astra's back curves to accept Marcel's hand in the small of it, and then the music shifts, too, curving like her spine.

I shrink back into the shadows beside the doorway and watch.

Suddenly, it doesn't seem so ridiculous—Astra and Marcel, together. She's still young, but she doesn't look so much like a girl, now. It's stage presence, that's what it is: as tall as Astra is, she always grows even taller when the spotlight is upon her. And now the collective spotlight of all of us— Colette and the redhead, Bruno behind the bar and me lurking in the shadows—shines right at her.

We watch Marcel as he leads, his hair oiled back from his forehead, gleaming; we watch Astra's body, trained by years of ballet to do just this, to perform, as it follows. But this dance isn't anything like ballet, not really. Ballet is structured, and formal, and it has rules. Probably those are the reasons that I love it.

This dance isn't that. There's something . . . wild about it. Something that scares me. They dance until the other couples cede the center of the floor, they dance until the music builds to a fever crescendo, until a fine sweat breaks on both their brows, they dance until the music swells and crests and peaks. They are impossibly alive, more alive than any of us.

It's *raw*, that's what it is. I don't know where the word comes from, but there it is. I reach for my cheek and find tears there, though I can't say why.

The song ends. Marcel tips Astra to her feet. She drops her gaze, opens her hand as if to receive, and the crowd breaks into thunderous applause. Then she scans the room—this time, looking for me. When she finds me, she grins, and the feeling I have is something like relief. Suddenly, she's my sister again—still beautiful, brilliant, shining Astra, but mine. I swipe my cheeks with the back of my hand.

"Your sister."

It's Conrad's voice and I turn with a smile, glad to have someone familiar here, but though he spoke to me, he's looking at Astra. His dark eyes, their golden flecks, follow only her.

Maybe Conrad has been in love with Astra since the day he walked into Madame Lucia's studio. He was too young to take over as accompanist—only fourteen or so—but then, we had needed an accompanist, suddenly and unexpectedly, and there wasn't any other choice. How nervous he'd looked, how charming his Adam's apple, bouncing up and down as Madame Lucia tapped her stick on the floor and said, "Girls, please welcome Esther's brother, Conrad."

We all turned to Esther then, wondering how it felt, seeing her brother sit on a dead man's bench. She shrugged and pushed her heavy glasses up the bridge of her nose, and I saw that they shared some features: the same wide eyes, the same broad forehead, the same wavy, copper hair. But where those features looked too big on Esther, on Conrad, they fit just right.

Still watching Astra, Conrad pushes his hair from his brow. Finally, he manages to tear his gaze away long enough to ask, with his familiar stutter, "Wh-What's Astra even doing with that guy? Isn't he . . . too old?"

Even though I agree, my instinct to defend Astra rises before I can stop it. "You're just jealous because she won't go out with you."

I regret the words as soon as I've said them. It's true that Conrad has twice asked Astra out—once to a movie, another time to a picnic at the beach—and twice been rejected. At the time, I'd believed this was proof that she meant to keep her long-ago promise to never fall in love. It's not Conrad I'm angry with; there's no reason for me to take things out on him.

"Sorry," I offer, and he nods.

Neither of us knows what to say next. It's not as if we're friends; we haven't spent any time together except at the studio, and there it's always him behind the piano and me on the floor with the other girls. When I visit Esther, he barely comes out of his room.

Astra's at the bar now, and Marcel is ordering her a drink. She accepts it and takes a sip. Another surprise.

The band begins another number, louder this time, and faster. Conrad taps the toe of his clean brown boot and closes his eyes as if to let the music take him. For a moment, it feels like it's just him and me there. I take the chance to study his long, soft lashes; his eyebrows, feathered up at the corners. His lips, pinker than a boy's lips should be, but it strikes me that I like them. I've never noticed a boy's lips before. His look soft, and more relaxed than when he talks. It occurs to me that he looks like this when he's at the piano. Maybe speaking through music is easier for him, more natural.

His eyes are still closed. His fingers drum a beat against his dark gray wool trousers, his thigh beneath. His top shirt button is undone—no, the buttonhole is ripped through. I have this crazy idea to offer to mend it, like I do Opa's. I have a vision of myself with his shirt in my lap, a needle and thread, each sharp, tight stitch piercing the fabric, bringing the torn edges together again. Conrad standing nearby, shirtless, watching.

Maybe he feels me looking at him, because suddenly, his eyes open. Their gold flecks catch light and reflect it. He looks at me—really looks at me, for the first time tonight, maybe ever. My face flushes hot with embarrassment, and my body feels like a jolt of lightning has hit it. Is this how Astra feels, when Marcel Goldmann looks at her? How Mama used to feel, when Father swept her up and kissed her? It's a strange feeling, but not a bad one. Maybe I'll step closer. Maybe I'll say something. But then—Conrad's gaze slips past my shoulder, focusing beyond me, and the moment breaks.

"Where'd she go?"

I turn and I scan the bar. Astra is gone; so is Marcel.

"I've got to find her," I say. "See you at the studio."

At the bar, I push between two men so I can speak to Bruno.

"Hey," I call. "Have you seen my sister? Tall, dark hair? The girl who was dancing, a little bit ago."

"The Jewess," says one of the men, then whistles slowly. "She's *your* sister?" He looks me up and down as if trying to see how Astra and I are related.

Bruno flicks his chin in the direction of the back curtain. "She's in the cardroom. And listen, kid—you want some advice?"

I nod.

"Your sister will want to watch herself with Marcel Goldmann."

"What do you mean?"

One of the men snorts. Bruno ignores him. "He's not a *bad* guy. Just—he's not exactly a one-woman man."

At that, the men at the bar laugh outright.

I shouldn't be dealing with any of this. I should be in our kitchen doing the after-dinner dishes, and Astra should be with me—probably not helping with the chores at all, but at least *home*, safe and sound.

Beyond the curtain, the air is even smokier; the acrid burn of cigarettes stings my eyes and throat. It's tight back here, barely enough room for an octagonal table with a green felt top, cards dealt across it. Each of the eight chairs is taken—in the one across from me is Marcel, a cigarette dangling from his lip and Astra perching on his knee. Seated beside him, holding the deck of cards, is someone I've met before—Mr. Weissinger.

I see Mr. Weissinger around town all the time. I can't say for sure what he does for a living; it must be something important, judging by his fine clothes and neatly trimmed hair. But I might not know his name, had he not once come to Opa's apartment with the intention of taking Mama out to dinner. He looks the same now as he did when he knocked on our door, and I answered: stocky, with fur-like hair on the backs of his hands. Round, wire-rimmed spectacles framing smallish eyes; hair, dark and thinning, combed straight back.

I remember Opa had joined me at the door; he'd put his hand on my head and said, "I'm afraid my daughter has come down with one of her headaches."

I remember how Mr. Weissinger clenched his hand before he answered. He wore a gold ring on his pinkie finger, black hairs poking out from beneath the band. "That *is* a shame," he said. "We will have to reschedule."

"My daughter is subject to frequent headaches," said Opa. "Best not to count on her for dinner company. Look elsewhere—that's my advice."

There had been a tense moment before Mr. Weissinger nodded sharply. To me, he said, "Please tell your mother I am sorry for her ill health," and then, to Opa, "Good evening, Mr. Fischmann."

He'd walked through the doorway, out of our apartment, and Opa had shut the door loudly behind him.

Now, as Mr. Weissinger shuffles and cuts the deck, I notice he's wearing the same pinkie ring. He deals, beginning with Marcel on his left, then to three men I don't know, then to Colette, and then another woman, this one much older.

And then, to the man in the last chair—oh, God.

It's my father.

Since the last time he left us, there hasn't been one visit. Not one letter. Not a single message. Until this moment, I haven't been sure if he was even alive. But now, here he is, arranging a fan of cards, a tumbler of liquor beside him.

He looks almost exactly as I remember. The same lock of hair falls boyishly across his forehead, his rolled-up sleeves display the same strong

41

arms that used to swing me onto his shoulders. I'm a child again, and it is childish the way my heart beats in my chest, with something like hope. The turn passes to him. "Check." I notice that his eyes are on Colette rather than his cards.

I glance at Astra; does she recognize our father, too? She meets my gaze, and I can read it perfectly: *Of course I recognize him, dummy.*

Colette wins the hand. As she leans to collect the money, her golden cross swings forward and her blouse falls forward, too, in a way that seems intentional. Coolly ignoring my sister, she says, "Marcel, I'm tired. Take me home, won't you?"

From her perch on Marcel's knee, Astra doesn't move, not a muscle.

Marcel smiles and leans back. He looks between the two of them, my sister and Colette. "Ladies," he says, palms open, "surely, we can all three of us come to a compromise. There's enough of me, isn't there, for you both?"

The men break into laughter, our father included. They're *laughing* at my *sister.* I don't stop to think. I step away from the curtain to grab Astra's wrist and pull her from Marcel's lap. "Come on, Astra. Let's go home."

"Freddie?" says my father. No one has called me that in seven years. Father's eyes go from me to my sister, recognition spreading across his face. "Astra!" And he stands, smiles, takes us both into his arms. Neither of us return his embrace, but he doesn't care, or maybe he doesn't even notice. "My girls." He sounds truly delighted.

"A family reunion, eh, Alfred?" says Mr. Weissinger.

I hate my father. I *hate* him, for abandoning us, for ruining Mama's life . . . but then I breathe in the scent of his hair pomade, vanilla and sweet licorice, a smell I'd forgotten entirely until—suddenly—I remember. Tears spring to my eyes and I feel myself softening. My cheek begins to rest on the warm, scratchy roughness of his coat. I close my eyes, take another breath.

That's when Astra yanks me away. It's Mr. Weissinger, for some reason, who stands, pulls back the curtain for us to pass through.

"Freddie," calls my father.

I stop, but I don't turn. Astra's hand still grips my wrist.

"Tell your mother to expect me tomorrow."

# FOUR

## HOW TO FIX THINGS

When we exit together from Café Europa, it's into snow—the first real snow of the year. Flakes of it land and sparkle in Astra's hair like pricks of starlight in a dark sky. Together, we go down the street, arms linked, our frozen breath mingling into a shared cloud.

There's a lot to talk about—Father, of course, and why he's back, what he might want from Mama, and what that could mean for us—but the question of Marcel Goldmann is even bigger, scarier. I can feel that we're on the edge of something, and I don't want to be the one to push us over. And maybe Astra feels it, too, because she bumps her shoulder into mine and says, "It doesn't *mean* anything. I'm just having fun."

"But Astra," I say, "he's so . . . *old*!"

She throws her head back, laughs loud. I feel a little leap of gladness in my heart, that I have made her laugh. Even now, when I'm so upset about everything.

"Marcel's not *that* old. Not even thirty, quite."

"So . . . he's, what, a *dozen* years older than you are?"

44

She shrugs, says again, "I'm just having fun."

What I want to say is: *It didn't* look *like fun, back in the cardroom.*

But I don't. Maybe this thing with Marcel will be like when Astra got so excited about violin, right after we'd moved in with Opa. She'd found his old fiddle in a closet and wouldn't put it down. She was great at it, very quickly—a natural, Opa had said. He'd been delighted; especially, as he said, since Mama had never taken an interest. But then one day Astra declared she was tired of the violin, and that was that. Back into the closet it went. No amount of cajoling from Opa could get her to open the case again.

"Listen, don't tell Mama and Opa about tonight, okay? There's no reason for them to worry."

"Mama already knows you were with Marcel at the market."

"She'll forget about that. She forgets about most things, if they're not in her face."

Astra's not wrong about that. "Okay," I agree, reluctantly. She throws her arm across my shoulders and kisses me on the cheek.

Marcel Goldmann will be just like the violin, I tell myself. Astra's having fun, trying something out. But she'll get tired of him, as she does everything, eventually. Everything except dance. And me.

The next day, as soon as Opa leaves for morning services, Father, for once, makes good on a promise.

When I hear his knock on the door, I'm sorry that I didn't prepare Mama. I would have told her he was coming if I'd believed him. But one thing I know about my father is that he shouldn't be trusted.

So he catches her unaware—dressed in a housecoat, hair in curlers. No lipstick. When she answers the door, I'm struck by how much older she looks than he does, though they are the same age. He is boyish, a rake; some lines around the eyes, sure, but well-tanned as if he's been abroad, traveling to exotic places, far away from everything happening in Czernowitz. She, by contrast, has deep grooves around her mouth—heavy parentheses framing her lips, even when she smiles—and around her eyes and between them, too, from the way her forehead pinches when she has one of her sick headaches.

When she sees our father, the first thing she does is touch her hair, the gesture so vulnerable, so expressive, that I want to cry.

Then she throws herself into his arms, her sobs muffled against his coat, and he makes soothing sounds as if to a child as he backs her into the apartment, closing the door with his foot.

He pats her back and he looks up to see us standing in the hallway watching. "Astra, Freddie, go to your room, eh?"

He speaks as if we're still bound by anything he says, which we're not; and yet, we obey. I go because it's too painful to watch Mama like this. I don't know why Astra does.

"We should have warned her," I whisper when we're in our room.

"Shh." Astra has her ear to the door, straining to listen. She doesn't need to strain for long; almost immediately, Mama's voice grows higher, laced with emotion.

"*Now* is the time you tell me this?"

"If not now, when?" Father's voice raises to match Mama's. "Love follows no man's schedule."

"Love." One word, only. But into it she puts everything—heartbreak; yearning; hatred.

"It's for the best. Maybe you'll finally move on."

I sit on the foot of Astra's bed.

Mama makes a sound I can't interpret—like a cat with her tail caught in a doorjamb. And then Father's voice drops, grows muffled, and I can't make out the words anymore.

Astra turns away from the door. She sits next to me, says nothing.

Mama's voice, again. "Did you *ever* love me?"

"Stupid woman. Of course I did."

Mama, sobbing.

A moment later, the front door slams.

The apartment falls deathly silent. I go to the door and press my ear against it.

Nothing.

"Do you think we should go out there?"

Astra has picked up a book—*Madame Bovary*, which she's read a thousand times. "*I'm* not going out there. Do what you want."

I do not want to go out there.

Mama is on the sofa. Her face is strangely calm. On the table are some papers. They're folded in thirds, but loosely. An image flashes in my mind—a bird, with broken wings.

"Mama?"

She looks up at me, then down at the papers, and then quickly away, as if the sight of them pains her. "Your father is divorcing me. He says he's fallen in love again. They want to marry."

"Oh." I don't know what else to say. "Who is he marrying?"

Those are the wrong words. Mama's face closes. She leans forward and picks up the papers. Unfolds them, pressing the creases flat. She tears them in half. "He can marry who he wants. But I won't be making it easier for him."

She stands and throws the papers in the dustbin.

The next day is Sunday, my favorite day of the week. This is the day I go with Opa to his shop.

The sky is bright and brilliant blue; it stopped snowing midday yesterday, just before Opa got home from synagogue. We spent the afternoon reading books and newspapers in the front room, a cozy fire in the hearth. Astra even joined us, making hot cocoa and bringing it to the front room on a tray. Three cups, only, for Mama had shut herself in her room after Father left. When Opa asked what was wrong with her, Astra and I told him about Father's visit, how he'd asked Mama for a divorce.

"And what did she answer?" For a moment, he'd looked hopeful—we both knew how Opa despised our father—and so I felt badly pointing to the torn divorce papers in the trash bin.

"Ay yai yai," he said, shaking his head and running his hand down his long beard. "Crazy times, crazy people."

This is something he says when things are out of his control, which made me think that the only thing we could do about Mama was wait for her to come around. So we settled in with our cocoa and books, and then later Astra and I took turns playing chess with Opa, who beat us both.

Other than Mama's sulk, it had been a really nice afternoon. Astra had been in a fine mood, and she spent almost the whole time with us rather than shutting herself in the bedroom with her books, as she usually did. The way she was acting made me feel more confident that the thing with Marcel was just a bit of fun for her. She certainly didn't *seem* like Mama, tied up in knots. Everything would be all right, if I just left it alone and let it run its course.

We take our time getting to Opa's shop; though it's cold, everyone on the street seems to be of the same mind: that today is a day for sunshine.

Maybe one of the last. A day for sharing.

On our way, we stop in at Marty Diamond's butcher shop—*Glatt Kosher,* reads the sign over his door. We don't need a cut of meat, but Opa wants to know Mr. Diamond's opinion on the cantor's voice yesterday—does the butcher agree it's just a cold, or perhaps something more serious? Then they get into a debate about the weather, if it's likely to change soon or if we'll have the sunshine for a few days longer, both of them oblivious to the line of matronly ladies waiting for their turn at the counter.

I stand patiently and watch, enjoying how animated Opa gets, the way he leans in, nods seriously, strokes his beard and then laughs. But when they pick up their years-long debate about which Brecht poem is his finest, I finally interrupt.

"Don't you have a whole boxful of watches to repair today, Opa?"

"Ach," he says, waving his hand at me. "Work is to support *life*, not the other way around."

Still, he wraps up his conversation with Mr. Diamond, and we continue on our way.

It's too cold for the cafés to put tables on the sidewalks, but the windows are full of fashionable couples, heads leaned conspiratorially together, discussing whatever it is lovers talk about. I have a hard time imagining what that might be. A newspaper is sprawled across one of the tables—it's the *Official Gazette of Romania,* and the headline reads "Results of the Revision of Citizenship of Romanian Jewry."

I quickly glance at Opa to see if he's noticed the headline but he's smiling at a baby in a pram, so bundled by a hat and blankets that nothing but its fat pink cheeks can be seen.

I know Opa doesn't want me to worry, and I do my best not to, but when I see a headline like this, all the worries rush in, whether I want them to or not. This "revision of citizenship" begun by the Goga-Cuza government means that Jews who couldn't show proper papers are no longer counted as citizens, becoming aliens in our own country. My family still has our citizenship, thankfully, but many others do not.

Along with the citizenship issue came a ban on Jewish-owned newspapers and Jews working in government service. The only people who can have political power are "Romanians with pure Romanian blood in their veins"—so, no Jews.

Suddenly, even though the sun still shines brightly, all I can focus on is the cold.

Opa senses my shift in mood. He drops his arm over my shoulders, pulls me close to his side. I want to ask him about the war, which seems both tremendously far away and terribly close, about whether there's anything we could be doing, to stay safe. But it upsets him to think of me worrying about these things. He wants me to be a child just a little bit longer, he says.

I remind myself that Opa lived through the last war. He's told me over and over that things were bad, but then they got good again. That's how it goes, he says; "Everything is cyclical." But the thing is, he's never gone into details about just how bad things got, so I have no idea of how bad things might get, this time.

We turn a corner and there is Opa's shop. As always, the sight of its door cheers me: etched in glass are the words *Heinrich Fischmann, Jeweler*. There's room on the glass below his name for another . . . maybe, one day, mine. Opa hands me his keys and I flip through them until I find the right one. I fit it in the lock; it turns with a satisfying *click*, and then we go inside, together.

I love everything about Opa's jewelry shop. This is a place where things are set to rights, where things run the way they should. That's how I feel, whenever I'm here. Like everything works, and what doesn't, can be fixed. Firmly, I shut the door and leave everything else outside.

Opa's repair table is in the corner near the front window, where there's the best natural light; it's a mess of opened watches, fine tools, loose parts. "The first thing I need," he says, approaching his table and unwinding his scarf, "is my loupe. I couldn't find it anywhere on Friday." He waves his hand in the general direction of the glass countertop at the far side of the shop, beneath which an assortment of watches and rings are stored in leather and velvet boxes. The counter is as big a mess as his worktable, if not worse; papers and tools and books stacked near-to-tipping, abandoned cups of wine and tea and water; plates here and there laced with crumbs.

"Opa," I groan, for when I was here a week ago, I'd spent most of the day clearing the counter. All the progress I made has been obliterated.

"I know where to find criticism, Rieke. It's my loupe that's lost," he says, his tone playful.

As I dig through the piles searching for the small brass instrument, he calls, "Careful. I know just where everything is in those piles."

"If you know where everything is, then where's the loupe?"

This, Opa ignores. I laugh and keep looking. There—tucked beneath a book, upon a far pile of receipts. I take it to Opa, who plucks it from my palm.

"Thank you." He holds it to his eye. "I don't know what I would do without you."

Opa is always saying things like that. But in truth, it's the rest of us who depend on *him*. He settles in to work and I plug in the electric kettle for tea. While the water heats, I tuck my things behind the counter and retrieve Opa's scarf and coat, which he's let crumple on the chair behind

51

him, completely forgotten as soon as he set to work. He's even forgotten to take off his tall felt hat, which makes me laugh. I bring him a cup of tea and pluck the hat from his head. He looks up; it takes a moment for his vision to readjust from peering at the fine filigree work of the ring he is repairing—and then he smiles, takes a sip of his tea. "Ah," he says, and then he sets the cup on the table. There's at least a 50 percent chance he'll get so absorbed in his work that the tea will go completely cold before he takes a second sip.

I carry my tea to the counter and begin to sort invoices. We work quietly, Opa and I, and I know he feels it, too—how nice this is. The tea's jasmine fragrance rises on its steam; I hear the tiny metallic sounds of Opa's tools against jewelry; my hands are set to work as well.

Right now, in this room, in this moment, everything is safe and sound. My earlier worries about the state of our city, the state of the world, feel far away. The problems out there are too big for me to fix. But I can fix this stack of papers; I can bring Opa the right tools.

And, as the daylight wanes and the shadows grow long, I can even be the one to diagnose a problem with a stopped pocket watch; the hairspring is bent out of round, and must be trued.

Opa stands from his chair so I can take the seat; he positions the lighted magnifier above the watch so I can better see my work. Now he's the assistant, and I'm the jeweler. He gives me the pliers, and slowly, delicately, I bend the tiny spring until the spiral is even again, no overlaps.

"Perfect," Opa says. "Just so."

It's near dusk when Opa says, "All right. Let's call it a day. What do you say?"

"I say yes."

He pats the pockets of his vest and his pants, looking for his keys. "Now where could they be?"

This, I know too—they hang on a nail on the back of the desk, near the register. I pull them from the nail, rattle them.

"Ah. Good girl." He joins me by the register. "Do you have your things?"

I get our coats and hold open Opa's so he can slip into it, and I see how stiffly he moves. His shoulder is giving him trouble from hunching over close work, all day.

He opens the register to take out the meager stack of bills, folding the money and tucking it into his coat pocket. Then he takes his hat from where I placed it on the small shelf above the coat hook and puts it on over his skullcap.

Still patting his pockets out of habit, Opa walks slowly to the glass-paned door. He turns the knob, and we are no longer insulated in our own little world. Cold air rushes in, and my skin rises in bumps. Opa goes out first, touching the mezuzah, and I push out after.

I find the key on the ring and lock the door, pushing it to make sure the bolt has slid into place, then hand the keys to Opa, making a mental note that he's placed them in the inside left pocket of his coat so, when he inevitably asks me where he's put them, I'll know the answer. Then we turn toward home.

I link my right arm through Opa's left. The wind is up, so we tuck our chins into our collars. The snow begins to fall now, slantwise, tiny punishments of ice. Opa's eyes are protected by the brim of his hat and his glasses, but mine are not. I lower my lashes and squint, trusting Opa to lead me safely home.

We stop at a corner to let an automobile pass. But rather than driving by, it pulls to the curb and stops. The driver rolls down his window; it's Mr. Weissinger.

"Heinrich, hello." Mr. Weissinger's hands are gloved in black leather; the cab of his car is rich in burled wood and fine upholstery. "May I offer you and your charming granddaughter a ride?"

I squeeze Opa's arm; it's not every day I get the chance to ride in a car, and it *is* cold out here.

But Opa answers: "No, thank you, George. We'll be fine."

"Are you sure? It's no trouble."

I'm about to say something, but Opa puts his hand on top of mine. "Enjoy your evening, George," he says.

Mr. Weissinger's mouth turns down. "Good day, Heinrich. Good day, Frederieke." And then he drives away.

I look wistfully after the departing automobile. "Opa," I ask, "what do you have against Mr. Weissinger?"

"Bah," says Opa. "It's better not to owe anything to a man like George Weissinger. When he collects, he always makes sure to make interest."

# FIVE

# WELCOME TO
# THE BLOOD YEARS

In the wake of Father's visit, Mama takes to her bed again.

Opa tries to rouse her. He tries shame: "How can you just lie there, all day long, leaving all the housework to the girls? What kind of a woman does that?"

He tries threats: "If you're not up and dressed by the time I get home from the shop, you won't *believe* what I will do!"

He tries pleading: "Anna, darling, please get up. I can't bear to see you like this."

But nothing he says moves her.

The days grow shorter and more bitter, and Opa's worries are divided: Mama, the war, the fact that fewer people come to his shop. It used to be that everyone in the city, no matter where they came from or what their religion or ethnicity, wanted Heinrich Fischmann to repair their watches. Now, the names on the invoices, the people who come to drop off and pick up: only Jewish names, only Jewish faces.

And the price of everything is rising—firewood, meat, even bread.

Higher prices, less income; more need, less help. I worry that Opa is drowning, and Mama, Astra, and I have no line to throw him.

Mama suggests a possibility, one of the few times she joins us for a meal at the table: "We could borrow some money from George Weissinger."

"That no-goodnik?" Opa exclaims. "Never."

She shrugs and returns to bed.

I can't make winter less harsh; I can't make firewood cost less or burn more slowly. I can't force people to bring their watches to Opa for repair; I can't shake Mama from her stupor.

And I can't stop Astra from being Astra.

Despite her promise that she's "just having fun" with Marcel, Astra's entire day is made or broken by whether or not he's outside the building when dance class ends. If we emerge from the studio to find him leaning against the side of the building and smoking, waiting to walk her home, Astra's body blossoms, unfolding as she goes to him. I watch the way his slick black head tilts to her, the way his arm snakes around her waist. When we arrive to our apartment building, I pretend to look away as they kiss. Astra's taken to wearing only flat shoes so that she's not taller than him; one could almost pretend they're equally enamored, the way their faces come together, neither above the other . . . but when Marcel walks away, it's Astra who moons after him, and he who never looks back.

When he isn't waiting outside the studio, his shadow still is, ruining Astra's mood and darkening the part of day that used to be our special time.

On New Year's Eve, Astra lies to Opa and tells him that a group of girls from dance is meeting at Café Europa to celebrate. I bite my tongue and when we get to the café, I watch her and Marcel dance and kiss in the corner, clinking their glasses together and laughing like fools.

1940 arrives. A new year; a new decade. It gets even colder in Czernowitz; the sidewalk is slick and black with ice. One day after dance, Astra and Marcel quarrel—she yells something about Colette, the name dripping with poison—and her mood stays as slippery and mean as the sidewalks until three days later, when Marcel finally shows up after class and Astra runs into his arms like nothing has happened.

I should be angry at her, but really what I feel is desperation. I've done what she asked. I've been patient. I've given her space and time to get bored with Marcel, to come back to me the way she always has before, the way she promised she would when she said that she was just having a bit of fun. And yet—it feels like she's drifting farther and farther away, like things between us are unraveling, and soon, she'll be too far away to ever return.

One night, when we've all turned in early because it's so cold and there's no firewood left, Astra and I lie in our narrow beds across from one another. I'm wearing both my sweaters, and still I shiver.

Astra's breaths are deepening. I know she's almost asleep when I burst out, desperately: "You said you'd never fall in love!"

A pause, so long I think maybe she's fallen to sleep. But then: "Rieke," she says, "you have nothing to worry about. Trust me."

I may not be sure about things like God, the way Opa is—Father and Mama never raised us to be religious—but I guess I've always believed in two things: that Astra would always be mine, and that things *circle back*. That there's a rhythm and cycle to the world, to everything. But then it hits me—Father didn't come back. So what makes me so sure that Astra will?

It's the first Monday in February, and for breakfast I'm having what's left of last night's soup while Opa winds my watch. My stomach hurts and I

57

don't much feel like eating, but I wouldn't think to waste food—not these days—so I'm taking slow sips. Opa, across from me, has a cup of tea. He peers down his nose at my watch, turning it over and rubbing it with a soft rag to shine it. He is just beginning to wind its tiny crown when I smell the sharp tang of cigarette smoke, drifting from beneath the bathroom door. Suddenly and all at once, Astra's secret becomes too heavy for me to bear.

I set down my spoon. "Opa," I say. "I need to tell you something."

This is the first time in my life that I've betrayed my sister.

"Astra!" His voice booms in a way I haven't heard since he used it on our mother, years ago when he rescued us from our apartment. "Come here at once!"

Not only does the bathroom door open, but Mama's does, too. Astra comes down the hallway, wary; Mama stays in her doorway, pulling closed her robe, but she's listening.

"Is it true what your sister tells me?"

Astra's gaze is so hateful that I look down, into my soup bowl. My stomach clenches again, and I push the soup away.

"That depends. What did the little rat tail say?"

I know it's a nasty thing to call someone—a rat tail—but always before, when Astra has said it, it's been with affection. This is the first time it feels like an aspersion. A shard of glass wedges in my heart.

"She tells me you've been seeing someone—a man. Is this true?"

Astra lifts her chin. "It's no secret. Marcel Goldmann and I are in love."

I have betrayed my sister—but with this declaration, she finally admits that she's betrayed me, as well. The glass shard deepens.

Casual as a cat, Astra reaches into her pocket, pulls out her cigarettes and matches, and lights one, right in front of Opa.

Opa roars. He stands, pounds the table, pulls his beard, paces. But all Astra does is cross to the counter and tap her ash into the kitchen sink. Eyes hooded, face neutral, she stays cruelly calm.

Mama cuts in—"At least he's a doctor"—and Opa's rage extends to her, then, too.

"You knew about this?"

Mama shrugs, nods. Astra turns to Mama, and the two of them lock eyes.

"There are worse things than Astra falling in love, and with a doctor," Mama says, more strongly now.

"She's just a girl," Opa wails.

"I'm not a girl." Astra turns the water on, lets it run over the butt of her cigarette. It hisses as it goes out. "I'm a woman, and you can't tell me what to do."

She throws the cigarette in the rubbish, goes up the hall to kiss Mama's cheek. Then she gathers her things, throws her coat over her arm, and goes to the door. With a hand on the knob she says, "You're stuck in the past, Opa. You wouldn't let Mama have a boyfriend after Father left. You don't want me and Rieke to grow up. It's funny—you make clocks work, but you want to stop time. Well, maybe Rieke and Mama are okay with that. But I'm not."

With that, she leaves the apartment—not *slamming* the door, but almost.

Mama returns to her room. Opa drops to his chair, shaking his head. I want to say something to comfort him, but I can't wait another minute for the toilet.

In the bathroom, I lock the door. What on earth have I done? I see now that telling Opa won't change anything; all it will do is push Astra

59

even farther away. My stomach cramps and I rush for the toilet; maybe the soup turned in the night, or maybe it's the stress of the fighting.

In the toilet bowl, I see red dripping into the water.

My stomach cramps again, this time with fear. The only thing I can think is illogical, impossible, but still—part of me feels certain that this is what comes of betraying my sister.

I wipe myself; there's more blood, bright red.

"Rieke!" calls Opa. "Your watch is ready." I can hear that he's trying to make his voice light, and I hear the strain beneath.

I stand and flush. I fold some toilet paper and place it in the crotch of my underwear, then pull them up.

I wash my hands and look in the mirror. My eyes are wide, my face pale. "Are you dying?" I whisper to my reflection. She shakes her head.

"Rieke," Opa calls again. "You'll be late!"

I grip the sink with both hands, lean my forehead against the mirror. I focus on how cold the glass is. My heart pumps quickly and I wonder if it will make me bleed out faster, so I try to control my breath, force my heart to slow down.

When I was very young, if I woke from a bad dream, Astra would wake, too. It was like she knew about the dream, even before I cried out. I would turn over in my bed and there she would be, her face bright as the moon, lifting her blanket and inviting me beside her. I'd climb into her bed, and she would pull my face into her neck—soft, sweet, warm—and I would close my eyes and breathe her in. The dream would fade, and her breath would touch my hair. I would start to drift to sleep again, and we would become exactly the same temperature, so that I could no longer tell what was her neck and what was my cheek, against it.

It has been many years since my sister held me in this way. Now that

I have betrayed her, she may never hold me again.

I go to the kitchen. Opa takes my wrist and threads the silver watch-band around it, fastens the delicate clamp. I hear the tiny sound it makes, counting away the time.

Astra isn't waiting for me on the street. I knew she wouldn't be, but still—I hoped. I take myself to school.

At the first chance I go to the bathroom and change out the bloodied clot of toilet paper for fresh.

"Something's wrong with me," I whisper to Esther in mathematics. Behind her glasses, her eyes glisten with concern, but before I can tell her more, the teacher clears his throat and looks pointedly at us.

When I go to the bathroom again at lunch, what a relief to find that there's almost no fresh blood; there's a brownish stain on the folded tissue, and only a streak of red when I wipe. Shakily, I fold a fresh length of toilet paper. I wash my hands at the sink; my reflection has bright red cheeks, my lips are still pink. If I were bleeding to death, surely I'd look like it. "You're going to be okay," the girl in the mirror and I tell one another. Does she believe it? I try to.

When school ends, I wait for Astra in the building's foyer. When she comes down the hall toward the door, she looks right through me as if I'm not even there. I follow her through the streets to the studio; she stays ten steps in front of me. Her silence is meant to punish me, and I deserve it. Near the studio, I jog to catch up before she goes inside. Gathering up my nerve, I reach out and grab her arm.

"Astra," I say, but when she turns to me, her eyes are so full of anger that I gasp and let go.

I have to compose myself before I go inside. I breathe in the cold air, counting to ten and then to twenty, and then to one hundred. Then I go inside, and head straight to the bathroom.

There's more blood, but not much. A glance at my wristwatch tells me I'll soon be late to the barre, and Madame Lucia despises lateness, no matter the reason. This is strangely comforting, the knowledge that I'll be in trouble if I don't hurry. I wash quickly and go to the dressing room.

It's almost empty. Only Ruth remains, smoothing her hair. "Hi, Ruth," I mumble, and unfasten my watch, tucking it into my bag before I loosen the laces of my shoes.

"Better hurry," she says, kindly, and then she floats from the room.

I do hurry, stumbling through my preparations. My hands tremble as they tug my slippers on.

Conrad is in his place at the piano, and when I push through to the studio, he lifts his fingers from the keys in a wave.

I find my place at the barre just before Madame Lucia enters.

"Begin," she says, tapping her stick against the floor, and we do—all of us, Conrad at the piano and the line of us at the barre, moving as one.

It's cold in the studio, and the hairs on my body stand on end as I move through the exercises. No matter how tedious exercises can feel—the same routine, every day for years now, pliés and port de bras, tendus and dégagés, rond de jambes, fondus, frappé, frappé, frappé—we move through the work as precise and regular as a clock.

No matter what, as my muscles warm with each movement, my mind clears and everything goes away, everything but the music and the movement. I am part of a machine.

"Frederieke."

The music tinkles to a stop. Up and down the barre, dancers' heads bob out of sync.

I turn to Madame Lucia. She holds, as she always does, the long wooden prod with which she runs the class, touching it to the tops of our heads, the backs of our legs, the place between our shoulder blades.

Now, she aims it at my thighs.

I look down. A streak of red snakes from beneath my tunic.

"You're excused to the restroom. Astra, go with your sister."

As mad as she is at me, Astra doesn't dare disobey Madame Lucia. Quickly, she leaves the barre and takes me by the wrist.

My head is down as I scurry across the floor, grateful for Astra's grip, even though it's rough. I feel the eyes of Madame Lucia, of the other girls, of—oh God, of Conrad—following us from the studio.

Behind us, Madame Lucia orders, "Begin."

In the dressing room, Astra drops my arm. She turns away, rifles through her things. She says nothing to me.

"I'm dying," I mutter, desperate to fill the silence.

Astra looks up. Her face does not change. The long oval of its beauty is placid, unfeeling. Then she turns back and digs deep into her bag until she finds what she's looking for—a little fabric pouch. "Come on."

I follow her to the bathroom.

"You're not dying." She closes the door, unties the bag, and pulls out a soft, thick rag. "You got your period, that's all."

*That's all*, she says. But I have no idea what she means.

"All women bleed, every month. It's part of growing up." She waves the rag at me, impatient. I've seen cloths like these drying in the bathroom. I don't know why I'd never wondered about them. They were just something that was there, like towels or curtains. "Mama didn't tell me anything, either," Astra goes on. "I had to figure it out myself."

"Oh." Relief seeps through me like warmth from a fire.

63

"Change the rags every few hours, so they don't smell."

"When will it stop?" I ask.

Astra's mouth is perfectly flat, like the edge of a knife, and there's a moment when I have no idea which way it will curve. I have never wanted anything more than what I want right now—for my sister to smile at me, like nothing's changed. The moment vibrates.

Then the corners of her mouth turn down. She takes two steps toward me and points her finger right into my face. "You telling Opa isn't going to change a thing with me and Marcel, you know."

I nod, miserable. I do know that, now; I'd hoped that somehow Opa could intervene, but I should have known better. Astra is a force.

"I've always been there for you, Rieke. Every time you needed me. But when I ask you for one little thing, you rat me out."

"I'm so sorry, Astra. Really, I am."

She turns, yanks open the door, turns back. "Another thing. You don't need me to walk you everywhere, and I certainly don't need you trailing me anymore. So stop following me, rat tail. I'm done with you."

The door slams behind her.

Alone, I sink onto the toilet. I put my head in my shaking hands, and sob until I choke. When there are no tears left, I dry the crotch of my underwear the best I can—I don't have another pair to change into—and pull everything back together. I splash cold water on my face and blot it dry. In the long mirror on the door, I see that the pad forms a strange lump; when I look at my backside, it shows there, too.

A hand taps at the door. Maybe Astra has taken pity on me and come back. Maybe she didn't mean what she said—*"I'm done with you."* Those words make me wish I *was* dying.

But it isn't Astra; it's Ruth.

Her smile is gentle. "Do you need help?"

At first, I shake my head, but then, miserable, I nod. "Astra gave me something for the blood, but I look like I'm wearing a diaper."

"May I come in?"

I step back to make room. Fresh tears sting my eyes.

"It's okay." Her kindness makes my tears flow faster. She reaches out and I allow her to embrace me. Her hair smells like lilacs—so different from Astra's rose, but still, it feels good to be held, even for just a moment, even here in the studio's bathroom. I close my eyes and breathe her in.

Eventually, she lets go. "Everything will be fine. Here." She unfolds something she's been holding, a piece of gauzy black fabric. A dance skirt.

She winds it around my waist, wrapping the long tie twice before tying a neat bow.

"There." She turns me to the mirror. "You look like a fairy-tale princess."

Dance slippers. The floral, gauzy skirt. My tunic, swelling at the bust. "I don't think fairy-tale princesses bleed."

"Of course they do. Where do you think little baby princes and princesses come from? A princess becomes a woman, and then she meets a prince, and then they fall in love and get married. Then, baby princes and princesses."

This is news to me. It hits me like a sack of rocks, how stupid I am. And then—anger. Why hasn't Mama told me any of this? She spent my childhood chasing after my father, lying in her dark room with her bed and her pills, shutting me out.

"I can't go out there. Conrad saw me."

"He's got a mother, doesn't he? And a sister? I'll bet he's seen it before."

"That's different." The thought of Conrad seeing me, knowing . . . my cheeks go hot just thinking about it.

Ruth stands behind me, hands on my shoulders. "There's nothing you can do about what's already happened. You just have to keep moving forward. Everything will turn out fine. Okay?"

It sounds like something Opa would say. I look from my reflection to Ruth's. She smiles at me, kindly. I nod.

"Now, come on. You know how much Madame Lucia hates to wait."

When class is over and the girls are filing toward the dressing room, as Conrad stacks his music into a folder, Madame Lucia says, "Frederieke. Stay for a moment."

I've been a student at Madame Lucia's dance school for five years. Never has she spoken to me other than to correct my form, and usually she does that with her stick rather than her voice.

She waits until the room has cleared. I stand straight as if in class, clenching my backside, feet turned out in first position out of habit. She walks toward me, tapping her stick on the ground with each velvet step. *Tap. Tap. Tap.* Up close, I see how her face powder sinks into the wavy lines across her forehead, the curved lines around her mouth. Though I'm not particularly tall, I loom over Madame Lucia. How can such a small woman take up so much space?

"I take it your mother could not be bothered to explain the functions of womanhood to you."

I blink. "No, Madame Lucia."

"I have very little patience for women like that." *Who does she have patience for?* I wonder. "Do you know *why* women bleed, Frederieke?"

I clear my throat. "Ruth says it has to do with making babies. But I can't see what one has to do with the other."

She taps her stick again. "Being a woman is bloody business. There's blood each month, for many years. Some dancers find they can stop its flow if they stay very thin." She shrugs, as if to say that she has no opinion on that one way or another. "If you lie with a man, there will be blood. If you give birth to a child, blood. You'll curse the blood most of the time, except for those times when you're awaiting it desperately, when it's the only thing you want to see."

I stand motionless. I can't imagine why anyone would possibly *wish* for this.

Madame Lucia looks at me shrewdly. "Tell me, Frederieke. Your sister says she wishes to be prima. We shall see. Lately, it seems she's had . . . other things on her mind. She has the talent of course but not the temperament. You—well, we both know you don't have your sister's talent, yes?"

This stings, but it's also a relief to hear someone speak frankly. I nod again.

"Good." Madame Lucia raps the floor hard, as if to punctuate the word. "So, then—I will ask you this question, as it seems your mother doesn't have the constitution for such conversations, and Astra seems to live half in a world of her own making: What is it that you want to do with your life? Now that you have your blood, it's time for you to start thinking about what you want. What you might choose to pursue. Mind you," she warns, "it's unlikely that you will get what you want, regardless. Most women don't. But I think it's better to have an idea. So. If not dancing, then what will it be? Are you a talented student?"

I'm not. Astra is the brilliant one, though she's fiercely lazy. I shake my head.

"Humph. A homemaker, then? Would you like to have a husband, children?"

I think of Mama, pulling Astra and me through the dark-night streets, calling for our father, begging strange men to find him for her. I remember our mildewed icebox, our empty stomachs. I can think of nothing I want less than that. Even though Astra's broken our vow, I have no desire to do the same.

"No. No husband. No children."

"All right. Knowing what you *don't* want is a good start. But tell me, Frederieke—what is it you *do* want?"

I knew the answer as soon as she asked the question the first time. I want to join Opa in his shop. I want to see my name etched in the glass beneath his. It's not an *ambition*, like dancing *prima* is, or becoming a doctor, or even raising children. It's a small thing—to work with Opa, selling and repairing jewelry. To open up the backs of watches and find what's broken, and set things to right. To be together.

It's all I want. This small thing. That, and for my sister to forgive me.

I almost tell Madame Lucia about the shop, but I see Astra's expression when she shoved her pointed finger at my face, and I hear her words—*I'm done with you.*

Those words make me feel a little death, inside me. I focus on the space between my feet, the whorls of gray and brown along each thin finger of wood. A tear slides down the bridge of my nose and falls like a raindrop to the floor.

"Ah." Madame Lucia is disappointed. "Still lost." She taps her stick again, this time more lightly. "Well, the future is uncertain for everyone—these days more than ever. Still, there are only two ways to go, Frederieke, in dance and in life. You choose your path, or it chooses you."

I don't know why, but after she says that, about paths and choosing, Madame Lucia's face droops, and her gaze drifts off. Just for a moment, she looks very old and very tired. And for the first time, I wonder how Madame Lucia, with her thick French accent, ended up here, in Czernowitz, sharing an apartment with the Jewish milliner and teaching a bunch of girls to dance. What had her path been? What had she wanted it to be, and how close is what she has now?

Then her gaze snaps back into focus, sharp as ever, and seeing me surveying her, she frowns. "All right. Hurry along now."

I drop a small curtsy and turn to go.

Just as I reach the dressing room door, Madame Lucia calls to me. "Frederieke. Welcome to the blood years."

# SIX

# BROKEN, AND BREAKING

Astra is as good as her word. She's done with me. I see her at dance, and at home we still share a room of course, but she looks through me as if I'm not even there. At mealtimes, she's polite but distant; it's like living with a stranger. It would be better if she'd yell—at least then I'd feel that I matter to her. I'd take her hate over indifference.

I try everything I can think of. I give her the bigger portion of supper, when I serve it; she leaves a wedge on her plate. I wipe down the bathroom sink when it's dusted with face powder; she knocks her eyeshadow compact against the porcelain, leaving another mess. I fold her clothes and set them on the foot of her bed while she sleeps; she wakes and kicks them to the floor.

Opa sees what's happening, but just like he couldn't change things with Marcel, he can't sway Astra from her pique. One afternoon when he sees me moping by the front window, listlessly watching the gray sky, he says, "Come, Rieke, and see if you can beat me at cards, eh?"

I don't feel like a game, but I don't like to say no to Opa, who's set aside his stack of bills to make time for me. So I get the playing cards from the end table's drawer and join him. I shuffle, he deals. Almost always, when the two of us play at cards, I lose. This time, though, I have a good hand—a run of four spades, a set of three queens, and two aces.

When Opa discards an ace, I almost can't believe my luck. Snatching it up before he can change his mind, I swap it out for my useless three of hearts and lay my cards in a fan, faceup.

"Gin."

Opa looks up from rearranging his cards, his thick white eyebrows raised like two arching caterpillars. "Is that so?" His eyes run across my cards, and then he folds his hand, tapping the cards upon the table, and sets them facedown. "Nice, Rieke. Very nice."

I can't help but grin, and it feels good to smile for a change. Opa picks up his cup and sips his tea, then fishes in his shirt pocket for a coin. "Tell you what, big winner, how about you go downstairs and fetch the paper. I'll let you have the art section."

Outside, it's very cold, frigid air biting my cheeks and bare legs. I turn my face up to the sky. Snowflakes drift toward earth, fat and white and thin as dreams, melting just as soon as they touch the ground. The newsboy stands on the corner with his stack of afternoon papers; snowflakes land, shine, then melt on the bill of his dark gray cap. This is *his* corner; he's stood there, waving his papers, every day, as long as I can remember.

*Forget Astra,* I tell myself. *She's not the whole world.*

I begin to cross the street to buy a copy of the paper.

Then, the newsboy calls: "Extra, extra! Death to the Jews."

A man exchanges a coin for a paper. The transaction is so quick, so casual, exactly the same as I've done with this paperboy so many times. Snowflakes land in my eyelashes. I blink; they melt on my cheeks. I'm

71

frozen in the street, unable to take another step forward. I don't want to know what the news story is that follows that headline—it's something terrible, of course, but I don't want to know the particulars. Standing there, I feel stripped naked. My eyes dart around; is anyone is looking at me? Does anyone on this street want *me* dead?

Finally, I get my legs to move. I go back inside. Opa looks up from the cards; he's playing a game of solitaire.

"There were no more papers," I tell him. Before he can speak, I say, "I think I'll lie down for a little while."

"Rieke," he calls, "are you all right?"

I can't answer. In our room, Astra ignores me, but for once, I don't mind. I want to be invisible. I want to disappear.

The next day, Opa tells me it's better if I don't come with him to the shop for a little while. He also says that Astra and I should come straight home after school and dance.

"There's more tension with the war," he says, "and there's been some . . . aggression against Jews in some of the villages outside the city. I don't want you to worry," he says, cupping my cheek in his hand. "I just want you to be safe."

I try to convince Astra to stay home, but she pretends not to hear me. And with Mama in bed and Opa staying at his shop later and later, hoping for business, Astra comes and goes as she pleases, with no one following her. I worry about her every time she leaves the apartment, but I don't want to tell on her again to Opa—she'd probably keep doing exactly what she wanted anyway, and I can't stand the idea of doing anything to push her even further away.

Mid-March, late on a Sunday afternoon, Astra sweeps into the apartment, gliding across the floor like she's on stage. I've been reading on her bed where the light is better and I scramble up, rush to straighten the blankets. But she strides right past our door and to Mama's, which she slams open with a bang. I hear the scrape and swish of the curtains being yanked open, and then: "Mama, get up. I need you. Marcel has asked me to marry him."

I'm standing in the hallway, listening, and my mouth drops open.

Mama screeches, a sound I can't interpret—excitement? Despair? Perhaps some impossible mix of both. The bedclothes rustle as she sits up at last.

*"Married?"*

"I'm not telling you one more thing until you brush your hair." Astra leaves the room, slamming the door closed behind her. She narrows her eyes. "Little rat tail, listening at keyholes?"

It has been six weeks and two days since I told Opa about her and Marcel; it's been six weeks and two days since the last time Astra spoke to me, at dance class.

I take a step closer to her. "Tails don't have ears," I say.

"Well, careful, then, or maybe I'll snip yours off." She grins and turns to the kitchen. I follow.

There are so many things I want to say. But I have learned my lesson. Six weeks and two days is a very long time to be without your heart. So, being careful to keep my tone light, I ask, "Are you really going to be married?"

"Don't get any ideas. There won't be a flower girl."

Mama bathes and arranges her hair and fixes herself a coffee. At the kitchen table, she lights a cigarette and says nothing when Astra lights one, too.

"Tell me everything," Mama insists.

"I have Conrad to thank, oddly enough," Astra begins. "He asked me to a concert at the Musikverein."

I feel something when Astra announces this; not jealousy, of course—even though Astra has broken her vow, that doesn't mean *I'm* planning to. Watching Astra fall for Marcel has only doubled my conviction that she was right . . . nothing good can come of falling in love.

"So, I accepted, and I made sure to tell *everyone* about it."

Mama leans in. "And Marcel didn't care for *that*, I'm sure, when the news reached him."

"No." Astra smiles, a slow, sly grin. "He did not. When Conrad and I arrived at the concert house on Mehlplatz, who do you think was waiting for us on the steps?"

"Clever girl," says Mama, breathily.

Maybe it's to have a place to put the anger I feel for Astra but can't express. Maybe it's because Mama is acting like she's a teenager rather than our mother. Whatever the reason, her reaction makes me sick.

Stubbing out her cigarette in the crystal ashtray, Astra nods. "Yep."

She describes what happened next like a scene from a movie, doing each of their voices:

"What do you think you're doing?" Marcel said to Conrad, smooth as could be.

"Wh-wh-what does it look like?" Conrad answered. It's so *mean* of Astra, to make fun of his stutter, but I bite my lip, say nothing.

"It looks like you're trying to steal my girl," Marcel said.

"And that's when I spoke up," Astra tells us. "Cool as a cucumber, I said to him, 'I thought *Colette* was your girl.'" She grins, and now plucks Mama's cigarette right from her fingers and takes a drag before returning

74

it.

Mama barely seems to notice; she places her lips where Astra's have been, sucks in. The tiny fire of her cigarette burns bright red. "What happened then?"

"I thought that maybe they would fight. But instead, Marcel dropped to his knees—right there!—and begged me to marry him." Astra shrugs, as if to say it's nothing. As if to say this is something that happens to people every day, and now, it's her turn.

"And you said yes," Mama says.

"Eventually. First, I made him ask a few more times."

I can't bear not knowing. "What happened to Conrad?"

"Oh." Astra waves her hand. "I'm sure he understood."

"Did you still go to the concert?" I know I'm being stubborn, but the idea of Astra and Marcel walking off, arm in arm, all kissy and disgusting, and poor Conrad left alone on the steps of the concert hall, two tickets for the afternoon performance clutched in his hand . . . well, it's just awful.

"We'll have to start planning," Mama says. "Money is tight, but it isn't every day that we have such a reason to celebrate."

I want to rage. I want to say *Have you lost your mind? Both of you?* I want to strike them with my fists and kick them in the shins and scream until my voice is worn to rags. But I'm a coward. Astra is apparently getting married, and if I'm not careful, she might leave and actually, truly, never speak to me again.

With a faraway look, Mama taps out her cigarette. "A wedding," she says.

"No wedding," says Opa, when he gets home. It is dark, and Opa struggles through the doorway carrying a large, heavy box. Mama and Astra assault

75

him with their news before he's even set it down.

"But, Papa," Mama beseeches, "they are young, and in love, and don't we all deserve a little light?"

I clear the plates and the teacups and push the ashtray to the side so Opa can set the box on the table.

"Thank you, Rieke." Then, to Mama and Astra, "One doesn't get married at a time like this. The world is at war. And anyway, you're too young to be married, Astra."

"I'm almost seventeen," Astra protests.

"I have news." Opa continues as if Astra has not spoken. "Something happened today. At the shop." He reaches to take off his hat, and his hand trembles.

"Opa. What happened?" I ask.

He shakes his head, lips drawn tight as if he isn't going to tell us, but then he looks at our three faces and sighs. He slumps into a chair, still wearing his coat, hat clutched in his hands.

"Papa," says Mama, "what is the matter?"

Even Astra shuts up.

"There was . . . a problem at the shop today."

"What kind of a problem?"

"Nothing, nothing," Opa says. But then, "Some hoodlums. They came into the store. They said some things."

"What sorts of things?" asks Mama.

"It's not for the children to hear. Later. I'll tell you later, Anna. But I think . . . it is time for me to close the store."

Astra goes to the cardboard box and pulls open the flaps. I peer around her shoulder. Watches, and rings, and hatpins, and cuff links. Bracelets. Necklaces. All of it, tangled and twisted together.

76

"Papa." Mama says just this word, but the tone—reverence, maybe? Fear?—sends a shiver through me.

Astra starts to dig through the box, but Opa says, "That's enough," and, for once, Astra listens.

Jewelry pours from her hands with a sound like tinkling rain, and then the apartment is silent.

"No weddings." Opa stands, slowly, and goes up the hallway, still wearing his heavy coat, still clutching his hat. He enters his bedroom and gently closes the door.

In the morning, it's not just Mama who doesn't come out of her room. For the first time in my memory, Opa's door stays closed.

Astra and I sit at the table as long as we can. I wind my own watch, though it's been Opa's tradition to do it for me.

At last, we have to leave, or we'll be late for school. We put on our coats, and for the first time in a long time, Astra doesn't try to walk ahead of me. I can almost pretend things are the way they used to be, except for this heavy feeling, about Opa.

Then Astra takes a left where she should take a right.

"Astra?"

She stops, holds out her hand. "Come on," she says.

I give her mine, and follow.

As we go up the Herrengasse, I watch the sidewalk closely for patches of black ice. Because my eyes are on the ground, I don't *see* so much as *feel* that we're almost to Opa's store. Together, we stop. Together, we look.

The window to the left of the door is shattered, but the window to the right is not, and there we see a crudely painted six-pointed star. Beside it, hastily written:

## DON'T BUY FROM JEWS
## JEWPIG, YOUR HANDS SHOULD ROT OFF
## VERMIN JEW
## DEATH TO THE JEWS

And, the last, simply:

## JEW

My breath forms a cloud before my face, but it's not the cold that numbs me.

Something on the ground catches my eye—the glint of metal near the doorframe. Has Opa dropped something, maybe a bracelet, in his hurry?

I kneel to retrieve it; it's not a bracelet. It's the mezuzah, the top badly dented. Slowly I stand and examine the doorframe. My fingers run across the splintered wood. Someone ripped the mezuzah clean out and dropped it to the sidewalk like trash.

"Sons of bitches," Astra growls.

"I don't understand." The mezuzah is so cold it burns my palm. "Why would anyone do this?"

"Because they hate us, dummy."

I know she's telling me something for my own good, the way you have to drink a spoonful of nasty medicine when you're sick. And honestly, it's a relief, to hear it spoken plainly.

"They hate us," I repeat. It feels good to say it out loud. Like lancing a boil and letting the pus run.

"The Iron Guard, the Lancieri, Goga, Cuza, King Carol. All those fascist bastards." Astra looks at me, and I see a constellation of emotions in her eyes—anger about what's been done to Opa's shop, and fear, maybe, but also desperation. It's this—the desperation—that terrifies me. "They want us dead," Astra says. "Not because of what we believe, or what we don't believe. It doesn't matter if we're religious like Opa or if we think God is the same thing as a fairy tale. They want us dead because of what we *are*. The whole country wants to kill us all."

"No." I shake my head. "Not *everyone*. Opa says this isn't Germany. He says things won't be so bad here." But even as I speak the words, I know that they aren't true.

"What's this, then?" Astra gestures to Opa's ruined shop. "Listen, rat tail, I know Opa wants you to believe everything is okay. But everything is *not* okay. It's time you open your eyes. You put Opa on a pedestal and he pretends you're still a baby. And if it makes you feel better to coddle him, go right ahead. But if Opa refuses to tell you how bad things might get, and if you refuse to see it for itself, I'll say it in a way you can hear it: things are bad, and they're only going to get worse. And Rieke, it's one thing to be ignorant, but it's another thing to be stupid, on purpose."

It's terrifying, to hear Astra speak this way. But it's electrifying, too.

"What are we going to do?" I ask, breathless.

"I don't know about *you*," Astra says, "but I'm going to *live*, while I can."

She reaches out, grabs me, pulls me close. Her chin rests atop my head. I don't move. I stand right there, perfectly still, as long as she holds me. After a long time, she lets go and turns away.

"Wait! Aren't you coming to school?"

Astra barks a laugh, then turns the corner and is gone.

# PART II
# THE RUSSIAN YEAR

Spring 1940–Summer 1941

# ONE

# THE GOOSE AND THE BEAR

Five years ago—two summers after Father left, and we moved in with Opa—Opa decided that we should go to the mountains for a couple of weeks, on holiday. I think it was his way of trying to shake Mama out of her depression.

A member of his minyan, Mr. Katz, told Opa about a woman who let rooms and provided meals; a charming place, he said, and though the woman was Christian, a large portion of her guests were Jewish. "My brother and his family live in the village," he told us. "Very nice neighbors. Fresh air."

Before we left, Opa said, "Rieke, come. I have a surprise for you."

Mama and Astra were still in the bedrooms and his hired girl, Milka, who came three times a week to do the cleaning and light cooking, was in the kitchen packing us a basket for the train. Opa sat on the sofa, opened the end table's little drawer, and pulled out a small black velvet box. I ran my thumb across the velvet, soft as fur. I waited as long as I could to open it, enjoying the anticipation, but when I couldn't stand it any longer, I hinged open the box.

Inside was a silver watch with a skinny, long face and whisker-thin arms.

I looked up at Opa, as if to ask if it was really for me. He nodded, took the watch from its bed, wound it. I watched his dear face as he did—his brown-gray beard, his nose with tufts of hair protruding from each nostril, his overgrown eyebrows, all the lines around his eyes and across his forehead. Each line, each hair, was perfect. "I love it, Opa," I told him. What I meant was "I love you."

He finished winding, held the watch to his ear to listen to its tick. Then he said, "If you take care of things—if you keep them clean and mind their delicate parts and watch out for them, they can stay with you for a lifetime. Okay?" Behind his spectacles, Opa's dark brown eyes were deep and serious, and I knew even then that he was speaking about more than just the watch. He was talking about us.

"Okay," I promised.

Opa nodded, and he fastened the watchband to my left wrist.

Then we were on our way. A carriage collected us from the apartment—it took two trips to bring down all the bags.

"They have rocks in the mountains, Astra, why are you bringing city rocks?" Opa joked as he hauled the second of Astra's heavy bags to the staircase.

"It's full of books," Astra said. "I doubt they have any of those where we are going."

Opa and the carriage driver loaded the luggage, the horses waiting patiently, and Astra, Mama, and I slid into the back, the leather seat already hot at ten in the morning.

The driver flicked the reins, and away we went.

That day, when I was not yet nine, when Opa's Persian rug still stretched across our floor, before I joined ballet, when the watch upon my wrist still felt foreign and new, the Herrengasse was full of people and cars and carriages and bicycles and businesses, and our carriage took its time winding through it all.

We made our way slowly but surely, the driver yelling in Romanian at a man who rode his bicycle right in the middle of the road and tipping his cap at all the ladies we passed. I counted pigeons as we went, and remembered the summer two years earlier, on the roof with Astra. The bread, the jam, the birds, the promise.

I was scrunched in the middle between Mama, who held a hatbox on her lap, and Astra, whose face was disappeared into a book but whose arm was linked through mine, and I strained to look across them, first one direction and then the other.

Up and down the street, every door was open for business. There was the bakery, and out its door came a woman with two loaves of bread tucked into her basket—a heavy loaf of dark rye and a thick yellow braid of challah. I remember thinking how funny it was that she looked like a loaf of bread herself, doughy and soft, her hair braided and then wrapped into a bun at the nape of her neck. The Herrengasse felt awash in summer sunlight; the stores gleamed yellow and ochre, and it seemed to me that the tiled faces of each doorway and window shone with the hope of a trip about to be taken.

The people were beautiful, even the ugly ones. Mothers pushing prams down the sidewalk; gentlemen smoking cigarettes and having a conversation on the corner, gesturing wildly as they spoke; the boys who ducked under their arms to avoid being burned by those cigarettes; a young man proudly walking his German shepherd, training him to heel. The shoppers with their parcels and bags. The young couple who walked slowly, arm in arm, turned toward each other rather than facing where they were heading, lost in one another. The grim-faced matron who pushed, shoulder first, through the dawdling crowd, as if wherever *she* needed to be was vastly more important than where everyone else was going—even *she* was beautiful to me that morning. A street photographer snapped a photo of the young couple. I felt like the photographer, and the couple, too. I was all of them. They were all me. On my wrist, my watch ticked merrily, steadily along. I remember that on that morning, all was right with the world.

The train station was massive, much larger than our school or our apartment house, a long sprawling building shining pink in the sunlight, rows of windows on each wing and, at the very center, a large green dome with a little windowed turret on top. In front of the green dome were three sets of statues—two figures in each, all naked. The central, tallest figure was a woman, bare-breasted, one hand holding a child against her side, her other hand raised in greeting or salute. Glass and iron and arches and peaks. Brickwork and metalwork and big swinging doors.

Inside, rows of dark wood benches spanned the center of the room, and everywhere people bustled about, as busy as a hill of ants. Opa stepped into the queue to purchase tickets, and I left Mama and Astra with the bags to go with him. He dropped his big hand onto my head and patted my hair.

In front of us was a tall man who wore a coat too thick for the summer weather. Beads of sweat sprung up around the neckline, along a ridge of flesh that sat above his collar, beneath his bristle of short hair. Next to him stood a beautiful woman. She wore a creamy yellow dress, almost exactly the shade of the dress I was wearing; like mine, hers fell just below her knees. She had on silk stockings and heels, these a deeper yellow that reminded me of the tiled entryways on the Herrengasse. Her hair was neatly arranged in the same manner as Mama's, in a low loose twist, but hers was much lighter—blond—and atop her head perched a small darling hat, like a yellow bird.

She must have felt the weight of my admiring glance, for she turned to look down at me. I smiled, recognizing how alike we were: both travelers, each about to embark on a holiday. Surely, I thought, her heart must feel like mine—full to bursting with excitement, and expectation, and the thrill of a train ride just ahead. I held out my wrist to show her my new watch.

At first, the lady smiled, but then she glanced up to Opa, whose hand was on my head. Her mouth went from a smile to a grimace; her eyes, icy blue, washed over me from head to toe, and I felt as chilled as if cold water had been thrown in my face.

She turned away and muttered a word, under her breath: "Jidani." The Romanian word for "kikes."

Atop my head, Opa's hand tensed. I didn't dare move a muscle. The tone in her voice, the turn of her head . . .

The thrill of our journey drained like a flush of the toilet.

The couple paid for their tickets and moved away, and then it was our turn at the front of the line. When Opa purchased our tickets, I felt such relief that the destination he named—Vizhnitza—was different from the destination of that woman and that man. Opa pocketed the tickets and his wallet, took me by the hand. "Come, Frederieke. Never mind that woman. We will give you a seat by the window, yes?"

It was too warm to hold hands, and I was perhaps too old for it then as well, but even so I held on tightly as he led me back to my mother, and when he had to drop my hand a moment later to pick up the suitcases, it felt empty in a way I couldn't remember it feeling before.

A uniformed conductor greeted us, taking our tickets and punching them. We followed Opa through the train car until we found our seats. Astra began to push past me to slide next to the window, but Opa's hand came down on her shoulder.

"No. I promised Rieke that the window would be hers today."

"Astra can have the window," I said. "I don't mind."

But Opa shook his head. "The window is for you, Rieke."

Across from us, Mama and Opa settled into their seats. I gazed out the window onto the platform, and I could feel Astra rest her chin on my shoulder, looking out as well. On the platform were the woman and her gentleman. She was saying something to him, and he nodded, a strained expression on his face, and he pulled a handkerchief from his pocket, dabbed his brow and the nape of his neck.

At that moment, our train screamed, and the woman jumped, clutched a hand to her chest. Loudly, slowly, we began to pull away. She looked up to our train and our eyes caught. My first instinct was to look away, or even to duck out of sight. But I didn't; instead, I made my face ugly, narrowing my eyes and screwing up my nose, and I stuck out my tongue as far as it would go. Her eyes widened, our train went faster, and we were away, away, away.

Sparks flew from the train's iron wheels as we sped from the city. Outside of Czernowitz, great golden fields lay like finely spread blankets, one after another, fences separating this land from that. Cows watched us mildly, ears twitching, chewing their cud. Here was a woman working in her garden; there was a thick green swath of grass along a stream's shimmering edge. We slowed but didn't stop as we rolled through each village. I leaned my forehead against the great glass window, feeling the sun's warmth and the train's vibrating motion together, feeling everything. The springs in the velvet seat beneath me. The press of Astra's weight as she dozed against me. The excitement in my stomach twirling and whirling.

And the other things I'd felt—the shock and shame at the word that woman had used, the anger and defiance that had spurred me to make a face and stick out my tongue—those things faded as if they had happened to someone else.

*This* was happening to me now, this train ride, this adventure, and I held my eyes wide open so as not to miss a thing.

And yet, still, when the train stopped with a hiss and a jolt, I was startled awake. My face, damp from being pressed to the glass, stuck as I sat up. I blinked and rubbed my eyes; the sun, which had been overhead just a moment ago, had moved in the sky.

"Waste of a window seat," Astra teased as she gathered up her things, which made me laugh.

The station was not much more than a wooden platform and a small structure beside it, nothing like our beautiful station in the city. We were the only party to disembark, and then the train left us there—Astra and me, Mama and Opa, and all our luggage.

"From here, now what?" Mama asked Opa, and I could tell from the way she held her hand above her eyes to shield them from the sun that one of her headaches was coming.

"A carriage will meet us to take us to Vizhnitza." Opa pushed back his sleeve to check the time. "Soon."

We shuffled with our belongings to the shade provided by the building's overhang. It wasn't long before a cart appeared around a bend in the dirt road.

"That is not a carriage," Astra said.

"It's most likely not for us," Opa said, but, with a dry puff of dust around the horse's feet and the wagon's wheels, the driver pulled to a stop and said, "Fischmann?"

Opa nodded, and the man hopped down to help with the luggage. He spoke Ruthenian, quickly and in an accent that made understanding him difficult for me and near impossible for Opa, who responded in slow, broken words. The cart driver wore a red kerchief tied jauntily at his neck. He smiled and offered each of us his hand, which Mama and I took, but which Astra and Opa waved away.

"Some shade would have been nice," Mama said, and she held her hand again across her eyes. But I didn't mind. The open air was clean and warm. The road was one lane, hard-packed dirt with a hump in the center, and the wide-backed horse pulled us up, up, up, into the Carpathian Mountains, through the trees' dappled shadows.

The lane twisted along the mountain's ridge. I remember how I peered over to a river below, shining like a mirror in the sunlight, and the delicious fear of being up so high. Then the cart turned up a smaller path and the trees thickened, a cool shadow draping over us.

We passed through an open white gate and spied our home for the next two weeks. Not an apartment building like in the city but a cottage as if from a fairy book, whitewashed and thatch-roofed, with a bright red door and a garden spread in front of it. A dog barked, and a woman opened the door and stepped outside. Her head was covered with a clean white scarf and around her middle she wore a white apron, just as clean. Enormous breasts strained beneath her floral-patterned shirt, and when she raised her hand to wave to us, the meat of her arm waved, as well.

Beside me, Astra snorted. "At least we know the food will be good."

When the wagon stopped, the woman came down the steps to greet us, arms open. I waved, shyly, and was shocked when she lifted me right out of the wagon and embraced me, speaking in a jolly, loud Ruthenian that even I could barely understand—I caught the words "happy," and "home," and "welcome," but that was all—and then she kissed me as if she'd known me all my life, one cheek, the other, and then the first again, before she set me down.

The woman reached for Astra next, but my sister stuck both her arms out in front of her and shook her head firmly. "No," she said, and the woman had no trouble understanding *that*. She laughed, as if delighted by Astra's rudeness, and held up her hands as if in surrender, and then she shook Mama's hand, and Opa's, and began to unload the luggage.

It was the dog's turn next—a great red setter with a feathery tail and velvet ears. He jumped up and stuck his tongue right into my face, greeting me with a sticky warm-wet kiss. I laughed, overcome and delighted. "What's his name?" I asked.

Our driver came over and rubbed the dog's head. "His name," he said, speaking slowly so that I would understand, "is Peter."

"Peter," I said to the dog, and he barked in recognition.

"Andrei." The man pointed to himself. "And my mother, Maria."

"I'm Frederieke. And that's my sister, Astra."

"And your . . . other sister?" Andrei nodded in my mother's direction.

"She's not my sister! She's my mother."

"Your *mother*!" Andrei still smiled, and now I felt that he was teasing me. "But she is too beautiful to be a mother."

"Well, she *is* my mother. Her name is Anna."

"Anna." He rolled the name in his mouth like a confection, and I was immediately sorry I'd told him.

"Come on, Peter," I said to the dog. "Show me around."

91

Peter barked as if he understood me and we went, all of us, together, into the house.

"Girls," Maria said, in Ruthenian, but slowly, "you'll share the room on the left."

Astra went straight for the bed under the window. I followed, dragging my suitcase, Peter circling around me. "No dogs in the bedroom," Astra said, taking him by the scruff and pushing him out of the room, shutting the door. Then she flopped onto the bed, kicking off her shoes and peeling off her socks with her toes. I sat on the edge of the other bed and looked around. The walls were whitewashed; the room was sparely furnished with gleaming dark furniture: a dresser, a small writing table with a chair. On the wall between our beds hung a wooden cross, and on the cross hung Jesus, a semicircle carved behind his head to form a halo.

I was used to religious things—back then, we were still allowed in public school where most everyone was Christian, and every morning they all prayed while the few Jewish kids awkwardly stood and watched. But having a crucified Jesus in a bedroom seemed like a step too far. Who could sleep well in a room where someone is hanging on a cross?

"Hey," I said to Astra, "want to go look around?"

"Later," she said, rifling through her things to find a book.

I followed the sound of voices and found my mother with Maria in a second bedroom; here, too, there was a cross on the wall, this one above the dresser. This room had just one bed, double sized, and like ours it was perfectly clean. Maria seemed to be telling Mama about mealtimes, from the words I could pick out. Mama seemed to understand about as much as I did; she nodded at all the right places, at least. Then she asked a halting question in broken Ruthenian, and Maria responded. It was boring to watch them discuss household affairs and anyway I needed to use the bathroom, so I went to find it.

I opened a third door to see Opa sorting his shirts and socks into a dresser; here, also, was a cross, above the bed; and then I came to the kitchen, and then a staircase. Could the bathroom be upstairs? I grabbed the handrail and began to climb.

"Hey," I heard from behind me.

I stopped and turned. It was Andrei; his kerchief was untied, and I could see a strip of skin where it had stopped the sun from tanning.

"Those are our rooms, upstairs," he said.

"Where is the bathroom?"

His brow wrinkled; was it as hard for him to understand my accent as it was for me to understand his?

"Bathroom," I said again, slowly, and louder, as if that would help.

"Ah." He nodded. "Toilet. Outside."

I must have misunderstood him. "Toilet?"

"Outside," he said, slowly and carefully, and he pointed through the back door. There, across the yard, was a small blue structure, no bigger than a closet. An outhouse.

Maybe I didn't have to use the bathroom as badly as I thought I did, I tried to tell myself, but it was no use. The more I tried not to think about it, the more I needed to go, so I went outside and down the steps, across the yard.

*"Honk! Honk!"* The sounds came in a rush of white feathers, of orange beaks and webbed feet. A cloud of them rushed at me—geese, and angry, from the sound of them. They charged, wings aloft, waddling and honking. I screamed and ran, but the gaggle was undeterred, closing the distance between their serrated beaks and my bare legs, and I ran faster, diving for the door of the outhouse, slamming myself inside just in time.

Panting, I leaned against the door to keep it closed. The geese were no longer honking, but I heard the low, rough sound of a man laughing. I peered through the crescent moon cut into the door. It was Andrei.

When I returned to the house—chased again by the geese—I found that a meal was ready for us, though it was far earlier than we ate at home. Maria had laid the table with roasted eggplant, and cabbage leaves that were stuffed with meat, and a stew that smelled of garlic and onions. There was fresh bread, still warm, with a dusting of flour on the crust.

The four of us gathered around the table; Maria served but did not sit, and Andrei was nowhere to be seen. First, there was a drink called tuica for the grown-ups, made of plums, served in little glasses and drunk very quickly. After the drink there was soup, clear and thin, mostly broth. Then came the rest of the food.

"What kind of meat do you think this is?" Mama asked as she took up a spoonful of the stew, but none of us knew the answer and Maria didn't seem able to translate the word.

Opa covered his bowl when Maria tried to serve him the stew; though he was willing to eat in Maria's kitchen, the meat was a bridge too far for him. Still, he encouraged Astra and me to have a second serving when our bowls were empty, saying, "Growing girls need their nourishment."

After we finished eating, Opa stood. "I think a walk in the country air will do us good. Who's with me?"

Mama said her head was still bothering her and that she preferred to rest, and Astra didn't answer at all, just wandered back to our room and shut the door.

"Can we bring Peter?" I asked.

"Peter?"

"The dog."

94

"Ah, of course! We will need someone who knows the lay of the land, yes?"

Peter understood us better than Maria and Andrei; he jumped right up and barked happily.

It wasn't yet five o'clock, and the sky was full of light, and the hard-packed dirt road cut a pretty path through the fields and flowers. Opa and I set out on it together, with Peter for a guide. The dog ran happily ahead, his tail a feathery flag.

It was a fine bright afternoon. Opa radiated happiness as he walked along, and I stood as close to him as I could as if to soak it in. I slipped my hand into his, and he squeezed it.

Opa breathed in deeply, as if tasting the air. "Ah," he exhaled. Then, raising his palms to the sky: "Hashem, you have outdone yourself." He dropped his hands. "Rieke, smell the air. Go ahead. Smell it."

I took a deep breath. Opa was right; the air was delicious here. We made our way up the winding road, and for a long time we didn't talk. We just followed Peter, who seemed to know where he was going.

Then we rounded a bend and found ourselves at a vista, above a sweeping view of farmlands. Red farmhouse roofs dotted the landscape, a house to each fenced-off parcel. Here and there were trees, or a great mound of hay, piled up. It was as still as a picture until I looked more closely, and then I spied movement: the flash of sun on a creek; the slowly migrating backs of sheep; a crow, cutting black-winged across the sky.

"It's beautiful."

"The world is full of beauty," Opa agreed. He squeezed my hand again, and I knew that was his way of saying that I was part of it, that I was beautiful, too. "Even if your mother and your sister don't always see it."

Peter trotted over and sat at my feet. I placed my hand on his sun-warmed head, as Opa sometimes placed his on mine, and the dog looked up with a wide white grin.

I loved it, right there, with the world spread out like a picture just for us. Sure, Maria was overly friendly and Andrei was mean to laugh at me, but in that moment, with the dog by my side and Opa, too, I was happy.

But still, something was nagging at me. "Opa," I began, "why did you bring us here?"

"It is good to get away," Opa said. "The city can be so oppressive."

"In the summer," I said.

"Yes," Opa said, but there was a catch in his voice. Or perhaps I imagined it, for a second later he said again, more firmly, "Yes."

I remember that moment, on the hill with Opa and the dog. I remember too, when I woke suddenly late in the night to a sharp pain in my leg and the hiss of Astra's voice. "Rieke. Wake up."

She was pinching me. "Ow." I pulled my leg away. "What are you doing?"

"I need to use the bathroom."

I rolled over and pulled the covers over my head.

Astra yanked them back. "You're coming with me." It was not a question.

I sighed, rubbed my eyes. I was wearing only my thin white nightgown, so I fumbled for a sweater to pull on, my fingers still awkward with sleep.

"Come *on*."

"Why do *I* have to come?" I whispered as I followed her down the dark hall, through the kitchen and to the back door.

"Because." Her hand was on the doorknob. "I need you to distract the geese."

There was no time to protest. The door was open and Astra, white as a ghost in the moonlight, was out into the cold night air. "Come on. Stay close!" And she broke into a run across the yard, straight as a shot toward the shadow-shape of the outhouse. I stumbled across the threshold and tried to catch up, but her legs were longer and stronger and faster than mine, and I never really had a chance.

I heard it first—the feathery thrash of wings, the whisper of the grass as the goose ran-flapped after me. I screamed and tried to go faster, but the sound I made seemed to fuel its desire to catch me, for, with an angry honk and a furious fluttering, it leaped forward and landed at my heels, its vicious serrated beak clamping hard onto the calf of my left leg, exactly in the spot Astra had pinched minutes ago. I screamed louder and kept moving, the goose anchored to my leg. Astra made it to the outhouse and pulled me inside fast. The goose dropped away, one of its wings caught in the outhouse door as Astra slammed it shut. It honked again indignantly before pulling free its wing.

"It bit me!" I reached down to my calf and my hand came away wet with blood.

"Good, we're even." Astra was peeing, now.

"For what?"

"For you taking the window seat." Astra finished, wiped with a square of paper, and dropped it into the hole. "Come on." She pushed open the door and peered outside. "The geese are gone. Now's our chance."

Before I could say a word, she grabbed my hand and ran for the house, pulling me along. With each step, I felt again the burn of the goose's bite, felt a pulse of blood.

We made it to the kitchen and latched tight the door.

"Some holiday." Astra headed toward the bedroom, but now, in the safety of the house, the pain in my leg hit me, and I felt tears on my cheeks.

When I didn't follow her, Astra looked back, sighed, and said, "All right, then. Sit down. Let's take a look at it."

She pulled out a chair for me and I sank into it. There was no electricity in this house, only a kerosene lamp, which she lit and brought over. Kneeling, she pushed up my nightdress to examine the wound.

"He really got you. There's a lot of blood." She sounded impressed. The words made me want to cry harder, but I sniffed back my tears and bit my lip.

Astra went to the sink and got a clean dishrag, wetted it. Coming back, she pressed it against the wound. It hurt, but I didn't flinch. She held it there for a while, stanching the blood. I sat perfectly still and looked down at the line of white between the dark wings of her hair.

Too soon, she pulled away the washcloth. She took it to the sink and rinsed it, then found a napkin and brought it to press against my calf. "There," she said. "Better."

Then, Astra noticed the watch on my wrist; I'd worn it to bed, not wanting to take it off even to sleep.

"Opa gave that to you?"

I hesitated a moment, worried that she might be jealous, then nodded. But all she said was "It suits you."

I looked down at the watch. "You wouldn't want one?" I asked.

"Nah." She offered me a hand to help me up. "It's better this way. You can keep track of time for both of us. Besides, it would probably get annoying, taking care of something so delicate."

Astra kept ahold of my hand as we went up the unfamiliar hallway. Moonlight spilled into the room like milk.

"Want to sleep together?" Astra offered, and I nodded, eagerly. We slid side by side into her narrow bed and she pulled the sheet and thin blanket up around my shoulder. Her arm thrown across my waist, Astra fell asleep almost at once, but I stayed awake as long as I could keep my eyes open, listening to the tick of my watch, feeling the warm, sweat-damp weight of Astra's embrace.

Was it worth it—the bite—for this moment?

Yes, I decided, my eyes too heavy to keep open any longer. Absolutely yes.

By the end of the first week, Astra and I had come up with a plan for dealing with the geese. They only went after us, never the grown-ups, and they were reasonably afraid of Peter, as well. During the days we'd make sure to take the dog with us whenever we needed to use the outhouse, and we kept two long sticks beside the back door, which we wielded as weapons, waving them wildly and thrusting them at the geese if they dared get too close. They continued to circle and honk and hiss, but mine was the only goose-inflicted injury. It healed well, forming a thick scab that I couldn't help but pick at until it bled again. By the end of our stay, it had healed for good, though it left a white scar, thicker at one end and thinned out at the other, shaped like a crescent moon.

We filled our days with walks and sunlit naps and books and card games. Astra sometimes joined Opa and me, and even Mama ventured out of her room from time to time, and soon two weeks had slipped away.

The day before we returned to the city, Opa and I set out for one final walk. Peter, seeing us tying our shoes, waited eagerly by the door, and when we opened it he shot out happily into the yard.

Nearly September, the air was cool in the early mornings. It was the perfect temperature for walking. Opa and I each brought along a basket for gathering; we'd pick enough berries to take back to the city for our neighbors, and Milka could make pies with what was left. We rounded the corner to the vista and stood, enjoying the view. It was familiar to me now, the layout of the farms and their houses, the flocks of sheep and the grazing cows. Peter sat beside us and when we were ready to go on, he trotted beside me instead of running off ahead, as if he knew this was our last walk together.

Opa and I picked our way down a trail that led to a stream. Thick, green-leafed bushes lined the water, practically bursting with berries of such a deep blue they seemed almost black and dusted with a powdery gray sheen, begging to be picked and eaten. And so, we picked and we ate, filling our baskets and our stomachs, both. And after a while, Opa began to talk.

"When I was a boy," he began, "it seemed the whole world was as ripe as these berries. My parents, Hashem rest their souls, made such a life for us! Everyone knew our name, up and down the Herrengasse, and everyone spoke it with a smile. 'Good morning, Mrs. Fischmann,' they said to my mother. 'Good day, young Masters Fischmann,' they said to my brother and to me. It was more than a neighborhood. It was *family*, that is what it was. Everyone knew our name, and we knew theirs. We still have some of that on our street, in our building, yes, but it is not what it once was. 'How is your mother, Mr. Warner?' my mother would ask. 'Tell your sister how beautiful she looked in her new dress on Shabbat, Mrs. Steiner,' she would say. It was a beautiful life."

Opa paused and stared off into the sky, his vision blurred as if he was seeing into the past. "A beautiful life." He shook his head. "That is all I want for you and your sister, yes? The life I had. You should have it, too.

100

It's true that times are not good right now, my girl, but it is true that things have been not good before, and that they got better then. They will get better now, yes? They will. We must have faith."

Opa got like this, sometimes—wistful, even longing, for the past, for his parents, for the time before Czernowitz had become part of Romania, when all the street signs were in German.

"Listen," Opa said. "I heard that woman at the train station. I heard her, and I saw what her word did to you. People will wound you. Strangers. Your own family, too. So, what do we do when we are wounded?"

I shrugged. "Fight back?"

"Sure. That is one thing we do. But it is not the only thing. It is not even the best thing, though sometimes to fight is a thing we must do. Rieke," he said, "Hashem chose us for a reason. You understand? We are Hashem's chosen people. And for why?"

He didn't wait for an answer, which was a good thing, as I didn't have one.

"It is because of our capacity to love. It is because we can love more persistently than they can hate. Scripture tells us, '*Olam chesed yibanei*. I will build this world with love.' That is what we are here to do, my girl. To build, with love."

It always made me uncomfortable when Opa started in with God. He knew that Mama wasn't religious. I didn't know what I believed.

Still, what I said was "I understand, Opa." Another way, I suppose, of saying "I love you."

"Okay," he said. "Okay. That's enough of that."

We went back to picking berries and worked until our baskets were nearly full. Peter had found a shady spot beneath a tree, and he rested there, eyes closed, his head upon his paws. Opa turned to his thoughts, and

101

I to mine, and we worked without words, enjoying the feeling of the firm berries, the way the stem of each resisted for a second before it released, enjoying the sound of the stream and the rustle of leaves and the rhythmic tug of berries from bushes.

I think it was Opa who saw the bear first, even before the bear saw us. Opa froze in place, hand outstretched; it was his stillness that caused me to look up and to follow his gaze across the stream. And there it was.

It was an adolescent, not large for a bear, I know now. But much bigger than Peter on all fours, and taller than Opa when, upon catching sight of us, it stood up on its hind legs.

Opa said nothing to me, but he shifted, just slightly, so that his body was between mine and the bear's. I knew Opa wanted to protect me, but I peered my head out from behind him. I'd never seen a bear, outside of pictures. In fairy books, they slept in houses and ate porridge from bowls.

But seeing this one, in real life, I was struck by a truth: a bear is not a person. Even if it stands on its hind legs like a person and clasps its hands like a person, it is not, and can never be, a human being. A bear is a giant, dangerous, wild animal.

I stood perfectly still. From across the stream, I studied its thick black pelt; its rangy body; its reddish-brown muzzle; its shiny black eyes. I didn't breathe. The bear didn't blink. Opa stood, forming a wall between us. The ticking of my watch was frantic and loud—before I realized it was my heart I was hearing, pounding in my ears. And if not for the beating of my blood, I might have thought that time stood still, as we did, Opa between me and the bear, that great black beast, so close to human in the way it held itself, the expression in its eyes. I was scared, yes—I was terrified—but I also knew that Opa would protect me. He would never let this animal hurt me. And I was right: finally—at last—the bear dropped to all fours and wandered away.

When it was gone, Opa let out a deep breath. I did the same. He reached back and put his hand on my head the way he liked to do. I was grateful for its warm, familiar weight.

"I think we have enough berries, yes?"

I nodded.

It wasn't until we were retreating up the path that Peter shook off sleep and rose to follow us.

"Useless dog," Opa chastised, and we both had a good laugh at that.

The next morning, we said our goodbyes, and I wept into Peter's neck. He licked my tears gamely and wagged his tail when I slipped him a piece of meat that I'd saved from the breakfast table. Maria managed to land a kiss onto Astra's cheek, which infuriated my sister and made me want to laugh, but I didn't want to insult Maria.

We were the only passengers to climb aboard at our station; Astra slid next to the window and threw her arm across my shoulders as I tucked in next to her. I suppose vacation must tire one out, because I don't think any of us managed to stay awake. Mama and Opa were asleep even before we'd wound our way out of the mountains; the pang of sadness I felt upon returning to the flatlands drew shut my eyes, and I slept the rest of the way home.

Unlike the coolness in the mountains, the air in the city was just as hot as when we'd left, made hotter by the press of bodies exiting the train station. All around me faces looked unhappy, irritated, on edge. It must be the weather, I thought; it was making everyone grumpy.

But then just outside the station Opa bought a newspaper, and his expression as he read the front page chilled me to my bones.

"Opa, what is it?"

He ignored me, scanned the street. "We need a carriage." And there, as if on cue, a carriage appeared. Opa shot up his arm and waved.

The driver slowed and pulled to the curb, but just as Opa reached for the carriage door, the driver said something—I don't know what, I couldn't hear him, but I saw his lips move—and then he snapped the reins sharply and yanked his horses hard to the left, back into the street.

"What was that?" Astra said. "Why didn't he stop for us?"

Again, Opa ignored us—as frightening as the driver's behavior. He saw another carriage and waved his arms again, then whistled—high and sharp, a desperate sound.

This time, the driver barely slowed. Again, he looked at us; again, he went away.

"Papa," said Mama, "what is going on?"

Without a word Opa thrust the paper in her direction and turned back to the street.

I went to Mama; I read the paper's headline. "Christians United Against the Jews," it read. Underneath was a photo of a young Romanian man—maybe twenty years old, with a short-clipped mustache, ears that stuck out, a half smile—with the words "Murdered by Jews—30 Arrested."

"Murdered? Mama, who was arrested?"

Like Opa, she ignored me, folding the paper and tucking it into her purse.

Astra stepped forward. "Let me try." Though Opa began to protest, Astra lifted an arm and flagged the next carriage.

This one stopped, though when the driver saw that Astra wasn't alone, he tried to pull away. Too late—Astra had already wedged herself into the back seat, pulling Mama in alongside her, and Opa was loading our luggage into the carriage.

At home, Opa opened the door, touching the mezuzah before stepping aside to let Mama, Astra, and me in first. Just past the threshold, I stopped and looked around. Before we had stayed in the small thatched-roof mountain house, I had never noticed how high and grand our own ceilings seemed. Opa's hired girl Milka had drawn open the long white curtains, and they billowed as Opa closed the front door. She had also prepared the apartment for our return. Fresh flowers filled vases on each table, and there was a small bouquet on the mantel as well. In front of our well-stuffed velvet sofa, magazines and newspapers from the time we had been away were fanned on the coffee table. All around were the knickknacks and doilies and framed photographs and vases and tables and chairs that I had seen all my life, or, rather that I *hadn't* seen, for returning to them now felt strangely as if I were walking into a brand-new room, or at least one I'd never properly paid attention to before.

Milka emerged from the kitchen. Her, too, I saw with fresh eyes. How lovely she looked, in her usual black dress and white apron, her small gold cross around her neck, and I almost teared up to see the familiar tilt of her head, the flat lines of her brows and lips.

But when she spoke—"Good day, Mr. Fischmann"—her voice was not familiar. It was distant, cold.

"Good day, Milka," Opa said. "I trust all has been well in our absence?"

I saw Milka's gaze flash to the newspapers on the coffee table before she answered, "For the most part."

"Did you restock the kitchen?" Mama asked.

Milka nodded. "All the basics."

"Good." Mama unpinned her hat as she walked across the front room, toward the sofa. "I think we'll have tea, Milka."

But Milka didn't move.

Mama said, "Is there a problem, Milka?"

"It didn't seem right to quit while you were away." Milka's voice grew softer, more familiar. "I wouldn't want you to come home to find the house not ready for you."

"Quit?" said Opa. "Milka, what is this about?"

Her hand reached up and she touched the cross that hung on a thin gold chain. "I've got your dinner started. There's milk in the icebox. Everything's been dusted." It seemed like she would say more, and all of us—me, Mama, Opa, even Astra—waited to hear it.

But then Milka cleared her throat, and she went to the coatrack, took down her purse. She nodded to Opa. "You've been good to me." And that was all she said. She closed the front door gently behind her.

"What on earth . . ." Mama said.

"Is she coming back?" I don't know why I asked. Even then, I knew the answer.

"Girls," said Opa, "go unpack your bags."

Astra started to protest—normally Milka would be the one to put our things away. But she must have thought of this, for she closed her mouth and, for once, did as she was told.

But in our room, Astra didn't unpack. She abandoned her suitcase by the door and pulled something out from beneath her arm—it was the newspaper from before, which Mama had put in her purse. Astra must have taken it when she went for her suitcase. She went to her bed and laid out the paper so that we could see the headline and the photograph all at once. It was in Romanian, of course, which I could read but found harder to understand. Astra, sensing my frustration, translated for me.

"It says the Jews were paranoid that something would happen to the

House of Yiddish Culture," Astra said. "It says hundreds of Jewish workers occupied the building day and night and refused to go home. But . . . 'Of course no such attack was planned, and it was only the Jewish tendency for hysteria that caused the fuss in the first place.'" Astra's voice dripped with derision, and her dramatic translation helped make it seem as if this was all just a story rather than a thing that had really happened, a thing we were reading about in the papers.

She continued, "'The clashes between the good citizens of Romania and the hothead Jewish youths escalated until finally it came to a head in the Volksgarten.'"

Here she stopped translating for me and scanned ahead quickly, her eyes flashing back and forth across the lines of print. Even though the day was warm, I felt a chill at the mention of the Volksgarten—the People's Garden. I knew that it was really just for *some* people, and not for Jews. When Opa was young, the Volksgarten had been a welcome place for everyone. But Astra and I were not to go there, Opa was very firm about that, and of course I wouldn't have dared to, anyway; there were posted signs at each entrance warning us that Jewish walkers entered at their own risk and could not expect protection from the police, who wished to stay neutral in such matters. It was a shame, as it was the nicest park in Czernowitz, but it was simply a fact that the park was not safe.

And yet the article Astra was reading said that a group of young Jewish workers had gone there.

"What else does it say?" I peered at the newsprint and tried to catch a thread of meaning.

"Rieke, go and get the Jewish paper from the front table. Bring it back here, quick."

"There's no way Mama will let me have it."

"Figure it out," Astra said, and so I did.

I opened the door slowly to keep it from making a sound and listened for Mama and Opa. They were in the kitchen; I could hear Mama's shoes clicking on the parquet and I heard the *tic-tic-tic* of the stove as she lit the burner. On tiptoes, I snuck into the front room. There on the coffee table was the Jewish paper, the *Ostjüdische Zeitung*. It was disarranged, having been picked up and set back down again in the time since Astra and I had left to put away our things. No one noticed me as I took the paper and snuck back to our room, and I closed the door with a sense of guilty triumph.

Astra grabbed it from my hand without a word. "You're welcome," I said haughtily, but she ignored me, lost in the paper. I scooted next to her on the bed, and she made room for me.

This paper was in German, which I understood easily, but the first thing I noticed was not words—it was a photograph. It was another young man, different than the one in the Romanian paper, but about the same age, with dark, wavy hair parted to the right. Small, round glasses. Kind eyes, a gentle smile. I knew this person—he was Edi Wagner, the pianist at our dance studio.

"Astra, why is Mr. Wagner in the newspaper?"

"Because," she said, her eyes still not rising from the page, "he's dead." Astra thrust the paper into my lap. "See for yourself." She scrubbed tears from her eyes and left the room.

I couldn't look away from the photograph of Edi Wagner. It was like he was staring at me. But at last, I read. The article said that there had been a fight in the Volksgarten the previous Wednesday—same as the Romanian paper reported—but rather than saying the Jews were to blame, this article said it had been a clash between fascist antisemites and a Jewish youth group. The leader of the Fascists had taken a knife wound to the heart and had fallen dead. No one knew who had stabbed him, but thirty Jewish youths—including Edi Wagner—were arrested.

"All were severely beaten," the story continued. "Police claim that Edi Wagner leaped from a second-story window during questioning, but others say he was thrown from the window by police after interrogation. He was brought by police, critically wounded, to the Central Hospital, and upon examination it was found that he had been beaten severely before he had suffered his fall. He died without regaining consciousness that night and was buried in secrecy with only his mother present so as to protect the location of his body from further desecration."

I set down the paper. Edi Wagner stared up at me.

I remembered, then, the bear in the mountains. If not for Opa, standing between me and the bear, I would have been dead for sure.

That was what I thought then, when I was a child. That Opa could keep me safe from bears.

Now, standing in front of Opa's ruined shop—a place where broken things were meant to be set to rights—I begin to think differently. Opa formed a wall the best he could. But if that bear had wanted me dead, I probably would have died. Opa couldn't have stopped it. All he could have done was die before me.

If I hurry, I can still get to class on time, barely. Before I leave, I look again at the words on the window. *Heinrich Fischmann, Jeweler.* Someone has defaced this too, partially covering it with paint, so the words now read *Heinrich Fischmann, Jew.*

If things do get worse, as Astra says they will, it'll be better for Opa's name not to be etched in the window for all to see. I pick up a fragment of glass, intending to scratch out his name. But with the first scrape, the glass fragment breaks, its sharp edge slicing into my finger. Blood wells and I gasp, drop the glass, stick my finger into my mouth, suck. The blood tastes of iron, which is so strange to me. Is there metal in me? It doesn't seem like it could be true. Astra, yes—but me?

I take my finger from my mouth and wipe it on my skirt. Then I shrug off my coat. I make a fist with Opa's mezuzah at its center and wrap the coat around it, and then I punch the glass.

As my fist goes through the window, I remember Opa's words by the river, before the bear: *"We can love more persistently than they can hate."*

Astra's right. I need to see the world for what it is. I won't be stupid, on purpose. But Opa's right, too. I'll also see my *them*, my family, with clear eyes—for what they are, rather than what I wish they were—and I won't stop loving them. So much is beyond me, too complicated and too big for me to change. But this, I can control. I will love my family. We will not fall apart. And if we must, we will stand together before the bears.

When I shake glass shards from my coat, they catch the light and throw rainbows across the ruined storefront, across the snow. I put on my coat and shove Opa's mezuzah deep into my pocket, and then I run to school.

# TWO

## WHEN FLYING MONKEYS ATTACK

In March, not long after Opa's shop is destroyed, the Germans bomb England.

In April, they attack Denmark and then Norway.

In May, they invade the Netherlands and Belgium.

German soldiers rampage through country after country. Now that I'm searching for it, news is everywhere: Adolf Hitler's unhinged, terrifying rants on the radio, which I turn on the moment Opa leaves for the synagogue to pray with his minyan; rumors in the hallways of our apartment building and on the streets, horror stories about Jewish families being ripped apart, men taken in the middle of the night from their homes, whole families shipped off to ghettos. In a town called Oswiecim in southern Poland, the German occupiers establish a detention center for political prisoners—nearly a thousand homes are demolished to build it. They are calling it Auschwitz.

"That could never happen here," Opa tells me, but now that I'm looking for it, I recognize that there is fear in his eyes. It's for love that he's lying—to protect me from the truth—and so I do the same. I pretend to believe him.

And people are saying that even if the Germans don't invade Romania, the Soviets might. Some say the Soviets might be the better of two devils. In the entryway of our building, as I return from dance, I hear Mrs. Oppenheim tell her husband that maybe a Soviet invasion could be a blessing in disguise. "At least they could protect us from the Germans," she says. Mr. Oppenheim doesn't disagree, just holds open their apartment door and nods, his short brush of a mustache twitching.

Then the Germans bleed into France. Though I've never been to Paris, I dream of it, we all do—the cinema, the dancers, the food—so when it surrenders to the Germans on the sixteenth of June, just two days after Astra graduates and school ends for the summer, it feels truly shocking. That great city, a place my own Czernowitz aspired to emulate, on its knees, a knife at its throat. Bereft, Madame Lucia closes our dance studio for two weeks out of respect for her homeland.

Astra's seventeenth birthday comes on the twenty-eighth of June. At breakfast, Mama puts a candle in a biscuit for her to blow out, and Opa gives her a golden brooch in the shape of a flower, tucked into one of the remaining velvet boxes from his shop, which makes my heart ache.

When breakfast is finished, Astra says, "So, rat tail, are you ready to go to dance?"

"It's closed until Monday," I tell her.

But Astra shakes her head. "Ruth told me that Madame Lucia wants us all there by nine o'clock sharp."

I look at my watch—it's half past eight. "Why didn't you tell me sooner?" I push back my chair and rush to gather my things. In my room I have the idea to bring along the few coins I have; if there's time on the way home from dance, maybe I can buy Astra a scoop of ice cream for her birthday.

"Straight there and straight back, and stay together," Opa says.

"We'll be home by two," Astra tells him, and she bends down a little to let him kiss her goodbye.

He kisses my cheek, too, and pats it. "Better hurry," he says.

But as soon as we emerge onto our stoop, there's Marcel, a cigarette dangling from his lip. Astra runs to him and he takes the cigarette from his mouth, blows out the smoke, kisses her.

They turn to go up the street. Astra says, "Thanks for covering for me. I'll meet you back here at two o'clock and we can go up together, okay?"

"Wait!" I call, but she doesn't hear me. She and Marcel have their arms around each other, and they're laughing. Her white summer dress dances around her knees; her bare calves are long and smooth.

I watch them until they turn the corner. Anger bubbles in my chest. What should I do now? The last time I ratted on Astra, she didn't talk to me for weeks. Six weeks and two days.

Sighing, I lower myself to sit on the front stoop. I remember the promise I made myself—I will love my family for who they are, not who I wish them to be. And my sister hasn't changed; she's being what she's always been—headstrong, selfish, passionate. I do love her for it. Even when she drives me mad.

At least it's a beautiful day. All up and down the block, the trees are in bloom.

"Hi, Rieke." It's Jeremy Applebaum, his mother behind him. I wave. "Where's Astra?" he asks, but his mother takes his arm and leads him away before I can answer. What would I say, anyway? I don't know where she went, or what she plans to do. All I know is who she's with.

Slowly, I head down the street. Briefly, I consider going to the little cove along the river Prut that we call Bird Beach. I don't know if it has an official name.

We call it Bird Beach both because of all the birds that go there to beg for scraps, but also for the people who flock to it as soon as the weather is nice. They bring picnic baskets and umbrellas and blankets. When Mama was so sick with headaches after Father left, Opa took Astra and me there all the time to watch the birds and the people, both. We stood along the shore, all of us with bare feet—even Opa, whose feet looked white and funny through the clear river water, like pale fish—and threw the bread to the ducks and terns and swallows that came to beg for it.

Once, we saw a young man—maybe twenty, in short pants—bend to his knee to propose to his girlfriend, a sallow-faced brunette who looked as if she might cry.

When she said yes, the young man jumped right up and rubbed his legs where they'd pressed into the sand. It was so hot it burned him, which made Astra and me laugh wildly.

"Love will burn you up," Opa had said, and that made us laugh even more.

"Love will burn you up," I say out loud to myself, thinking of Astra.

I want to go to Bird Beach, but I know I shouldn't head that far away from home by myself. Anyway, it's too hot and humid for such a walk, and so when I pass in front of the building where Esther lives, on a whim, I decide to see if she's home.

Like us, Esther's family lives on the second floor. The stairwell smells like cooking oil and baby diapers, and I hear a child wailing somewhere up above. When I knock, it's Conrad who answers the door. The first thing I see is the soft divot at the base of his throat, right at the place where his shirt splays open. Then I glance up, to his Adam's apple, his chin, speckled with the beginning of a beard—copper, like his hair—his mouth.

I swallow.

"Hi, Rieke." He widens the door, turns to look over his shoulder. "Esther! Ri-Rieke's here." He steps back to make room for me. "She's probably mooning over one of—one of those magazines of hers."

I step across the threshold. I try to think of something to say but can't seem to form words, and I'm relieved when Esther finally comes out of her room. She's reading a magazine as she walks toward us, not bothering to watch where she's going. Her glasses have slipped down her nose and I'm worried that either her glasses are going to fall off or she's going to run into a wall, or both. But by some miracle Esther makes it to us in one piece, and then she finally looks up. "Hi, Rieke! What are you doing here?"

I almost tell her about how Astra lied to me and ditched me for Marcel but then I remember that could be a sore topic for Conrad, so I shrug and say, "I was just passing by and thought I'd stop in."

"Well, you're just in time," Esther says, grinning now. "Want to go see a movie with us? It's at the Savoy!"

I have the coins in my pocket, and I won't be buying Astra ice cream, now. "Which movie?"

"It's called *The Wizard of Oz*. And it's in Technicolor!"

It turns out that Conrad doesn't want to watch the movie but was planning to walk Esther to the theater so she wouldn't be alone. I like the way he walks, rolling up onto the balls of his feet with each step. The way he folds the cuffs of his trousers so that the tops of his brown leather boots show. The way the hair on the back of his head whirls counterclockwise.

There's an energy in the air, a crackle of something like electricity.

Everyone we see seems keyed up, irritable. Mothers keep their children extra close, everyone hurries, hurries, no one stopping to make conversation. It's hot, so that's part of the reason why people are anxious to get off the streets, but it feels like more than that.

It would be faster to cut through the Volksgarten, but of course we don't. I don't know if Esther and Conrad think about Edi Wagner every time they pass it, the way I do. We could take the trolley, but none of us has extra money for that, so we walk the longer route down the Herrengasse, past the string of shops—cafés, a bookstore, the pharmacy where Mama gets her pills. It feels even hotter in the Ringplatz, where there's so much concrete and so little greenery; trolly cars rumble down the street with no regard for pedestrians. We pass city hall, its tall spire casting a long sharp shadow across the monument—a monstrous thing, there's a life-sized bull, and two enormous eagles, all beneath a pedestal with a sculpture atop it, a solider and a peasant, together kissing the Romanian flag.

Nearby is a wall where notices are posted, and today it's plastered with advertisements for summer holiday stays, the Vatra Dornei spas in the mountains, resorts near the Black Sea. It doesn't go together—seeing these vacation posters on our way to the cinema, while just beyond our borders is war.

There's a sharp, shrill scream, and all of us—me, Esther, Conrad—gasp together. Conrad grabs Esther's collar and yanks her close. But it's just children playing in a fountain, trying to cool off. We laugh, but there's a nervous energy in it, right beneath the surface.

Conrad tells us he'll be waiting for us when the movie is over. Inside the cinema, it's dark and cool. Esther and I find two seats together near the back. We're not the only people who thought to escape the heat in here. Before the film begins, there's a newsreel, images of German soldiers as tall as trees on the screen in front of us, and my chest tightens. I don't want to watch, so I say I'm going to use the bathroom.

In the ladies' room, I bend over the sink and splash water on my face. I close my eyes and press my palms against my eyes until I see little stars. I shouldn't have come. Even if Astra wants to run all over town with Marcel, I should be home with Opa and Mama. But it's too late now, I've paid for my ticket. I pat my face dry and go back to the theater and I'm glad to see that the newsreel is over.

The movie begins, and for two hours, I'm somewhere else—first a flat gray land called Kansas, where the people don't look so different from us, and then, incredibly, beautifully, somewhere else. Somewhere filled with color, with music, with magic.

"Isn't she amazing?" Esther whispers as Dorothy Gale sings about somewhere over the rainbow.

I nod. She really is.

When the film is over, the theater erupts in applause. I clap, too, even though no one who made the movie can hear us. We join the crowd pushing out of the theater. Everyone is talking about the movie—the Technicolor, the songs, the costumes.

"That's what I want to do," Esther tells me when we get to the lobby.

"You want to be an actress?" Esther doesn't much resemble Judy Garland. And she's not a very good dancer, either; she's one of the girls Madame Lucia doesn't often bother to correct.

"I don't care what I do if it has something to do with the movies. I'll do anything. Style hair. Sew costumes. Type copies of the script. Sweep the sets."

This doesn't seem like too much to ask. It could happen for Esther. I've never met anyone as crazy about movies as she is, after all.

But then we push through Savoy Cinema's glass doors and we're back in the humid, oppressive heat, and I remember where we are, and who we are. I remember Opa's shop. I don't have the heart to look at Esther, who practically floated out of the theater. She feels it, too—how the heat is like a hand on the backs of our necks, pushing us down, the electric snap in the air.

Conrad is waiting for us, arms crossed, a muscle jumping in his cheek. As soon as he sees us, he grips Esther's arm. "We need to get home." He walks quickly, pulling her along.

I rush to keep up. "Did something happen?" When he doesn't respond I grab his sleeve. "Conrad. What happened?"

He stops, turns. There's a look in his eyes that I don't know how to describe. His eyes, wild, stormy, frantic—remind me of the music that was playing in the movie, when the flying monkeys attacked.

I can barely speak. "Is it— Is Astra okay? Did something happen to her?"

"What?" Conrad shakes his head. "N-no. Nothing like th-that."

My relief is so intense that I almost have to sit down on the curb. It's so intense that I only half hear what he says next, even though he doesn't stutter.

"It's the Russians. They're coming."

Conrad explains as he rushes us back to our neighborhood. "Everyone on the street was t-talking about it, as soon as the afternoon paper re-reported it. While you were in the—in the theater."

The Russians, fortifying their hold on Eastern Europe against Germany's aggression, have made an ultimatum. Romania can either cede territory peacefully and take its military out of Bessarabia and Bukovina, or the Soviets will take those areas by force.

Czernowitz is part of Bukovina. *We* are part of Bukovina. The Savoy Cinema, the sidewalk beneath our feet, is part of Bukovina. And the Romanian government has ceded it. Has ceded *us*.

"Our military is fleeing like t-ticks off a drowning dog," says Conrad. We're at the corner near the wall posted with advertisements, waiting for the streetcar to pass. *Take the Waters,* one of the posters reads. *Get out of the City and Relax.* Conrad yanks Esther away, and together, we break into a run.

Conrad and Esther leave me in front of my building. But I'm not going inside without Astra. I look at my watch; it's nearly two o'clock, when Astra said she'd be home. I pace and up down the block, waiting for her, but at half past two, I make a decision to try to find her.

The only place I can think she might be is Café Europa; that's her and Marcel's favorite place. I rush there, as fast as I can without running. I don't like being on the street by myself, but I don't want to draw attention, either. I breathe a sigh of relief when I get to the café and step inside. She and Marcel aren't there. But Mr. Weissinger is.

He sits at a table in a far corner. I see him in profile: the thin rim of his glasses; the glisten of his oiled-back hair; the looseness of skin around his jowl and a thin sheen of sweat across his brow, which he blots with a fresh white handkerchief from his pocket. In front of him is an espresso, a biscuit, and a stack of paper currency alongside a notepad. Compared to how electric the street felt and how fast my heart is racing, Mr. Weissinger's calm demeanor is strangely disorienting.

Maybe it's that sense of being thrown off balance that grounds me where I am. It feels like Mr. Weissinger is the center of something, and that feeling intensifies when, behind me, the bell dings and a man enters. With him comes the warm afternoon breeze. He takes off his hat as he goes to Mr. Weissinger's table, waiting to sit until Mr. Weissinger gestures that he may.

The waitress circles by, but the man shakes his head. Then he leans in close to Mr. Weissinger. I can't hear what he says, but the *way* he speaks—beseechingly—sends a shiver up my back, even though it's warm in here. Under the table in his lap, he clutches the rim of his hat, twists it.

Mr. Weissinger listens, expressionless, and when the man is finished, he nods, once.

The man collapses into his chair. Relief changes everything about him—his shoulders relax, his hands go still, his mouth curls in a momentary flash of a smile. Mr. Weissinger makes a note on his pad and then counts several bills from his stack, folding and handing them to the man, who takes the money quickly and tucks it into the pocket of his shirt.

"Excuse me, darling," the man says on his way out of the café, lighter now with whatever business he'd settled behind him.

Mr. Weissinger looks over, following the man's voice, and sees me by the door. He beckons. "Frederieke, hello." He stands to greet me. He has such fine manners. "Please." He gestures to the seat across from him. "Join me."

He waits for me to sit before he sits down again. Neatly, he stacks the bills inside the notebook, folds it closed. "All alone?"

I nod. "I'm looking for my sister. I don't suppose you've seen her?"

"Ah." Mr. Weissinger looks amused. "The future Mrs. Goldmann. I hear congratulations are in order."

Is he mocking me, Astra, our family? It feels as if he is.

"Have you heard about the Soviets?" I ask him.

"Of course, of course." He nods. "It means it will become even harder for most people to find the things they need." There's an expression on his face—not a smile, exactly, but a look of contentment.

The waitress arrives and asks me, "Would you like something?"

I shake my head, but Mr. Weissinger says, "Bring her an omelet, some toast, a cup of coffee—no, make that lemonade."

The waitress makes a note.

I start to say, "I don't need any of that," but she's already walking away. So instead, to Mr. Weissinger, I say, "Thank you."

He waves as if it's nothing, which, given the stack of bills I saw on the table, I suppose it is, to him. In a flash I see my opa slumping into our apartment, carrying his last box of wares from his broken shop.

"Your sister is headstrong, like your father," he says. "She goes after what she wants. And that temper, hmm? Same as your father."

I narrow my eyes. It's one thing for *me* to think these things. It's another thing entirely for Mr. Weissinger to say them.

Mr. Weissinger sees my cross expression, laughs, holds up his hands in mock surrender. "Okay, okay. You're loyal to her, I can see it. Nothing wrong with that. Nothing wrong with a little loyalty. Who do *you* take after, I wonder?" Here he stops, tilts his head, looks at my face very carefully, like he is reading fine print. "More like your mother. Am I right? You look like her, that's certain."

Do I? I shrug.

"Your hair is lighter than your mother's, and you have a smaller nose. Same mouth, though."

I push back my chair, about to make my excuses and leave—maybe Astra's back at our building, waiting now for *me*—but just then the waitress returns with my food, and I can't think of a way to refuse it, and the sight of it makes me realize how hungry I am.

The omelet is delicious. Buttery melted cheese. Fluffy eggs. Little wedges of red pepper. The lemonade is wonderful, too. Icy cold, the tall glass weeps. Mr. Weissinger sits back and watches as I eat. I try to keep myself from stuffing my mouth, but I'm not entirely successful.

I pat my mouth with my napkin, attempting to recover a shred of manners. "Thank you."

The waitress delivers a fresh espresso to Mr. Weissinger. "It's nothing," he says. Then, "Let me ask you a question, Frederieke. What happened there?"

He points down, at my calf—the scar where a goose took its bite all those years ago. I remember how terrified I was. I remember the serrated orange beak, sharp as a knife.

"I cut it on a piece of metal at a play yard when I was young." The lie slips out without my even planning it. I know why I lie—it's because I don't want to give a sliver of my time in the mountains to Mr. Weissinger, not even the bad parts.

"Ah. A shame." He clears his throat. "Listen, Frederieke. I want you to know that I am someone you can come to. If you need things, you come to me. You ask me. All right?"

I remember what Opa said about Mr. Weissinger: that he's the kind of man who always collects interest. I twist the napkin in my lap. "That's very nice. I really appreciate it. But right now, all I need is to find my sister."

"Perhaps I can help you with that. Have you tried Marcel's apartment?"

"I don't know where he lives."

"Luckily, I do."

Mr. Weissinger gives me the address. It isn't far. "Thank you," I say again, standing. "Now I'm indebted to you for the meal *and* the information."

I smile to show I'm joking, but Mr. Weissinger's mouth stays flat. "Another time."

As I go through the door, I look back. Mr. Weissinger is removing his notebook from his pocket, folding it open, setting the stack of bills alongside it again, as if he's open for business once more.

It takes me a full minute to get up the nerve to knock on Marcel's apartment door. Muffled music, the same sort of stuff the Café Europa band plays in the evenings, tells me that someone is definitely home. There's another sound, too, one I can't make sense of.

Finally, I knock. No one answers.

My watch says it's just past three o'clock. Opa will be so worried. I try the doorknob; it turns, the door opening to reveal an empty room.

The music is coming from a record player on a table. Sunlight shines through the window above, reflecting off the ridged black circle, pinned beneath a needle, spinning. It's a clean room, smaller than ours, but nicely appointed with a rug, a bookshelf, lamps, tables, and a green velvet sofa. Photographs line the mantel, mostly of Marcel with various people his own age, others with an older woman who must be his mother. His diplomas, framed, hang on the wall. The place smells different than our apartment. Musky.

There's an open doorway into a kitchenette and a thin hallway. The apartment is small enough that I can see into the open door at the end of the hallway—the bathroom. To the left is another door; this one is cracked open as well. That is the room the other sound is coming from—a sort of frantic yowl, a keening rhythmic cry. It's Astra's voice, and though I am unclear on what exactly is happening in the bedroom, I know enough to not go any deeper into the apartment. But I can't quite bring myself to leave, either.

Astra's cries grow louder, more frantic. The music plays on, and on. The same trumpet sounds, over and over and over. With a jolt, I realize that the needle has hit a scratch and it's caught in a groove, on repeat. It will continue to replay those same notes until someone moves the needle or unplugs the record player.

I want to leave and pretend I was never here—I almost do. But then I picture Opa, pacing the length of our sitting room, stopping to pull back the curtain and look down on the street for us, worried, worried.

I close my eyes, breathe deeply. Then I set my shoulders, go to the record player, and lift its arm. The music stops, though the record spins on.

"Astra!" I call.

Just as the record goes quiet, so too do my sister's yowls. There's a beat of absolute silence, and then—laughter, hysterical laughter, from Astra and Marcel both. My cheeks flame with embarrassment. I fold my arms across my chest. I am aware of every inch of my body, from the top of my head to the tips of my toes.

The bedroom door cracks open, and Astra's head peeks out—her hair is a mess, half up and half down, and her mouth looks swollen—from kissing, I'm sure. Her shoulders are bare, leaving no doubt that the rest of her must be, too.

"Rat tail!" Rather than sounding furious, as I expected, the lilt of her voice is light. "Give me a minute." Her head disappears; the door clicks shut.

I hear their voices, just the sound of them, masculine and feminine, but not the words. Still, I understand the cadence, a sort of music—he's

124

trying to convince her to stay, cajoling, begging, and she's coyly resisting.

I'm beginning to wonder if she'll ever come out when she emerges, dressed in the white sundress she left in, holding her shoes. Her hair is still a mess and she runs her hand across it as she comes up the hall to me, stumbling slightly.

"Are you—drunk?"

She laughs again, reaches me, kisses my forehead. I smell the alcohol coming off of her in waves.

"Sister," she says, and she wraps her arms around me, the wooden soles of her shoes hitting me in the back. "Look at you, sniffing me out." She kisses me again, this time on the tip of my nose.

"Astra." I take her by her arms. I almost tell her about Russia, but I decide to stick with the basics, for now. "Do you have any idea what time it is?"

"Nope," she says. "That's *your* job, remember?" She grabs my wrist, narrows her eyes to make out the time, but she must be too drunk to focus; she drops my wrist and shrugs.

"It's nearly four o'clock. We're almost two hours late coming home from dance. Opa will be beside himself!"

"If Opa is beside himself, would that make *two* Opas?" She laughs sloppily.

"Come on. Let's put your shoes on."

I lead her to the sofa, push her to sitting. Together, we manage to get her into her shoes.

There's the sound of bare feet crossing the wooden floor. Bare feet, bare legs—muscular, hairy men's legs, making me blush anew. Marcel is knotting the belt of a dressing gown, rich burgundy-and-white brocade with a velvet collar the color of wine. Like Astra, his hair, which he usually keeps scrupulously pomaded, is rumpled. He's grinning down at both of us.

"*Coitus interruptus,*" he says.

I have no idea what that means and don't intend to ask.

I want to scream at them both, but there's no time. I stand, yank Astra by the arm. Marcel wiggles his fingers in a wave, his mouth a crooked grin.

# THREE

## WHEN TIME STOPS

There's no way to hide what Astra did from Opa; when we get home, Astra's arm across my shoulders, my arm around her waist, he's waiting on the front steps, face as concerned as I knew it would be. And he must be able to read at least some of what happened on my face, in Astra's entire body. With a deep sigh, he comes down to the street and takes Astra's other arm, and we lead her up the stairs, together.

After she's delivered to her bed, where she falls asleep immediately—facedown, still in her shoes—I try to apologize.

Opa shakes his head. "A girl like that, she does what she's going to do," he says. "The rest of us have to live with the consequences."

She's not allowed out all weekend, which she doesn't complain about, probably because she's too hungover to *want* to go anywhere. On Monday, Opa himself walks us to dance and waits until he sees us both inside. Madame Lucia wears a black band around her arm in honor of her city, and all of us offer hushed condolences.

There are a few girls missing from the dressing room; Penny Meyers, who always takes the longest at the mirror, is nowhere to be seen. Didi Liebermann, who always speaks as if she knows everything, says, "She's not coming back. Penny's family is rich, and the Soviets hate rich people. They'll be leaving town for sure."

"My family says we should feel lucky," says Connie Schneider. "The Soviets say we're all the same. Jews, Christians, it doesn't matter. Things will get better now."

"That's because your family is poor," says Didi.

I blush on her behalf, but Connie doesn't seem insulted. "That won't matter," she says. "We'll all be equals."

If that's true—that the Russians coming will mean we're all equals—I wonder what might have happened if they'd come earlier. Maybe Opa's shop would have been spared.

Again, the jewelry store's window flashes into my mind—*Death to the Jews*. Opa said that "hoodlums" came into the shop—I imagine that now, too, a group of young men pushing through the door. I can see them in my brain, as clear as *The Wizard of Oz* had been on the theater screen. I see them pushing Opa's tools off his worktable. I see them yelling in his face. I see Opa standing behind the counter, doing his best to keep calm, maybe trying to convince them that he's no different than they are, not really.

I see them rip the mezuzah from the doorframe and drop it to the ground.

Out front after dance, Opa is waiting for us. He looks relieved to see us emerge together, as if he suspected that Astra might have snuck out the back or something. I ask him if we can go by Penny's apartment on the way home.

When we get there, we find the building's door propped open. I pull it open the rest of the way. Opa says he will wait outside. Astra doesn't come in, either.

Penny's family has a huge apartment on the ground floor. Their apartment door is open, and Penny's mother is in the doorway. I recognize her from our recitals and the one other time I came to their apartment; she has Penny's same dark blond hair.

"Leave the books," she snaps at a boy—Penny's younger brother, Nathan, who I think is eleven years old. "Take the silver."

Nathan sets the books on an end table, next to their telephone. Penny's family is one of the only families I know with a telephone. I wonder what will happen to it. I suppose they'll have to leave it behind.

The books aren't stacked properly, and as soon as Nathan puts them down, they topple to the floor. He leaves them like that and heads for the sideboard to collect the silverware.

"Mrs. Meyers?" I say. "Is Penny here?"

"She's in her room." Mrs. Meyers waves vaguely to a hallway that branches to the right. "Nathan," she says, her heels clicking on the shiny parquet floor as she crosses to help him, "don't forget the second drawer."

I feel strange wandering through Penny's apartment; we aren't close friends, and the last time I was in her home was several years ago, for a birthday party that all the girls in dance were invited to. The party was opulent: fine food, a beautiful cake, small gifts for each of us to take away after, and a real clown performance.

I find Penny sitting on the edge of her bed. She's holding a glass horse, and tears streak her cheeks. I stand in the doorway awkwardly, feeling that I'm watching something private. Astra was right not to come inside. I'm just about to turn away when Penny looks up.

"Frederieke?"

"Hi." I step into the room. "I'm sorry to bother you. It's just—Didi said you were moving away. I just wanted to see if it was true."

Penny nods, a tear falling from her cheek onto the glass horse. It's beautiful—delicate legs, a mane and a tail that feather and glisten in the light. It's sort of purply-pink.

"Father says we have to, or the Russians will send us to Siberia."

"Oh." I don't know what to say to that; I have no idea what might happen. I'm not even sure I know what Siberia is.

Penny wipes her cheeks and stands. "Here. You might as well have this. It's too fragile to bring, and I'd rather you have it than some Soviet solider."

She holds it out, and I don't know what to do except to take it. I feel terrible, going to her house just two times, and leaving each time with a gift. "I'll keep it safe for you, just until you come back," I tell Penny as she walks me to the door. I hold the glass horse with both hands.

She begins to answer, but then her mother calls, "Penny! I need your help with the jewelry."

Penny shrugs, says, "Goodbye, I guess," and closes the door.

I stand there, staring at the door. I know I should have said something more, but I don't know what.

I hear Penny's muffled voice from inside the apartment: "Coming, Mother." And her footsteps fade away to nothing.

By Friday, we are Soviets.

"Well, it's a good thing we're not rich or religious," Astra says, reading an article in the paper about the frantic evacuation of many Czernowitzers.

"Opa's religious."

Astra ignores me. But this is important, so I say it again, louder. "*Opa's*

130

religious. Do you think the Russians will send him to Siberia?"

Mama says, "If he keeps his religion to himself, he'll be fine. They can't lock him up for *thinking* things."

Astra puts down the paper. She pinches her lips together, then says, "He'll need to stop gathering with his minyan. That's the sort of thing they'll be watching for."

"How do you know—" I begin to ask, but then I realize it's probably something Marcel has told her. And at that moment, I'm glad for him, saying aloud what Mama and Opa won't.

She leaves the paper a mess on the table and goes out of the kitchen. There will be no getting in the bathroom for at least an hour.

Mama picks up the paper and folds it. "Opa will be fine. It's a blessing he shut the store when he did. The Soviets aren't fond of business owners."

"Then where do people in Russia get the things they need?"

"The government owns everything. People either get things from the government, or they don't get them at all."

I look at my watch; it's almost time for dance, but I feel nervous about going through the city. "Should we go to dance today?"

Mama has begun reading the paper she'd been folding and has sunk into Astra's chair.

"*Mama.*"

"What? Oh. No. It's best if you stay home, I think."

Opa is in the front room. It's strange to see him with empty hands. He always used to be busy repairing something, reading a book or the paper. But now his hands are flat on his lap, and he stares in the half distance out the window, eyes unfocused.

"Opa," I say when I can't stand looking at him like that any longer. "Maybe it will be better now. With the Soviets. Maybe it won't matter anymore, about us being Jewish." I'm not convinced it will be, but I want to comfort him.

"Never pray for a new king." Opa sounds as if he's quoting something.

I don't point out that he's the only person in our house who ever does any praying. "I'm going to go sit on the stoop for a while."

"Hashem," he says, raising his hands to the ceiling, "you know I love you, but this is a terrible decision you've made, sending the Russians to our city. I don't know what you're thinking, I really don't." His hands drop to his lap. To me he says, "Don't leave the front steps. Stay close."

Outside, the street is full of carts and carriages packed with boxes and even small pieces of furniture. Everyone is in a hurry; few stop to greet one another or chat, rushing here and there, eyes on the ground or far off in the distance rather than looking one another in the eyes. And yet, it's beautiful outside. Little songbirds hop about in planters and flowerbeds. In the trees are birds I can't see; I hear them chirping and rustling, feathering their nests, maybe, or just enjoying the weather. Pigeons in the gutters and in the street, looking here and there for crumbs. And it's less humid today than when we went to the movies. Maybe that's a sign. Maybe it means something.

The door opens behind me, and the Fischers from down the hall emerge. Mrs. Fischer, who's pregnant again, carries little Sophie, and Mr. Fischer struggles down the stairs with the pram. I take the other side and help him.

"Thank you, Frederieke." We settle it on the curb. "How is your family?"

I shrug. "When is the baby due, Mrs. Fischer?"

Her hand rests on the large, hard lump of her belly. "Soon. August at the latest."

We could talk about the Russians—I see the shadows in their eyes, same as in mine, I'm sure—but we don't. It's like we're working together to hold on to something already almost too far gone to grasp.

Mrs. Fischer puts Sophie in the pram, and they go up the street, Mr. Fischer pushing, Mrs. Fischer with her arm linked through his. They go slowly, Mrs. Fischer waddling a little, and I watch them all the way to the corner, where they disappear.

I sit on the top step, letting the sun warm me. As people pass, I hear snippets of their conversations.

"The Mendelssohn family didn't even lock the apartment door behind them."

"I heard that in Poland things got bad fast when the Soviets arrived. Jails full of merchants."

"Better than the Germans, that's for sure. I'll tell you what, this is a relief—you'll see!"

"Who knows what this will mean for the—"

This last snippet comes from a broad-waisted lady in a purple coat, and she cuts herself off mid-sentence when she looks up and catches my eye, realizes I'm eavesdropping. She shuts her mouth tight and frowns at me.

I sit on the stoop all morning, watching the people, watching the birds. Around eleven o'clock, Opa comes outside. He pats my head and I watch him walk slowly up the street. An hour later, he returns with a loaf of bread. "Lunch soon," he says, and pats my head again. I nod, and Opa goes inside. Now the sun is high above my head, and I stretch my legs on the steps and lean back on my elbows, warming myself like a dog. The heat, the feeling of doing nothing, reminds me of the trip we took to the country, when I was young. I remember Peter, the red setter. I wonder what he's doing right now—if he's off on a jaunt, or if he's taking a nap on the back porch of his house.

That's when the first Russian soldiers turn onto our street.

There are about a dozen of them. From a distance, it's clear what they are; they're carrying rifles and are dressed in military uniforms, and they march in two parallel lines down the middle of the road.

Hope flaps in my throat like a swallowed bird. Maybe, maybe. Maybe this will be a good thing.

There's a man driving a cart in front of them, and he pulls his horse to the side to get out of their way. People walking on the sidewalk freeze in place, watching.

As the men get closer, I see that their uniforms aren't neatly pressed or fastidiously clean the way I'd expect them to be. Some of the soldiers' jackets are faded and some of them are torn. Several of the men wear boots in disrepair, one with the sole of his left boot flapping like a tongue. It is this soldier who peels off from the group and stops in front of my stoop.

He beckons me to come down the stairs. At first, I can't move. It's like two things—hope and fear—are tearing me in opposite directions, and the result means that I'm paralyzed.

He smiles at me, beckons again, and hope surges forward, loosening me to stand. I smile back and go down the stairs to the street.

He speaks to me first in Russian, which I don't understand. He tries again, this time in Ukrainian; I know enough to pick out the word "time."

Then he points at his wrist, as if he wants me to tell him what time it is. It's five minutes after noon, but I don't speak Russian at all or Ukrainian well enough to tell him this, so instead I hold out my wrist so he can read the watch for himself.

With one hand, he grabs my arm—hard—and with the other he

134

deftly unstrings the watchband. His hands are stained with dirt, black lining the whorls of his fingers, and a thick line of grime beneath each fingernail. My watch falls from my wrist into the soldier's hand, and he tucks it into his pocket. Then he turns on his heel and rejoins his group.

My arm hurts where he grabbed me. His fingers have left red marks and a streak of dirt.

The soldiers take a sharp left at the corner, and then it's as if they were never on my street at all. But for the marks on my arm and the disappearance of my watch, I could fool myself into thinking I imagined the whole thing.

My hands are shaking. The red marks are darkening already into bruises. I stumble backwards to the stoop, and when the backs of my legs touch the step, I sink to sitting. My wrist looks naked without my watch. Oh—what will Opa say?

"Stupid, stupid." I make a fist and pound it into my thigh, again and again, focusing on the pain there, the deep ache. I hit myself until it hurts so badly, I can't feel anything else. And then I cry like a little girl.

# FOUR

# THE MOISEYEV DANCERS

"You can take any watch you want from the box," Opa says.

I tried to hide my wrist, but it was no use. That very night at dinner, he sees the watch is missing, and he sees more—the ring of finger-shaped bruises on my wrist; my face, swollen from crying.

I can't stand to look in his eyes—anger and helplessness, flashing back and forth until they blur into one.

"It was my fault. I should have been more careful."

Opa shakes his head. "No. Not your fault."

"Really," I say. "It was."

"What do you want to protect the Russians from?" Astra says. "Bunch of thieves."

"Astra, hush," says Mama. "Please. Don't say such things."

"What things? *True* things?"

"Dangerous things," says Opa. He takes off his glasses, pinches the high point of his nose between his eyes. It's something I've seen Mama do countless times.

I think it upsets Astra, seeing Mama's gesture. "Don't worry, Opa," she says. "I know better than to say anything like that in public."

"How could you?" It comes out in a bark—harsh, not like our Opa.

Astra's head jerks back as if she's been struck.

He puts his glasses back on. He says it again—more softly this time, mournfully. "How could you?" A moment passes, and then, "You girls can't know." He shakes his head.

"Opa," Astra says. She puts her hand on top of his.

"I wanted to give to you what I had when I was young. That's all. That's all." He's still shaking his head back and forth, back and forth.

I blurt, "I don't want any other watches, Opa. Not until everything goes back to normal. Okay? When everything is normal again, you pick a watch for me."

Opa stops shaking his head. He looks up at me. He's still holding Astra's hand. With his other, he reaches for mine. His hand is warm, gentle, just like it's always been.

"Okay," he says, squeezing both of our hands, and then releasing them. "Okay. When things are back to normal."

Later, in our room, Astra says, "You know there's no more 'normal,' right? Not for a long time—maybe never."

I want to disagree. But I don't; I just nod. Then Astra pulls me into her arms, and we stand like that for a long time, together.

For the first few days after the Russians' arrival all of us stay home, nervous about what might happen outside. Astra doesn't even try to sneak out to see Marcel. But there's only so long we can hide in the apartment; it isn't long before we have to go out for supplies.

There are soldiers on the street, and they go into markets and take what they like; no one has the nerve to stop them. But we find we can avoid them if we're careful, and all our Jewish neighbors keep saying, "At least they're not the Germans." They sound just like the stuck record at Marcel's apartment.

I guess people can get used to almost everything, because by mid-July, I no longer feel a shock of panic when I see a Russian soldier. The day after the Russians arrived, Madame Lucia closed the studio again, but finally it reopens, and on our first day back, there's a feeling of euphoria in the dressing room. Along with Penny, two other girls are missing—their families both fled—but the rest of us are here, and glad for it.

Astra's the only crab; I hear her telling Ruth, "I drank too much and my head is killing me."

I ignore this, as I've ignored the last two nights when she slipped out of bed and went to the front door to sneak Marcel into our apartment. I heard them in the front room, laughing and sshing each other. I have no idea if Mama or Opa heard them, too, but it embarrasses me even to think about it.

Esther's sitting at the far end of the bench; she's in her tunic but her hair is down around her shoulders, and she's hunched around a notebook, scribbling something. I lift my wrist to check the time out of habit, but of course my watch isn't there. Still, it must be almost time to get out to the studio.

"What are you doing?" I ask.

She looks up, startled, like she's been somewhere far away. It takes her a second to adjust her focus from the notebook to my face, hazel eyes blinking behind her glasses. "Oh. Take a look."

She hands me her notebook. I can see that she's working on something.

138

The Hatch in the Floor

by

Esther Glassman

FADE IN —

A young girl, KATIA, is bent down in the kitchen of her
apartment. She's looking at something on the floor, but we
can't see what. MOTHER walks in.

MOTHER

Katia, what are you doing?

KATIA looks up, startled. Her hand covers something on
the floor.

KATIA

Nothing, Mother.

MOTHER crosses the kitchen and yanks her hand away.
Under her hand is . . . nothing! Just a dark burl in the
wooden plank.

MOTHER

Enough with the daydreaming, Katia. We need to get dinner on the table for your father and brothers.

KATIA

Yes, Mother.

KATIA stands and gets busy at the counter chopping
vegetables. But as soon as her mother leaves the kitchen, she
drops back down to the floor, pulls open the burl as if it's a
little door, and peers inside.

KATIA

139

I can't let anyone else know about this secret hatch! Who knows what they would do?

That's just the first page. I flip through the notebook and find it's half-full.

"Esther! You're writing a play?"

She takes the notebook back with a bashful grin. "It's a screenplay."

I've never known anyone who wrote anything before, outside of assignments for school. "What's on the other side of the knothole?" I ask.

"Oh, it's—"

But just then Ruth comes over and tells us we need to hurry. The screenplay will have to wait.

The studio is even hotter than the dressing room. It's too hot to dance, but we do anyway, sweating in a line at the barre. Madame Lucia sweats, too, as she beats out the rhythm with her stick against the hardwood floor. Up and down the row we plié in unison. I'm behind Ruth, whose chestnut hair is wrapped into a thick, neat bun at the nape of her neck. Little sweat curls form in her baby hairs.

"Lazy, lazy." Madame Lucia taps my rear end with her stick. Immediately, I tuck. She moves up the row, passing by Ruth, whose form is perfect even in this swampy heat, to tap *Astra* under the chin—she barely ever corrects Astra, but I can see that my sister is struggling today. If she's upset at being corrected, it's her own fault.

I'm thinking about Esther's play and what the girl Katia might be seeing through the knothole—the downstairs neighbor's secrets?—when there's the click of the studio door opening. Though I want to, I don't look to see who entered; that would guarantee extra exercises. But in the mirror, I catch a flash of brown and green: a soldier. Beside him, two men in street

140

clothes—one fat, one tall.

Immediately, every muscle in my body tightens in fear, and my sweat turns clammy and cold.

Conrad meets Madame Lucia's eyes, wondering if he should stop playing, but she shakes her head; he goes on, we keep dancing, all of us intensely aware of the three men waiting in a line near the door. Madame Lucia ignores them until we finish our work at the barre.

After we complete our final exercise, Madame taps her stick, twice. "Center in five." We rush to change from soft slippers to pointe shoes. As we do, the fat man and the soldier converse in quiet voices with Madame Lucia. The other man—the tall one—doesn't talk, just stands, rolling one ankle and then the other. He is incredibly handsome. Broad shoulders, narrow waist, cheekbones slashing across his face almost violently. Dark eyes, nearly black, and hair just a shade lighter. He catches me looking at him, grins with bright white teeth. I look away.

I can't make out what the men and Madame Lucia are saying. But my attempt to eavesdrop slows my ribbon tying, and when the others stand, I'm just half-finished.

"Frederieke," says Madame Lucia dryly, "do you need more time?"

I flush with shame. Quick as I can, I tie the last knot and scurry to join the girls in the center of the room. No one makes eye contact with me, as though Madame Lucia's displeasure is contagious.

"Girls," she says, "these men are from the Moiseyev Dancers. They have traveled here from Russia, bringing their culture to our humble city."

If you didn't know Madame Lucia, you'd think she meant every word. But every dancer in the room can tell from her one arched brow that she's not convinced by what they believe they have to share with us.

"They will be performing in Czernowitz in the coming months. One of their dancers suffered a turned ankle on their journey, however, and so they are in need of a replacement. They wonder if someone here has the talent to dance alongside them. Everyone, line up. Astra, Ruth, to the front." She bangs her stick to the floor, loud as a gunshot.

Astra steps forward at once, waves of pride practically radiating from her, any hint of her hangover evaporated. Ruth follows.

"Tendu, dégagé, tendu, dégagé, tendu," Madame Lucia orders. Conrad brings his hands to the keys, and we're off.

The heat is oppressive, but you would never know it by watching Ruth and Astra. Though sweat falls from their brows and dampens circles beneath their arms, their backs stay straight, their arms and legs slice through the air with precision and grace. It seems as if *they* move the music, rather than the music moving them.

The rest of us just do our best to keep up. Madame Lucia calls out more moves to add on to the combination, and now we're turning and jumping as well, and the rhythmic beat of her stick on the floor, the increasing intensity of the piano, the energy emanating from Astra and Ruth, like twin suns, inspires all of us to jump higher, spin faster, hit our marks cleaner.

"Again," calls Madame Lucia, and we spin, our sweat raining against one another's faces.

"Enough." It's the first word from any of the men, and spoken not by the solider, but by the thicker, older gentleman who stands between the others. The piano stops; we do, too. He turns to the younger man, a dancer most certainly, from the shape of him, and says something in Russian. The two of them confer, heads close. Madame Lucia waits with her mouth turned down. The rest of us stand still, trying to catch our breath. My legs are shaking; I want to sit on the floor, but, of course, I don't.

At last, the men turn to Madame Lucia. The heavyset man says, in slow, painful French, "Let's try the girl on the left."

Astra.

To the male dancer, the man says, "Anatoly," and gestures for him to prepare.

Madame Lucia waves Astra forward. "The rest of you—against the wall." We are glad to comply, leaning against the far wall to watch.

Each of Astra's steps tells a story as she takes center stage. The dancer—Anatoly—shrugs out of his shirt and unlaces his shoes. He takes a pair of slippers from a pocket and pulls them on, stretching briefly before he takes up space behind Astra, rolling his neck. Astra, tallest always in every class, comes up only to Anatoly's chin. They look handsome together.

He places his hands on her waist, Madame Lucia nods to Conrad, and the music begins.

Together, they dance. Together, we watch. Though they haven't spoken a word, they move as fluidly as two glasses of water poured into a single vase. So lovely are they, that the anxiety I've felt since the men entered the studio seeps out of me, and I feel myself straighten with pride, watching Astra.

"Enough," calls the heavy man, and then the dance is over. Anatoly steps away from Astra and bows. She drops into a small curtsy.

"The other," says the man, and Ruth steps forward.

Conrad begins again. And if Astra and Anatoly were water in a vase, *Ruth* and Anatoly are the river. It's clear the moment they begin, as Conrad's first notes chime through the studio, as soon as Antoly's hand touches Ruth's, that they're designed to move as one. Her chestnut hair perfectly matches the dark swoop of his, her brown eyes lock with his, first in the mirror and then, as he spins her, his eyes become her spot for each

143

revolution.

No one calls, "Enough." Even Madame Lucia's stick falls silent. We watch until the last long note fades, Ruth bent backward across Anatoly's knee, and then all of us break into applause.

Well, nearly all of us. Astra's hands stay at her sides.

I don't know when it happened—when Ruth surpassed my sister. Maybe Astra's just a little off today because she's hungover. Or maybe while the entirety of Astra's world became Marcel Goldmann, Ruth blossomed.

Anatoly returns Ruth to her feet and bows to her, then to us.

"Dismissed." Madame Lucia waves vaguely in our direction, and she goes to confer with the men.

His full name is Anatoly Tokarev, we learn when Madame Lucia comes into the dressing room, which she hardly ever does. "Ruth," Madame Lucia informs us, "is to replace his partner."

A smile breaks on Ruth's face as her head falls, and a few of the girls gather around her in a hug, all of them jumping up and down together.

I rub my wrist where my watch used to be.

"Madame Lucia, is that— What I mean is, will Ruth be safe?"

The other girls fall still at my words, even Ruth.

Madame Lucia sighs. For a moment, it looks like she might sit on the bench—but then she remembers herself, straightens, and says, "Ruth will be as safe as any of us." And then she turns, and leaves.

The girls go back to congratulating Ruth, a bit subdued, but Ruth blushes with excitement. Astra, I notice, doesn't say a word. She places her pointe shoes and slippers into her bag with unusual care, then leaves the dressing room, head high.

On the street, I find her lighting a cigarette. I don't know what to say, so I just stand beside her. Cigarette lit, she turns toward home, and I follow half a step behind.

We walk like that for several blocks. Astra finishes her cigarette and flicks the butt into the gutter. I catch up to her when the smoke is gone.

"I'm sorry they didn't choose you."

I'm not sure if it's the right thing to say; with Astra, everything is a gamble. Something that might be the best thing to say one day can be the absolute wrong thing to say the next.

But Astra just shrugs. "She's the better partner for him. They made the right choice."

I try to say something else, something to make her feel better, but she waves her hand at me. "It doesn't matter. What will be, will be."

This doesn't sound like my sister at all. But what can I say? Instead of speaking, I match my steps to hers, my left with her left, my right with her right, two hearts in one rhythm.

The next day, Astra says she won't be going to dance.

"Madame Lucia was furious when you didn't show up that one time. What do you want me to tell her?"

My sister sits on her bed, using the mirror in her compact and the light from the window to apply mascara. I don't know where she got the money to buy such a thing. "Tell her whatever you want."

"I'm going to tell her you didn't come to class because you're in a jealous rage."

No reaction.

I try something else. "You said yourself they picked the right dancer for Anatoly. It's nothing personal."

Astra snaps shut the compact. She points it at me. "Everything is personal. Remember that."

I return home after dance, exhausted and sweating, but the sight that greets me as I push through the door astonishes me into stillness. It's Marcel, sitting across from the fireplace on the sofa, his arm slung up over the back of it. The thin mustache on his upper lip, straight and dark like a line of ink, dances happily as he laughs. Nestled up against him as contented as a cat is Astra. Her shoes are off; her legs are tucked beneath her.

I stand in the open doorway and stare. Mama slumps in the armchair, face puffy and eyes red. Opa doesn't sit at all, but paces in front of the tall set of windows.

"There you are," Astra says, as if they've been waiting for me, as if she didn't send me to dance class without her. "Rieke, we have news."

Marcel leans toward her and kisses her temple, and Astra blushes.

A pain creeps into my stomach, a feeling just like hunger. I close my eyes. I see myself and Astra, young again, on the roof.

*"I'll tell you one thing, Rieke—I'll never fall in love. And I'm never getting married. You can count on that."*

In spite of everything Astra has done—getting engaged, sneaking out to meet Marcel, sneaking Marcel *into* our apartment—I have held out hope that she would keep her vow. That if I made myself accommodating enough, if I loved her strongly enough, if I accepted enough, remained loyal enough, still—somehow—she would return to me.

I open my eyes.

"You got married."

"You *knew*?" Mama wails, and tears spill as if they've been waiting for an excuse. "I can't believe you knew about this and kept it from me. I've been cheated out of attending my own daughter's wedding."

146

"I didn't know," I say, but Mama isn't listening.

"Don't *cry*, Mama," says Astra.

"Astra," I say, "how could you?"

She meets my eyes across the room. She doesn't speak, but she raises her chin, defiant.

"A wedding is a joy, is it not?" It's a voice I don't immediately recognize, until a man saunters in from the kitchen, carrying himself as if he lives here. He strolls to the sofa, pushes Astra's feet out of the way, and makes himself right at home.

My father.

I am so stunned that I feel my knees buckle and stumble forward to catch myself.

"A *wedding* can be a joy," Mama says, sniffing and dabbing her eyes with a handkerchief she pulls from her sleeve, "but this is not a *wedding*. This is a—a—"

"An ambush," declares Opa, slamming his fist on the mantel.

"Heinrich, you have always been dramatic." Father sips, pulling the coffee through his teeth to cool it. "I've missed that about you."

Poor Opa practically turns purple.

I turn to my father. "What are you doing here?"

"One needs a witness for a wedding, and for a father to bless it." And he shrugs, as if he's done this as a favor. But I know what this is—revenge. For Mama still having not signed the divorce papers.

"Anyway," says Marcel, "what's done is done."

I drop my dance bag near the door and sit on the arm of Mama's chair. She reaches over and takes my hand. Is this what it feels like when someone you love dies? An opening, and a falling in—into a pit inside of you, a pit you didn't know about but maybe *always* was there, waiting?

I've lost people and things before, in different ways. Father, when I was young. Mama—to her headaches, to her own dark pit. My dream of working with Opa at his shop. My watch. But this loss . . . I'm upside down and tumbling, tumbling from a great height, a great gray mass of feathers and wings all around.

I squeeze shut my eyes. Tears press against my lids, but I refuse to let them escape. They burn, and I focus on that pain until they recede, until the feeling of falling recedes, as well. I know that if I allow myself to cry, I won't be able to stop.

I need to be *angry*, instead.

I open my eyes. Astra is watching me. I don't speak until I'm sure I can control my voice, and then I say, "So you're moving out?"

"Wouldn't you love *that*, rat tail." Astra arches a brow at me. "The Russians are requisitioning the apartments of single men. And it will look better if Marcel offers his rather than waits for them to come for it. We'll live here, together."

I pull my hand away from Mama's, and cross my arms. "Where?"

"You can have the room off the kitchen. Bring up one of the cots from the basement."

"What? The *pantry*? It's tiny, and there's no window."

Astra shrugs. "Then you can share with Mama." She waves her hand dismissively—I see a flash of gold on her ring finger—and laughs, her beautiful, mean bell of a laugh. "What, do you expect me and Marcel to squeeze in with Mama? Or with Opa?"

She laughs again, and Marcel does, too, and Papa joins them, and I hate all three of them, this line of laughing selfish fools who've taken the best seats in the room, who take and take and take.

Mama stands, slowly. "Come, Rieke," she says. "Help me get supper."

148

By the time supper is through, I have no energy to empty all the dry goods and other supplies from the pantry and lug up a cot from the basement. So, after Father leaves, after Opa disappears into his room with an uncharacteristic slam of the door, I climb into bed alongside Mama. She falls asleep, the sweet waft of her cocoa-buttered skin taking some part of me back to earliest childhood.

I'm almost asleep when I hear them. Astra, and Marcel—in bed, together. *My* bed, and Astra's, which they'd pushed together with a terrible scraping sound.

A rhythmic squeaking. A moan. A sigh. A laugh. A gasp.

And then, stillness.

Rolling onto my side, I make myself into a thin line at the far edge of the mattress. Here I am, forced to share a bed with my mother.

And Astra, on the other side of the wall, doing exactly as she pleases. Again.

# FIVE

## HONEYMOONS, WAXING
## AND WANING

For Astra, the next few weeks are a honeymoon. She stops going to dance altogether—something else for Mama to mourn. Madame Lucia tells me not to hold my breath for her return, saying, "Marriage has ruined more dancers than flat feet."

When Marcel isn't working at the hospital, they close themselves in their room, laughing and smoking, and drinking. It's harder to get things like cigarettes and alcohol now, and ordinary things, too, like candles, butter, milk—the Russians have "requisitioned" almost everything worth taking. But Marcel is the kind of man who makes friends easily, and soon he's found some Russian buddies that slip him extra rations. He also takes as long in the bathroom as a woman, making me late for dance twice before I learn not to expect any time in the bathroom at all, brushing my teeth at the kitchen sink and waiting to use the toilet until arriving to the studio.

He takes up space at the dinner table, serving himself first and Astra second. It's true that his Russian connections mean there's more food on our table than there otherwise would be, but it's still *Opa's* apartment, isn't it?

He takes up space in every conversation. Of course, he *is* a doctor, but that doesn't mean he knows everything about everything, the way he thinks he does. And when he speaks, the rest of us are supposed to listen. Marcel's voice is his favorite sound in the universe.

He even takes up space in his absence. In early August, he doesn't come home for dinner. All of us—Opa, Mama, me—sit with Astra in the front room. All of us are worried; anything could have happened to him, or maybe he's just late coming home from the hospital. Astra paces and wails, and none of us dares speak, silently keeping vigil as the minutes tick by on the mantel clock.

It isn't until close to midnight, when Astra throws on her coat over her nightgown, that Opa finally speaks.

"You cannot go out. It's too late."

"Rieke will come with me."

I remember the Russian soldier grabbing my arm, stealing my watch, bruising me. Still, she's my sister, and so I'm about to get my own coat when Opa cuts in.

"No, she won't."

Silently, I'm relieved. But Astra is not. She leaves her coat half-buttoned and looks between the two of us, her face wide in surprise and wet with tears.

I swallow hard. "You shouldn't go out either, Astra. It isn't safe."

This sets her fingers back to buttoning. When she speaks, her voice climbs up and up, to the edge of panic. "Well, I can't just *leave* him out there! He could be dead in the street, for all I know!"

A shiver goes up my spine; it's Astra's voice, but Mama's words.

Opa shakes his head, tight-lipped. "It isn't right." I don't know what he means—that it isn't right that Marcel isn't home, or that Astra wants to go after him. But he must understand that there's only one way to keep Astra from going out, and it isn't by forbidding it, so he takes up his own coat and hat. "You will stay here; I will find him."

The last thing he says, before going out the door, is "Like it or not, he's family." I don't know if he's speaking to us or himself.

After Opa leaves, we heat up some milk and sit around the kitchen table. Astra barely touches hers and soon a skin forms across it.

"He'll come back," Mama soothes Astra. "Opa will find him."

"What if he's been gambling again, and lost? What if he angered some Russian soldiers? He gets belligerent when he drinks." And then, as if this thought is even worse, "What if he's with another woman?"

Mama can't say that this is an impossibility. How could she? The best she can offer is "You're young. You're beautiful. He will come back."

I can't stand it anymore. "What is *wrong* with you both? Opa's out there all by himself. He doesn't speak a word of Russian. What if something happens to *him*? Because of *Marcel*?"

They both look up, as if being woken from a dream. They're so obsessed with their men—Astra, with Marcel, and Mama, with her lost dream of our father—that they aren't paying attention to *our* man, Opa. Astra and Mama, in this moment, are exactly the same.

I want to scream. I want to shake Astra, to force some sense into her, to yell: *Don't you see what you've become?* And maybe I would have, but it's at this moment we hear the key in the door. Astra rushes from the kitchen; Mama and I stay at the table.

"Astra, my beauty." Marcel's voice, slurred with drink.

Mama relaxes. She smiles as she stands. "Thank God," she says, and I follow her into the living room.

There he is, leaning heavily on Opa. His free hand, he waves in the air as if conducting an orchestra. "Astra, my beauty," he says again, singsong, and unwinds himself from Opa's support, stumbles across the room and into Astra's arms.

"You stink," she says, but she's laughing with relief.

"If I stink, you'll stink soon, too." Oblivious to the rest of us, Marcel runs his hands up and down Astra's body, kissing her sloppily.

"Stop," Astra says, but she doesn't mean it. She kisses him back, and the rest of us turn away.

"Time for bed," Opa declares, and then, under his breath, "not that anyone listens to me."

He heads toward the hallway. As he passes me, he pats my cheek and says, "Crazy times, crazy people."

Even *this* is part of the honeymoon. Even is the night, in late August, when Marcel doesn't come home until daylight, when Astra rages and raves, when her eyes look as round-white and desperate as Mama's did, all those years ago. Even this.

If Astra is having a honeymoon, Ruth is, too. She falls in love with Anatoly Tokarev each time they dance. Though things like food and oil are in short supply, the Russians love to host celebrations: parades and concerts and dance recitals, each opening with speeches in praise of Mother Russia and Father Stalin, and followed by performances—food for the soul, they tell us.

No one can take their eyes from Ruth and Anatoly when they take the stage, her spinning and spinning, his arms the fulcrum that holds her straight, and when they do lifts . . . oh! The audience gasps. His long fingers practically span her narrow waist, featured so prettily in the boned, corseted ivory bodice, her graceful legs bare beneath the flare of her cloud-white tutu. Wherever the Moiseyev Dancers perform—inside, on the stage of the Palace of Culture, or outside, in the park—they are all I see, Anatoly Tokarev and Ruth, their chestnut hair gleaming under the stage lights, under the sun. Passion blazes from their flesh in a woozy pink aura. They are perfect, and perfect for each other.

I fall in love with them both, and the city watches them falling in love with one another all summer long. Ruth doesn't come to class anymore, and neither does Astra, but they grow thick as thieves, now that they're both in love. Anatoly promises to marry Ruth when the war is over, Astra tells me. He'll take her home to meet his family.

I take to tagging along when Astra and Ruth meet at the Volksgarten, which, with the Russians in charge, is at last safe for Jews. They've flanked the entrance to the garden with a huge portrait of Stalin on one side, and Lenin on the other. The Russians love to pipe in music all along the Ringplatz—what they call the Red Square—and we can hear it in the park, giving the whole place a feeling of celebration. Chopin is playing one morning when we see Mrs. Fischer in the Volksgarten, pushing her new baby in Sophie's pram, and Sophie, a big sister now, trotting at its side.

"We named him Moses." Mrs. Fischer is gorgeous with pride as she pulls back the draped blanket to reveal him—so small, so pink, like an apple, his mouth sucking the air as if he dreams of his mother's breast. Little Sophie brushes her brother's palm; he grips on tight without waking, each little finger absolutely perfect, each tiny nail, thin as tissue, delicate as glass.

A pretzel man wanders up and down the pathways with his cart, another man sells flowers, a third poses couples near the fountain and snaps their picture for a coin. Girls in their best dresses walk by on the arms of their suitors; a cloud of geese passes overhead—I scratch the scar on my leg at the sight of them—and land together in the pond. It feels peaceful and almost normal, even with Stalin and Lenin looking down on us like gods. Maybe it's a good thing the Russians have come. Better than the Germans, that's for sure, if the news out of Poland and Western Europe is any indication.

Sitting close together on a bench in the sun, Astra and Ruth conspire about love—ways to wear their hair, the best fragrance one could make from combining flower petals and a bit of alcohol, even whispered conversations about pregnancy, and how to keep it from happening.

"Have you read van de Velde's *Ideal Marriage*?" Astra says, low.

Ruth shakes her head.

"You must get a copy."

Ruth looks at me, as if she isn't sure I should hear about such matters, but Astra says, "Who knows? One day, maybe the little rat tail will have use for such information."

I don't tell them that I snuck her copy of *Ideal Marriage* when she was out with Marcel and thumbed through it hungrily, cover to cover, gulping as much knowledge as I could before they returned home. I learned more from that one book than from my mother in all my life. It makes me look at people differently; I have no problem imagining Astra doing the things described in that book, but my mother? *Opa*? I wonder—does Conrad know about these things? Does *he* do them? The thought makes me blush deep red, makes me feel tight and swollen between my legs in a way that's both uncomfortable and wonderful. All I say is, "I know all about babies, Astra."

"Do you?" My sister laughs. "Good."

Everything ends. Once, Opa's shop was a haven, until it was not. Each year, summer arrives with a fresh promise—even this summer did, the summer of the Russians. I suppose this summer is a honeymoon for us all, in a way—a break from the fear of a German invasion. But by summer's end, the honeymoon ends, too.

When you marry a man, he makes you change your name. That's happened again with our city; it's Chernovtsy now—not Cernăuți, no longer Czernowitz—and you'd better not forget it. We soon find out that if a Russian soldier asks you for directions and you don't know the new Russian names, you might get arrested as a dissenter or a spy. The Russians change the names of the parks and meeting places, of course. They also change the laws about religion. Now, it's not just Jews who feel the burden of faith. No one is to practice religion of any kind.

As summer comes to an end, there are more arrests. One can be jailed for any number of reasons—for questioning the actions of a Russian official (even when their actions are unjust); for speaking out against communism; even for being wealthy.

It's an unsteady marriage, between the Russians and our city.

The end of the honeymoon comes in late August, the hottest night of the summer. We've flung open all our windows to catch any scrap of breeze. I'm in my "room," trying to get comfortable on the cot's thin, hard mattress. The air is heavy and hot. I can't sleep, even with the covers thrown back. I lie in the dark, itching in the sweat-damp sheets, wondering if I should go for a glass of water, when I hear a sound I've never heard before.

It's a wail, a sharp rising keen, an animal.

156

I jump from bed and run through the apartment to the front window. I search the street—what could make such a sound? A cat, maybe? A stray dog? The night is deep-dark and moonless. The streetlamps are extinguished, no lights shine in other apartments' windows. At first, I see nothing, and I blink into the darkness.

The sound comes again—high-pitched, frantic. And then, words. "Not my son!"

It's Mrs. Applebaum.

Her building's door bangs open and light pours out, along with people.

There is Jeremy. He's flanked by two Russian guards, and he stumbles down the front steps. At first, I think he's stumbling because the men are pushing him, but then I see that something's wrong with his leg—it bends strangely at the knee, bowing out to the side rather than swinging back and forth as it should.

His mother is behind them. She's dressed in a nightgown; her hair is covered in a scarf. I think this scares me more than the sight of the guards or even the sight of Jeremy's broken leg; I've never seen Mrs. Applebaum with a hair out of place, let alone in her night things. She isn't even wearing slippers.

"Don't take my boy! You can't take him!"

By now, my family is gathered behind me—Mama, Astra and Marcel, Opa.

Mrs. Applebaum grabs the sleeve of one of the Russian guards. He turns sharply, knocking her hand from his arm, yells at her.

"What did he say?" Astra asks Marcel. He's already proficient at Russian. He's had to be; working at the hospital, he's been assigned to work alongside Russian medics. But his Russian is likely coming along more quickly from drinking vodka and playing cards than from work.

"He said Jeremy's an enemy of the state. They're sending him to the white bears."

The expression—the white bears—makes me shiver in spite of the heat, remembering the bear I met once, long ago.

I doubt Mrs. Applebaum understood what the soldier told her. She's screaming now. They shove Jeremy, his leg buckling unnaturally, and he nearly falls at the curb before they hoist him into a wagon.

"Ma-ma—*Mama*!" He's as plaintive as a babe. The wagon doors slam shut.

"Enough is enough." Opa heads for the apartment door.

"Papa, what are you doing?" Mama says.

"I've got to help the boy. The Soviets will kill him. He's no spy—he's a do-nothing laze-about."

Marcel strides around Opa and blocks his path, standing in front of the door.

"You'll stay right here. If you cross the street, they'll take you, too."

"Nonsense. What good am I if I let them take that boy?"

"What good are you to our girls if you're dead?"

This gives Opa pause. But then he shakes his head and reaches around Marcel for the doorknob.

Marcel puts his hand on Opa's sleeve. "I can't let you go," he says. "I'm sorry, old man."

The air is gone from our apartment. The rest of us are statues. A tear of sweat traces down my back.

Then another wail from the street. Opa shakes free of Marcel's grip and shoves past him. He grabs the knob and tosses open the door. He leaves the apartment and Marcel, shaking his head, follows.

Astra dashes back to the window, and Mama and I go with her. The carriage is gone now, and Jeremy with it. Mrs. Applebaum is collapsed on the sidewalk, wailing. Her scarf is undone, her hands clutch her hair.

"That poor woman." Mama goes to get her dressing gown, and then she leaves, too.

Astra shakes a cigarette from the pack she keeps on the mantel. She lights it, and we watch as Opa and Marcel cross the street, then, a moment later, as Mama joins them. Together, they help Mrs. Applebaum to her feet and shepherd her back into her building. The door closes, and the street is dark again.

"What will happen?" I don't know why I think Astra will know. But there's no one else to ask.

"They'll send him to Siberia." The ember of her cigarette glows bright red. "He'll die there, most likely."

If you didn't know Astra, you'd think from the way she acts so casual—the way she carries on smoking, the flat expression on her face— that she really doesn't care about Jeremy. But I know that's not true. I can see it in the way she wraps her arm around her own waist, the way she stands and stares at the blackened window. I see it in the way the edges of her lips go white. I see it in the ash of her cigarette, the way it grows and grows as she holds the cigarette close to her mouth but not taking another drag. The ash lengthens until I think it will surely fall on the floor; then, with ruthless precision, Astra turns to the hearth and taps the end of the cigarette. The ash breaks and disintegrates as it falls, turning to nothing.

Later, Opa and Marcel return. But Mama doesn't come home until morning. When she does, she won't talk. She just shakes her head and goes to her room. Marcel leaves for the hospital; Astra buries herself in a magazine; Opa takes up his hat and goes out. The apartment is quiet as a tomb.

What can I do? The dishes. Then the dusting. Then, I straighten the books on the shelves and the items on the mantelpiece.

Finally, Astra snips, "Rieke, cut it out. You're driving me mad. Here." She tosses a magazine at me. I fumble to catch it. "Sit down."

I sit, and I flip through the magazine, but I barely see the photos or the words. I hear Mrs. Applebaum's cries all day, and the memory of them wakes me each night for a week.

# SIX

## MASKS ON

When school starts in September, there's no segregated Jewish school anymore. Now we're all comrades, and we will attend public school together. We're to be mixed not only by religion and family background, but also by gender—for the first time, I'll attend classes with boys and girls together.

I'm on my own; Astra graduated in the spring and is taking a bookkeeping course. Marcel says that when the war is over, he's going to open a private practice and Astra will be in charge of the numbers.

"Astra," I say, when I catch her alone for a minute, in the kitchen. "You're not a secretary. You're a *dancer*."

But Astra shrugs, indifferent. "I don't know who you all think you're dancing for. It's not coming back, Rieke—the way things were. That life is over. You've got to look up, look around, and take what you can, now. Instead of chasing a memory, or a dream."

I ignore how what she's saying sounds so much like the promise I made myself outside of Opa's ruined store. "You're just trying to justify how selfish you're being," I tell her. "You don't care who you're hurting."

161

She laughs. "Believe what you want, I guess. You're just as stubborn as you've always been."

*That's* something—Astra calling *me* stubborn. But before I can tell her what a hypocrite she is, she says, "Anyway, I'm still dancing. Every night. Just—horizontally." She grins, drops a wink, walks away.

Because all comrades must be industrious, Astra also works part time at the hospital, where Marcel finds her a job filing papers. Each morning, all of us leave the apartment together: me, to school; Astra and Marcel, to the hospital; Mama, to her new job at a government-run bakery; and Opa, to a shoemaker's cooperative, where he's been put to work making rubber soles.

A "house administrator" has been installed in each apartment building—basically, a government spy. Ours is named Vadim Glazkov; he and his wife are like two mean cats, always skulking around, on the hunt. Even inside our own apartment, everyone's too scared about being overheard to speak freely.

When we leave home, we must carry a Soviet-issued ID booklet. It's called a passport, but it doesn't allow us to travel anywhere. Opa's lists his employment simply as "Clerk," and again we're all relieved that he closed his shop before the Soviets arrived. Business owners who kept their doors open, and people who own their home rather than rent, are issued a "Passport 39." We don't know what that means, but it seems better that Opa's booklet lists him as a member of the proletariat. Until the Russians arrived, it was a *good* thing to have money, to own a business . . . it's like everything's upside down, now.

The photo in my booklet makes me look older than my age—I turned fourteen just after school began this year, celebrated hastily by my family at home—and in the picture I look quite beautiful, though I'd never say

162

so aloud. I keep looking at it and wondering, is this really me? But across from my picture, under the section marked "Nationality," is the designation "Jew." Not Romanian, not Russian. No matter what this place is called, still, it doesn't name me one of its own.

At school, everything is different. Not only are most of our days taken up with Russian history lessons, but our teachers seem anxious that they're being judged by how closely they follow the new curriculum, how dedicated they are to Stalin. There are new teachers, too, who speak no German or Romanian—just Russian—and they're terribly frustrated with us, for hardly being able to understand a thing they are saying. But it doesn't matter. All they seem to want us to learn about are Stalin and the Communist party. About how lucky we are that we're now part of Russia, and how much Stalin loves us all, especially the children.

I don't feel loved. I feel hungry.

Because even though the Russians tell us that communism means that everything belongs to everybody, the reality seems to be that no one I know owns much of anything, at all. Russian officials preach that food belongs to the people . . . but food becomes increasingly difficult to find. Opa says it's because the new government won't allow farmers to set their own prices. "Without being able to control what they charge," he says, "why would they bother coming into the city?" And anyway, the Russian soldiers feel entitled to take what they like without paying anything at all, the way they did with my watch. If anyone complains, the best they can hope for is a slap across the face.

By the time the leaves are turning, one can't help but taste how flavorless the soup has grown, how thin each slice of bread, how rare a treat a pat of butter.

Hunger makes me weak, and weak is no good for dance.

"If you have no energy, *act* like you do," Madame Lucia yells at me. Her mood has been foul; I heard a rumor that her roommate, Miss Rosen, was taken in for questioning, but she must have been released because I saw her bringing down a boxful of green caps from her shop just this afternoon. She's been conscripted into making military wear.

Since the Russians arrived, Madame Lucia has been compelled to instruct us in the Russian method. Now, we train to make our leaps bigger, bolder, more athletic. Our arm movements are to be more dramatic, our expressions more intense.

"Circus dance," I hear Madame Lucia mutter, just once. I agree with her.

Today's class is worse than usual. I haven't eaten much—a dry crust of bread in the morning, with coffee, and a little slice of eggplant, fried in oil, at midday. My legs feel as weak as a kitten's, and I feel the rhythmic thrum of my heart beating in my head. When it's finally over, I wait for Astra outside the studio. Though she doesn't come to dance anymore, she passes by on her way home from work, and we walk the rest of the way together. I'd rather walk alone, but Opa insists we stay together, as much as possible.

I lean against the wall, closing my eyes and turning up my face to the fading October sun, and wonder—what was the point of it all? Of Opa's sacrifices, of Astra's anger, of all the *work* ballet took? Now, Astra has quit. Dance was Astra's joy, and I was the tagalong. And I . . . I am so tired that each day of dance seems to drain a year of my life away.

All I want is to sleep. Or, even better, to be a child again, warm and safe in Opa's shop.

Then, as if I've called him into being just by thinking about him, I can feel that Opa is nearby. I open my eyes and scan the street. There—across the way, near the corner. He's with Naida Glazkova, the wife of our house administrator. Their heads are close, and she's looking at something in Opa's hand. I glance at Astra; she sees him as well, though her expression is flat.

Slowly, I pull myself away from the wall. In the street, a draft horse pulling a cart meanders past, blocking my line of sight. "Come on," I say to my sister.

Astra rolls her eyes, but she follows me down the block to get a better view, just in time to see Naida Glazkova take some bills from her pocket, exchanging them for whatever Opa is holding. This, she tucks away. With a nod, she's on her way, and Opa on his.

"Let's go home," comes Astra's voice from behind me.

"Did you see that? The house administrator's wife just gave Opa money. I think he sold her something!"

"No!" Astra mocks. "I thought he was saving the jewelry for your dowry! Now you'll never get a husband."

"The jewelry? From his shop?"

"Of course, the jewelry from his shop. Is there other jewelry?"

We go home. When Opa arrives a little later, it's with a loaf of dark bread and a freshly killed chicken. Mama takes both into the kitchen.

Opa looks very tired. I help him with his coat, and I hang it and his hat in the closet.

"Would you like some tea?" I ask.

"Sure, sure," says Opa, patting his pockets. Then he calls after me, "Just hot water is fine, Rieke. No tea."

I turn back to insist—surely it isn't too much to have tea after a long day!—but seeing Opa sitting on the sofa, counting through a meager stack of bills, I close my lips. I'll have hot water, too.

We're eating dinner when we hear a knock. Mama gasps and chokes on her bite of chicken. I jump to get a glass of water, and Marcel pounds her back, and Opa says, "You should be more careful! You've bolted your food since you were a child. How many times have I told you?"

It's Astra who goes to answer the door. Mama manages to cough up the food into her napkin and is sipping water, but her face is still red when Astra returns, followed into the kitchen by Vadim Glazkov, the house administrator.

My sister's face is unreadable, void of expression, but I know she's nervous; she carries herself as if she's on stage. Which, in a way, I suppose she is.

"Frederieke," she says, "get an extra plate. Perhaps the gentleman is hungry."

I rush to take a plate from the cabinet. There isn't much left—just a quarter of a potato and one leg of the chicken—but I scoop it all onto the plate and place it on the table, allowing Vadim Glazkov to take my seat.

What is he doing here? Has he come to take back the money that his wife gave Opa for the bracelet? Or, worse, to confiscate the rest of the jewelry? Or—worst of all—has he come to take our opa?

Vadim Glazkov says something in Russian. I've never been so glad to have Marcel here; he answers quickly and goes to the front room. I hear the clinking of glasses and then he returns, holding a shot glass with vodka, which he places in front of our guest. The house administrator thanks him, raises the glass in salute, and throws back the drink. He lets out a sound of satisfaction, then makes short work of the food I've served. The rest of us are statues in our own kitchen, waiting.

When he's finished, he stands and speaks again. Marcel responds in the affirmative and goes to the radio on the counter. He unplugs it, wraps

166

the cord tightly, and hands it to the house manager, who takes it. Before he goes, he looks at Astra, and then me, and says something to Marcel with a slow grin. Marcel laughs and responds; Vadim Glazkov laughs in reply, slapping Marcel on the back.

Marcel walks him to the door. The rest of us stay where we are. I hear the door open, then, a moment later, shut again. I hear the bolt turn. When Marcel returns, he looks like Mama did when she choked on the bite of chicken—wide-eyed, frightened.

"Why did you give him our radio?" Astra demands. "We'll never be able to replace it!"

Marcel frowns. "Don't be obtuse."

Astra crosses her arms like a child.

"What did he say?" Opa asks.

"He said that the Oppenheims told him we had a radio. And that the authorities have declared that all radios are to be turned in to house managers immediately."

"The Oppenheims." Astra's voice drips with resentment.

Marcel shrugs. "What can be done?" he says, but it's not really a question.

"What else did he say?" I ask. "Before he left?" *When he was looking at me and Astra.*

"Nothing important. Just making conversation."

I don't press. I take the house administrator's plate and fork to the sink. He hasn't left a crumb behind.

We barely have a fall before winter comes—early this year, and bitingly cold. I have always been slender, but what little fat I had disappears, and my period, with it. I think about food all the time: I dream about the blackberries Opa and I picked down by the river that summer in the mountains. I fantasize about chicken fat, cooked crisp and brown. I smell phantom bread baking, only to find our oven cold to the touch.

We eat the little we have more slowly than we ate when our plates were full; we sit at the table together in the evening as if we all hope that maybe if we sip onion broth slowly enough, if we cut our potato into small enough pieces, that someone, magically, will offer us more.

In late November, I catch a cold that keeps me home from school for two days. I'm not feeling fully myself when I do go back to school, but it's not a good idea to miss too many days in a row; that can draw attention from the new Russian teachers, and it's better to not stand out in any way. I feel better for a week or so, but then the fever comes back, this time with a cough. Sometimes at night I sweat in my little cot as if it were full summer, waking up drenched and then shivering again in the wetness.

I should see a doctor, but there's no money for such things. When Opa fusses around me, I tell him not to worry, that it's just because of the cold weather, that I'll feel better as soon as the warmth returns.

In December, Opa insists on lighting the Chanukah candles. When I was a child, this was something I looked forward to each year. We would set the menorah proudly in the front window and I would stand beside it, gazing into the dark night, counting all the other menorahs in all the other windows up and down the street, shining and blinking as if in response to ours.

This year, Opa sets the menorah on the table where no one will see. And he lets the candles burn for just a few minutes each night, because we really can't spare them.

"Some miracle," Astra scoffs.

But Opa says, "It's the lighting that's important." And each night, he stubbornly lights them, saying the blessing as the flames multiply, then snuffing them out, one by one.

It's the last night of Chanukah, just after the final candle has been extinguished, when Marcel announces, "I heard there's to be a New Year's Eve celebration. A masquerade ball."

"Come on," Astra says. "You're teasing me."

"I never tease."

This of course isn't true. Teasing Astra is Marcel's favorite hobby—telling her there's something in her teeth when there isn't, or pointing out gray hairs that aren't there, then laughing hysterically when she runs to the mirror to check. But he's telling the truth about the masquerade ball. I've heard the same news from Madame Lucia.

"It's mostly for Russian officials and their friends, but Madame Lucia says they want the girls from dance to go," I tell them. "I guess they need extra dance partners. I heard Ruth will be there, too."

"Oh, Ruth." Astra waves her hand the way she does. I don't know what happened, but the two of them aren't spending nearly as much time together, anymore.

"Is she that cute brunette?" Marcel asks.

Astra frowns. So *that* was what happened. "She's not that cute."

"Jealous girl," says Marcel, teasing.

I don't want to go to the party. I'm still sick, and it's cold out, and all I want to do is sleep. But everyone says there is going to be food there—lots of it—and I've gotten so thin that Opa thinks I ought to go to eat, if nothing else.

Marcel and Astra are going—the Russian who told Marcel about the party invited him—so I trail behind them to the Palace of Culture.

The three of us huddle through the doorway, breathing into our hands to warm them, and look up to find ourselves surrounded by surreal bounty. The benches and chairs that usually line the floor are cleared away to make room for dancing. On the stage, flanked by oversized photographs of Stalin, musicians play feverishly, loudly, horns and strings wailing and screaming. On the floor, dancers match their pitch, jumping and swaying and spinning, as if this is the last party they'll ever attend.

It's a masquerade ball, so most everyone is wearing a mask, but the biggest mask is the ball itself. Just like the parades and concerts the new government likes to host, this is a celebration of Russia and communism. There hasn't been enough food for months, but here, suddenly, we're surrounded by bowls full of punch, cheese trays, cold cuts. By cigarettes, raised glasses, and high-pitched excitement. People swarm the food tables, shoving the delicacies into their mouths and pockets.

Astra wears a mask cut from purple felt, decorated with some stray sequins and a patch of lace; Marcel has a top hat and a matching purple mask, minus the sequins and lace. As soon as we're through the doors, they disappear onto the dance floor. I stand awkwardly holding my coat. There are Esther and the other girls from dance, standing together by the punch bowl. I'm tempted to go over and ask Esther about how her screenplay is coming along but it's too loud to make conversation, and I feel too tired from sickness to try to talk to people I can't even hear. So I find a spot in a corner to watch the band and the dancing.

A haze of cigarette smoke clouds around me, along with the sounds of the band and the heat of dancers and revelers. Languages dance along with the smoke and the sounds and the bodies—Russian, most loudly, and German, and Romanian, some Ukrainian, a few words of Yiddish here and there. People toss back shots of vodka. Heads tilt close to light one cigarette from another, for lovers to kiss. I haven't eaten all day, and so I should be by the food, shoveling in everything I can get my hands on, but I feel nauseated. I want to sit, but there are no empty chairs, so I stand as still as I can, making myself small.

Then I see Ruth. She's dancing, of course—she's always dancing—held close in Anatoly's arms, the whole length of her body pressing against his. She follows beautifully as he leads, a hand on the small of her back, their faces just inches apart. There's no space between them, not a hair's span.

She looks so happy, so carefree as she moves through the crowd, so trusting that Anatoly will guide her where she needs to go.

The room spins around me, too hot, too crowded by far.

"Rieke."

It's Astra. Her mask is pushed up on her forehead, and she crackles with furious energy.

"Come on," she says. "We're leaving." She starts toward the door.

I shake my head to clear it. "What about Marcel?"

I can hear her words clearly, even over the music. "He'll do what he likes, just like he always does."

I don't point out that this is exactly what Opa says about *her*; I'm just so relieved to be heading home that I don't care why we're leaving. I'm feverish and short of breath, and I should have never come in the first place.

"Wait a minute." I stop to pull on my coat. My hands shake and my fingers do a poor, slow job on the buttons, but finally, I manage to do up the last one. "Okay. I'm ready."

But Astra is ignoring me; she's caught someone's eye behind me and is smiling, waving.

171

Conrad.

He smooths his hair as he makes his way through the crowd to Astra. She reaches out both her hands and he takes them.

"Hello!" Astra is all smiles now. "How have you been?"

Performing, again. For an audience of one. Marcel, if he's watching. I sigh. I desperately want to sit, and my breathing is labored.

"All right, I suppose." Conrad offers Astra a cigarette and lights two, hers and one for himself. "H-hey there, Rieke."

"Hello," I say, but he's turned again to my sister.

"Where's Marcel?"

Astra shrugs as if she doesn't care, sucks on the cigarette.

"Listen." Conrad steps closer, his mouth close to Astra's ear. I can't hear what he says, over the noise. I watch the movement of his mouth. I see Astra's tilt upwards in response.

The band's revelry reaches a fever pitch. The room around me narrows to the size of a pin and I am spinning.

A moment later, Astra's eyes are on me, and her mouth is open, but her words are far away. I want to tell her that I'm fine, but I can't make my voice work.

Someone's hands are beneath my arms, and I'm lowered to the ground. It's strong and sure beneath me, hard against my head in a way that both hurts and feels comforting. My eyes flutter open; Conrad's face is close, staring down at me, brows knit together in worry, cigarette dangling from his lower lip. Above him, still standing, is Astra. She flicks ash onto the ground.

"I'm okay," I manage to say.

Conrad gives me his hand and helps me sit up. Someone passes him a glass, which he holds to my lips. "Here," he says.

172

I take a sip—vodka—and it burns my mouth and tongue, sets my chest aflame. But it seems to clear my head, and after a minute I'm ready to stand. Conrad helps me to my feet.

"Drama, drama," Astra says.

"Don't be mean," Conrad responds.

She raises one of her beautiful eyebrows and sighs. And then, I see something in her expression, a softness that hasn't been there since Marcel came and ruined everything. "All right, little rat tail, let's get you home."

"Should we f-find Marcel?" Conrad asks.

"No," Astra answers sharply, and so Conrad says he'll walk us home.

Outside, the cold air feels good. Fresh. And though I have a rotten headache, I feel better than I did indoors. Conrad keeps a hand around my waist as we walk, and though I know it's only there for support, I let myself enjoy the feeling. When was the last time I was held, by anyone? I can't remember.

From the Palace of Culture, we hear a great cheer go up. It's midnight. It's 1941.

"A new year," Astra muses. "Do you think it will be better than the last?"

And she drops the butt of her cigarette onto the icy sidewalk, grinds it out with her toe.

173

# SEVEN

## THE NARROWING GYRE

Marcel doesn't come home for two days.

Astra is meaner than a snake the whole time. Even Opa gives her distance. And when Marcel finally returns, it's with a black eye and a torn collar, reeking of vodka and cigarettes. Astra doesn't speak to him for a full day after that, and the apartment is as icy inside as the street is out of doors.

Then there's a screaming fight, and broken dishes.

Then the reunion.

For this last part, we do our best to give them space by taking a walk around the block. It's miserably cold, but none of us complains. When we go back to the apartment, Marcel is singing in the shower and Astra lounges on the sofa in her dressing gown, a cigarette in one hand, a drink in the other. It's so ridiculous that it's funny, and it feels good to have something to laugh about. I find that I'm relieved Marcel has come home. Whether I like it or not, he's family now, I suppose. And if doing those things with Marcel makes Astra less miserable to live with, then I'll walk around in a snowstorm, if necessary, to give them space.

Winter is long and dark. We all know that even worse things are happening out in the world than here, but no one we know has a radio anymore, and where once our city prided itself on its numerous news sources—even after the Jewish publications were forced to stop printing, there were still nine newspapers—now there's just one, a Russian paper called *Red Bukovina* that does nothing but praise Stalin and print exaggerated accounts of the successes of farmers and workers.

Opa continues to sell privately the wares left over from his shop, but only when absolutely necessary; each time he takes a piece out on the street, he's taking the risk that someone might beat him up and steal it or report him to the Soviets for selling on the black market.

One thing we get lots of practice at is waiting in lines. Everything I once took for granted—coffee and tea, milk, bread, cheese—is now as precious as the jewels in Opa's dwindling collection. We take turns waiting to purchase the goods we're "entitled" to, but sometimes by the time I get to the front of a line, it's to find that our rations have been cut in half, or there's nothing left to buy at all.

And my illness only gets worse. My cough doesn't go away, and often I'm feverish and weak. In school, I do my best to focus, but it's difficult when I haven't slept. At dance, I struggle to keep up, missing my marks and feeling as though I'm moving my limbs through water, as if I'm wearing invisible weights. I'm starting to agree with Astra—what *are* we dancing for? Are we like the musicians on that British cruise liner, the *Titanic*, who kept playing as the ship went down? When I first learned about the ship, I thought the musicians were heroes. They kept playing to keep the passengers calm. But now . . . I don't know.

In the food lines I shiver, then sweat, then shiver again. One day at dusk, walking home at the end of a long day, there's a loose wetness in my lungs; it rattles when I breathe deeply, making me gag and then cough. I stop on the corner and put my hands to my knees, trying to catch my breath, as passersby dodge around me. When I hack up phlegm and spit it to the gutter, I see it is laced with blood.

Dread thuds in my gut like unleavened bread. This can't be normal.

"Calm down." I speak aloud, quietly. "You thought you were dying the first time you got your period too, remember?"

An old woman, bundled from chin to toes and leaning on a cane, is watching me from the side of her eye, probably wondering what sort of a crazy person I am to be standing here on the corner talking to myself. I ignore her, blink down into the gutter. "Bodies bleed sometimes," I say, this time to myself. "Remember how stupid you felt before, when you made such a big deal over nothing."

I'll go home and find Astra. I'll tell her what happened, and she'll roll her eyes. "Rat tail," she'll say. "Do you think you're the only person who coughs up blood now and then?" Imagining her reacting this way calms me, and my lurching heart returns to normal. I step over the gutter and cross the street toward home. "You think *that's* something," I imagine Astra saying, eyebrow arched, one arm folded across her middle, the other bent, a cigarette perched between two fingers. "Once, I coughed up a clot as big as an egg, and you don't hear *me* complaining."

My pace quickens. I'll feel better when I'm home, with my family.

But when I reach the apartment and open the front door, I hear voices from the bathroom, and a choking sound—a sob.

"Astra?" I call.

No answer.

Slowly, still in my coat, I go down the hallway. The bathroom door isn't latched; I peer through the crack.

Astra is naked, sitting in the tub. She is crying.

I can't remember ever seeing Astra cry. Ever.

Mama kneels beside her. She dips a washcloth in the bathwater and pulls it across Astra's back. "Shh," she soothes. "Shh."

I don't breathe. The only sounds are Mama, saying, "Shh," and the soft splash of the washcloth dipping into the water, and Astra's broken sobs. She rocks back and forth, back and forth.

At last, Astra sucks in one more breath of air and composes herself. Then she takes the washcloth from Mama and dunks it in the bathwater, rakes it across her face.

"We can never tell Marcel," she says. "He'll get himself killed."

Mama says, "No one needs to know. It will be like it never happened."

Astra shakes her head. She drops the washcloth in the water. Then she nods.

"All right," she says. "Okay. Get me a towel."

Mama climbs to her feet to fetch a towel, and I back slowly away, then go silently up the hallway to the living room. I open the front door, quiet as a mouse, and slip outside. I shut the door and wait, I don't know for what.

My hand is shaking. I watch it as if it doesn't belong to me, trembling like a poplar leaf. I wait until it stills, until I have control again. Then I open the door and go inside.

"Hello," I call, feigning cheer. "I'm home!"

I don't know what happened to Astra. If I were braver, I would ask. But I'm not the brave one. Astra is. I tiptoe around her for a few days while she mostly sits in silence, often holding a book but staring past it. Until, at last, I'm collecting mugs strewn on the tables in the living room and she flicks a cigarette butt in my direction. "Hey," she barks. "Rat tail. Cut it out, why don't you?"

I manage to jump out of the way of the cigarette, still burning. I pick it up and dunk the ember in the dregs of water at the bottom of one of the dirty cups.

She seems to get better after that; maybe being mean to me is some sort of balm for Astra. And there's no more blood when I cough, and maybe I'm even coughing less. It seems that way.

A few days later, Astra comes home from her job at the hospital and calls me into her room.

It's the first time I've been in here since Marcel moved in; with wistful fondness, I look at the corner where my twin bed used to be. Now it's pushed together with Astra's to make one large bed in the center of the wall. The room smells different, too; like cigarettes, of course, and Astra's perfume, but also like the musk that Marcel wears, and a staleness, too, perhaps from having the windows closed all winter long, perhaps from what they do in bed.

"I have something to give you." Astra sets her purse on the bureau and rifles through it. She pulls out two small packets and sets one aside, then offers me the other on her flattened palm. As I reach to take it, she closes her fingers and yanks it out of my reach. "Careful," she says. Her voice and face are serious. "This isn't kid stuff."

Then she holds out her hand again, her fingers opening like the petals of a flower, and this time she lets me take it.

It's a small wax-paper envelope, folded over. Inside is a pill.

"What's this for?"

"Emergencies," Astra says. "Listen. If you get in a situation that you can tell is going to be terrible—*really* terrible, the kind of thing that isn't worth living through—you can take this pill."

"What will it do?" It's small and white, like something for headaches. It looks harmless.

"It'll kill you, dummy."

The packet slips from my fingers to the floor. I stare down at it.

"*Careful*," she repeats. She picks up the packet and holds it out to me again. I'm not sure if I want to take it. "It's better to have it and not need it than need it and not have it."

I suppose I can't really argue with that. I take the packet. "Where'd you get this?"

"There's a pharmacist at the hospital who's making them."

I want to ask her about what happened. About why she was crying in the bathtub. I look into her eyes; they are the deepest, most beautiful brown, almost black. I see her pupils dilate, and it feels like she's pulling inward, pulling away from me. "Astra," I say, stepping toward her, but she shakes her head.

"Get out of here, rat tail. I've got things to do."

She's gone again. I turn to go.

"Hey." Her face is softer now, her eyes gleam. "You can actually survive a lot worse than you'd think."

"Okay," I answer. Then I leave.

Back in my room, I tap the pill out of the wax-paper wrapping and hold it up to the window. It looks perfectly ordinary. I have a necklace I rarely wear; I dig it out of the top drawer of my dresser. It's the locket that Father gave me, years ago, when he returned from one of his absences with presents for all three of us. Where is he now, I wonder. We haven't seen him since the day Astra and Marcel got married.

I pry open the golden heart with my thumbnail. Tiny photographs—one of Opa, and the other of Mama, much younger and with baby Astra on her lap. I set the pill inside the locket, snap it closed. Then I slide the locket deep into the far corner of my top dresser drawer.

I can't think of anything so terrible that it would make me not want to live anymore. Opa would be devastated if I ever did anything to hurt myself, for one. And as far as I've gone from *believing* Opa's dictum that "everything is cyclical," I guess I can't help but *hope* it's true, that somehow, things will improve—the war, my cough, all of it.

Snow falls heavy, dampening everything. When we aren't at work or school, we're at home in the apartment. We play cards and read books and try not to drive one another crazy. I decided not to tell anyone about the blood—it's only happened one more time, during a particularly cold week—but there's no hiding my cough. And everyone has an opinion.

"She needs honey in her tea," Opa insists one day upon returning home, and produces a small jar of it from his jacket pocket. It's obvious he went out to buy it with the money he made from selling his gems.

"Opa, you shouldn't have, it's too dangerous," I say, but he makes a sound—"Pfftt"—and waves his hand at me.

He's right; the honey does help. When there's no tea we stir the honey into hot water, and that's almost as good. He fusses around me like a chicken.

"Faking it for attention, I'll bet," Astra says, but she drops a wink at me to let me know she's kidding, and she gives me one of her pillows so I can sleep without lying down so flat. That helps, too.

From the hospital, Marcel brings home some tonic. "The Russian doctors have been prescribing this for coughs," he says, and shrugs. "It might not help, but it certainly won't hurt."

"You need to dry out, that's all," says Mama. "You'll improve in the spring."

At last, spring does come, and with the warmer air, I do feel stronger. It's a relief to be able to open the windows for a change. Out there, the birds must not know about the Russians, because just like every spring, they return. The trees grow fresh waxy green leaves, same as they always do. But though I do feel better, I'm not *well*, not really. My cough doesn't go away, or the feeling that my lungs are wet and spongy. I'm too weak to dance, but I go to the studio anyway. I need the distraction, and besides, I don't want Opa to worry more than he already does. At the studio, I sit in a corner on the floor, watching the other girls.

It's the middle of the night in May when I awake from a dead sleep to a pounding on the door. I blink into the night-black room, trying to adjust my eyes.

I lie still and listen to the thumping of Marcel's steps, and the slower movement of Opa, both heading to answer the door.

Voices, then silence, then voices again. I sit straight up, holding the sheet to my chest. My heart flutters, and I take shallow breaths, trying my best not to cough.

Marcel's footsteps, coming up the hall, through the kitchen. He knocks on my door and opens it at the same time.

"Get up," he tells me.

In the front room, the others are pulling on coats over their sleeping clothes.

Marcel says, "We have to hide. The Soviets are coming for your grandfather—he's on the list for Siberia."

Those words—*The Soviets are coming for your grandfather*—immobilize me. Immediately, liquid fills my lungs, my eyes, and I am drowning. "No, no, no," is all I can say, at a whisper. Around me, the others pull on coats, wrap scarves around their necks.

Astra asks, "Who was at the door?"

"Vadim Glazkov. He says we should go to the basement." Marcel grabs my coat from the closet, thrusts it at me.

"The house manager?" Astra says. "Why would we listen to him?"

Marcel doesn't answer. Beside me, Opa sits on the sofa, tying his shoes. He has on his coat. He looks up and me and smiles. "Don't worry, Rieke. It will be okay."

I manage to swallow the liquid rising in my throat. "What do they want with Opa?"

Astra has finished buttoning her coat. She comes over and yanks my coat from my hands, holds it open for me.

"They're rounding up all the merchants." Marcel throws on his coat over his pajamas and begins lacing up his boots. "Someone must have told them about your grandfather selling the jewelry from his store. The Oppenheims, I'd guess."

Outside our apartment, the hallway is silent. Straight across from us is the Oppenheims' door. Could it be? Our own neighbors, telling the Soviets about Opa? Our radio was one thing, but to tell them about Opa's wares . . . Why? How could they?

We tiptoe down the hall, past other doors, behind which other families sleep. We make our way to the staircase and go down to street level, and then take another staircase—this one thinner, steeper, and dusty—to the basement. Opa feels along the wall and finds a light switch. Boxes are piled up, crates of things that belong to various residents. Far in the back is a sofa covered over with a sheet. We go to it and sit in a row. Then Marcel returns to the light switch to flip it off. He makes his way back to us, knocking into a crate and swearing under his breath before settling in next to Astra.

I'm smashed between Mama and Opa. It's a tight fit, all of us hip-to-hip like sardines in a can.

We do our best to be silent. I take careful, shallow breaths to keep from coughing. It doesn't seem real, sitting here like this. Hiding. The room is so dark that I feel like I'm falling into nothingness, so I shut my eyes. But behind my lids I see visions of Soviet soldiers bursting through the basement door, boots pounding down the stairs. I see them grab my opa's arms and pull him to standing. I see myself crying out, "No! Don't take him, you can't take him!"

I open my eyes again, but nothing changes. Open or closed, it's murky black, unknowable. We are completely without power, without agency. If the house manager decides to betray us, they'll take Opa. They could take all of us.

"We are safe, we are safe, we are safe," I say inside my head over and over again, though it doesn't feel true, until, at last, I sleep.

It must be midday when the door opens and a shaft of light spills into the basement. We listen and squint to see who descends, all of us blinking against the brightness. Is this it? Is this the end?

It's Vadim Glazkov. He stops halfway down and speaks quickly in Russian. "All clear. Go home."

He goes up the stairs, leaving the basement door cracked open.

"Do we trust him?" Astra asks.

"If he wanted us dead, he'd have brought the Reds down here already,"

Marcel answers, and so we stand, stiff and cramped, and make our way back to the apartment.

There we find the door unlatched. We go inside, and Mama begins to cry.

It's a mess. Chairs knocked over, cushions on the floor, the liquor cabinet wide open and emptied of all the bottles. Mama runs to the sideboard to see what's been taken. The plates are still there, but all the silver is gone, even Opa's mother's heavy Sabbath candlesticks.

Almost everything of value, gone. Mama's fur and her few pieces of jewelry, taken. Astra's silks and Marcel's watch, stolen.

"We have nothing," Mama moans.

"They left my books," Astra says, wryly. "Must not be big readers."

I want to tell Mama and Astra that we don't have "nothing." That Opa is still here, and that's all that matters.

"We don't have nothing," says Opa, echoing my thoughts. He takes off his coat, and shows us—stitches along the seams, raised lumps at regular intervals.

"Clever, Opa," says Astra, impressed.

"I'll be needing something for Vadim Glazkov," Marcel says. "It wasn't out of the goodness of his heart that he warned us."

Opa finds a stitch ripper in the sewing kit and sets to work. A moment later he hands Marcel a gold ring.

"They'll come back," Marcel says, grim. "Soon, probably."

But he's wrong. It's worse than that.

Though that night the Soviets rounded up merchants and bourgeoises from all around the city, and though they doubtless would again if they were given the chance, they don't get that chance. Because on June 22, the first German bombs fall.

It's a Sunday. I wake to the sound of thunder, but when I get out of bed and go to the window, the skies are clear. The street below looks normal—mostly empty, as it's still early, but nothing out of the ordinary. I'm about to draw the curtain when I see something—a Russian soldier, running. Each of his footfalls ricochets off the buildings that line the street. I don't know why, but I pull my head back inside and step behind the curtain. Through its gauze I watch him run. His cap flies from his head and lands in the street, but he doesn't stop.

Then I see a column of smoke rising into the sky near the far edge of town. Uneasy, I draw the window closed.

Moments later, Mrs. Oppenheim from across the hall—the very one who told Vadim Glazkov about our radio, the one we suspect of telling the Soviets about Opa's jewelry—is banging at the door.

"They blew up the airport!" She's out of breath even from just crossing the hall, or maybe from fear.

"Who did?" Marcel is dressed for the day in his shirt and tie; Mrs. Oppenheim doesn't seem to care that she's in a housecoat and slippers. She pushes past him into our apartment. Her hair is in curlers, covered over with a silk scarf. Normally, Mrs. Oppenheim is the sort of woman who wouldn't let anyone see her without lipstick perfectly applied onto her wide trout mouth.

"The Germans," she says, breathing hard. "They've attacked all along the border. The Russians are running. And we are in terrible danger."

I know who she meant by "we"—the Jews. When the Russians weren't serving up Chopin on the speakers along the Ringplatz, from time to time they played broadcasts, as well—our only access to news from the outside world. We've heard Adolf Hitler's speeches. We know what's happening in

185

Germany, and elsewhere.

Or maybe by "we" she means herself and her husband. After all, they've cozied up with our house manager and have been vocally supportive of the Soviets.

As soon as Mrs. Oppenheim leaves, off to spread the news to the other neighbors, Mama says, "We'll need to get whatever supplies we can. Who knows what will happen now?"

Everyone agrees. Opa and Marcel pool the bit of money they have—both Russian rubles and Romanian lei—and decide we should buy all the essentials we can, as we can't know how long the currency will be worth anything at all. Astra and Marcel go to see about buying kerosene, in case the electricity gets shut off, and Mama and Opa go in search of flour, yeast, potatoes, and cooking oil.

They leave me home. "You'll just slow us down, with your cough," Astra says, but Opa softens her harsh words by saying, "We'll need someone to stay here in case anyone else drops by with more news, yes?"

The door shuts loudly behind them. I go to the window; a moment later they emerge from the front door below, Astra and Marcel first, linking arms and heading briskly in one direction, then Mama and Opa, moving less quickly but with equal determination in the other.

Tears fill my eyes. There's no one to see me cry, but still I hold them back.

I don't expect visitors, but indeed there is a knock, about an hour later. I crack open the door and peer out.

I freeze. "Mr. Weissinger?"

He runs a hand across his dark, oiled hair. "Frederieke. Might I come in?"

"No one else is home."

"That's all right. This won't take long."

I only hesitate a moment before I open the door and step out of the way. Mr. Weissinger enters and makes himself comfortable on the sofa. I stand beside a chair across from him.

"Can I offer you something to drink?" We have no coffee or tea, much less liquor. I hope Mr. Weissinger will turn me down to save me the embarrassment of admitting it.

"No, thank you. Frederieke, you're old enough now, surely, to realize that things are likely to get quite bad. I came to speak to Heinrich and Marcel, to let them know—to let your family know—that I will do what I can to help."

"Why?" I blurt as I sink to the chair. Horrified, I cover my mouth with my hand.

Mr. Weissinger laughs. He has good, white teeth, with two gold ones in the back.

"Look." He leans forward and puts a hand on my knee. "It's times like these when we have to stick together. And I know your father would do the same for my family, if I were a family man. So, if you find yourselves in need of anything, you can reach out to me, all right? I will make a loan, and I will give you better rates than you will find anywhere else. That, I promise."

I hear his words, but not really, because all I can focus on is his hand on my leg.

Before I can decide what to say, he pats my knee—once, twice—and then pulls his hand away. He reaches into his pocket and takes out a pack of cigarettes and a chocolate bar. He puts them on the coffee table and stands.

He looks at me for a moment before heading to the door. "You've grown into a beautiful young woman, Frederieke." And then he's gone.

When the others return, they bring news—the Russians are fleeing the city like rats from a drowning ship. I have news, too. I tell them about Mr. Weissinger's offer to loan us money if we need it. I give them the chocolate and the cigarettes. Astra cracks open the cigarette pack immediately, taps one out.

"Oh-ho," says Marcel. "So George is making the rounds, the old snake." He says it with something like admiration.

Opa shakes his head. "That Weissinger fellow—you girls stay away from him."

Mama, peeling open the bar of chocolate, says, "He's not so bad."

Opa makes a sound, shakes his head again. "He's no good. Men like that, making a profit off others' misfortune, their weaknesses. What sort of a man does that?"

"A *rich* man," Astra answers, lighting a cigarette.

"Rich like that, he can keep it."

Mama holds out the bar of chocolate. Astra takes a chunk, and Marcel does, too, but Opa says, "Bah," and turns away.

When he's left the room, I take a piece of the chocolate. I can't remember the last time I've tasted something so rich. I let it melt on my tongue.

The retreating Red Army leaves a trail of destruction in its wake. At night, thousands of Russian troops march through the city. We sit at the windows and watch them go, listen to the boots, the trucks, the tanks. The smell of diesel, permeating our apartment. The street echoes with clanking and rumbling.

I look down at the soldiers, moving like a long snake through the street. Which one of those men has my watch? Where will he take it?

Day and night, everyone stays indoors with their curtains pulled tight as soldiers loot stores and take what they like from anyone who crosses their path. They go to the building where all the confiscated radios are stored and set it on fire. They destroy the electric utility station. There are beatings, even killings, say the whispers of the people who gather in the building hallways—anyone who gets in their way, and some people who try to stay out of it.

None of us leaves our apartment, not for anything. We huddle together in the front room, waiting . . . for what, we don't know.

On the Monday of the Russian exodus, in the middle of the night, we hear a string of rapid explosions.

"They've blown up the bridge," Marcel says. "That's the only thing over there for them to destroy."

I don't believe him. I don't know why I don't, maybe just because that bridge has been there all my life and my mind can't accept that it isn't there anymore. But when the sun rises in the morning to reveal a smoke-heavy sky, there's no denying it.

We peer out the window and I catch the eye of a man looking out of his, across the way. We stare at each other, unblinking, for a long moment. Then he steps back and draws closed his curtain.

The smoke from the bombing of the bridge hasn't yet cleared when the air fills again with thick black smoke—a fire, and nearby. The smoke makes my chest hurt even more than usual. Marcel heads outside to see if our building is in any danger.

"It's the post office," he tells us when he returns. "Apparently the Russians stored explosives in its cellar, and they've detonated them so no one else can set them off. Complete destruction. Now the fire is spreading."

"The fire department will extinguish it before it gets too far," Opa says.

Marcel shakes his head. "The Russians took all the firefighting equipment with them. There is no fire department anymore."

It sounds too nightmarish to be true. But it is.

Before long, the Romanian mobs arrive, clearing out what the Russians left behind, like vultures on a carcass wolves have eaten their fill of. Like the soldiers, the mob knocks down doors, busts out windows, grabs what they like with impunity. They concentrate mainly on shops and street-level apartments, but we're constantly listening for footsteps in our hallway, checking and double-checking the lock on our door. Imagining what Opa's shop must look like now, I'm glad for the hundredth time that he doesn't go there anymore. Down below, the street sparkles with broken glass.

A looter walks down the middle of the street, his boots crunching the glass into powder. "Kill all the Jews!" he yells in Romanian.

At this, I do as the neighbor across the street did; I pull my face from the window and draw the curtain shut.

Between the Russians and the looters, every comfort, every convenience, is destroyed. Then, at last, they're gone. The city falls still, hushed. We hold our breaths.

Marcel returns to the hospital, despite Astra begging him to stay home. "I have a duty," he tells Astra.

"You have a duty to *me*, but that doesn't stop you from whoring," she spits.

After he leaves, Astra retreats to their room, and slams the door.

# EIGHT

## WHAT HAPPENS TO RUTH

The next day, Ruth comes to our door.

Her braids, always neat, are loose and disheveled, and her face is swollen from crying. Her breathing is fast and shallow; I'm afraid she's going to hyperventilate.

"I need to speak to Astra," she gasps.

"She's in her room. Come in."

Ruth follows me. I knock on Astra's door.

"Go away," says the voice on the other side.

I open the door anyway. Sprawled on her stomach, reading, Astra looks up irritably. Then she sees Ruth. She rolls over and stands. "Hey! What are you doing here?"

Ruth's tears turn to sobs, and she goes to Astra, who takes her in her arms. I shut the door and sit on a chair in the corner, awkwardly. Astra leads Ruth to the bed, and they sink to it together, Ruth crying into Astra's chest. She says something, but I can't make out the words.

"He's just a man, Ruth," Astra says. "There will be others."

"Not for me," Ruth cries, lifting her head from Astra's chest. "Never for me."

"What do you mean?" says Astra.

"He left me!" she says. "He's gone! I begged him to take me with him. He'd promised he would! But—he *laughed*, Astra, he laughed in my face."

"Son of a bitch."

"And he told me—" Ruth sobs. "—he told me that—Astra, he has a *wife* and *three children* back in Russia! I thought he was going to marry me . . ." She collapses again, as if the words have taken everything she has left.

Astra holds her, rocks her roughly. "Shh," she says. "Enough. You're young, you're beautiful, you'll be fine."

Mama's words, coming out of Astra's mouth.

More snuffling, more crying. Then Astra pushes Ruth away and hands her a tissue. Ruth blows her nose.

When Ruth speaks again, her voice is full of something else: fear. "I did something."

The tone of her voice scares me.

"You slept with him," says Astra. "So what? Wait—are you pregnant?"

"No. Not that. I . . . took something. After he left."

"You took something? What do you mean? You *stole* something?"

"No." She pauses, and now the tone of her voice scares me. "I took pills. I swallowed them."

"Ruth," says Astra. I can tell she's scared as well. "Ruth, what did you *do*?"

Ruth answers, but her voice turns to jelly as her tears redouble, and then Astra takes her by the wrist and yanks her to standing. I follow as she pulls Ruth by the wrist through the apartment and out the front door. Opa calls after her to stop, that we cannot leave the apartment, but Astra pays him no mind. I want to go with them, but I know I won't be able to keep up—my cough has been better since the summer arrived, but I know I wouldn't be able to run more than half a block, so I stop on the apartment threshold. And then she and Ruth are gone.

Ruth has always been incredibly kind to me. It was Ruth who comforted me when I got my first period; Ruth who greeted me, my first day of dance.

I remember that Astra got me safely to the studio, but the second we were in the building, she crossed the foyer and disappeared into a dressing room. When she pulled open its door, the group of girls, each in a black tunic putting on their things for class, turned with bright smiles to greet Astra, and I was forgotten.

When I got my courage up to follow her into the dressing room, no one noticed me at first; the girls went about their business—this one fitting her feet into her dance slippers, that one adjusting the straps of her brassiere, there, a girl pinning up her hair. I slipped as quietly as I could onto the edge of a bench and began unlacing my school shoes.

"Oh," said a girl. "Aren't you adorable!"

I can still feel how my face turned red. How nervous I was.

"What's your name?" she asked.

"Frederieke," I mumbled.

"Frederieke!" she exclaimed. "You're Astra's baby sister?"

I nodded. In the pocket of my skirt was a pair of brand-new ballet slippers, and I pulled them out.

"You'll need elastics sewn on those," the girl said. She looked to Astra, who was deep in conversation with two other girls. "Here, I have some." She went to a locker and rifled through it, returning with a length of pink elastic, scissors, some thread, a needle. The other girls filed out the door to the dance studio. "Tell Madame Lucia that we'll be there in a minute," she called after no one in particular. "Now," she said, "let me see your slippers."

I handed them across and watched her measure out a length of elastic, double it up, and cut it in two. Her dark braids fell forward as she worked. She set aside one length and threaded her needle. She sewed quick, small, neat stitches. When she finished the first slipper, she handed it to me and said, "A princess's slipper for a princess. I'm Ruth, by the way."

I watched as she affixed a length of elastic on the second shoe. It didn't take long. She handed it to me, and I slipped them on while she put away her sewing equipment. She quickly wrapped and pinned her braids at the nape of her neck, and then we went together from the dressing room and into the dance studio, where the other girls were already lined up along the barre, a great wall of mirrors behind them.

I think about the elastic, about Ruth sewing it onto my slippers, as I wait for Astra to return. I think of her bringing me a dance skirt when I got my period. How she danced like she was a princess, like she thought all of us were princesses, and for each princess there would be a prince, and a fairy tale. The way she lit up the day she was chosen for Anatoly, the light that shone from her, always.

Astra doesn't get home until dusk. She's with Marcel; they're holding hands. He nods to me, kisses Astra on the forehead, and goes to the bathroom. Astra heads to the mantel, for a cigarette; there's only one in the pack. She looks at it, contemplating whether to smoke it, and then taps it into her hand. She crumples the empty pack, throws it into the fireplace. Pushing open the sash and collapsing into the window seat, Astra lights the cigarette.

I watch her do all of this. Finally, I can't stand it anymore. "What happened to Ruth?"

Astra sucks hard on the cigarette and blows a cloud of smoke into the sunset. "She's going to die."

"Don't be awful."

Astra shrugs, as if it doesn't matter if I believe her or not. "She took a bunch of her grandmother's pills—something for her gout. Then she got scared and came here to tell me. But it's too late—the hospital gave her charcoal to try to soak it up, but Marcel says it's no good. She's going to die from it. And over a man. Stupid cow."

It can't be true. It *can't*.

Another long draw on the cigarette, another cloud of smoke. "She'll be dead in two days. Three, tops. The medicine is poisoning her organs. They're shutting down."

"You're lying." I clench my hands into fists.

"Believe what you want." Astra's face is a cold mask . . . but for one moment, it slips, and I see her heart, breaking.

Still, I won't believe her—not until the next day when Astra takes me to visit Ruth at the hospital where she lies in clean white sheets; when I see how her face has begun to yellow; when I see her mother at her side, clutching her hand, sobbing without cease; when I see her father standing by the window, his face gray as the ash of Astra's cigarettes. Then, I believe her.

Ruth is dead and buried before the Germans arrive in force. May her memory be a blessing.

# PART III
# A VERY LUCKY GIRL

June 1941–May 1942

# ONE

## THE NAZIS

Many families leave with the Russians, the Oppenheims among them. They'd so publicly aligned themselves with the Soviets—loudly praising communism, reporting on the rest of us, and getting close with our house manager and his wife—probably they felt they had no choice. Whether or not they were ever true believers in the communist movement, they're smart enough to know that whatever happens next, Soviet supporters are going to be in danger.

So are the rest of us, with the Germans coming.

Before they leave, Mrs. Oppenheim knocks on our door. When I open it, she's holding Mitzi. It's a large, fluffy cat that looks like it's eaten more over the last year than my whole family put together.

"Frederieke," Mrs. Oppenheim says, and her tears began to flow. "You must promise to take care of my baby. It's impossible for me to bring her with me." She holds out the cat.

I take a step back. "Oh, Mrs. Oppenheim. I don't think that is a very good idea."

"It's the *only* idea," she insists, shaking the cat a little to emphasize her point.

I don't know why I nod. We have no money to feed it. But what else can I do?

Mitzi seems completely apathetic about this exchange; Mrs. Oppenheim, though, burbles with tears and kisses the cat, one cheek, then the other, then the first again. "What is the world coming to?" she says, to no one in particular, and then she leaves.

I'm certain that my family will be furious with me—after all, we don't even have food enough for ourselves—but instead, they're delighted.

Astra rushes to me, pulling the cat from my arms. She coos like a mother with an infant, cradling her, rocking her back and forth. Immediately, Mitzi purrs like a motor. I swear the cat even smiles.

Marcel is happy because Astra is happy, and I think Mama and Opa are glad for the distraction, too.

"But what are we even going to feed it?" I ask, crossing the room and sitting down. My cough has been better, or at least not as frequent, but I still feel weak with illness.

"*Her*," corrects Astra. "Mitzi is not an 'it.'"

"What are we going to feed *her*?"

"We'll make do." Opa scratches the cat's head.

"You said the Oppenheims are already gone?" says Mama.

"I think so. Mrs. Oppenheim looked dressed for traveling when she brought me the cat."

Astra raises an eyebrow, sets Mitzi on a footstool, and opens the apartment door. She crosses the hall and knocks on the Oppenheims' door. No answer. She rattles the knob. "Locked."

Marcel, who has been standing back, watching, looks up and down the hallway, then throws his shoulder against the door. With a loud *crack*, the doorjamb splinters, and Marcel falls forward into the Oppenheims' apartment. Mama gasps; Astra, though, laughs and claps her hands. A moment later, we hear Marcel exclaim, "Will you look at that?"

I get up, and Opa, Mama, and I cross the hallway, too.

There, in the front room, is Opa's beautiful Turkish rug, covered in cat hair, just as I imagined. We walk across it and go into the Oppenheims' kitchen, where we find Marcel and Astra staring into the open pantry.

I haven't seen anything so beautiful since childhood. In front of me is a larder filled with dozens of jars and canisters and sacks of food. Jars of jam and olives and pickles; rations of flour and sugar and salt; bins of potatoes and onions. There are even a few tins of herring and sardines.

It's clear that a part of the pantry was recently emptied—I'm sure the Oppenheims took whatever they could carry—but compared to what we have across the hall, it's the difference between a dried-up creek bed and a flowing river. My stomach grumbles.

"Some communists," Marcel mumbles.

But Astra is as awed as I am. "We'll eat like movie stars," she sings.

"If we take it all for ourselves," Opa says, "we are no better than the Oppenheims."

That kills the feeling of celebration. I look around; the apartment is full of other things of value that must have been deemed too heavy for the Oppenheims to carry away with them.

"If we don't take all this," says Astra, "others will."

"We'll take the canned fish," Opa says, "in payment for taking care of their cat. But no more."

For once, Astra obeys. "Okay, Opa. We'll do as you like. We can come back later, I suppose, if you change your mind."

"No mind changing," Opa says. "A person has to have morals. If not, what is a person?"

We take the fish. Everything else, we leave, just as it is.

We spend the next hour together in the living room—me, trying to keep the cat calm with limited success, Astra reading, Marcel smoking, Mama pacing—until Opa announces he's going to lie down for a nap.

As soon as he's left the room, Astra and Marcel exchange a glance. Then, they get up in unison and head for the door.

"Where are you going?" I ask, though I already know. I get up, too, letting the cat leap to the ground.

Once we've crept across the hall, Astra and Marcel go straight for the pantry. "Check the icebox," Astra tells me.

"What are we doing?" I ask. "There's no way Opa is going to let us keep any of it."

"Your opa is sweet, but he's completely wrong," Marcel says.

"He's an idealist, but he's not stupid," says Astra. "Once the food is in our apartment, there's no way he's going to make us bring it back. And if he tries to, you just look at him with your big puppy eyes and tell him how hungry you are, okay, rat tail? He'll do anything for you."

I hesitate before I go to the icebox. I understand that to Opa, there are moments that define a person. And when he sees what I've chosen, he will be disappointed in me.

The icebox is empty. "I'll go look for valuables," I say.

Marcel nods. His arms are full of potatoes and onions.

We take every morsel of food. And then we go back for Opa's rug.

When Opa wakes from his nap and sees what we've done, he sighs and shakes his head . . . but he doesn't insist we return it. Instead, he says,

202

"Okay. If we take the food of one neighbor, then we divide it evenly with those who remain."

"What?" says Astra, indignant. "That's ridiculous!"

But Marcel sides with Opa. "It will be good for building relations. We scratch their back now, maybe later they can scratch ours."

"That's not for why we share," says Opa, as indignant as Astra was a moment ago. "We share because it is the right thing to do—the *human* thing."

"You have your reasons, I have mine," says Marcel. "The result's the same, isn't it?"

And there's nothing Opa can say to that.

Marcel, who's still working at the Jewish Hospital, comes home nightly with reports from the outside world. He tells us that the people living in villages a few miles away from the city aren't waiting for the full might of the German army to arrive. Along with the Benderovtze, who descended from the mountains, the villagers are rampaging. "They say all Jews are communists, and Russian collaborators," he tells us. "They're killing any Jew they can find."

Opa shakes his head, back and forth, slowly.

"In Banila pe Siret," Marcel continues, "the villagers killed two Jewish men and cut them into pieces, then used their blood to grease the axles of their carts."

"That can't be true. No one would do such a thing. Opa," I say, turning to him, "tell Marcel that can't be true."

"I wish I could say that, Rieke. I wish I could."

It is July, the temperature is blisteringly hot. Suddenly freezing, I shiver, and I go to bed.

As it turns out, it doesn't matter that Astra quit dancing, because within the week, Madame Lucia closes her studio. Or, she doesn't close it so much as she simply disappears. One day, she is there; the next, she and Miss Rosen are gone. No one knows where they went, or how.

I understand why Miss Rosen left—she's Jewish, and lots of Jews are taking their chances by leaving. But Madame Lucia isn't Jewish; most likely she'd be fine staying in Czernowitz. Probably she'd even be safer here now, with the Russians gone.

"They must have been very close friends, for Madame Lucia to leave with Miss Rosen," I say to Astra. "Where do you think they'll go?"

"Friends." Astra laughs. "Dummy. They're lovers."

"They *are*?"

"Of course they are. One thing you can be sure. Wherever they went, they went together."

I've never heard of two women being lovers. I hadn't even known that was possible.

Madame Lucia's words: *"You choose your path, or it chooses you."*

And I see them, clear as a picture: Madame Lucia and Miss Rosen, tapping together the rims of their martini glasses. Choosing their own path—I hope—together.

The morning after Madame Lucia and Miss Rosen disappear, Marcel calls a family meeting.

The five of us sit around the table, Mitzi curled on Astra's lap. We each have a cup of precious coffee, the one thing we took from the Oppenheims' apartment that Astra insisted she *wasn't* sharing with the neighbors, no matter what Opa said.

"So," says Marcel. "It's time for us to make a decision."

Opa nods; Mama does, too. Astra strokes Mitzi, gathering fingerfuls of loose fur, which she lets drift to the floor beneath the table.

I know what Marcel is talking about—should we stay, like the Fischers have opted to do, or leave, as the Oppenheims, Madame Lucia, and Miss Rosen have?

"The feeling among my minyan is that to stay is the wiser choice," Opa says. "It's dangerous, as you know, in the villages beyond the city, as well as on the roads—bandits and robbers, and no place to stay at night. What's more, to leave is not legally permitted. Those who are captured face terrible fates."

Mama bemoans, "If we still had our radio, we'd know more of what's happening in other places where the Germans have invaded. We'd be able to better weigh our options."

"You can bet it's nothing good," Marcel says. "One of my colleagues got word from a relative in Warsaw—there, the whole Jewish population and also the Romas of the city have been corralled into a tiny walled-off section of the city, a ghetto. They are treated like animals in a pen."

"So where would we even go, if we left?" I ask.

"That's the thing," says Marcel. "Even with a sponsor in a place like the U.S. and money for passage—neither of which we have—there's no guarantee we'd even get beyond Romanian borders. If we crossed the path of a soldier, we could be shot on sight. It's open season on Jews."

We all sit with that for a moment. I don't know what the others picture, but I see us running, and in my mind, I hear a shot ring out, and I see my opa fall.

Marcel clears his throat. "I think we should vote. Whether to try to figure a path out—mind you, I don't think there is one—or to accept that this is still our home, for now. My vote is to stay. Either way could mean death, but here at least we've got a bed and a toilet." He speaks plainly, and it's a wonder to me how he manages to keep his tone so even, talking about such terrible things. Maybe it's the doctor in him, evaluating symptoms and making a diagnosis. Or, just as likely, it's his inner gambler, assessing risk and then placing a bet.

"I vote we stay," says Astra. "Mama?"

I turn to my mother and see with a shock that she has tears running down both cheeks—she hasn't made a sound. "Stay," she manages to choke out, "if that's what you think is best."

Opa agrees, and so do I, remembering the promise I made to myself the first night I slept in this apartment—to never leave, ever again.

On July 5, the SS, along with the Romanian military, marches into Czernowitz. They set up a headquarters on the Ringplatz and take over the Hotel zum Schwarzer Adler. They rip down the portraits of Stalin and Lenin that flank the entrance to the Volksgarten, burn them, and hang their own flags—twin black swastikas, dangling like venomous spiders above our heads.

I've seen images of this symbol printed in newspapers. I've heard Adolf Hitler's speeches on the radio. At the cinema that day with Esther, before I escaped to the restroom, I saw the straight-legged march of Hitler's SS troops—the flatness of their expressions, the rigidity of their gate—but to see the swastikas, the Nazi army *here*, in the heart of our beautiful Czernowitz . . . nothing could have prepared me for the way this makes me feel—naked, and terrified.

Over loudspeakers set on poles on the Ringplatz, an SS officer makes an announcement. The Germans, along with the Romanian government that the Russians had ousted, have retaken the territory together, "driving out the scourge of communism." Now, the Romanians and the Germans are allies—"Two hands of the same body," says the disembodied Nazi voice. It continues: "Day-to-day work of the city's administration is to be run by the Romanian military. Larger issues of war, the Germans will decide, guided by our Führer. We are united in philosophy and force. More orders to follow."

Days later, Marcel brings home a pamphlet from the hospital. On the front is an illustration of a doctor looking through a microscope, and then a close-up of what he sees; it's a terrible, six-legged crab, meant to represent a "bug" you can catch, but its face is human, and is clearly a caricature of a Jewish man. It has a long hook nose, a scraggly beard, a skullcap on its balding head, a hunched back. He's rubbing his claws together and grinning as if he's plotting something terrible.

Inside, the pamphlet reads:


TUBERCULOSIS
SYPHILLIS
CANCER
WE MUST DO AWAY WITH THE GREATEST OF
SCOURGES . . . THE JEW!


On the street, pasted-up propaganda posters, one of a Jewish man half in shadow, hiding behind a Soviet flag. Beneath, the inscription: **BEHIND THE ENEMY POWERS: THE JEW.**

And notices are hung:


**EFFECTIVE IMMEDIATELY, ALL JEWS ARE ORDERED UNDER CURFEW. NO JEWS ON CITY STREETS 7PM–7AM.**

## ANY JEW ON THE STREET DURING THESE HOURS MAY BE SHOT ON SIGHT.

Apartments left vacant by retreating Russians and fleeing Jewish families are occupied at once by the Romanian military or Nazi officers—neither seems better than the other. In our building, the Oppenheims' apartment is taken almost right away by a Romanian general named Ioan Chelaru and his wife.

"See?" says Astra, to Opa. "I'll bet you're glad now we went back for the food."

"There are some things more important than food," Opa says.

"Bullshit," says Marcel. "Maybe sex, but that's debatable."

Astra laughs, but Opa sighs and shakes his head. "Sex, and food. The chief concerns of animals."

"We *are* animals," says Marcel.

"We are more than animals." Opa lifts his hands to the sky. "Hashem, do you hear what I put up with? Do you hear this?"

"He's not listening anymore, old man," Marcel says, "if he ever was in the first place."

The next morning, along with the rising sun comes a voice from the sky. But it's not God—it's the SS officer again, issuing orders over the loudspeaker on the Ringplatz. Under the penalty of death, all Jewish men are to report to the Palace of Culture.

"You can't go!" Astra is in her nightclothes still—we all are—and she holds Mitzi tightly.

"I don't see what choice we have," Marcel says. "They have a list of all the residents in the city. It's either go, and see what they want with us, or

208

stay, and be arrested. Our new neighbors will make certain of that. And with the Nazis, being arrested probably means we're dead."

It isn't yet five o'clock in the morning. Opa hasn't even had his coffee. But still, he gets ready to leave. He pulls on a light jacket and puts on his hat over his skullcap, as if he's heading to the store or maybe for a chat with a friend.

Mama cries hysterically, her eyes swollen shut. She is completely useless. I feel the way she looks, but I don't want to be completely useless. So I do the buttons on Opa's jacket.

"Opa," I say. I don't know what to say after that. Some things there just aren't any words for.

He puts his hand, warm as always, to my cheek. "Don't worry, Rieke. We'll be home before you know it."

I reach up and grasp his hand. "Promise it."

"I promise," he says, without hesitation.

It's a lie. I don't know why it makes me feel better, but it does.

Astra and Marcel are kissing, the cat squished, yowling, between their bodies. Then Marcel opens the door for Opa. Before he follows, Marcel blows Astra one more kiss. The door closes.

Mama, Astra, and I stand silent for a breath, and then we rush to the window. We're there before Opa and Marcel come out of the building. They line up with other men already in the street. German soldiers are checking names against a list, and then they are marched away. Silently, I try to will Opa to turn and look up at me. *Please, Opa*, I pray, *look back*.

But he doesn't.

The whole day passes like that—the whole hot summer day. The sun shines cruelly, so beautiful it makes the sky. And there is nothing to do but wait. Astra smokes cigarettes and picks fleas off Mitzi, drowning them one by one in a cup of water. Mama cries until she gives herself a headache, and then she goes to her room, closing the door behind her.

Even though moving about makes me cough, I can't sit still. Whenever I stop pacing, I imagine all the terrible things that could happen. I imagine Opa and Marcel, marching in a line to the Palace of Culture, the soldiers who were on the street pointing their guns at their backs. I imagine them caught up in a stampede of fleeing men, pushed to the ground, trampled on. I imagine Opa saying one of his prayers or talking to God the way he likes to do, and being punished for it. I can't rest, so I do what I can to make the house nice for when Opa and Marcel return. I wash the dishes, sweep the floor, straighten up the pillows and cushions and aging magazines and dust the knickknacks until Astra says, "Enough! You're driving me mad."

"There's nothing else to do, anyway," I tell her, and I fold the dust cloth neatly.

"You can say that again," answers Astra, and I know she feels as helpless as I do.

I set the dust cloth on the end table by the sofa. Then I sit, and wait.

The beautiful, awful sun makes its way all the way across the sky, and still they don't come home. The moon rises, and still they do not come.

Astra goes to bed, taking Mitzi with her. I sit and look at the moon. It's like a cake cut right down the middle. I don't know if it's waxing or waning; I try to remember what the moon looked like last night, but I can't. It frightens me terribly that I can't tell, for reasons I can't explain.

At last, I cry. I try to do it quietly, so as not to disturb Mama and Astra, but I am overcome. I hold the dust cloth to my face to muffle my sobs. I cry until my breath leaves me and I begin to cough. When at last I have some control over myself again, I look at the dust cloth and by the moonlight see a dark shadow, a splatter of blood.

I turn to face the moon straight on, the closest thing I can think of to the face of God—it seems fitting that it's half disappeared. "God," I say, but the word sticks in my throat, comes out garbled. I clear my throat. "Listen. I'll make a deal with you. If you return Opa safe and sound, if he isn't killed or hurt—you can take me instead. You can have *me*, God. I'm not as good as Opa. I know that. But I'm younger, and maybe that's something. I promise, God. If you keep my opa safe, I'll do anything. I won't even complain if I die. I promise."

Something brushes against my ankle. I gasp and choke again.

It's only Mitzi. Shaking, I scoop her up, so soft and warm. She purrs. I press my forehead against her side, letting her purring calm me, and I whisper into her scruff, "I promise. I promise. I promise."

I'm whispering those words as sleep finally finds me; I whisper them silently all the next day, as Astra, Mama, and I sit in the living room. I whisper them until the sun has nearly set, and a knock comes at the door.

When we first hear it, we all clench tight. No one moves to answer.

Then, Marcel's voice. "Let us in. We're home."

Mama starts crying again, sloppy uncontrollable tears, and Astra rushes to unbolt the door. Marcel takes her in his arms, and they hold each other close. Mama takes Opa's hands in hers and kisses them. And there's someone else with them.

Conrad.

It takes me a minute to recognize him, for the light has gone out of his eyes.

All three of them come inside, and then I bolt the door.

"Get them something to drink, Rieke, quickly," Mama says. I go as

211

fast as I can to the kitchen to draw three glasses of water.

In the front room, the men take off their coats and leave their shoes, crusted with dirt, near the door. I pass around the glasses and see that their hands are nearly as dark with dirt as their shoes. Their faces are dirty, too, and streaked either by sweat, or tears, or both.

To Opa I say, "You came back."

He pats my cheek. "I said I would, didn't I?"

"It's been nearly two days!" Mama says. "Tell us what happened."

The men settle into the chairs and on the sofa. Their pants are dirty, too, but no one complains about the upholstery.

"It's because of Conrad that we're here," Marcel says, nodding to him.

Conrad shakes his head. "It was nothing."

"Not nothing," says Opa. "Not nothing."

"They took us to the Palace of Culture," Marcel begins. "And made us stand in lines. All the chairs and benches had been removed; they packed us in tighter and tighter as the day went on. The soldiers—Nazis soldiers, Romanian soldiers, different coats, but the same words—all of them said, 'Whoever moves will be shot,' so of course we did our best not to move. As the hours went on, it got harder to stand like that, especially for the older men. Trying to keep up our spirits, some men began to sing, and others joined in, but then they came with a whip and they struck the men who were singing, and the ones who stood nearby for good measure. So then there was silence." He takes a sip of water. "All day and all night, we stood there. When it fell dark we took turns holding each other up. Some men could not wait any longer and soiled themselves, there in line. It was awful." He stops, shakes his head. "It was a full twenty-four hours—not until this morning—before the command came: 'Turn around and march!'"

Next to him, Opa barks a hard laugh. "March," he repeats.

"So," says Marcel, shrugging, "we marched. Some men we had to hold up, as their legs got used to moving again. But we went out into the street, and they marched us past the university. I didn't know where they could be taking us, but I knew it couldn't be good. There were hundreds of us, maybe a thousand, walking together. Guards whipped anyone who fell back. One man went down, and I don't know if he got back up."

Marcel clears his throat. I've never seen him like this, overcome by emotion.

"That's when Conrad found us," he says, when he continues at last. "I don't know how he found us, but okay. I guess sometimes God takes with one hand and gives with the other."

He says this last part with a sideways grin; if I had to guess, I'd say Marcel is less of a believer than any of us.

"It was Mr. F-Fischmann I n-noticed first," Conrad says. "By the way he—the way he walks."

"He made his way over to us," says Marcel. "And then he said, 'This isn't going to end well.'"

"Yes." Conrad nods. "That's what I—that's what I said."

"We knew he was right," says Marcel, "but what could we do?"

Conrad picks up the story. "I s-saw there was a break in the hedges up—up ahead, just a little gap, and I don't know what made me do it, b-but I grabbed Mr. Fischmann's arm and I said to Marcel, 'Run.'"

I think these are the most words I've ever heard Conrad speak in a row. He looks exhausted by the effort.

"He did," says Marcel. "So I grabbed Heinrich's other arm, and together we shoved him through the break in the hedges, and we ran!"

"I haven't moved that fast since . . . I don't know when," Opa says.

Marcel says, "An officer chased us, yelling for us to stop, and then we

213

heard 'Bang! Bang!'"

"They shot at you?" Mama cries.

Everyone ignores her.

"We didn't stop. We didn't look behind us. If they were going to shoot us, it was going to be in our backs. We just kept going. And I don't know why they stopped chasing us, but eventually, they did. We ducked in an alley and caught our breath."

"I could kill them all," says Astra. "I could murder them." Her hands are in her lap, clutching fistfuls of her skirt.

"But that must have been hours ago," Mama says. "Where have you been since then?"

"I wish that was the end of the story," says Marcel. "We waited in that alley behind some bins of trash, for hours. At last we decided we couldn't live with the trash cans forever, so we headed for home."

"Almost as s-s-oon as we were—we were—we were out of the alley, w-we were caught," Conrad says, his stutter growing worse.

Marcel takes over. "A different group than the one we'd been in before was coming down the street. About fifty men in this one, being led by three German guards. One of them pointed a gun at our heads when he saw us. There was no getting away. So, again, we marched. In this group, two of the prisoners were pulling carts full of shovels."

"They took us to Bird Beach," Opa interrupts. He's been staring off into middle distance, almost as if he's been asleep with his eyes open. "You remember Bird Beach, yes, Rieke?"

Unable to speak, I nod.

"They took us to the riverbank," Marcel tells us. "And there we saw—" Here, his voice breaks. He puts a hand to his face, shakes his head.

Conrad picks up when Marcel cannot bring himself to continue. His voice is as flat as his eyes, and this time, he barely stutters. "We saw the men who had been in the first group. The gr-group we had run away from. All dead. Their bodies f-filled with bullets. The guards stood around with their machine guns slung over their shoulders. They were smoking cigarettes."

Marcel makes a sound that at first I think is a laugh, but it isn't a laugh. It's just that I've never heard him cry before.

Finally, he says, "The German guards told us to bury the men in the first group. The men we'd stood with all day and night."

"A friend of mine was among the dead," Opa says. "Marty Diamond, the butcher."

I picture Marty Diamond in his white apron, standing behind his counter and debating the merits of Brecht's poems with Opa. I picture him facedown in the sand.

"Did anyone see his son?" asks Opa.

Marcel and Conrad shake their heads.

"So we dug pits and buried the men," Marcel says. "We tried to remember who we saw, so that we could tell their families what had happened. But there were . . . so many of them. After a while, it was like my brain couldn't hold any more faces." He looks at Astra, desperate. "I tried to remember them all."

"Shh, shh," she says, touching his face with a tenderness that I've never seen.

All of us are quiet.

Finally Mama says, "And what, then? After the men were buried?"

Conrad begins to speak, but Opa interrupts. "That was it. After that, they let us come home."

"Well—" begins Marcel, but Opa claps his hands once, sharply.

"We came home," Opa says.

215

Marcel pauses for a moment, then nods. "We came home."

With that, we prepare food for them, and they eat, and then Conrad gets up to leave. "I have to get back to my f-f— I have to get back to my family."

Astra walks him to the door. Before she opens it, she kisses him right on the mouth.

Later, when Opa is in the bathroom cleaning himself up, and Mama is busy in the kitchen, Marcel says to me and Astra, "Listen. Your grandfather clearly doesn't want you to know the rest of the story. But I think knowing is better than not knowing."

"Tell us," says Astra, and though I'm not sure I want to hear what he might say, I nod.

"After the bodies were buried," Marcel says, his voice low to keep the others from hearing, "they lined us up against the wall near the top of the beach. You know that wall?"

I do. Opa and I used to sit in the shade it cast on days when the sun got too hot.

"They lined us all up, and they told us to put our hands above our heads. And they took aim at us with their machine guns. I was on one side of your grandfather, and Conrad was on the other, and we were going to die there. You understand? And then they began to shoot—but not at us. Up in the air. Two men dropped to the ground right then—whether they fainted, or worse, I don't know. One of them didn't get up again. But none of us was hit by a single bullet. And the soldiers—they laughed and laughed. It was a joke to them. And *then* they told us to go home."

Marcel turns, and with Astra's arm around his waist, they go to their bedroom. He walks like an old man, like Opa.

216

And I—I go to the bureau in my room, and I fish out my locket.

*"It's time for you to start thinking about what you want."*

I hear Madame Lucia in my head; her voice feels as far away and fanciful as something from a fairy story. The problems that seemed overwhelming before the Germans, before the Russians—now I wish they were the scope of my concerns. To be upset about whether Astra would forgive me for telling Opa about her love affair! It feels . . . quaint, I guess. Bittersweet.

I unlatch the locket and tip the pill into my palm. It's so light that I can't even feel it. The pill is round and white, a tiny moon, as strong as God . . . maybe stronger.

What sort of God would send Opa to Bird Beach, the place we loved so much, and allow Nazi soldiers to force him to dig the graves of his friends? What sort of a God would bring him home with dirt from those graves crusting his hands, dusting his beard? What sort of a God would let any of this happen, at all?

I've heard Adolf Hitler's speeches on the radio. I've heard about the terrible things his soldiers are doing across Europe. I guess I thought I understood what it would feel like to have the Nazis come to my city. But I was wrong. There is no way to prepare for something like this.

I suppose it's possible that we're in the middle of a cycle, and I just can't see the curve toward better times from where I'm standing now. But it's just as likely—and I'm beginning to fear, even *more* likely—that there is no cycle. What if there's only bad, and worse?

The day that Astra gave me this pill, how ludicrous it had seemed— that I would ever need such a thing. It doesn't seem ludicrous, anymore. I put the pill back into the locket, snap it shut.

Then I fasten the chain around my neck and tuck the locket inside my shirt.

# TWO

## NEVER PRAY FOR
## A NEW KING

For two weeks after the roundup and mass killing of Jewish men, no one in our family leaves the apartment except for Marcel, who's compelled to continue his work at the hospital. Each day, we are restless until he returns. Each evening, when he comes through the door, it's to a hero's welcome. All of us, even Opa, fuss over him, giving him the best chair, bringing him a cup of tea, rushing to fetch a snack for him. Then, we gather close and listen to whatever news he has to share.

"Up and down the street, you can't move ten steps without hearing the muttered phrase 'the Jewish solution,'" he tells us.

"Solution!" Astra scoffs. "As if we're the problem!"

Marcel nods vaguely, but he's looking at the wall across from him, not Astra.

"You should hear the rhetoric over the loudspeakers," Marcel says. "The Romanians blame us for what happened during the Russian Year, all the corruption and the abuses by the Russians; they claim that Jews greeted the communists with open arms, with cheers and wreaths of flowers, and have been hoarding the wealth they shared with the communists."

"But," Mama spurts. That's all she says. We know what she means.

"They've given badges and guns to the Romanian youth," Marcel continues. "They've fashioned themselves as vigilantes, and they're leading German soldiers to the homes of 'communist Jews' across the city—they're reporting their Jewish neighbors, their doctors, their friends, even. It's smart, really, of the Nazis. Those boys are in a race, practically, to turn over the most 'enemies of the state.' It's a point of pride for them."

"They're making arrests?" Opa asks.

Slowly, Marcel shakes his head. "Not arrests," he says. "Worse."

He tells us that thousands of Jewish Czernowitzers have been murdered in their homes in the two weeks since Bird Beach.

One day, Marcel comes home from the hospital, ash-gray; his mentor, Dr. Lerner—the man who got him through medical school, who told Marcel that he refused to let him waste his talent, despite what Marcel admitted was a staunch determination to be wasteful about nearly everything in his youth—has been shot and killed in his home. "He was a good man," Marcel tells us. "And such an excellent doctor."

In the hallway of our building, Mr. Fischer whispers to me and Astra that something terrible happened to his friends the Sternbergs, who lived just three blocks over. He told us that they heard the SS at their door and hurried to escape through the back window. "Mrs. Sternberg had just two days before given birth to their daughter, their firstborn," Mr. Fischer says, and there he drifts off, imagining, I suspect, *his* daughter, Sophie, not to mention Mrs. Fischer and their baby Moses. "He managed to hoist her through the window and hand her the baby," he continues at last. "But as he climbed out after them, the SS broke down the door and shot him dead." Mr. Fischer shakes his head back and forth, back and forth. "Mrs.

Sternberg and her child made it to her in-laws', thank God."

Astra drops her hand atop his. "He died a hero," she says, and Mr. Fischer bursts into tears.

After two weeks, we have eaten through the last of the Oppenheims' food. Marcel tells us that the violence has begun to die down, and that order is returning to the streets. "As long as we follow the rules exactly and only leave the apartment when they allow it, we should be safe," he says. Opa says that he will be the one to do the shopping, but Marcel suggests that he not go alone. "I'd do the shopping myself, if I had time outside my work," he says.

Mama leaves with Opa; three hours later, she returns with half a loaf of stale bread and the news that, just two blocks away, on Molnitzergasse, the bodies of hundreds of murdered Jews lie in the street. Opa tries to shush her, to spare us, but she can't keep it to herself.

"Mothers, babies, children, men—it's too much," Mama wails. "Too much. And the *flies*," she says. "The *smell*." She sets the bread on the table and goes to her room, where she stays for three days.

One day, a knock comes at our door. It's Mr. Katz, from Opa's minyan. He stumbles over the threshold, collapses into Opa's arms. At last, he manages to tell us that his brother, his sister-in-law, and his three nieces have all been killed. "Every single Jew in Vizhnitza, and the farmland around it—men, women, children—dragged from their homes by their own neighbors, corralled into the court building," Mr. Katz cries. "All of them, slaughtered by machine gun fire. My whole family," he wails. "My brother!" Opa comforts his friend the best he can, and they pray together. But when Mr. Katz must leave before curfew falls, he stumbles, still weeping, into the hallway.

It was Mr. Katz who recommended the place we went on holiday to the mountains. Vizhnitza. "Very nice neighbors," he had said. "Fresh air."

We ate at their table. We slept in their beds. Is it possible—could Maria and Andrei have been involved in such an atrocity? How could it be true?

The news keeps coming: Stoning. Hanging. Raping. Shooting. Stabbing. Flogging. Clubbing. Whipping. Any way a person can be killed, a person is killed.

Of course, they burn the synagogue where Opa worships. Dr. Mark is woken in the night and summoned, along with Cantor Perlstein, and is forced to unlock the synagogue doors. The Germans take what there is of value, then set fire to the building. It burns to the ground, and the rabbi and cantor are taken away, no one knows where.

In short, Opa was right—never pray for a new king.

Have they always hated us this much, our Romanian neighbors? Or is hatred as easy to catch as a cold, as quick to spread as my own illness has, in my body?

Why do we live, while others die? Why is no one in our building taken? Maybe because we live on a street that's traditionally been occupied by mostly Christians, and the more tolerant kind—those who didn't used to mind living and working beside Jewish families. Maybe because none of the Romanian residents in our small building of sixteen apartments are teenage boys or young men, who have been leading the raids into individual homes.

Or maybe there's no reason at all that we survive and others do not. Maybe it's just luck. From the highest levels of power all the way down to the lowest, it seems the city takes delight in what is happening to us. Marcel brings home a series of memorandums and tosses them on the coffee table with disgust; published by Dr. Nandris, president of the Society for Culture and Literature as well as president of the Society of Christian

Doctors, the memorandums suggest and then demand the extermination of the "Jewish element," proclaiming, "It will be a cultural triumph if such a thing can be accomplished."

Another day, Astra and Opa bring home a suspicious-smelling fish wrapped in newsprint. When I unwrap the fish to prepare it, I see the paper's masthead: *Porunca Vremii*. The front-page article reports on Romanian efforts to exterminate its Jewry, claiming its actions will be a model for the rest of Europe to follow. "The die has been cast," writes the editor. "The liquidation of the Jews in Romania has entered a final, decisive phase. Present-day Romania is prefiguring the decisions to be made by the Europe of tomorrow." My hand trembles as I move the fish onto a plate and shove the newspaper to the bottom of the rubbish bin.

Once, when I'm waiting in a line with Mama for kerosene, a familiar-looking woman passes by. It's Milka, the girl who used to work for Opa! She's a little older, and a little fatter, but it's *her*, I know it is. And she's holding the hand of a little boy, four years old or so—he must be her son. He has the same red cheeks, the same fine blond hair. Milka is a mother now. Reflexively, I raise my hand in a wave—I know she saw me and Mama, I'm sure of it—but she swings the boy up onto her hip. She walks right past us.

On the first of August, a new order is posted on streetlamps and buildings across the city: all Jews, no matter the age or sex, must, within three days, affix a yellow "Jewish star" to the left breast of our clothing. No exceptions. Any Jewish person found out of doors at the end of those three days without the yellow star will be subject to punishment, the order says.

So we make stars. I have the old yellow dress that I wore to the mountains—to Vizhnitza—and Mama, Astra, and I cut the shapes from it, a sunny constellation. Mama's stars are the most symmetrical, though Astra has always had the steadiest hands. I suspect my sister made hers purposefully catawampus, as a small rebellion. Still, Mama then takes pains to even them out, along with mine.

They look ridiculous, these stars on our clothing. I see my reflection in the mirror, the yellow patch just above my heart, and I'm filled with a strange mixture of fear and shame.

When I go outdoors, the star becomes a target. Little children hurl insults and rocks. Women coming up the street in the opposite direction, who once would have shared the sidewalk with me, seem to grow like balloons when they see the star. They fill the sidewalk with their enormity, forcing me into the gutter.

Each morning at six o'clock, a different neighborhood is searched, and any able-bodied Jewish men are rounded up—someone's got to repair all the damage the Russians did as they fled, and so Jewish men are conscripted into labor. Sometimes, the laborers come home in the evening.

Sometimes, they never come home again.

And, through it all, as summer ripens in Czernowitz, I grow sicker. I try to hide it, as Mama and Opa have enough to worry about. But it's difficult to mask the lethargy, the exhaustion. It's like an animal growing inside of me, taking up more and more space, eating away, hollowing me out. I fear it will consume me, and that I will be unable to do anything about it. I consider asking Marcel to examine me, but he's barely home— an "essential," he spends most days at the hospital, and only comes back to our apartment on the nights when he wants to. And, perhaps, I'm afraid of what he might discover.

But then, what could he discover about the illness inside me that would be worse than the one that has taken our city?

Astra doesn't know where Marcel is sleeping on the nights he doesn't come home, and because of the curfew she can't go out and search for him the way she once would have done. She barely ever leaves her bedroom, other than when we have to go out for supplies. She just smokes cigarettes when she has them, and grooms Mitzi when she does not.

One day in mid-August, Astra and I wait and wait in the bread line— all afternoon, and into evening. Opa and Mama are off trying to sell Opa's lace tablecloths, the ones his mother made by hand that were overlooked by the Russians who ransacked our place. Astra and I finally make it to the front of the line—just as the vendor flips his sign to "closed."

"It's not even seven o'clock yet," Astra says to the man, an edge of exasperation in her words.

I squeeze her hand, trying to remind her not to talk like that—her tone could draw attention to us. A vision flashes in my mind—Astra and me, kneeling, facing the brick wall in the nearby alley, guns pressed against our backs.

She sighs, squeezes my hand in reply, tries again. "Please," she says, a word I know she rarely uses. "Anything at all. Please."

"What are you, stupid? We're out!" He slams shut his window.

Astra is silent, but seething. Behind us, the ragged line dissipates, everyone trying to get home before curfew.

"Come on," I say. "Let's just go home."

She shakes her head. "You give up too easily, rat tail."

I'm in no mood to be cajoled. "Astra, I'm exhausted."

Her chin is set in the way that tells me she's not done arguing, but she must see something in my face that convinces her I really am tired, for she softens, takes my arm. "Okay, rat tail. Let's get you home."

We head toward the apartment; up the street in our direction comes a Romanian official. He carries a whip, rolled, over his shoulder. I know before he reaches us what's going to happen. His eyes go like a magnet to our stars, he never even looks at our faces. Then he pulls the whip from his shoulder. It unfurls, his wrist flicks.

Astra lunges in front of me and we fall to the ground together. The leather whip bites at my arm, at Astra's back, like a venomous snake. Blood flecks the sidewalk.

"Dirty Jews," he spits. "Get home."

Astra pulls me to my feet and we run as quick as we can, trailing drops of blood like breadcrumbs. We slam open the building door and rush into the foyer, breathing hard. Quickly, we go up the stairs. Outside our door, Astra wipes the tears from her own face, then from mine. She puts a finger to her pursed lips to warn me to be quiet.

Pushing open the door, she calls brightly, "We're home!"

Then, she leads me to the bathroom, where she cleans me up. The flesh on my forearm is split like an eye and weeps blood. "You know," she says, wrapping a piece of gauze around my arm, "it wouldn't work for me, but I'll bet if you weren't wearing a star, no one would even guess you're Jewish."

I look up from my arm into her face. "You—you want me to go out there? Without the star? Alone?"

"Of course I don't *want* you to," Astra hisses. "I'm just saying—you could, and I couldn't."

Perhaps she's right. Astra, with her dark hair and eyes, her full lips, likely wouldn't be able to pass. But, looking at my reflection now, I suppose I can. My hair and eyes are the lightest in my family, and when I wear my braids pinned up over my head, I look almost the same as the photographs of the smiling German women on the propaganda posters we see on the Ringplatz.

Still, the thought terrifies me. "Do you really think I should try?"

Astra shrugs. "I'll bet they don't run out of bread in *their* food lines."

The next day, wearing a long-sleeved blouse to cover the wound on my arm, and with the star tucked into the pocket of my skirt, I leave our building as soon as curfew lifts. I decide to go to a market I know in the next neighborhood over, hoping no one will recognize me.

*"Hope for a miracle, but don't rely on it,"* Opa used to say.

I queue up behind a group of women. They chat comfortably about the warm weather and their children. "A good day for the park, I think," the woman in front of me says to the woman in front of her.

I try to arrange my face and body to mimic theirs. We step forward as the line slowly moves.

At last, it's my turn. The grocer looks at me with blank ambivalence, the most welcome reaction I can hope for. I ask for the same things the woman in front of me ordered, but when the grocer tells me how much I owe, I blanch—it's nearly double the amount I have.

"I'm sorry—" I begin to say, but then a man's hand reaches past me and waves a bill at the grocer, more than enough to cover what I owe. A hand covered with dark hair.

"Oh," I say, turning. It's Mr. Weissinger. His round glasses glint in the sunlight, rendering him, briefly, a man without eyes. Then the light shifts, and he has eyes once more.

Indifferent to who's paying, the grocer takes the money and gives me my groceries.

"Thank you," I say as we walk away together. "I'll repay you, I promise."

He nods. "It's a good thing I came along when I did." And then he looks at my shirt, where the star should be. Mr. Weissinger, I notice, also wears no yellow star.

"Are you here alone?" he asks.

I nod.

He smiles, warmly. "I'll walk you home."

He walks quickly, and I try to keep up. But with the bag full of groceries, my breaths are shallow, and I can't manage it. I begin to cough and grow lightheaded, and as the familiar feeling overcomes me, I lean against the wall of a building. I close my eyes, trying to calm the frantic beating of my heart as I drown, for a moment, in my own lungs. My cough grows harder, rattling my chest, and my knees begin to shake.

I pull a handkerchief from my sleeve and hold it to my mouth. Even with my eyes closed, the world swirls around me. I don't know where the ground is or the sky. A strong hand grips my upper arm, tightly, and I'm grateful for it.

At last, I get control of myself. My eyes flutter open. Mr. Weissinger peers down at me as if I am a specimen in a zoo.

"You're ill."

I nod.

Still grasping my arm, he looks up and down the street. "Come. I know a doctor who lives nearby."

I should say no—Opa told me not to take anything from Mr. Weissinger, and it seems I can't stop disobeying . . . the omelet, the chocolate, the money for the groceries. But in a strange way it feels like it would be rude to refuse this favor, especially as Mr. Weissinger picks up my bag of groceries, which he paid for.

And, as Marcel once said, what Opa doesn't know won't hurt him.

It takes us a quarter of an hour to arrive at the doctor's apartment building—it's not far, but we have to stop once more for me to regain my breath.

At last, we're here. Mr. Weissinger knocks at the door of the ground-floor apartment. There is no answer. He knocks again and calls, "Flor! Open up. It's George Weissinger."

From the other side, a shuffling. A pause. And then the sound of a chain being pulled, a bolt turning. The door opens. A face peers out—small, deeply wrinkled, with a tight, pointed beard. "George? What are you doing here?"

"I've brought you a patient."

The old man, Dr. Flor, pulls open the door farther, and Mr. Weissinger motions for me to go inside. I hesitate for a moment—I know Opa would *not* approve of me going alone into the house of a stranger, doctor or no—but I don't know what else I can do now that we're here, so I cross the threshold. Mr. Weissinger follows, and Dr. Flor bolts the door again.

"Is she *in trouble*?" Dr. Flor asks, looking me up and down.

"Not *that* kind of trouble," Mr. Weissinger says. "She has a worrying cough."

"Ah." Dr. Flor motions for me to sit at his kitchen table. It's piled high with medical texts and journals. "Excuse the mess. The savages forced me out of my offices. No more private practice."

Mr. Weissinger makes a conciliatory sound, shakes his head.

"What is your name, girl?"

Mr. Weissinger answers for me. "Frederieke Teitler. She's Alfred's younger girl."

"Oh-ho, Alfred," says Dr. Flor, and his eyes light with pleasure. "That rascal." He rummages around in a big leather medical bag. "Take off your blouse," he says absently, withdrawing a stethoscope.

Mr. Weissinger makes no move to leave the room, just takes a seat at the table.

Slowly, I undo the buttons of my blouse. It's August and the room is warm, but I feel my flesh rise in goose bumps. I feel naked, even though I'm wearing a thin undershirt, and I hunch my shoulders forward.

The doctor fits the earpieces of his stethoscope. He places a hand on my shoulder, puts the cold mouth of the stethoscope on my back, beneath my undershirt. "Breathe."

I breathe, and I cough. Dr. Flor listens. Mr. Weissinger watches.

When Dr. Flor is done listening, he looks in my eyes, my nose, my mouth. He indicates for me to put my blouse back on, but then he notices the wound on my arm. He goes to his medical bag and brings back an ointment which he smears on the wound, and he wraps it in a piece of gauze. He doesn't ask how I was injured.

When I'm dressed, he asks, "How long have you been coughing?"

"A while. A few months."

"Sputum?"

I must look confused, because he says, "Are you coughing anything up? Phlegm? Blood?"

"Oh. Yes. Um . . . phlegm. Sometimes blood."

Dr. Flor nods and turns to Mr. Weissinger. "It's impossible to say for sure without an X-ray, and of course, that can't be done." He waves his hand around his apartment, clearly irritated by the state of what has become his office. "But I can't say for certain it's not tuberculosis."

The word takes my breath away, what little I had. I don't know very much about tuberculosis, but I know people die of it, and that's enough.

"I'd recommend good nutrition, full rest, and fresh air," Dr. Flor continues, still speaking to Mr. Weissinger. "A stay in a sanatorium would be ideal. But, of course, conditions are not ideal."

"No," Mr. Weissinger agrees. "Not ideal."

"May I use the bathroom?" I ask.

Dr. Flor nods and points up the hall.

I don't need the toilet; I just need a moment alone. I put my hands on the sink and stare into the mirror. There I am, blinking back. Around my neck, I see the glint of my golden locket.

How will it happen? Will my lungs fill with liquid, until I drown in them? Will I go to sleep one night, and not wake up in the morning? Will I cough so hard that my lungs rip in shreds? Will it hurt, to die?

My head starts to clear, and I hear the men talking in the living room.

"Without treatment, if the disease continues to progress . . . it's hard to say. It could be a few months. But it could perhaps be several years."

"Any of us would be lucky to have several years, right now."

"True."

The men fall silent. Perhaps, on that side of the door, they are contemplating their own deaths, as I am, here in the doctor's bathroom.

Eventually, I emerge. I thank the doctor for examining me.

"Go home, child," he says.

Mr. Weissinger walks with me all the way to my building, this time carrying the groceries himself. The day is beautifully warm, the streets around our home are nearly empty. We pass one SS soldier, but he pays us no mind.

At the front of my building, he hands me the bag of groceries.

"Thank you, Mr. Weissinger."

He bends his head and kisses me on the cheek. His lips are damp. "Call me George."

# THREE

## INTO THE GHETTO

Fall comes early, as if Europe itself is turning more quickly away from the sun. And as the days grow colder, my health worsens. On Yom Kippur, Opa insists I eat, even though he fasts. "Hashem would understand," he says, pushing a slice of bread buttered with margarine into my hand.

At night alone in my little room, I'm glad for the smallness of it, the way it wraps around me. I lie on my back, head propped by two pillows, and feel the edges of my cot, run my hand along the rough texture of the wall, picture in my mind each corner of the room, each drawer of my dresser, each item of clothing within each drawer. It comforts me, to walk myself through the things I am sure I know.

After I've journeyed through my room, I venture with my mind to other places in the apartment. First, the kitchen, which adjoins my room. This, I imagine as it once was rather than how it is now: squatting on the stove is the heavy iron pot briskly boiling matzo balls, lid tight, steam escaping, doughy scent warming the air, orange flame beneath merrily flickering. My mother stands at the sink—it's the mother in my earliest

231

memories, when I could not have been older than three, and Father was still around—singing along with the radio as she washes dishes, the sink full of froth and bubbles and clinking glassware, a song itself. Opa rests at the table, a stack of his favorite newspapers beside him, all the ones that would be banned—the Jewish papers, filled with news about births and weddings, as well as obituaries for those who have died, nearly all celebrating long lives, surrounded by family and love, with a proper shivah for each one. He winds my watch, wipes it on a soft cloth, and fastens it to my wrist, just so.

Then I wander down the hallway to find Astra in her room—*our* room, still, in my mind. The twin beds are split, the way they used to be, with matching white coverlets pulled up tight over the pillows. Astra sits on her bed with a book in front of her and leans half out the window smoking—for even in my imaginings, I can't separate Astra from her dear cigarettes. The cat is there, too, because Astra loves her so much, and Astra smokes with one hand and strokes Mitzi with the other, all the while reading her book, until she sees me standing in the doorway. Then, she grins and calls, "Hey! Rat tail! Quit lurking in the doorway, will you?" She gestures with a flick of her chin for me to come inside, and she stubs out her cigarette and shuts her book and pushes Mitzi from her lap and opens her arms to me. There we are, wrapped in a plume of her rose scent and the sharp tang of cigarettes, and she holds me.

That's as far as I ever get in my imaginings, for there is no further I wish to go. My mother and Opa, safe and well in the kitchen; Astra and me, as we were, and light shining down upon us all.

I haven't told my family about my visit to Dr. Flor, or about George Weissinger paying for the groceries that day. And yet, the word "tuberculosis" enters our home, anyway. It's Marcel who utters it one morning before he goes to the hospital.

Astra's still in bed, and Mama and Opa are in the kitchen. I'm sitting by the fireplace, where I'd gone after a coughing fit to sip a cup of hot water—no more honey, it's gone and irreplaceable. He stops by the mantel to put on his cuff links, and looks at me, mouth downward. Cuff links on, he comes over to my chair, puts the back of his hand on my forehead. I realize with a shock that this is the first time we've ever touched. His hand is warm.

He crouches down. "I ran into George Weissinger yesterday. He tells me he took you to see Flor."

I swallow, nod. "I didn't tell Opa," I whisper. "He wouldn't approve, and also, I don't want him to worry about me. Please don't tell him," I say, and immediately hate asking Marcel to share a secret with me.

He chuckles. "Your opa and his opinions. Don't worry, I won't tell him about George taking you to see Flor. But it's a relief that someone finally told you—Astra and I have been saying that you have a right to know what's likely happening in your own body."

A feeling overcomes me, something like what I used to feel in dance when I was young and didn't yet know how to spot—like I've lost my orientation and I'm spinning wildly, my head floating free of my body.

"You—know? Opa, too? And Mama?"

Marcel nods. "It was clear to all of us that this was more than a common cold, but your mother and grandfather thought it would be best to keep it from you. What good could it do you, at a time when we can't be sure we can get care for you? That was their reasoning, anyway." He sniffs, as if he disapproves of them.

I have to say it plainly. "They all believe—and you agree—that I have . . . tuberculosis?"

"Well," he says, sounding now like the doctor he is, "the only way to know for sure is through testing, at the hospital. But, if I had to guess, based on your symptoms? It's the most likely explanation."

Again, I'm spinning. "Am I— Do you think I'm going to die?"

"Well, we all are, eventually." He grins, and I see the charm in him that Astra so loves. It maddens me.

My expression must show my feelings. He clears his throat, and casts a glance toward the kitchen, where Opa and Mama are still talking, unaware of me and Marcel. "I've seen people with worse cases than yours live for years . . . There's a treatment we could try. For that, you'd have to go to the hospital."

I roll my eyes. "Sure, Marcel. But I'd like a private room."

"If your condition continues to worsen, we might not have a choice," he says, not responding to my joke. "But it's not a good idea to let it be publicly known that you're ill. It's happened in other places that the sick and lame have been rounded up, taken away, or—" Here he cuts off suddenly, but I know what he means: or killed. He clears his throat and then continues. "For now, Frederieke, the best thing you can do is try not to cough. If there's a blood clot in your lung, a violent cough might throw it, and then you'd be dead."

As chilling as his words are, I appreciate Marcel's bluntness. "All right. I'll do my best."

He puts on his coat, his star pinned to the lapel, and goes to the door. Before he leaves, he drops a wink at me. "You won't die. There's no way Astra would let that happen—and God knows," he says, ruefully, "Astra gets what Astra wants."

October 11 is a Saturday. And it's not just any Sabbath; this day is Simchat Torah—The Joy of the Torah. Opa doesn't like to say such things, but I know how deeply it wounds him that he can't be at the synagogue today, and that there is no synagogue for him to go to anymore.

He's sitting across from me, his Chumash open in his lap to its final pages. I watch him as he traces his fingers along each line. It's Deuteronomy 34, the very end of the Torah. This is a day that Opa looks forward to every year, but today, he pulls on his beard forlornly as he reads the final words. With a sigh, he closes the Chumash. His eyes drift to the window.

"Opa," I say. "Tell me about Simchat Torah." I know by heart the words he'll say—he's said them to me each year before he heads to synagogue to celebrate. But I'm not asking for me.

"Oh, my girl," Opa says, his gaze returning from its far-off place to focus on my face. "What a joyous day! Today is the day, as you know, that we complete the yearly reading of the Torah. We celebrate the end of one cycle, and the start of a new one."

"Because you'll start reading again, from the beginning, right away," I say.

"Yes, yes." He nods. "It's a thing without end, even as it has an end, you see. It's a closed circle. Like the rings I craft at my shop. And like the hands on the face of my watches, around and around it goes. It's a happy day. And we should be together, celebrating."

His gaze drifts to the window.

"Well." I bang my fists into the table. "*We* are together, aren't we? Let's celebrate!"

He startles and laughs. Behind his spectacles, his eyes widen. "Yes, you are right. We *are* together. All right, then, Rieke! Up!"

He stands, taking the Chumash with him, and pulls me to my feet.

He tucks the book under his arm and takes up both my hands, and he starts to bend his knees and bounce, a grin spreading across his face as he sings. I don't know much Hebrew, and yet, I understand: Opa is praising God, giving thanks for every blessing, he's praying for success and deliverance. His voice grows louder and louder as he begins to bounce in a circle, taking me along.

Mama emerges from the kitchen. Marcel and Astra come out of their bedroom still dressed in their nightclothes, Mitzi in Astra's arms. And then, to all of our surprise, Marcel begins to sing, right along with Opa. He grabs Astra by the waist; Mitzi, yowling, leaps from her arms, and he sings as he dances her into the sitting room, around and around, and even Mama peels off from her bedroom doorway and comes to join us, clapping and laughing as we dance like fools.

It hurts my lungs, of course, to dance, but I hold back coughing as long as I can. I don't want to this moment to end.

"L'chaim!" yells Marcel. He dips Astra dramatically, just as he did that night in Café Europa. He stands her on her feet and kisses her on the mouth.

"L'chaim!" answers Opa, swinging me around and around.

And then we're all yelling it—"L'chaim, l'chaim, l'chaim!"—*To life!*

I don't know what we're thinking. It's like someone had shaken a bottle of champagne and the pressure had been building and building until it's too much, the cork can't restrain it any longer, it *has* to explode. That's what we're like—an explosion. An explosion of joy.

Until—suddenly—there's a hard knock, like the crack of a gun, on the door. All of us fall silent, hands frozen mid-clap, bodies stopped midswing. I feel the blood draining from my face, I feel the cough I've been suppressing rise up, and I sink to the sofa and cough into my sleeve.

"Shh, shh, it's all right," Opa says, his hand upon my head as if I were a little girl, still. "Everyone calm down," he says. And then he goes to the door.

Opa opens it a crack. We hold our breath, together, and then—

"Joseph," Opa says. We all hear his relief and let out our shared breath. His posture relaxing, Opa widens the door. "Come in, come in."

It is Mr. Strasberg, an old friend of Opa's whom I haven't seen since the Germans arrived, though I know he's a member of the Jewish Council, which means he is a sort of liaison between the Jewish population and the government officials. He wears a long beard and carries his hat in both hands in front of him.

"I can't stay," Mr. Strasberg says when Opa offers him a seat. "I wish I came with better news." He clears his throat and then begins. "There's been an order that all Jews must move to a designated section of town. The streets from the Steingasse to the Neueweltgasse, ending at the Judengasse and then down to the train station. Nowhere else."

"What do you mean—move?" asks Opa.

"We're being evacuated, Heinrich. Herded like cattle into the poorest part of town. The Germans mean to make a ghetto for us, as they have done all over Poland, in each city they occupy."

I was happy, just moments ago.

"No." Astra's voice is so sharp that it scares Mitzi, who yowls and arches from her embrace, then darts back into the bedroom.

"Bring what you can carry," Mr. Strasberg says, ignoring her. "Your warmest coats. Food, if you have it. Bedding."

"By when do we have to move?" Marcel asks. "We'll have to get things in order. And find a place to stay. It will take a while."

"Any Jew not within the designated area by six o'clock this evening

237

will be shot. Bring your apartment keys in an envelope with your name and address on the front. Someone will collect them." Mr. Strasberg lifts and drops his shoulders. "I wish I had better news," he repeats, and then he goes.

Opa bolts the door. His shoulders curl inward; his chin drops to his chest. He stands with his back to us, his hand on the doorknob. The rest of us are quiet, too. I think all of us are in shock.

The neighborhood Mr. Strasberg mentioned isn't nearly big enough to hold every Jewish person in Czernowitz. It's a run-down neighborhood, not very large. It's mostly poorer Jewish families, but not entirely—the apartments there are cheap and so some non-Jewish people who need a good deal and don't mind intermingling live there, too. Where will we possibly go?

Opa turns around. His dark brown eyes look sunken. "Who do we know who lives near the railroad station?"

"I know a doctor who lives on the Judengasse," says Marcel. "But he has a large family—five children, and his mother-in-law."

"Ruth lived on the Steingasse, with her parents and grandmother," Astra offers. "I think it was just the four of them. Three of them, now."

I think of Ruth's family, still mourning her.

"We'll try there first," Mama says. "If they won't take us in, we'll go to the doctor's."

With that, Mama and I rush to the kitchen to pack all the food we have, which isn't much. Marcel sweeps through the house, collecting anything of value that we might be able to trade—the second-rate silverware from the sideboard, all that's left after the night we spent in the basement; Astra's and Mama's few pieces of jewelry; his own cuff links. Astra and Opa fold blankets and sheets and lay out everyone's warmest sweaters and coats.

In the doorway to my small room, I stop and look around. There isn't much in here, and the blanket from the cot is already added to the pile near the door. Penny's purple glass horse is the only adornment on the bureau; it's too fragile to take with me, just as it was too fragile for her to take along when she left the city.

Maybe we should have left when Penny's family did, back before the Russians invaded. But where would we have gone? Penny had distant relatives in Ukraine, I believe—that's probably where they headed. But so many things could have happened to them along the way, and even if they made it to their family, then what? Like Romania, Ukraine has fallen to Germany now, too. So, then what? Is Penny in a ghetto, just like the one in which we're about to live? Is she even alive? Is she any better off than she would have been if she had stayed?

It's impossible to know. I leave the horse, tucked in among my delicates in the bureau's top drawer.

At noon, we sit at the kitchen table, all together, and eat what's left of a pot of soup Mama made the day before, as well as some hard brown bread. Steam rises from the bowls. We sit around the table, napkins on our laps. The soup is thin, but hot and good. Mama even puts out the last of the margarine. I tear off pieces of the bread and soak them in the broth, then fish them out again with my spoon.

When we have all sopped up the last dregs of soup with the last crusts of bread, Mama collects the bowls. She takes them to the sink to wash them, but Astra says, "Why make it nice for the vultures? Leave the dishes, Mama."

Mama shakes her head and turns on the water, but then Astra slams her fist on the table.

239

"Leave them," she shrieks. "Leave the goddamned dishes!"

Mama freezes. We all do. The only sound is the water, running.

Then Marcel stands, his chair scraping as he pushes it back. He goes to the sink and turns it off.

We tie the bedding into bundles; we each wear two sweaters and a coat, a scarf and a hat; we put on our sturdiest shoes and tie the laces tight.

Opa tucks his prayer book into the breast pocket of his coat, close to his heart. Astra manages to fit Mitzi, yowling and fighting, into a box. Marcel, who knows better than to argue with her, punches airholes in the top and ties the box closed with a length of twine.

Together, we wait in the hallway as Opa makes a final pass through the apartment, shutting off lights and looking for anything of value that we might have forgotten. Then he emerges, swiping at his eyes, and he turns the key in the lock. He puts it in an envelope; I see he's written his name and our address on it. He seals the envelope and tucks it in a pocket, then pats his coat the way he always does.

"Okay," he says—to himself? To us? "Okay," he says again.

He bends and picks up his bundle. Together, like vagabonds, we go down the stairs and out into the street.

As we leave the building, we're greeted by a cold slap of wind in our faces; sleet comes down sideways, dirty snow lines the gutters. The icy air freezes my lungs, and for a moment, I can't breathe at all. The whole family is obliged to wait as I gasp and choke and try to get air.

Opa pats my shoulder. "It's all right, Rieke, it's all right," he says, which isn't true.

Our street is clogged with others just like us: bundled fat with sweaters and coats and scarves, lumpy pillowcases full of housewares, anything of any value slung over shoulders, boxes and bags gripped and grasped by anyone old enough or strong enough to carry anything. Across the street, heading in the same direction as us, our neighbor Mr. Fischer lifts the baby, Moses, onto his wife's back and uses a sheet to sling him there, freeing her hands to carry a bundle of blankets. Little Sophie's face is thinner than I remember—it looks like an old woman's, so drawn and worried. She carries a box that looks much too heavy for her, but she manages it somehow.

All of us, each family, are locked in our own private misery. At the same time, we function as one animal, moving together down the street and through the neighborhood, flushed out of our own homes and carried, as if by a mighty current, to some unfathomable place.

On the sides of buildings, on lampposts, in windows and on doors, notices tell us what we already know:

**ALL JEWS OUT BY 6 PM**
**NON-COMPLIANCE WILL BE PUNISHED WITH DEATH**

We walk for blocks on the uneven cobblestones, only stopping to shift our bundles from this hip to the other, to sling our heavy pillowcases from that shoulder to this.

Up ahead I see Esther and Conrad; I call to them, but they don't hear me, and it isn't until they have disappeared into the crowd that I realize it seemed that they'd been alone, just the two of them, without parents.

I find myself craning my neck, looking for my father. Is he out here, with us, part of this mass of humanity? Where will he shelter? Who will he be with? But I don't see him. He could be anywhere.

It hurts me to watch Opa carrying such a heavy load. He is an old

241

man. He should be sitting in a rocker by a fireplace, having an afternoon cup of tea, thumbing through a book, maybe listening to a program on the radio. Gentle filtered sunlight should be touching his cheeks. He should be safe. He should be warm.

"Rieke," he says to me, "give me another bag. You are carrying too much."

"No, Opa. It's better this way. They balance me out. If you take one of my bags, I might fall right over."

Opa shakes his head. "Silly girl. Let me know when it gets too heavy, yes? I will help."

"Sure, Opa, yes."

It would not matter if the blankets and sweaters turned to rocks. Under no conditions will I add to Opa's burden.

At last, we arrive at the section that has been sanctioned for us. Several uniformed Romanian officials are collecting envelopes from families as they go by. In that moment, I know what they will do with our addresses, with our keys: they'll go like pirates to each apartment and strip them of all the things we could not carry. They'll piss in our toilets, cook on our stovetops, sleep in our beds.

Maybe Opa has the same thought. Maybe he simply forgets that he was meant to turn over our key. Maybe sometimes when you don't count on a miracle, one happens, anyway. But for whatever reason, the guard nearest us gets into an argument with another guard just as we approach them. It's clear they've been drinking, and their voices get louder, and one of them shoves the other, and just like that their backs are to us and my family slips on by, no key turned in, no envelope with Opa's name and address given over.

It is a small triumph. Of course, a door can be opened without a key—as Opa says, locks keep out only the honest. But still, when we go into the ghetto, our key goes with us.

Astra leads us to Ruth's building on the Steingasse. It's an old building, run-down compared to ours. The ground floor's windows are covered with black grating, and the door looks like it hasn't seen fresh paint in my lifetime.

"Which floor is Ruth's family on?" I ask.

"Fourth floor," says Astra. "The top."

I only make it to the second floor before I have to stop and rest.

"Wait here," says Marcel. "I'll take my things up and then come back down for yours."

I nod and sit on a stair, where I close my eyes and focus on breathing. *Don't cough, don't cough, don't cough,* I remind myself, which only makes me need to cough more. I manage to control it; my heart flutters like a scared, trapped bird.

Footsteps. My eyes flutter open. It's another family, carrying bundles nearly identical to ours. Behind them is another family, and then another. In spite of all the people coming up the stairs, there is no conversation. One baby cries out, a sharp chirp of sadness, and she seems to speak for us all.

At last Marcel returns for me.

"Are they letting us stay?"

"Your sister is pleading our case," he says dryly.

Marcel takes my burdens, and I use the handrail to hoist myself to standing. He motions for me to go up the stairs, and he puts a hand on my back to help me forward. I feel I can trust him to keep me standing. He won't let me fall.

On the fourth floor, we find that Astra has been successful, for the door to the Keplers' apartment is open and my family is inside, setting down their parcels.

"We can never thank you enough for this," Mama says to Ruth's father.

Marcel and I go inside, and Marcel closes the door. Now, I see that we're not the only ones who have come to the Kepler apartment; there's another group: a middle-aged couple with two boys who appear to be between my age and Astra's, neither of whom I know. They look as awkward as I feel, standing clumped together by the far window.

"What can be done?" says Mrs. Kepler, Ruth's mother. She has this strange way of not quite looking at any of us; she looks past us, or to the side, as if she's hoping, somehow, to catch a glimpse of Ruth.

Before six o'clock, two more families have moved into the Keplers' apartment. It isn't *our* home, so it isn't fair for my heart to drop each time more people arrive . . . still, it does. I'm not proud of the feeling.

Mr. and Mrs. Kepler move Mrs. Kepler's mother out of her room and into theirs; they take her bed, wedging it, with the help of the boys—who, we find out, are Mr. Kepler's nephews, the sons of his sister—into one corner of the bedroom. This leaves a mostly empty bedroom for Mr. Kepler's sister's family, in which there are a half-dozen children, ranging in age from six to sixteen.

We establish a space for ourselves in the front room; Opa is given the sofa, and Mama gets a chair with a footstool. Astra and Marcel, along with Mitzi, make a nest of blankets underneath the piano. I lay a blanket on the carpet in between Mama and Opa.

The other families find space in the dining room and kitchen. We take turns using the bathroom before bed; it takes nearly half an hour.

It's all so tight and terribly awkward. There is no privacy.

That night, trying to make myself comfortable on the floor in this strange room, I wonder about the families from our building, people I've held the door open for, people who have borrowed or loaned a cup of flour, an egg. Some of them are Jewish, like us. Where did they go? Did they make it into the borders of the ghetto in time, before the six o'clock deadline? Some of them are not Jewish. Did they watch from their windows as we moved, laden, away from our home? Have any of them broken through, yet, into our apartment? Is someone sleeping in my bed? Is someone rummaging through my bureau drawers?

In the dark, someone is crying, softly. It's not Mama or Opa, nor Marcel or Astra. Isn't that strange, how you can know from the sound of a sob if it belongs to someone you know? I have heard my mother cry many, many times—it's an anthem of my early childhood. Her sounds are many, and varied: the woebegone wail of abandonment; the high-pitched gasp of panic; the deep, gut-turning riot of despair, when hope that my father may someday return was finally extinguished. And then it hits me: each of my mother's cries is tied to my father. Could it be that I have never seen her shed a tear about anything else? No—when Astra married. She cried then, too.

Then there's Astra. Her tears, though infrequently spilled, have always come when she's been angry . . . except that one terrible day, when Mama washed her in the bath.

And Opa. I've never heard him cry, and I pray I never will.

The sobbing I'm hearing now comes from the dining room. It's a woman, and the sound is muffled, as if she's pressed her face into something—a chest. The married woman, then, crying beside her husband.

After a while, the sobs lessen, there's a hiccup or two, and then—silence. Or as silent as an overcrowded apartment can be. Above me, on the couch, Opa's soft snores fall into a gentle rhythm. Across from me, Mama rustles around on the chair, trying to find a comfortable position. I hear the sounds of bodies all around, drifting into sleep. They comfort me.

I wake from a dream, still on the floor of Ruth's apartment. I badly need to cough but know that it would disturb the people sleeping all around me, so I sit up and try my best to suppress it.

There is Mama, curled into a ball in the armchair; there is Opa, sleeping flat on his back with his hands folded across his chest. I see Astra, curled around Mitzi, with Marcel curled around her, all beneath the black piano. I hear the breathing and snoring and farting of strangers who sleep all around us.

Then I blink, and it's as if that movement—that flutter of my eyelids—causes the four walls of the apartment to come loose from their moorings. They creak and groan and fall free, and the ceiling disappears, too, and then we're on a platform surrounded by open sky. It's the platform in Vizhnitza, from our long-ago summer trip. I turn with delight to Opa, but though he's standing next to me, he's asleep. My whole family. A bitter wind blows through me. Why is no one else awake? I reach for Opa, touch his arm. His skin turns to dry autumn leaves beneath my hand. Horrified, I try to pull away, to keep from hurting him worse, but I can't move. His skin begins to crackle, and I know that the next burst of wind will blow him away from me. I pray for the air to stay still, I pray for calmness, I pray into the empty open sky, but with horror I feel a rattle in my chest, and I know I won't be able to contain it, though I try, I try.

And then I cough, a knife turning in my chest, and Opa turns to dust

246

and blows away, my hands clutching desperately at nothing.

"Sit her up and give her air."

Hands pull and push and move me; I'm being yanked up from some deep darkness, even as I continue to cough. Someone puts a glass to my mouth; it strikes my teeth and I try to turn my head.

"Just a sip." It's Opa's voice, so I obey.

My eyes open. Faces form a ring around me—my family, and Ruth's, and one of the teenage boys.

I could have been embarrassed, but I'm just so glad to see Opa safely there, and, behind him, solid walls containing us.

"I'm sorry." My voice is barely a whisper.

"Give her room," Marcel says again, and the others back away. Then Mama takes my blankets. She tells us she is going to make a bed for me in the bathtub—so I'll have air, she says. There's nothing I can do but follow her, while everyone watches.

Through the blankets, I feel the porcelain, hard and cold. Still, exhausted as I am, I sleep.

The Keplers' apartment overlooks the train tracks. The first morning we awake in that apartment, we hear the rumble of a train, and all of us gather to the window to peer outside. I don't know what we hope to see. Some miracle coming to save us? Some sign that something, somewhere, still works?

What we see is a long, slowly moving train—cattle cars, one linked behind the next.

Astra asks, "What's that? In the train cars? Do you see, through the bars?"

I squint. One of the boys—his name is Leo—says, "I think they're arms. People reaching."

Astra leans closer to the glass, cups her hands around her eyes to cut the glare. Then she cranks open the window. I step away; cold air always makes my cough worse.

"Shh," says Astra, though no one is speaking. "They're saying something."

We listen. At first all I hear is a murmur, but then I recognize words, tangled together:

"Giurgiu!"

"Putyla!"

"Dubova!"

The people in the cattle cars are calling out the names of towns and villages. The names of their homes, the names of the places that have expelled them.

"Where do you think they're going?" Leo asks. He sounds as horrified as I feel.

"Nowhere good." Astra cranks the window closed again, shutting out the sound of their voices. Now that I know what's on the train, I can't look away. I feel compelled to watch the whole train pass. To bear witness to their passing.

I stare out the window, against the glare, until the train shrinks to a speck, then disappears on the horizon.

We're lucky, I'm told, as the Keplers' building still has running water; the neighboring buildings don't. By the second day in the ghetto, the stench is inescapable: toilets don't flush without water, so everyone is forced to dump the excess waste from the influx of new residents in gutters and alleyways. The hallways and staircases become as populated as the apartments.

There's no electricity anywhere in the ghetto, and no one has any way to heat their spaces, even if they're fortunate enough to have a space.

Mr. Kepler estimates that there are fifty thousand of us crammed into a neighborhood intended for several hundred families. Everywhere you turn are people: sitting shoulder to shoulder in hallways, lined up on sidewalks, mothers nursing their babies on stoops, alongside piles of filth.

By the end of the first week, the conscripted ghetto is enclosed by a hastily constructed wooden fence, three meters high, with barbed wire looped along the top. There are only two openings in the fence, each guarded day and night by Romanian commandants who happened to live within the boundaries of the ghetto before the fence went up, and now find themselves armed with both rifles and authority.

Few Jews are allowed beyond the fence for any reason; Marcel, as a doctor, is one of them. He's able to bring back some food, sometimes.

The rest of us do our best to stay human. This is difficult as we become hungrier and filthier, as the stench of our bodies and our waste grows stronger and thicker, seeming to congeal in the air.

As the second week in the ghetto begins, there is news, announced in the streets by the man we've come to know is the commandant of the ghetto, Major Nicolai Jacobescu.

"Residents of Fraazengasse, Dreifaltigkeitsgasse, and Franzosgasse! You are to report in the morning first thing to the train station for relocation. Bring your belongings. There will be no exceptions."

The apartment we're staying in isn't on any of those streets. That evening, huddled together in the Keplers' apartment, we wonder where those who have been ordered to report to the train station will be taken.

"The Romanians call it Transnistria," says Mr. Moritz, the father of the two boys. "The place where people are being taken. They're rounding up the Roma along with the Jews."

"Transnistria?" Mama says. "What the hell is Transnistria?"

"It's Soviet territory. Beyond the Dniester, and to the east," says Mr. Moritz. He turns to his wife. "We should go."

"But we aren't staying on those streets," she says. Mrs. Moritz is a tiny woman, dwarfed by her husband and two sons, all of whom dote on her as if she's a porcelain doll. She's the woman I heard crying, that first night.

"Those who go sooner rather than later are sure to get the best housing," Leo argues.

"It's a good point," says his brother, Nitek, nodding. Nitek, two years younger than Leo, agrees with him about everything.

"But how will we know if it's safe?" Mrs. Moritz's eyes brim with tears.

"Life was hard under the Soviets, but we were safer than we are with the Germans," Mr. Moritz says. "We have no wealth left. We're better off with the Communist devil than the Nazi one."

None of us can guess if they are making a good decision, or a bad one. At least they're making a choice, though I suppose the rest of us are, too, by staying.

And so it is that the Moritz family packs their belongings and says their goodbyes. We watch from the window as they exit onto the street as the sun rises, tiny Mrs. Moritz surrounded by her husband and sons. As they turn the corner, I know that we will never see them again.

In the late afternoon I feel a fever coming on, and I go into the bathroom to splash cold water on my face. In the mirror, my reflection shows dark smudges underneath both my eyes, sinking shadows.

I turn off the water with a shaking hand and lower myself to the edge of the bathtub. It's too early to sleep, but the nest of blankets in the tub seems to call to me. And anyway, what is there to be awake for? I slide into the tub and pull a blanket up to my chin. Though I'm hot with fever, I'm cold, too. How can one person be two opposite things at the same time? I lie there all afternoon, shutting my eyes and pretending to be asleep when others come in to use the toilet, pretending I don't hear the sound of urine hitting the water in the bowl, pretending I don't smell their bowel movements. The dying afternoon passes like that and turns to evening, and then to night.

This time, I dream of Ruth. She is sitting next to me on the edge of the tub. I feel the cool stroke of her hand against my forehead.

"Why would you do it?" I ask her, though my mouth doesn't move.

She doesn't answer. She smiles like a statue, and pushes my loose hair, stuck with sweat, away from my brow. Her eyes hold a secret, one she's not telling, and that only angers me.

I struggle to get up, but Ruth's hand grows firm, pushing me down. And now the bath is full of tepid water—had it always been? The water is the same temperature as my skin, and my skirt floats in it, and my braids float, too, and wrap like ropes around my neck as I toss my head, and soon the water will be at my lips, and then it is. Water pours into my mouth, my nose, my eyes, my ears, and still Ruth holds me under. I see her face, wavy through the water, that gentle smile distorted now. I don't want to die. I want to *live*, but Ruth is stronger than I am, and so I will drown.

"She needs to rest," I hear.

It's my mother's voice, and it pulls me like a rubber ring from beneath the water, buoying me to the surface. I hear her voice through my sleep, and another voice, as well, though somehow, I cannot wake up.

"I need to speak with her," Ruth's mother says. "It's urgent."

"She's sick. She needs to sleep. You can talk to her in the morning."

I want to protest. I want to speak with Ruth's mother, but I can't get my mouth and tongue to form words.

"You'll speak in the morning," Mama says—to Ruth's mother? To me?—and then the undertow of sleep takes me again, this time to a place without dreams.

When I wake, I find that I feel better. My fever has broken, and I'm hungry.

I go out of the bathroom and find my family arranged in an anxious circle around the table, Astra with her cat. The other families who share the apartment are crowded in the living room, as if to give us space. The Keplers are nowhere to be seen.

"What's going on?" I ask.

Tight-lipped, Mama shakes her head.

"You might as well tell her," Astra says. Since she has no more cigarettes to smoke, her hands seem to never stop stroking Mitzi.

Mama shakes her head again, and Astra sighs, her annoyance clear.

"Ruth's mother went out the window last night." Astra motions with her chin to the large window in the front room.

I stand rooted to the kitchen floor. "She—fell?"

"That's one way to put it," says Astra.

Marcel says, "She jumped."

My eyes go to the closed bedroom door, where the Keplers sleep. "Is she all right?"

"Stupid," says Astra. "She's dead, of course."

"No." I go to the front window. I don't know what I expect to see out there. The other families part as I walk by.

Out the window, down on the sidewalk below, I see what looks to be an oddly shaped shadow, but nothing is casting it. It's not a shadow—it's a stain.

Her body . . . it's here in the apartment, I know it must be. Behind the closed door to the bedroom. Her family—what's left of it—must be in there, with her. Sitting shiva, together.

Again.

My stomach is empty, but bile rises in my throat. I cough, once, twice, a third time. Everyone around me shuffles, uncomfortably.

"But . . . why?" Even as I ask the question, I know how ridiculous it is. There are too many answers.

"Why *not*?" says my sister.

"Astra," Opa admonishes. "That's enough."

She shrugs. "Everyone's thinking it."

I go to where my mother is sitting, kneel beside her. "Mama. Did Mrs. Kepler try to visit me last night?"

"You were resting. There was no reason to wake you in the middle of the night."

"I wonder what she wanted to say to me."

No one has an answer for that.

Everyone in the apartment is whispering now. Each family turns inward, but there is no room for privacy here. We stand around, desperate, disparate, unsure.

It's Opa who finally does something. He goes to the bedroom door, knocks, enters. He's in there for a long time. At last, he emerges, holding Mr. Kepler by one arm, and Mrs. Kepler's mother by the other, who both look as if they'd collapse if Opa weren't holding them upright. Mrs. Kepler's mother can't stop crying; Mr. Kepler's face is blank, unmoving. Opa brings them forward and others reach out to receive them, become the support that keeps them on their feet.

Then Opa stands in front of the window from which Mrs. Kepler jumped. He reaches into the breast pocket of his coat and pulls out his prayer book. Well-worn, it falls open easily; he flips through the pages until he finds the prayer he's looking for—the mourner's prayer. The kaddish.

Normally, prayers like this would be said at the synagogue, among his minyan—all men—but today no one is excluded. Opa brings his feet close together, faces us, and begins to pray. Rather than singing it, as he would most other prayers, he chants the words, swaying slightly forward and back. At first, many of us aren't sure what to do—those of us who aren't observant don't know the words, and the observant women aren't used to being part of such a thing—but when Opa reaches a break and looks up, all of us, discordantly, respond, "Amen."

He continues, his voice warm and smooth. Everyone listens; each of us leans forward with him, and back. We become water lapping the bank of a river, moving forward, back, forward, together, as one. When the next break in the prayer comes, we know what to do: this time in unison, we respond, "Amen."

I don't know what Opa is saying. I don't know what the words mean, or who he's praying to, or if any God is listening. But I answer "Amen" along with the others, and it feels right and good to do this, to do *something*.

When Opa takes three steps backward, then bows to the left, Ruth is standing there, beautiful Ruth with her chestnut hair, who lived and died by a fairy tale. And then he bows to the right, and there is Ruth's mother, who has eyes only for her daughter, whose face looks, at last, at peace. He bows again—a third time, this time to us, and I feel as if a great golden thread runs between us all, living, and dead.

Finally, Opa takes three steps forward—away from the dead, back to us, the living—and I love him so much, I feel my heart could break.

# FOUR

## UNEXPECTED HEROES

Two days later, the soldiers come to our street. They announce through bullhorns that all residents of the Steingasse—the street we are on—are to report at sunup to the train station for relocation to Transnistria. Street by street, they are determined to empty the pen they forced us all into.

No one sleeps. I lie awake in the hard porcelain tub, aware that this might be the most comfortable bed I will ever have again. I'm terrified that if I sleep, Ruth might return to me, or her mother. Each time my eyes grow too heavy to hold open, I see the stain on the street below.

Our family prepares to leave before the sun has risen. The other families are packing their belongings, too. Opa, Mama, Marcel, and Astra have redistributed my burden so that I'll have less to carry—in fact, there's only one thing that's apparently my responsibility, as I discover when Astra thrusts Mitzi's box into my arms.

"We can't take the cat," I say.

"Shut up," she answers.

Marcel looks like he has something he wants to say—maybe he agrees with me about the cat—but he holds his tongue until after we've said our goodbyes, until we're down the first flight of stairs and are clustered together on the landing between the second and third floor.

"Listen," he says, "it doesn't make sense for us to go to the station. I don't think we should go."

"What do you mean?" Mama says. "What choice do we have?"

"Even Ruth's mother had a choice, and she made it," Astra says.

"They're talking about Transnistria at the hospital. First, do you remember the cattle cars we saw when we first got here? That's not a train for humans. They're shoving in so many people that some are being smothered. And the ride lasts four days—*four days*, no bathroom, no place to sit, you understand? And then, when the train stops, word is that it's desolate. After the train ride, it's a three-day walk to the Dniester River. A bridge to cross. All along the way, people dropping dead like flies. And those who make it alive to Transnistria, they find themselves in shacks, without food or fresh water. The best you can hope for is to barter with local peasants. Heinrich, we could use your jewels to survive for a while, but . . . I don't think Frederieke would survive the journey, let alone the destination."

The picture he's painted stuns us all into silence.

At last, Opa nods. "Yes. We must not go. But what can we do? Our street was called. It's being cleared—everyone must report to the trains."

"There's somewhere else in the ghetto we might be able to stay," Marcel says, and I notice his eyes flick hesitantly in Astra's direction. "An apartment on a street on the far side of the ghetto that hasn't yet been cleared. I know someone there."

With that, it's decided. We go down the last sets of stairs and out into the frigid morning. Instead of turning left, toward the train station, we turn right. "Quickly, now." Marcel leads the way up the street. There's a

256

guard on the corner, watching us come toward him. I feel sweat begin to drip from my armpits, even though it's freezing cold. I smell the stink of my own fear.

But Marcel walks like a man with a right to be there. When he comes up alongside the guard, he says, "We need to get to the Neueweltgasse. I am a doctor and there is a patient there, waiting for medication." He shows the guard his identification card, which the guard examines. Then he looks at the rest of us, a motley bunch. The box in my arms yowls.

He raises an eyebrow, amused.

"We'll take care of the patient, then be right on our way to the station." That's when Marcel hands the guard something else—money.

The guard takes the cash, nods, and returns Marcel's identification. "Quickly, now," he says, and we rush by.

No one speaks as we follow Marcel through the tangle of streets toward the Neueweltgasse. But all of us feel he is a hero, in that moment. I don't know where we are going or what will wait for us there, but I know I'm grateful to be walking up the street rather than down. Especially when we make it to the Neueweltgasse with no other problems. Even Mitzi in her box seems to relax.

Marcel leads us to a building near the end of the street—a grim-looking place with a big tree in the front that was probably quite lovely in the spring and summer, but now is just a sharp-tipped bundle of bony sticks.

Marcel pulls open the door and leads us down a hall to apartment 1C. He taps a rhythm on the door, then turns to Astra. "Okay, listen," he says, that hesitant look in his eyes again. "Now isn't the time to do that thing you sometimes do. You understand?"

"What *thing*?" Astra asks, dismissive. "I don't do a *thing*."

The door opens. And there stands Colette.

She's smiling, big and bright, and in that moment, I realize that the rhythm Marcel knocked must be some sort of special signal. But when she sees the rest of us, her smile disappears. "Oh," she says.

It's as if someone poured out gunpowder and then struck a match, and we're all suspended in the moment between the striking of the match and the burst of flame, then the explosion.

But Astra does not flame, she does not explode. She just draws herself up to her full height, taller than any of us, her long neck so lovely, her chin tilted just as on stage.

Without a word she sweeps into the apartment as if it's her own. There's nothing for Colette to do but to step out of the way. The rest of us follow. The room is cheaply furnished, with a chintzy fabric spread across the table and no rug on the bare floor, but it's scrubbed clean. A row of books lines a shelf; like Astra, Colette has a copy of *An Ideal Marriage*. I wonder how many of the nights on which Marcel doesn't return home are spent here. It seems almost quaint to worry about such things.

No one is sure what to do with their bags, except Astra, who sets hers down like she's just returned home from shopping. I hand Astra the box with Mitzi in it; she opens it right away, and Mitzi climbs out. She puffs up and arches her back, distrustful of the new environment, and gives a low growl.

"There, there," Astra coos.

"Marcel!" Colette is saying. Her voice is high and panicky. "You can't *all* stay here!"

We hear the emphasis she puts on the word "all," making it clear that it's the rest of us who are unwelcome, not Marcel.

Once again, it's Astra who is in charge. "We'll let the two of you talk," she says curtly. She nods at Opa and Mama to set down their bags, which

258

they do, and then leads the rest of us into the adjoining kitchen. There, outside of Colette and Marcel's view, Astra allows herself to unclench. She sinks into a chair and puts her head down on the table. Mitzi joins her, leaping up to the table, purring loudly.

I feel terrible for her. But when I lay my hand on her shoulder, Astra twitches it off.

"Once a rat tail, always a rat tail."

"I can see why Marcel prefers it here," I shoot back. It's meaner than I meant it to be. I regret the words as soon as they're out. But if anything, my meanness invigorates Astra, who laughs.

"Marcel prefers to be up inside any available skirt." She stands. "But only *this* skirt is wrapped around his wife."

Mitzi in her arms, she goes into the front room. I guess she's reconsidered leaving Colette alone with Marcel. The rest of us stand awkwardly waiting, pretending to give them privacy but of course we can hear every word, especially once Astra joins them.

"You keep a cleaner home than I would have guessed." Astra manages to make a compliment into an insult.

Colette doesn't rise to the bait. "You can't possibly stay here. You must have seen the ordinances—'Anyone who harbors Jews or other undesirables will be immediately put to death.' I'm sorry, I really am, but you'll have to go."

"It won't be for long. Just for a couple of days, at the very most." Marcel's tone is the same one he uses when he's trying to calm Astra after he returns home from staying out all night, drinking. I wonder how it feels to Astra to hear him use it on another woman.

Colette shakes her head. "Absolutely not."

I find myself in the odd position of hoping Marcel can wear this woman down with his charms, and I can tell from Mama's and Opa's faces that they're hoping for the same thing. But all of us are to be disappointed; Colette holds firm. "Look, there's an attic in this building that's barely used. You can try hiding up there if you want. But if anyone asks, it wasn't me who told you."

Marcel must feel that this is better than nothing, for the next thing I know he's in the kitchen, motioning for all of us to get up. Colette follows. Her face is grim, her arms crossed beneath her bosom.

We take up our bags. Astra puts the cat back into the box. Marcel opens the door.

I'm the last to leave. "Here." Colette holds out a loaf of bread and a jug of water. I take it, but my loyalty to Astra keeps me from thanking her.

Behind us, I hear Colette bolt the door.

The attic is not nice.

It's drafty and dirty, with only one small, grimy window. Mouse droppings and dust carpet the floor.

"Maybe Mitzi will earn her keep," Mama says.

We set down our bags once again, and spread some blankets down on the hard wood. There's nothing to do but stare at each other, or the cat, or at the slice of light that comes from the window, and wait. For what, we don't know. We've avoided getting on today's train, but it feels that we've just delayed what's beginning to feel like a terrible inevitability.

Astra voices my fears. "So we're safe for a night, maybe two," she whispers to Marcel. "But then what?"

For half a second, I dare to hope that he has a plan. That he'll be able to get us out of this mess. But he just shakes his head.

The night is miserable. The attic has no insulation, and frigid air creeps in like ghost fingers all around. Of course, there's no toilet, so we use a bucket we find, which we position behind a sheet that Mama strings up across one corner. The curtain, however, cannot hide the sounds and smells. The only one of us who has a good night is Mitzi, who kills and eats two mice, and decides, without permission, to make one of our blankets her toilet.

I sleep fitfully and wake to a red, itchy rash on my arms, my legs, my neck.

"It's fleas." Marcel scratches his head forcefully.

We spend the day picking as slowly as we can at Colette's loaf of bread and taking the smallest sips we can manage of her water. The second night is even worse than the first. I dream that thousands upon thousands of fleas descend on me, covering my skin like a thick dark crust, a moving, breathing scab. They bite me and suck my blood until I'm completely dry. Then they scatter, and without them to define the shape of me, there is nothing left, nothing at all.

I awake with a sharp intake of breath, a gasp that turns into a fit of coughing. The horror on my family's faces at my coughing, that it might give us away, is terrible to witness. Mama presses a blanket to my mouth, trying to muffle the sound, pressing harder and harder as I am unable to stifle, until I can't find air at all, and blackness creeps into the edges of my vision, and I see my hands as if they're someone else's hands, scratching and clawing at her until I'm too lightheaded to do anything but lie still.

At last, the coughing fit passes. As Mama takes away the blanket, she and I both see the blood on it. I gasp and lie on my side on the dirty bare-wood floor. I want to cry, but for what?

We make Colette's bread and water last as long as we can, but both are gone by midafternoon of the third day. The only one of us who's eating decently is Mitzi; her belly is distended with mouse feasting, and she purrs even in sleep. The attic stinks of our excrement and the sharp acidic tang of cat urine.

The third night in the attic, when darkness falls, Marcel creeps down the stairs to knock on Colette's door and see about getting some more water and food. A tense hour passes during which none of us says a word, and then, at last, Marcel returns, bringing with him a fresh jug of water—and news.

"There's been a change of plans." Marcel is breathless with what he's learned. "It seems the Romanian administration has realized that, without its Jews, Czernowitz actually doesn't run all that well."

"What are you talking about?" says Astra.

"They're going to issue permits to stay in the city. Not everyone will be deported to Transnistria. Some of us will be allowed to stay. Eventually, perhaps, *to go home.*"

We erupt into questions—who will get to stay? Who is determining such a thing? How can we apply?—but Marcel puts a finger firmly over his mouth. "Shh! I'll tell you what I know, but quiet!"

We force our tongues to stillness. Mitzi curls in Astra's lap. Marcel passes around the water, and we each take a sip. Then, he explains, the best he can.

"There are jobs that need doing. You know that the Russians left the city a mess. Now the government recognizes that many of the people qualified to make repairs to streets and buildings, to service power and water lines, all sorts of jobs—are Jews. If they send us all to our deaths, who will maintain the phone lines? Who will write contracts? Who will diagnose illness and prescribe medicine? So, there will be a registration process. The Jewish Council is to create lists of various professionals, and we can go put our names down on them. Then, our names and skills will be reviewed by German authorities. We can go tomorrow to register—Frederieke's old school is one of the registration sites; it's not far from here."

A small crack opens inside my chest, something like hope, but Astra narrows her eyes. "How do we know this isn't just some trick? Maybe as soon as we go to the school, they'll shoot us the way they did to the men down on the beach. Have you thought about that?" Though she keeps her voice to a whisper, her words cut sharply.

"Of course I've thought about it." Marcel's whispered retort has the same biting edge. "But I don't think it's a hoax. The city *does* need us, no matter what it thinks of us."

"Not all of us are doctors," Mama says softly. "What will become of the rest of us, Marcel?"

"There will be exemptions for family of essential workers." Marcel seems to grow a little taller as he speaks. "It's a good thing you managed to trap me, eh, Astra?"

"*Trap* you," snorts Astra, but she's grinning now, too, perhaps feeling something like hope herself.

"And as for the rest of you," Marcel says, "Heinrich, you're an engineer, yes?"

"I'm a jeweler."

"Nonsense. You repair watches. Watches are machines. You're an engineer. And if your word isn't enough to get your name on a list, I'm certain a gift could encourage the authorities to write it down."

"I have some loose stones, still," Opa says, sitting taller. "And several rings."

"Then it's settled. Tomorrow, we'll go to the school. We'll get our names on the lists for doctors and engineers. And if we must, we'll bribe them."

Before Marcel had gone down to Colette's apartment to fetch water, it seemed that we'd reached the end of a tunnel—there was no light in front of us, no way forward, just a great stone wall. But now . . . now, I feel that maybe there is a crack in the wall, a pinprick of light.

I don't know about the others, but for me, there is no sleep. The bit of hope wedges like a shard of glass in my heart.

In school, we read a poem by the American poet Emily Dickinson. It said, "Hope is the thing with feathers." But I don't agree. Hope is a thing of glass—incredibly delicate, and intricately painful, if it pierces you.

We leave Mitzi in the attic and go to the school first thing in the morning. When we emerge on the street, I see that my family looks like a bunch of vagabonds—sickly, dirty, greasy haired. I'm sure I look the same. But there's nothing to be done about that. It is terribly cold—maybe because my body has eaten up all its fat. My bones ache, and even the cloud-filtered sunlight feels too bright. I squint against it.

Snow fell in the night, sugaring everything around us, and the air, though cold, is fresh, a pleasure to inhale. I pull off a glove and run my hand along the railing, scooping a palmful of clean white snow, which I eat. I close my eyes as it melts; it feels like fire in my mouth and throat, but after I swallow it, my head feels clearer, sharper.

I open my eyes. Across the street, a dog steps out of the alleyway. He stops short, stares into my eyes. His head gleams red in the sun. For a moment I'm back in the mountains, on the trail with Opa, and this is Peter, here to lead the way. The feeling in my body—a quicksilver flash of remembered joy, as intense and cleansing as the swallowed snow. Until I blink, and he's a mangy stray—skinny, half-starved. Once someone's pet,

264

now he's feral and alone. Slowly, he backs into the shadow of the alleyway.

We make our way to the school. I haven't been here since the Germans chased the Russians out of our city, and it feels like I'm entering some storybook version of childhood that I've grown much too old to believe in anymore.

Student papers and artwork still hang in the downstairs hallway, relics of a different time. Mama, Astra, and I duck inside the girls' bathroom not far from my old classroom. What a relief to use an actual toilet! And then to wash ourselves at a sink, to arrange our hair in front of the mirrors. To make ourselves human again.

When we emerge, we find that Opa and Marcel have taken advantage of the teachers' restroom. Their hair is damp and slicked back, a small thing that makes such a big difference.

We join the lines of people waiting to register. Being in my old school gives me a strangely hopeful feeling, and I crane my neck, looking for anyone I know from school and dance. Perhaps even Esther and Conrad? My memories of them feel so far away as to be from someone else's life.

I used to attend classes in the building. I used to walk from here to Madame Lucia's studio. I used to fear losing a hair ribbon, or missing my marks. That we're here now, like this—that that was once my life—it's surreal. Absurd. Impossible.

And yet, here we are.

Tables are set up in the auditorium. Behind the tables sit members of the Jewish Council, including Mr. Strasberg. "Let's try to get in his line," Opa whispers to Mama and me. I nod.

Ahead of us, Marcel and Astra step forward. "Doctor and Mrs. Goldmann," Marcel says. "Here to register as medically essential."

Mr. Strasberg is still busy with another family when a space opens

265

in another council member's line, someone we don't know. The people behind us grow impatient; we cannot wait.

"State your name and profession." The man doesn't look up; the top of his head greets us, his skullcap an unblinking giant eye.

Opa seems to lose his ability to speak. He is, I know, a terrible liar, so I speak for him. "Mr. Heinrich Fischmann, mechanical engineer. And family."

Now, the man looks up. When he sees Opa standing there, clutching his hat by its brim, he raises an eyebrow. "Mechanical engineer, eh, old man? Where did you study?"

This, I have no answer for, and beside me, Opa's mouth opens and closes wordlessly. The sliver of hope still wedged in my heart begins to dissolve to powder.

"He went to school in your mother's bed, how do you like that, Abrams?"

At these words, the councilmember—Mr. Abrams—grins wildly and laughs.

I turn, and see my father.

Mr. Abrams stands and reaches past us to shake his hand. "Alfred, you scoundrel, keep my mother's name out of your mouth."

"It's not my *name* she wants in her mouth."

Mr. Abrams guffaws, slapping the table. Distractedly, he scrawls Opa's name on the "Engineer" list. "Dependents?" he asks, and Mama and I tell him our names.

Can it really be this easy? It doesn't seem possible, but then nothing that is happening seemed possible.

"Alfred," says Mr. Abrams, turning his attention back to Father, "are you here to register as well? What list should I put you on?"

266

My father shakes his head. "No list for me, not today, Abrams. You take care, all right?"

Then Opa, Mama, and I follow Father away from the tables, into the hallway.

"Alfred," says Opa. "How can I thank you enough?"

It isn't like my father to get emotional, especially about us, but that's exactly what happens next. His eyes brim with tears and he looks at us, one to the other, as if we are his whole world.

*"Everything is cyclical,"* Opa has often told me. All my young years, I believed him—if things were bad, that must mean they would be better, soon. But then, things got worse, too bad to ever get better again. That's when I stopped believing in cycles; that was when I put the locket with Astra's pill around my neck. But now—look! It's my father, returned to us, at last.

He pulls Opa into a rough embrace, something I have never seen him do. Mama's mouth drops open. "It is I who should thank *you*," Father says. "You've taken care of my girls all this time." He sniffs and swipes tears from his eyes.

Maybe he will stay with us now. There is nothing good about war, and yet, still, perhaps one good thing will come of it: maybe my father has realized he needs us, his family. And that we need him.

He sniffs, pats Opa hard on his back once, twice, then holds him at arm's length. "Keep taking care of them, okay, Heinrich?"

Opa nods. "Always."

"Wait," I say. No one hears.

"You're not going to try to get on any of these lists, Alfred?" asks Mama.

"No. I'm going to take a train."

267

"What?" Mama is aghast. "You're going to Transnistria? Voluntarily? But why?"

My father shrugs. "There's a woman."

Of course, there's a woman. With my father, there always is.

"She was sent already. She has three small children, and no one else."

"Are you out of your mind?" I grab the sleeve of his coat. "Listen, maybe you don't know. Marcel told us what it's like over there." I'm a kaleidoscope of emotions. I was hopeful, then angry, and now, suddenly desperate. "Please, Papa, stay with us. Please don't go."

I haven't called him "Papa" since I was a little girl. I take his hands, beseechingly. He squeezes my hands, smiles at me; with a shock I see that he has a fleck of green in his right eye, in exactly the place I have the same fleck of green. I don't remember ever noticing this before. Now, it feels somehow like this huge thing, this connection I didn't know I needed, and I feel myself break open with yearning, with desire to know this man, my father—but he's leaving us—he's leaving *me*—again.

Mama tries to argue; he cuts her off by letting go of my hands and leaning into her, wrapping her in his arms, and kissing her cheek. He does the same, to me.

"Take care of them, Heinrich," he says again, and then he walks away. He pushes open the school's heavy front door. Before it shuts, I see him jog down the top few stairs. His breath puffs out like a cloud of smoke around his head.

Then the door slams closed, and my father is gone.

# FIVE

# IN MR. WEISSINGER'S
# APARTMENT

It's not quite as easy as that, as managing to get our names on Mr. Abrams's list. From there, as Marcel said, the lists will go from the Jewish Council to German officials. Final approval will be in their hands.

Within days of our visit to the school, deportations cease. We have no way of knowing if Father climbed aboard one of those last trains, or if he's still in the city. I spend more time thinking about him than I have since I was a little girl: wondering where he is, and who he's with. Grateful, at least, that even though he's not with us, he won't be alone.

With the deportations stopped, we feel safe to leave the attic. Anyway, we have no choice—officials are moving the barriers to shrink the ghetto, and Colette's building, which has been inside the borders, will now be outside, part of the greater city. Since our names have been recorded on the lists of Jews whose evacuations have been temporarily stayed, we don't need to hide anymore, but we do need to stay within the ghetto boundaries. The day the border fence is set to be moved, we again arrange our belongings, leaving the blanket Mitzi turned into her toilet, and head down the stairs.

We find Colette waiting on the ground floor, a bag in her arms. "Marcel," she says, thrusting the bag at him, "take this. It's not much—a blanket, some cans of fish. There's a bottle of wine, the kind you like . . . I was saving it. And another loaf of bread. I'm sorry I can't do more."

It's clear from the way Astra stiffens that some part of her would like to see Marcel refuse the bag, but of course she's practical enough not to insist on such a thing. He accepts the bag, shifting his other bundles to take it. Then he leans in to kiss Colette—on her cheek, but close to the corner of her mouth. I swear that at that moment, Mitzi, in her box, growls.

So, there it is. Nothing to do but go back into the street.

Each time we go outside, it's colder. Though it's the second week in November, winter has come to Czernowitz.

November. Only now do I realize that my birthday has come and gone, and not one of us remembered it. I am fifteen years old.

We have to head left, up the street, in the direction of the train tracks, even though we have no intention of going to the station. There, at the far corner, officials and workers are busy reassembling the border wall. Nearly as many men are directing the work as actively working. The men who appear in charge are all dressed in uniforms, an even mix of Nazi and Romanian; those working are Romanian men in plainclothes.

I know that I should be used to shifting borders at this point. But this fence—the same fence that had been on one side of Colette's apartment building, that is now on *this* side—it makes me feel both powerless and angry. That the rules can change so fast, that we have absolutely no control over what those rules will be, even though we're the chess pieces who are forced to move in step with them, who will live or die because of them.

I'm angry, and at the same time, I know my anger means nothing.

Look how quickly they put up the chain link, the barbed wire! Look how good they are at it—at building such a structure, at dividing a city, cutting it up first this way, then this other way.

We're forced to turn and walk along the wall until we come to the new checkpoint. It's guarded by two Romanians, each armed with a rifle. As we reach them, the guard on the left says to his partner, "Look at these rats. What are you doing out of your cage? You'll contaminate the good people with your filth."

"They don't even wash themselves," the other says. "Do you think they enjoy the smell of their own filth, or do you think they are immune to it?"

Their words pin us to stillness. Opa and Marcel flank the three of us—me, Mama, and Astra—and all of us are freshly terrified.

"Gentlemen," Marcel says, but it's the wrong thing to say.

The guards bark out laughter, the one on the right spraying spit from his mouth as he laughs. "Listen to how he talks," he says, then, mockingly, "'*Gentlemen.*'"

"Let's see your papers," says the first guard, all business now.

Opa and Marcel rush to find the temporary permits they were given by the Jewish Council. But before they can present them, there comes a shout from up above, a man high on a ladder, stringing coils of barbed wire.

"Hey," he calls down. "I have to take a piss. One of you take over for a while."

The two guards begin to argue about whose turn it is to climb the ladder. We move past them, no one stopping us. And just like that, we're within the ghetto's new boundaries, and I breathe a sigh of relief. It's amazing to me that just moments ago I was so full of anger and resentment, and now all I have room for is relief, even *gratitude*, that the man on the wall, the one who was stringing barbed wire to keep us from escaping, had to urinate.

It's too much to fathom. I can't even think about it, or I fear I'll swoon, as I did in the Keplers' apartment, as I did in the attic when Mama was silencing me with the blanket. So instead I focus on my breathing, my footsteps, and nothing more.

We walk for a while with no specific destination. I think all of us want to get as far away from the border wall as we can. And we're moving slowly. My family does not say it, but I'm sure they're all thinking that if I fall into a coughing fit, if I pass out, we'll be in even more trouble.

Finally, Astra suggests, "We should try to get a place near the school." It's a good idea, as that's where Marcel and Opa will have to complete their interviews in the coming days to get a permanent permit to stay in the city.

There's an apartment building just across from the school, but there are so many people crowding the foyer that we know the rest of the building must be just as packed. We keep going, turning a corner onto a smaller street.

"George keeps an apartment on this street," Mama says.

"Who?" says Marcel.

"George Weissinger," Mama answers.

"Did I ever tell you that he tried to date Mama, after Father left?" asks Astra.

Marcel shakes his head.

"Opa did *not* approve," Astra says with a wry smile.

"Do you think he'd let us stay?" Marcel asks Mama, ignoring Astra.

Mama raises her shoulders. "He might."

"I don't like that idea," Opa says, as I knew he wouldn't. "He's not a trustworthy man."

"Come on, Heinrich," says Marcel. "So he does a few things not quite by the book. That's not a bad man to know in times like this, if you ask me."

Opa shakes his head. "I don't trust him."

"You'd be a fool to trust anyone these days," Marcel answers. "But do you have a better idea?"

For some reason, Opa looks at me, questioningly. I do not want to go to Mr. Weissinger's apartment, but we need a place to stay, and there's no better idea. Opa must be thinking the same, because he lets his head drop, and then nods.

We follow Mama to a building halfway down the block, then up the stairs of one of the nicer-looking apartment buildings. Inside the main door, the air is as frigid as outside, but at least it is still. We stop for a moment and adjust our bundles. Mama smooths her hair.

"Which floor?" Astra asks.

"I've never been to this apartment," she replies.

"We'll just start knocking on doors, then," says Astra, taking charge once again.

The first door opens just a crack when Astra pounds on it. The drawn face of an old woman peers out.

"We're looking for George Weissinger. Do you know which apartment is his?"

The woman shakes her head and closes the door fast, as if she fears we might decide to force our way into her apartment when we can't find the one we're looking for. We have no more luck at the next three apartments, either.

But a man behind the fourth door we knock on tells us, "He's in 3B."

273

And so we climb, again.

As we reach the door marked 3B, Astra pushes Mama forward. "Your turn, Mama."

Mama clears her throat and raises her hand. She hesitates for a moment, and then, so gently, she taps.

"No one could possibly hear that." Astra reaches past Mama to bang on the door.

"Astra," says Mama, horrified.

A moment, and then we hear a lock turning. Just before the door swings open, I notice something: tiny nail holes in the doorframe, at eye level. A mezuzah once hung there, but no longer.

Mr. Weissinger opens the door. If he's surprised to see us there, crowding his doorstep, he doesn't show it.

"Anna." Immediately, he pulls the door wide. "Please. Come in."

If we were hoping that Mr. Weissinger's apartment would be one of the ones within the ghetto boundaries that wasn't crowded with refugees from elsewhere in the city, we are wrong. He's allowing several families to stay here, including a young man with the keen, intelligent look of a professor and his heavily pregnant wife; an older gentleman, close to Opa's age, whose skin smells as if he has been pickled in nicotine; a family of seven, with children as old as me and young enough to be held by their tired-looking mother; and a number of other people who huddle together in a far corner and hardly look over as we arrive. As Mr. Weissinger introduces us, we discover that the man who looks like a professor turns out to be a composer; the older gentleman is actually a professor, of chemistry.

Mr. Weissinger leads us through his sitting room and into the kitchen, where he helps us set down our bundles. He manages to not look shocked when he takes a box from Astra and it yowls.

"Hello, Frederieke." He doesn't speak to me directly until the others are busy getting settled. "How are you? How is your health?"

"Hello, Mr. Weissinger. I'm doing as well as I can, I suppose."

He nods, as if what I have said is very wise.

"Thank you so much for letting us stay here," I add. I don't know Mr. Weissinger well, but I know him well enough to be confident about what things I can say that will make him happy. "It's very generous of you."

"Oh, it's nothing," he answers, with a wave of his hand. "I seem to have developed quite the habit of saving you, Frederieke, haven't I?"

His words are light, but there's something beneath them I cannot name. All I say, though, is, "Yes, Mr. Weissinger."

"I told you," he says, "call me George."

After telling him about my illness of late—Mr. Weissinger doesn't mention taking me to see Dr. Flor, for which I'm thankful—it's agreed that I should take the bathtub. No one wants to sleep close to me, and I don't blame them. We eat—not much, just a part of a loaf of bread, tasting suspiciously of sawdust, with a piece of hard cheese for each of us—and then Mama spreads a blanket for me. I climb in, completely exhausted by the morning's move. As the familiar feeling of cold porcelain cradles me, I feel worse than I have since that night that Mama had to stifle my uncontrollable coughs.

"George, how can we ever thank you?" Mama asks, as they look down on me in the tub.

"For what would you thank me?" Mr. Weissinger says. He hands Mama another blanket. "For being human?"

"Not everyone is." Mama covers me with the blanket, and I close my eyes.

Maybe I sleep. Maybe I faint. Each breath is hard to catch, and shallow. Inside my head the world spins and spins. It's quiet, at least. I feel a shift as my mother sits on the edge of the tub. Her hand brushes my forehead. Then it pushes away the top blanket and undoes the buttons of my sweater. I feel her hand slip inside my shirt, just above my heart, but the hand is heavier, larger than it should be.

My weighted eyelids are hard to lift, but I manage to. It's not my mother's hand; it's Mr. Weissinger's. I cry out, a chirp, but he says, "Shh, close your eyes, I am monitoring your heartbeat to report to the doctor."

I squeeze my eyes shut. I hold my breath. But my heart beats on, even as his hand shifts lower, even as his fingers squeeze my nipple, even as I hear a belt buckle being undone, even as he squeezes my breast as if it were bread dough, kneading, kneading, rhythmically, roughly, until he makes a terrible sound, his fingers tightening so hard that I can't help but cry out.

Then, only then, his hand slips away. I keep my eyes squeezed shut; I hear him standing, I hear a shift of fabric, I hear the belt rebuckle. Still my eyes stay closed.

Then, "Rest," Mr. Weissinger says, and he leaves the room.

I don't open my eyes. I squeeze them even tighter, until I see bright flashes of white in the darkness. I try to count the flashes, to make them stay still, but they elude me.

My breast is sore from Mr. Weissinger's grip. *Don't think about that,* I tell myself, but my mind keeps replaying the incident, the way his fingers felt when he first slipped them into my shirt, the way he rolled my nipple in his fingers as if it were a lucky bead, a keepsake.

*Shut up, you stupid cow! What's wrong with you? You're the dumbest thing to ever live.*

The words help. So then I speak aloud, in a whisper. "You're a fucking dummy," I tell myself. I put my hand into my own shirt, over my left breast. I feel my heart beneath my skin. "It's just skin," I say—and, to prove it, I pinch my nipple hard as I can, until all I can feel is this fresh pain, until the tears that squeeze from my eyes are about this, this pain, that I am causing, right now, myself.

I consider telling someone what happened in the bathroom. Not Opa— the thought of the look on his face, if I told him, makes me physically ill. Not Mama, either. The only thing I can imagine that would be worse than her not caring would be if she did.

Astra. Would she care? She would, I decide. She would be angry. I could confide in her. But then what? What could she do, other than tell Opa, or Mama? She would surely tell Marcel, which would be terrible in a whole different way. And what good could come of telling *anyone*? If Opa found out, he'd insist on leaving Mr. Weissinger's home. My family would be on the street, because of me, because of such a little thing.

As the days slip by, I convince myself that maybe he *had* been monitoring my heartbeat, and in my imagination, I'd made it into something larger than it was. There is a part of me that knows this isn't true, that whispers—*It happened. You know it did*—but when that voice speaks I shut it up. *You fucking dummy*, I tell the voice. *How stupid can you be?*

Each day, no matter the weather, we wait outside the school, which has become a military station, hoping to hear our names called. We stand outside for hours and hours, sometimes in slushy snow, sometimes in biting rain. I cough and cough, and Opa can barely stand some days; it would be better to leave us at Mr. Weissinger's apartment while the others wait, but if our names are called, we need to be present for the interview. So we all wait, together.

The crowd thins as the Transnistria deportations start up again to carry away those whose applications are rejected, and as a slow trickle of lucky people are granted permits by the governor, allowing them to leave the ghetto and return to their apartments to see if there is anything left for them there.

It's on the fifth day of waiting that Marcel's name is called. "Mr. Laufer, Mr. Menschel, Dr. Goldmann, Professor Spiegel," announces an official from the steps of the school, reading from a list on a clipboard. Marcel surges forward, clutching Astra by the hand, and up the steps they go, and through the door.

It's neither raining nor snowing today. The sky is gray. The sidewalk is so cold that the bottoms of my feet have gone numb, though my toes tingle painfully. The entire time Marcel and Astra are in the building, Opa, Mama, and I stare at the door.

The first time it pushes open, I hear Mama catch her breath, but it's one of the others, either Mr. Laufer or Mr. Menschel or Professor Spiegel. Whoever he is, he comes down the steps looking a good deal happier than he looked when he went up.

A few minutes later, the door opens again. This time, it *is* Astra and Marcel. I study their faces as they come down the stairs, but I can discern nothing. They seem to be walking quickly, but that could mean good news, or bad. It isn't until they're right near us that I can glean from the set of Astra's mouth that fortune has favored them.

"Thank Hashem, thank Hashem," Opa says, when Marcel and Astra show us their permits. I close my eyes tightly, and I, too, thank God. Though whether or not He exists is questionable at best, and whether or not He's watching feels even less certain, I can think of nothing I've ever felt more grateful for, ever, than knowing that my sister is safe, at least a little while longer.

Though the official soon announces that the office is closed for the day without having called Opa's name, there is still cause to celebrate—if not all of us, at least some of us have been permitted to stay, to live. Those paper squares, each with a pale yellow star in the background, each with official signatures and stamps, are more precious than gold, and back at Mr. Weissinger's apartment we take turns holding them, examining them.

"You'll go back to our apartment, then," Mama says. "We will follow, when we get our permits."

Astra shakes her head, emphatic. "We will stay here with you. When you get your permits, we will go home, together."

This touches Mama so that she immediately bursts into tears. She throws herself, sobbing, into Astra's arms. Astra holds her up; when she catches my eye, she rolls hers, and we smile.

"You are my angel," Mama sobs. "Always, you have been my angel."

It might have made me jealous if the whole scene wasn't ridiculous—Mama clutching Astra, and Astra looking as if she wishes she were absolutely anywhere but here, even though she's just decided they'll be staying. And Marcel, behind them, dubious.

"Well, Astra, let's talk about this," he says.

But Mama isn't done sobbing, so Marcel is forced to wait a bit longer, until she has herself under control.

Then he clears his throat and tries again. "I'll be needed back at the hospital, and the apartment is much closer. And there's no reason for the two of us to keep imposing on George's generosity, now."

Astra waves a hand at him, dismissing his arguments. "We'll stay here. We'll go later, together."

279

"Your husband is right, Astra," Opa says. I think this is the first time I've heard him call Marcel Astra's husband. "You should go home."

But neither of them knows Astra as well as I do. If they did, they would recognize the set of her chin, the angle of her shoulders, the resolute energy that comes from her in waves. Astra has made up her mind.

It's in that moment that I feel certain we will get a permit.

Two days later is the heaviest storm so far. Mama, Opa, and I cluster together as close as we can get under the partial cover of a tree. Because it's winter, the leaves have all fallen away, and the bare branches barely give any cover. Still, it feels better to be under something, even something so insufficient, than to be out in the open. I wonder if this is an instinct, this desire to be covered from above, the way that little animals rush beneath a bush lest the hawk in the sky sees their bare heads and swoops down to pluck them from the ground. Whatever the reason, though, we're squeezed together under the tree's skeleton canopy when the official comes out to the step and calls, "Mr. Fischmann, Mr. Hoffman, Mr. Blau."

"Oh, thank God," Mama says, and we surge forward, through the rain and up the steps. But at the door, we find ourselves among four families, not three. It turns out that there are *two* Misters Hoffman: a man about Opa's age, with his wife, and another man, much younger, with no wife but two small children clinging to him.

"Which Hoffman?" the younger Mr. Hoffman asks the officer, who refers to his list.

"Joseph."

Deflated, the younger Mr. Hoffman descends the stairs, his children begging to go inside, and we go with the others whose names have been called into the school.

This time, the commission we find ourselves in front of is composed of uniformed German officials. When it's our turn, we step forward, Mama and me half a step behind Opa.

"Heinrich Fischmann," says the German official. He has a long, drooping mustache, the corners of which he pulls into his mouth and sucks in a most disgusting manner. He looks up from his papers. "It says here that you are a mechanical engineer. Tell us, where did you train?"

"I am . . . self-taught," Opa answers. My heart begins to quicken, so nervous is he. How I wish I could help him, but all I can do is stand here.

"A self-taught mechanical engineer," says the mustached official, turning to the man who sits beside him and laughing. Laughing, at my grandfather. "Tell me, old man, what are the most important projects you have worked on? Why does the city need *you*? It seems to me we would be doing the city a service if we sent you out of it."

Opa reaches into his pocket and extracts two things: a ruby ring, set in gold, and a loose stone—a small diamond.

"These are some of my accomplishments—stones I've cut and set myself, by hand. I am also a watchmaker, and am adept at watch repair. But I have no watches to show you today."

Quick as a viper, the man reaches out and snatches up the jewels. "You think you can bribe us, old man?" he says, and my stomach twists painfully in fear. But then he tucks the jewels into a pocket and motions to his partner to stamp our permits.

And that is that.

We contain our excitement until we've left the building and the heavy main doors shut firmly behind us. We emerge to find the rain has eased to a fine mist, and going down the stairs together we practically burst, so intense is our relief.

But then we see the other Mr. Hoffman. He stands with his

children—the younger one he holds, now sleeping on his shoulder—still waiting, still hopeful, but with an aura of desperation clinging to him like oil.

Opa stops and offers him a hand. They shake but do not speak. What is there to say?

Then we continue up the street, back to Mr. Weissinger's apartment. I turn before we reach the corner to look back at Mr. Hoffman and his children, but I can't tell anymore which of the bodies are theirs; all the waiting people blend together, indistinguishable.

"Come, Rieke." Opa reaches out and takes my hand.

This time, packing our things feels different. We know where we're going—*home*. I throw my things as quickly as I can into a pillowcase. By the time I am ready to go, the gratitude I feel for what happened today extends to Mr. Weissinger and his generosity this past week, overshadowing the incident in the bathtub, which I resolve to set in the past. For the final time, Astra wrangles Mitzi into her box and ties it shut; Mama folds blankets one inside the other; Marcel slicks back his hair in front of the hall mirror as if he's going to the theater rather than just home.

*Just home.* There is no such thing as *just home*, anymore. The word feels like a dream, too much to hope for anymore.

Marcel insists on leaving the wine Colette gave him. "It's all we have to thank you," he says, when Mr. Weissinger protests.

"At least, stay for a moment and let's drink it together." But the cat is already in the box, our hats already on our heads, and all of us are too anxious and excited to stay here any longer.

"Well, then." Mr. Weissinger holds the bottle by its neck. "I'll toast to your health when I drink." And he raises the bottle in salute.

282

He embraces each of us as we leave—Opa, he clasps warmly by the hand, Marcel, he slaps on the back, Astra and Mama he kisses, this cheek and then the other, and then the first again.

Then it is my turn to say goodbye. "Mr. Weissinger." I lean in and brace myself for his fleshy lips on my face. "How can I ever repay you?"

He kisses my left cheek, my right cheek. "We'll find a way," he says. And then, with a final kiss, "I asked you to call me George, yes?"

I pull away and nod. "George." His name comes out in a whisper. "Thank you."

I follow my family into the hallway. Mr. Weissinger, still holding the bottle of wine, waves as if he's saying goodbye after a dinner party. "Be safe," he calls.

When we reach the street, even though it's raining, again, I don't mind. In fact, I turn my face up to the rain, close my eyes as the droplets hit my cheeks, my lips, my chin.

"Come *on*, Rieke," Astra calls, and I hurry to catch up.

# SIX

## HOW LUCKY

Our home is haunted.

That's the first thing I think when we arrive back to our own apartment building. Outwardly, nothing is different—the same five steps up to the same double door, with the same inset glass along the top. The same handrails. The same stoop. But I can't shake the feeling that I'm walking not into the place I've lived in since I was six years old, but instead one that's been taken over by some malevolent spirit. I climb the stairs slowly, nervously, but force myself to smile as Opa holds open the building's door for me.

If I suspected I was being watched by invisible specters when we were outside, I'm sure of it once we're inside. The feeling grows as we cross the foyer; it grows as we climb the stairs. Part of it is how *quiet* the building is; usually, we hear movement and voices, sometimes music, from behind the doors. And the aroma of cooking meals—that's missing, too. Now, there are no signs of life; none of our fellow Jewish tenants have yet returned, and it seems that the Germans and Romanians have moved out as well, though I'm not sure why they've abandoned the building.

At last we reach our apartment door, pausing before it. None of us has said it out loud, but I know I'm not alone in believing that when we left our home, it was to never return.

And, yet, here we are—returning, as if from beyond the grave. With a flourish and a wink, Opa pulls his key from his pocket. The key slips into the lock with a sound I hadn't realized I knew, a sound that brings tears to my eyes . . . but then, when Opa goes to turn it, he frowns.

We look, then, at the doorjamb. It's been forced; the door is already unlocked.

Marcel moves Opa out of the way—gently, but firmly—and puts his hand on the knob. Slowly the door cracks open.

"Hello?" Marcel pushes it wide. There is no answer. The apartment is empty.

But it's not as we left it.

In the front room, wind howls through the window; though the middle and right panes are intact, the left pane has been shattered. The curtains have been ripped, and they tangle and whip in the wind and rain. Our velvet couch looks like a disemboweled body, cushions ripped open, stuffing pouring out. The tall lamp is shattered; the table lamp is gone. The bookshelf is a mouth with teeth punched out, Astra's fine collection torn asunder, most of the books splayed across the floor, others knocked flat.

We stand together in the doorway. Of course, we knew it was possible—probable, even—that our home would be broken into while we were gone. But knowing it and seeing it are two different things.

Marcel recovers first, pacing loudly across the room to pull the rain-drenched draperies. Opa shuts the door and tries to turn the lock, but the doorframe is damaged, so he must content himself with pushing it closed and then dropping his bundle in front of it. Mama goes straight to the kitchen; her wail tells us that the kitchen has been torn apart, too.

Astra takes Mitzi in her box through the house and to her bedroom, calling triumphantly, "The window is fine in here!" When she emerges, she closes the bedroom door tightly to keep Mitzi safely inside.

I stop in Mama's room to assess the damage there. It's as I expected: her lovely bedspread is gone, everything from her vanity stripped away, and a long crack runs down the center of the vanity's mirror. The drawers have been yanked open, and are empty.

I pass through the kitchen—Mama is opening every drawer, every cabinet, looking to see what's left. One thing hasn't changed—the dirty dishes we'd left in the sink are still right where we left them, now speckled with mold.

In my little room off the kitchen, I go straight to my bureau to see if it's been raided, too, but before I reach it, I see something on the floor.

I kneel down. It's Penny's glass horse. Someone has crushed its head and torso, along with the front two legs. It's only the back half—the purply-pink tail, the spindly hind legs—that remains. I left it here to keep it safe, and yet still it has been broken.

I want to believe what Opa told me that day in the country: that our capacity to love is greater than their hate. But . . . *is* it? The hate the Romanians and the Germans have for us is powerful. Their hate is enormous—as wide as the sky—but also so petty and small that it will go into the littlest room in a family's apartment, seek out the one scrap of delicate beauty, and destroy it.

How can anything we do to hold on to our lives, to hold on to one another, compete with hate like this?

I want to throw the remains of Penny's horse into the waste basket. But I can't do it. Instead, being careful not to let the sharp edges of its severed body cut me, I tuck it to the back of my top drawer.

This becomes our work for the next several days: restoring order to a disordered world. We have no water for scrubbing, no soap or cleaning supplies, and there's no way to fix the big front window. The best we can do is take down the door to my little room and nail it across the broken pane, which keeps out most of the cold air and the sleet but also blocks out much of the light. And the electricity doesn't function anywhere in the building, so the front room, which used to be a place of warmth and light, feels now like a cave. This, I imagine, is why the Germans and Romanians who had come to live in our building have left.

Still, we're home. And that's a thing I'd nearly given up hope for a week ago.

Life finds a new routine as November marches forward: each morning Marcel leaves for the hospital, and each evening we hope he'll make it safely home. The rest of us are allowed on the streets just two hours a day under a new, stricter curfew, so if we want any chance of getting the things we need from the government vendors, we are left to split up. Opa, Mama, Astra, and I—when I feel well enough to go—leave together at precisely ten o'clock in the morning, racing against time to gather what we can before noon, when curfew falls again. We need firewood, and kerosene, and food, and even water, now, as the water to our entire building has been shut off along with the electricity. Without running water to flush the toilet, we have to pour in water from a bucket—and water isn't so easy to come by, so we flush as infrequently as possible.

Two hours a day isn't sufficient for gathering all these things. The lines are still long; Jews still aren't permitted to shop alongside the Christians; and as for the yellow star we are still compelled to pin to our clothes . . . Wearing it means getting the mealiest piece of bread, the dampest stick of firewood. It means glares on the street, or worse, being spit at by people who, a few years ago, would have surely smiled at me. It means possibly feeling the crack of a whip from a German or Romanian soldier, who seem to delight in such things.

But not wearing it and being caught can mean worse—being beaten, arrested, disappearing without a trace. Which is why Opa can't stand the thought of me risking being caught without the star pinned to my coat. And so I learn to unpin it only after I've left the apartment. Once outside, I find a private corner and, back turned to the street, I unpin the star, then refasten it beneath my lapel so that the wool flap hides it. In this manner, I can avoid most harassment on the street, but if I feel in danger of being found out, I can tuck my lapel inside my coat so that the star is visible.

One morning, preparing to go out, I arrange my hair in front of Mama's cracked vanity mirror. I plait it into two braids, then cross them behind my head. This is a style I've worn all my life, but I also know it's the way I look the least "Jewish"—the way I look most like the Aryan woman on German propaganda posters. I turn my head this way and that, making sure the braids are even.

The crack in the mirror splits my face in half; the left side is higher than the right, the bridge of my nose bends oddly. I blink, and my eyes blink back, but they seem to belong to somebody else.

There are many ways for a place to be haunted. Though I see no ghosts, our apartment doesn't lose the quality I felt that day we came home. The girl in the mirror could be a ghost after all—some dead version of me, or a vision of who I might have been if a different fate had befallen our city. If I had not been born Jewish. If I had not been born a Czernowitzer.

Or maybe the girl in the mirror is a vision of my future. Of the breaking that is to come.

"Or maybe it's just a broken mirror, and you're stalling," I say out loud.

One day in late November, Marcel brings home news. The governor, whose signature is on our permits, had ceased issuing them, leaving thousands of Jewish residents in the ghetto awaiting certain deportation to Transnistria—but the mayor of Czernowitz, Dr. Traian Popovici, managed to obtain consent from our capital, Bucharest, to issue permits to people still stuck within the ghetto boundaries. He himself signed a permit for each and every remaining Czernowitz Jew. The ghetto is to be dismantled, and the entire remaining Jewish population—a fraction of what it once was, but still over three thousand people—will be permitted to return to their homes in the city.

"Mayor Popovici is a righteous man," Opa says. "He has always been a friend to the Jewish people."

And so, in the two days that follow, some of our Jewish neighbors come home. When I first see Mr. Fischer pull open the building door, holding young Sylvie, my heart leaps with gladness—until Mrs. Fischer comes in behind him, and I realize that their baby, Moses, isn't with them. Mrs. Fischer's arms are devastatingly empty.

When it seems clear that everyone who is going to come back *has* come back, still our apartment building feels hollow.

Then, on the cusp of December, there comes a new edict: the entire Jewish population still living in Czernowitz must report to city hall to have our permits reviewed and validated. No exceptions.

"We cannot go," Mama says that morning. "They will kill us all."

"Anna, hush," Opa says. "You'll scare the girls."

We're already scared, of course. Who wouldn't be?

"There's nothing for it, Mama, but to go," says Astra. "Chin up, all right?"

Mama nods, wipes her face, and gets her coat. Together, we leave our apartment. Once more, we have no way of knowing if we will ever return.

It's the sort of day I would have once thought beautiful, an icy blue sky above and a fresh layer of shiny white snow all around. The city looks fresh and clean and new. If you were to fly over and look down on us, you'd think that our city is something from a fairy story. Something good. Something pure.

When did it happen, my loss of innocence? When did I first come to understand that something can *look* pure, but still be rotten inside? It was the morning that we took the train to the mountains. I remember Opa stringing my watch on my wrist. I remember leaving our apartment with a sense of awe, a hope of adventure. I remember how we traveled through the city on our way to the train station, how I had felt part of something—that I belonged to this place, and it to me. And I remember exactly the moment that feeling was taken from me. When the woman in the yellow dress looked down at me, sneered, and named me—*kike*. When I understood that my own home could hate me.

*How much* it could hate me, and what it could do with that hate— that, I've been learning ever since.

Hundreds of fellow Jews are leaving their homes along our route, and we join in a river of anticipation and dread, flowing in one mass of bodies toward city hall. Yellow stars flutter like flowers on our lapels. Mothers clutch the hands of their children. Husbands place protective arms around the shoulders of their wives. All of us together think one thought, pray one prayer, no matter how devout we are or aren't:

*Please, God. Let us stay. Let us live.*

We arrive at city hall. Already the steps are full, and so we wait our turn, Opa and Mama in the front, then Astra with Marcel, and me, last. I look at the backs of their heads, the square of their shoulders.

Astra leans in to whisper to Marcel, her arm linked through his. "This is where we were married. Remember that day?"

Marcel turns, his lips brushing her ear. "I remember that *night*," he says, and Astra laughs—such a sound here, now, absolutely irreverent, even profane. Mama and Opa turn in disapproval, and strangers, too, look at her, aghast, but I—in my bones, I am *proud* that this is my sister, that she can laugh, despite everything.

When Astra married Marcel and broke all our hearts, she laughed that laugh, and I hated her. But today, right now, I couldn't love her more.

*"I don't know about you,"* Astra once told me outside Opa's ruined shop, *"but I'm going to live, while I can."*

As much as her decisions have hurt me, as angry as it made me when Astra threw away dance with both hands in favor of marrying a man who treats her just like our father treated our mother . . . Astra made a choice. She made a choice to live, while she could. She is doing it, still. My beautiful, terrible sister.

The line moves at a steady pace. Less than an hour passes before it's our turn to go through the doorway into city hall. I've never been inside this building before, but I'm too nervous to pay much attention to my surroundings, and within moments we're funneled up the hall and then into a large room. Three walls are lined with tables that form a horseshoe, where a dozen or so officers sit. Small lines are forming before each of them, and it becomes clear that the lines are designated for last names, in alphabetical order.

This is where we will part. Astra and Marcel will go to the "G" line; while Mama and I are Teitlers—Father's name—we will follow Opa, to "F," for Opa's last name "Fischmann," as our permits rely on his.

Before Astra moves away, she leans in close to me, her eyes serious. "Don't cough, rat tail." It's a command, not a suggestion.

As soon as she says that, it's like a trigger to my unconscious and I feel the need to cough more than ever. But I manage to suppress it as we queue up with Opa. There's an adjacent room off to the right, and two men in SS uniforms stand guard outside its door. The sight of them makes me shiver; I don't know what's on the other side of the door, but I do know that we definitely do not want to find out.

I study the faces of the officials seated behind the table at the front of our line; the man in charge of "F" is young, with a wave of dark blond hair that lies foppishly across his forehead. He looks like he could have as easily been a star in the movies as an officer in the military, and he wears his uniform—an olive-green wool jacket, a shirt and tie underneath, and on his left arm, a red armband with a black swastika insignia prominently displayed—like it's a performance. Next to him, the man in charge of the "G" line is older, maybe fifty. He sits stiffly in his black jacket, with an armband identical to the blond man's; he looks proud of himself, of the symbol on his arm. I shiver, glad that we're in our line rather than his, and hoping the harsh-faced man will be kind to Astra and Marcel.

The line moves quickly, but still, the wait is agonizing. Out of the corner of my eye I watch Astra. She doesn't look over at me.

The foppish officer at the front of our line examines a set of permits belonging to the middle-aged couple just in front of us. "Here your name is spelled with an 'ei,'" he says, "but here, on your wife's, the name is spelled with 'ie.'"

"Yes," says the woman. "It's just a mistake, it's nothing."

The blond officer sets down his pen. He looks up at the woman. Her husband tries to hush her, to make apologies, but it's too late. The officer smiles coldly. "You presume to tell *me* whether something is important? I decide what is nothing. This, I think, is not 'nothing.'" The officer half stands and calls to the guards outside the small room, waving them over.

Now the woman is panicking. Her voice is shrill and tight with tears. "Forgive me," she begs. "I am stupid. I didn't mean to offend."

But it's too late. One of the guards crosses the room. The blond officer hands him the couple's permits and lifts his chin to indicate they are dismissed. "Inspector Cojocariu will look into this matter," he says.

The woman wails. Her husband supports her with his arm around her waist; she might collapse if not for him. They follow the guard. When they pass us, my eyes go straight to the floor. I do not want to look into their faces. I don't think I can bear to.

When it's our turn to have our permits reviewed, the blond official barely looks at them. Maybe he was satisfied with what he did to the people before us. Maybe we are just lucky. Either way, our permits are stamped. So are Astra's and Marcel's.

As soon as the permits are returned to us, we hurry away from the table and head quickly for the exit, chased by a wailing cry. I can't see the woman; the guards block the door, their bodies forming a wall. However, they can't block out her cries, her pleading, her misery. Those sounds follow us after we leave city hall. Though our permits are approved—though we are safe, today—no one feels like celebrating when we get home. Instead, drained to exhaustion, all any of us wants to do is sleep.

It's Astra's idea to scavenge the apartments that have remained empty. She suggests it to me and Marcel one night after Mama and Opa have gone to bed; she knows that Opa would never allow it, and that Mama is unable to keep a secret.

"It isn't as if we would be stealing from *people*. The people are gone. We would simply be . . . liberating their possessions." Mitzi, curled on her lap, purrs as if she agrees.

Marcel considers for a moment. "I don't know. The apartments have already been picked over. Anything of value would have been taken. Think about what this place looked like when we returned."

"What was valuable to the Romanians a month ago could be different than what we might find valuable today," Astra shoots back.

She's probably right. The people who ransacked our apartment took most of the food, but they hadn't thought to look deep in the corners of our cabinets, where Mama kept the potatoes, and so those had been left behind; they hadn't known about the stash of cigarettes Astra keeps hidden inside a carved-out book—hidden from Marcel, who has a habit of stealing them from her—so now she has nearly a pack, which she smokes as conservatively as possible.

Still, a voice is speaking in my mind. Opa's, perhaps, or the ghost I see when I look in the mirror. "We would have to keep track of what we took, and whose apartment we took it from," I say. "That way, if the families come back, we can return what we borrowed, or pay them back."

"Sure, sure," Astra says. I already know she doesn't care, or have any intention of making a record of what we take. She's Astra, after all.

But that's not why I say it. *I* will keep track. I will remember.

We sneak off together, Astra and I, the next day, when Marcel is at work, Mama is out, and Opa naps. We decide to start on the top floor and work our way down.

When I have to stop to catch my breath on the way upstairs, Astra waits, arms crossed. How is it possible that once I was a dancer, when now I can't take stairs without pausing like an old woman? That version of me is another ghost, haunting me.

When we reach the top floor, we stand very still and listen. I realize I'm sweating; nervous to be caught, nervous about the look of disappointment on Opa's face if he were to find out what I am about to do.

We hear nothing; we smell nothing. The air is frigid and still. On cat feet, Astra and I go to the first door. This apartment, I remember, was home to a spinster and her brother who left along with the Russians. I don't know who's lived here since.

Astra knocks. We wait, and then, when no one answers, she tries to turn the knob. It doesn't budge.

We won't break anything or force any locks; that, Astra promised me. So we move on to the next door, and then the third. I can tell from her look of irritation that she's regretting making the promise.

And who knows if she would have kept her word—Astra rarely does—but luckily the fourth door—an apartment which once belonged to a Jewish baker and his family—swings open.

Others have been here before us, that much is clear immediately. As with our apartment, this door was forced previously, the apartment scavenged. Furniture and shelves are torn asunder; the sideboard is bare, all the silver taken from the drawers and cabinets. A whole stack of porcelain dishes lie shattered on the parquet wood floor. I can see the arm that swept the dishes from the cabinet, shattering them for no reason other than the

295

childish pleasure of destruction.

We move carefully past the broken dishes and into the kitchen. The main reason we are here is food. I can no longer remember a time when I didn't feel the constant, dull press of hunger. And Astra's body, which has always had an angular beauty, is now more angles than beauty; following her into the kitchen, I can see the shape of her shoulder blades through the back of her sweater and the knobs of her spine up her neck.

Every cabinet is thrown open like a chorus of screaming mouths. Not a scrap of food remains. We dig through every empty cabinet, each drawer; we scan all the shelves in the pantry. But we find nothing. Not one cracker, not a single turnip.

I didn't realize that I'd been holding on to hope of finding unclaimed treasure in this apartment until our search proves fruitless. "It will be like this in all the apartments," I despair.

"Little rat tail doesn't have a bit of gumption," Astra answers, and somehow, it makes me feel better. I suppose it's nice to know that even in the midst of everything, I can rely on Astra to stay the same.

I follow her through the bedrooms. There isn't much to find, but we do take a quilt from the foot of one bed. From the bathroom, Astra extracts a bar of soap wedged beneath the sink, and a dressing gown hanging from a hook on the back of the door. It has a gold rope belt with tassels on each end. I picture the baker's wife wearing it, but while I can imagine the general shape of her—the fact that she was short, the fullness of her bosom—I can't bring her features to mind. In my imagination of her in the dressing gown, her face is a clouded-out blur. It unsettles me, that this is something I've lost.

When we leave, we pull the door closed. The door reads 4A, and I make a mental note: *Apartment 4A, the baker's family. One quilt, one bar of soap, one dressing gown.* I will write this down when we get home. And in the moment, now, it feels right—to keep track not only of what we've taken, but who is missing. Someone should write it down, some record that they were real, that they were *here*, before they blur in memory like the face of the baker's wife.

Two more locked doors and then, another open apartment with nothing of value for us to take. But as we are leaving, a stack of books on the entry hall table catches Astra's eye. She peruses them as if she were at the library, selecting two. "I haven't read these!" She sounds nearly as pleased as if she had found a can of vegetables or a sack of potatoes.

*4E,* I tell myself, *the grammar school French teacher. Two books.*

On the third floor, 3A is locked, but 3B is not, and when the knob turns, we walk in.

But this time, the apartment is not empty. There, sitting on a sofa near the window, is a girl. When we barge in, she gasps with fear, clutching at the collar of her dress. The dress hangs loosely on her thin frame, and she has no hair.

"Oh," says Astra as she and I begin to retreat, "we're so sorry for intruding—"

But the girl squints, then stops us with a word. "Rieke?"

The face is that of a stranger, but the voice belongs to— *"Esther?"*

I step closer, hesitant. The girl nods, stands.

And then I rush to her.

Astra waits as Esther and I hug, cry, hold each other at arm's length to look into one another's faces. It's still difficult for me to recognize her without her remarkable crown of hair—copper colored, thick, it had fallen in waves halfway down her back. It was forever breaking hairbands and bending hairpins, I remember. But when I speak, what I ask is, "Where

297

are your glasses?"

"They took them. Right off my face."

I don't ask who "they" are. I just hug her, again. Astra and I are thin, but Esther's body in my arms feels completely wasted, nearly a skeleton.

"I thought maybe this was your building, but I couldn't remember for sure," says Esther. "I only came here once or twice, before."

I nod. "We're on the second floor."

Ester smiles, a shy, small tilt of the mouth. She squishes up her nose as she squints at us. "We live here, too. Well, *now* we do."

I don't think I've ever seen Esther without something to read or write in, except for when she was dancing, but there's no book, no notepad, nothing at all on the table beside Esther's seat. What had she been doing before we walked in? What has she been doing since last we saw each other?

"What happened to your hair?" Astra asks.

Esther's hand reaches up and rubs across the short-shorn dark shadow. "Lice."

Both Astra and I nod. Along with rats and cockroaches and fleas, lice were a common ghetto terror. My own scalp feels itchy just thinking of them.

"Is your family with you?" I ask.

"It's just me and Conrad."

I'm flooded by a great warm rush of relief when she says Conrad's name. I let out a shaky, ragged breath.

Then Esther says, "Our parents are both dead."

"Oh, Esther." It's all I can say. Astra doesn't speak at all, she just grabs Esther in a rough hug and holds her for a long time. When she lets her go, Esther sinks back onto the sofa, and I sit next to her, taking her hand. Astra sits in a chair across from us.

A couple of minutes pass during which none of us says anything. Finally, Astra says, "Do you want to tell us what happened?"

Esther shakes her head. "It's too much." But then she tells us, anyway.

"Maybe you knew this and maybe you didn't. But our father is . . . was . . . an amputee. He lost his left leg just above the knee, in a streetcar accident when he was young. Just after he and Mama were married. She was pregnant with Conrad when it happened. He was always in a hurry, my father, and he had been running to catch the streetcar. It was pulling away and he jumped to catch it, but he slipped and fell, and his leg was mangled beneath the streetcar."

Astra makes a sympathetic sound; I picture the young man Esther describes: wearing a jaunty hat, perhaps, incautious and bold, and then, in an instant, changed forever.

"It was a terrible thing, of course, but he always said it wasn't much of a loss. He was an intellectual. Now if he'd lost his *head* in the accident!" Esther laughs a little, like it's an old family joke that she heard a thousand times and is now repeating to us.

"He lost his job at the university in 1937, along with the other Jewish professors. He made some money as a private tutor for a while, but when the Germans came, his missing leg . . . well, it suddenly mattered. He was taken during the first sweep. And our mother, you see, was very devoted to him. She loved us, of course. But never as much as she loved our father. So when he was taken, she went with him."

"She left you and your brother alone?"

Esther shakes her head. She stares again out the window, and her eyes lose their focus. Her face looks intimately bare, without her glasses. Astra and I wait for her to come back, and eventually Esther blinks, turns to us. "I don't want to talk about it anymore."

299

Astra and I nod. "Well," Astra says, "you're here now."

"Yes. I suppose that's true."

We hear movement at the door, and then in comes Conrad, his hair shorn close, too, like Esther's, his similarly beautiful copper waves gone. He's carrying a small bundle of foraged wood.

He stops short when he sees us. "Astra," he says. "Hello."

Esther's face comes to life with relief and pleasure. "Conrad, you're back!"

"Of course I am." He steps into the apartment, closes the door, and sets the wood by the fireplace. "I always come back, don't I?" Then, he turns, finally, to me. "Hello, Rieke." There, in his eyes—I see a flash of gold in them, proof of something, I don't know what.

"I'm so sorry about your parents."

Conrad's mouth tightens. He nods.

Astra stands, and so I do, too. We gather up the things we plundered from the other apartments. "Well," Astra says, "it's lovely to see you again. We'd better be getting back before our family starts to wonder where we've disappeared to."

"If you need anything," I tell them as we go toward the door, "we're in apartment 2C."

In the hallway, Astra pinches the back of my arm, hard.

"Ow!" I knock her hand away. "What did you do that for?"

"'If you need anything,'" she simpers, mocking me. "Dummy. Like we have so much to share."

"You don't *always* have to be awful, you know."

She grins, then links her arm with mine. "Sure, I do," she says. "People would be disappointed, otherwise."

I groan, and roll my eyes, but I don't pull my arm away. We go together to the staircase.

When we're back to our apartment, I realize—Conrad didn't stutter. Not one time.

The next afternoon there's a timid knock on our door, and when Opa answers it, I hear Esther's voice.

"Forgive me, Mr. Fischmann," she says. "Is Rieke home?"

We make quite a pair, Esther with her roughly shorn hair, and me with my coughing fits, which I try so hard to control. But each of us is glad for the other, and we soon find that we have more in common than dance—Esther shares my enjoyment of cards. We play hand after hand of rummy, keeping a running score on a scrap of paper. Esther is marginally craftier, but I'm luckier.

She visits regularly after that day. Each time she does, I hope Conrad will be with her, but he never is.

Having a visitor in the apartment seems to do Mama some good; though we have little to offer, she brings us cups of tea when there is tea to have, and plain hot water when that's all there is.

I've resolved not to push Esther to talk about anything that might upset her, and for a few weeks, she seems to only want to disappear into the distraction of our card game. I've gone through the building's residents in my memory and have decided that the apartment she and Conrad are staying in either belonged to a man who'd come to help us with a clogged drain a few times over the years, or to the lawyer who never smiled.

But one day, after she's won three hands in a row, Esther feels like talking, and it turns out I was right—her uncle was our building's plumber. "He was the one who told Conrad to put down 'plumber' when we went to register," Esther says, laying down the three of clubs in the discard pile.

"He said that 'musician' wouldn't qualify as essential work. And it's a good thing Conrad listened—did you know that nearly all of the plumbers in Czernowitz are Jewish? When drains started clogging and toilets started backing up, the Romanian authorities decided to listen to Mayor Popovici, who suggested that all the plumbers and their families should be spared from being deported."

"So, then, where's your uncle?" I ask Esther.

"We don't know." Her eyes drift up from her hand of cards. "We came here, thinking he'd show up, too, but he never did." She stares at nothing for several moments, and I do, too, picturing the stain on the sidewalk below the Keplers' apartment. Esther might never learn what happened to her uncle; I will never know what Ruth's poor mother wanted to say to me before she jumped.

A different day, Astra asks Esther if Conrad has a girlfriend.

Esther shakes her head no. "And anyway," she says, "what's the point of romance these days? It's not like anyone would want to bring a baby into this world."

To this, Astra answers, "One can have romance without making a baby."

This causes Esther to blush wildly and change the subject.

Once, when we're sitting around doing nothing, I make the mistake of asking Esther about her screenplay. "Did you write any more of that story you were working on? *The Hatch in the Floor*?"

Esther's mouth flattens to a line. She shakes her head. "I don't like movies anymore."

I don't bring it up again.

Now that we're home again, there's talk amongst my family as to whether

I should be taken to the hospital for an examination and testing. Opa especially wants me to go.

"There are always risks to the treatment, but they're elevated these days," Marcel says. "We're understaffed and low on supplies of every kind. The possibility of infection is high—as careful as we are, without adequate supplies, there is only so much we can do. And there's a different sort of risk—as little as a Jewish life is worth to the Nazis, the life of a Jewish *invalid* is worth much less. There haven't been any evacuations of our hospital yet, but it's happened in other places, where Jewish hospitals are cleared out."

I remember what Esther told us about her father—how, because of his missing leg, he was taken in the first sweep, to die.

"But the benefits," Astra says. "What about those?"

"Well, Astra, I'm a doctor, so of course I think the benefits are many," Marcel says with a grin. "I'd put myself out of a job, otherwise."

"What about the expense?" I ask.

Opa waves his hand, like money doesn't matter, but I know better, of course. Any money put toward treatment for me means food taken away from my family. That's just the truth of things.

"It's not inexpensive," Marcel concedes. "And you'd have to stay in the hospital for quite a while, to insure proper rest and rehabilitation."

"We'll find the money," Opa says, as if the question is settled.

But I say, "No. I don't want to go."

"Rieke," says Opa.

"I don't feel any worse than I did a month ago. I think I even feel better, just being home."

"But you can't get well without treatment," Opa says.

"You heard what Marcel said. I could get *worse* at the hospital, too.

303

And it could be dangerous even. Please, Opa. I know what I need—just to stay home, with you. To rest. If things get worse, I promise I'll go."

Opa looks from me to Marcel, his dear eyes so worried behind his glasses.

Marcel shrugs. "Normally, I'd insist that she go to the hospital, and eventually, she will need treatment. But these days—I don't know, Heinrich. It might be best to wait for a while, and hope things ease up."

Finally, Opa nods. "For now," he says.

Eagerly, I agree. "For now."

We can measure time passing by the growth of Esther's hair; by February, it begins to curl around her temples, just as coppery as I remember. By April, Esther takes to winding it around her fingers when she's been dealt a particularly good hand, a tell that wins me more than a few games of rummy.

We're hungry almost all the time, and desperately cold, but we feel reasonably safe, as long as the men in our lives remain useful to the Romanian government. Stories begin to trickle into the city about the fate others are suffering across the river, in Transnistria—a terrible typhus epidemic is killing the very old, the very young, and the weak; those left alive are slowly starving, as there's nearly no food; and no one comes to collect the dead, forcing families to live alongside the bodies of their relatives for weeks at a time.

We know how lucky we are. Even when the weather drops below freezing and my illness gets so bad that I often can't find the strength to get out of bed, even when I fall into coughing fits that last for minutes on end, even when each breath comes with a sharp pain in my right lung—even at those times I know that, compared to others, I am lucky.

One morning, after Opa has left to wait in line for bread, and Marcel has left for the hospital, and Mama and Astra have left together to try to find some fuel for cooking, I hear a knock on the door. Thinking it must be Esther coming for a hand of cards, I pull it open.

It isn't Esther. It's George Weissinger, holding two packages.

"Frederieke," he says. "Have I caught you alone?"

It's a funny way to ask if anyone else is home, but not "funny" in a way that makes me want to laugh. "Mr. Weissinger," I say, and then remember. "George. Hello! Yes, everyone else is gone—too much to do, and only a couple of hours in which to do it."

He nods and looks pointedly at my hand on the doorknob; the door is only partway open, and I'm blocking the entrance.

"Oh." I make my hand open the door the rest of the way. "Please, come in."

He shifts his bundles to one hand, takes off his hat with the other. There's a sheen of pomade in his hair, and he smells of cologne—things no one else I know has access to. And his shirt looks recently cleaned, the collar stiff with starch. Who sends their clothing out to the laundry, anymore?

He holds out his hat; I take it, place it on the little table near the door. Then he goes to the sitting area, places the packages on the coffee table. He straightens his shoulders in a way that makes it clear he'd like me to help him with his overcoat, so I come up behind him and put my hands on the shoulders, receive the coat as he shrugs out of it. It's a rain slicker, and it's damp, which means that my mother, sister, and Opa are getting drenched. Shame twists in my gut, shame that I'm inside, because of my fragile lungs, while they're out there.

"I brought a few things for you and your family." Mr. Weissinger makes himself comfortable on the sofa, pats the seat next to him. I hesitate before joining him.

"There," he says when I sit. "That's better." He flourishes his hand at the table. "Go ahead. Open them."

Each box is wrapped in brown paper and bound up with twine. I pull the first box closer and am surprised by how heavy it is. Mr. Weissinger sits forward and watches each of my movements in a way that makes me feel as if I am performing, opening the boxes for his entertainment.

Inside the box are twenty-four cans. Some are wrapped in white labels with black type; other labels are red with a mustard-yellow frame around red lettering. Canned tomato soup. Canned bouillon cubes. Tins of meat. Evaporated milk. All of the cans are labeled in German.

"Mr. Weissinger," I whisper.

"Go ahead. Open the other." He's leaning back now, pleased with himself.

Hands trembling, I reach for the second box, but I'm shaking too hard to untie the string.

Mr. Weissinger smiles; he seems to find this charming. "Here, let me." He reaches into the breast pocket of his coat and pulls out a pocket-knife. He folds it open; it's a very nice knife. There's mother-of-pearl inset along each side of the handle. The blade is clean, it opens smoothly. It cuts through the twine as easily as if it were a single hair. He refolds the knife, tucks it back into his pocket, gestures for me to continue.

I carefully wrap the twine into a little ball and press flat the plain brown paper, folding it neatly. I know that we can make use of it all, if I'm careful with it. Then I open the box. This one is full of things we haven't been able to afford in months. Three pairs of silk stockings. A case of cigarettes, the kind Astra likes. Several books—not new, but in good shape. A box of matches. Two chocolate bars.

"Frederieke," he says. "Why are you crying?"

Am I? I reach up with my trembling hand, touch my cheek, find it is wet.

"There, there," he says, and reaches again into his breast pocket, pulling out a white handkerchief, perfectly folded and pressed. He takes my chin in his hand, turns my face to his. Gently, Mr. Weissinger dabs the tears from my cheeks. Then, still holding my chin, he rotates my face slightly to the left, and then the right, and then straight again.

"Such a beautiful girl," he sighs. And then he leans in, and his lips are on mine, his teeth pressing hard against my mouth, and it's with his mouth that he pushes me back, his hand at the nape of my neck, until he's laid me down on the sofa and the weight of him is upon me.

I know immediately what he is going to do. I read Astra's *Ideal Marriage*; I know what it is that happens between a man and a woman. Except this is not *between* us.

His hand goes up under my blouse and squeezes my breast, his mouth moves from my lips to my neck, his hand leaves my breast to lift up my skirt and move my underwear aside. There are his fingers, pulling me open and pushing inside of me, and I turn my head to the coffee table, I read the labels on the cans as he takes away his hand, as he undoes his trousers, as he adjusts himself, and then thrusts his penis inside of me.

*Brüh-Würfel*
*Hähnchenfleisch*
*Alpen-Milch*
*Kondenssuppe Tomate*
*Brüh-Würfel*
*Hähnchenfleisch*

*Alpen-Milch*

*Kondenssuppe Tomate*

*Brüh-Würfel*

*Hähnchenfleisch*

*Alpen-Milch*

*Kondenssuppe Tomate*

*Brüh-Würfel*

*Hähnchenfleisch*

*Alpen-Milch*

*Kondenssuppe Tomate*

He shudders, and I close my eyes.

Finally, Mr. Weissinger lifts his weight from me. He redoes his trousers, moves to rearrange my skirt, stops when he sees a smear of blood on the inside of my thigh. He still has the handkerchief; tenderly, he blots away the blood.

"Truthfully," he says, "I'd expected that the Russians would have gotten to you first. Or, if not them, the Germans. You're really a very lucky girl, Frederieke."

I look at the table full of food and dry goods. I look at Mr. Weissinger neatly folding his handkerchief, my blood hidden now at its center, tucking it into his pocket.

"Lucky," I say. "Yes. Very."

# PART IV

# WHAT IT COSTS

May 1942–December 1942

# ONE

## RIGHT NOW

Spring comes, then summer. This remains true each year, no matter who's in charge of a country, no matter if our city sees us as citizens, or trespassers, or communists, or vermin. In May, flowers bloom, even if a man visits your home and, if he finds you alone, uses your body as he likes. In June, the sky is beautiful and the air is warm, even if one is slowly dying of an illness that never, ever goes away.

There are some things we have control over. Everything else, I suppose, we learn to bear. Or else, we die.

I do consider it, briefly. I go so far as to unclasp my locket and look down at the pill Astra gave to me. But I can't bring myself to take it. As sick as I am, as disgusted as I feel about Mr. Weissinger's visits, still—I don't want to die. I suppose Astra was right, about surviving. Most of all, it's Opa that makes me click the locket closed. The thought of him, looking down on my dead body, the way Ruth's family was made to look at hers, and then her mother's . . . that, I cannot bear.

After the third time Mr. Weissinger finds me alone, takes what he

311

likes, and leaves a box of canned goods, Astra corners me in my room.

"So," she says. "It seems we have a benefactor."

My eyes fill with tears. "I suppose we do."

She nods. Pauses, as if unsure about what to say—a rare thing, for Astra. "Look. I can stop him coming."

I look up, sharply. "How—how would you do that?"

"I could tell Marcel to have a talk with him. That would end it, I imagine."

I imagine Marcel confronting Mr. Weissinger, pushing him in the chest, yelling in his face. I imagine Mr. Weissinger stumbling, falling to the ground. And I almost cry at the thought, the relief.

But then—I remember Mama's delighted squeal when the three of them returned empty-handed from their attempt at shopping just as curfew fell to find the open box of dry goods on the coffee table. "George Weissinger is our angel! Our family's angel," Mama had cried. Opa said nothing, but the look of relief that flooded his face was enough.

The truth is, Mr. Weissinger's gifts are keeping us going. Each week brings new restrictions on our rations. Already, there isn't enough for all of us. And if my sickness gets worse, or Opa falls ill from starvation . . .

"No." The word is a whisper. I clear my throat, say it again, more forcefully. "No. Don't say anything, Astra. I can handle it."

There's a storm in my sister's face. I can see it; I see the battle waging inside her. But after a moment, the storm passes.

"Sometimes we choose between bad, and worse," she says.

I nod.

"Not everyone is strong, you know. Some people—like Opa—they can't make choices like this. They throw out bad and worse and for what? For honor?"

The way she says the word—*honor*—makes it clear what she thinks of the concept.

I nod again. "I know. Just—please. Promise me you won't tell Opa." My voice cracks. I look up at her; she's a blur, through a scrim of tears.

"Of course not," she answers. And she leaves me alone.

The truth is—things can always be worse. I keep learning this lesson, again and again and again.

I learn it once more, on a Saturday night in July.

It's well after midnight when there is a fierce banging on our apartment door. I sit straight up in bed with a gasp that sends me into a fit of coughing that paralyzes me.

"Open up," shouts a man's voice. "Military business."

Moonlight spills through my doorway. When I finally stifle my coughing, I gingerly step out of bed into the light, and follow the moonbeam.

Everyone else is already in the front room. It's Marcel who opens the door, motioning for the rest of us to step back.

Three German soldiers, so similar in build and expression as to be nearly indistinguishable, fill the doorway.

"Mr. Fischer?" demands the man in the middle.

Marcel shakes his head. "No. I'm Goldmann—Dr. Goldmann."

The man on the left holds a rifle across his chest, and with its barrel he pushes Marcel aside so he can peer around him at the rest of us. "Which of you is Mr. Fischer?"

"None of us," Marcel says. "We are Goldmann, Teitler, and Fischmann."

"Fischmann, Fischer, what's the difference?" the third military man

313

says. "Give us those named Fischmann, then."

Opa steps forward. "I am—"

"The Fischers live across the hall, two doors down," Astra interrupts him. "The whole family."

"Astra!" Opa shouts, silencing her.

The soldiers look between themselves, questioningly.

Opa steps forward again. "My name is Fischmann. I am old, my life is nearly over. The Fischers—they are young. They've lost so much already. Take me. You said yourself—Fischmann, Fischer, what's the difference?"

The uniformed men look at Opa. All of them do. My dear opa, I can see how frightened he is. The way he has his hands at his sides, the way they tremble. Selfishly, I pray—*Please. Not Opa.*

Then one of the soldiers laughs. Then, the others do. Three of them, three Nazis, laughing at my grandfather in his own house.

The man in the middle stops laughing first, wiping his eyes as if Opa has told a joke so funny that it brought him to tears. "We may be back," he says, and they leave.

Marcel shuts the door softly.

We hear footsteps moving down the hall, a moment of silence, and then, banging, again. "Fischer! Open up!"

Opa reaches for the door, but Marcel blocks him, shakes his head. "I'm sorry, old man." Opa does look old, never has he looked older than he does now, as we stand in our living room, imagining what's happening down the hall: Mr. Fischer, in his summer pajamas, stumbling to the door. Mrs. Fischer clutching closed her robe, peering from the doorway of the bedroom. The trio of military men entering, demanding, their loud voices waking young Sylvie, who starts to cry. Mrs. Fischer, ducking into the nursery to tend to her.

That much, I can envision. What will happen next will depend on what the men want. Are they there because Mr. Fischer has committed some minor infraction, something forgivable? If so, perhaps they'll demand a bribe. If Mr. Fischer has done something worse, or if they feel in the mood for violence . . . well, then, worse things will happen.

I close my eyes as if I can keep myself from seeing what might happen to our neighbors. The visions continue behind my eyelids. A guard slamming the butt of his rifle into Mr. Fischer's temple. Mr. Fischer falling, unconscious before he hits the ground, unable to break his fall. His head hitting the sharp corner of the coffee table, splitting open. His blood, spilling on the floor; Mrs. Fischer running into the room, screaming, crouching down, the trim of her dressing gown soaking up her husband's blood.

I open my eyes to banish the vision, and I see on the others' faces that each of us is imagining our own horrors. Marcel still blocks the door.

Now, I wait to hear a gunshot. But no shots come. Outside our apartment, all seems so quiet that it's almost possible to imagine that the whole thing has been a hallucination, that perhaps we dreamed the whole thing, until we hear the pounding of military boots coming back up the hallway, toward our door . . . and then, mercifully, past it. I think I hear someone cry out, or maybe it's a cat yowling on the street. The footsteps fade to nothing. Still, Marcel blocks the door.

"Back to bed, everyone," he says, but we go to the front window instead, all of us.

There's a military truck parked in the middle of the street. It has an open back, and in the moonlight, I can see several people sitting in it, along with awkward shapes of hastily packed bags.

The Nazis exit our building. Following them is Mr. Fischer, and Mrs.

Fischer, and young Sylvie, too, in her arms. None of them—thank God— looks harmed.

One of the men opens the back of the truck. Mrs. Fischer hands Sylvie to her husband, then climbs up. Mr. Fischer gives her back their daughter, then a couple of bags, and then he clambers in alongside his family.

The engine rumbles to life and the truck rolls away. Then, it's gone.

My body doesn't know how to feel everything at the same time—desperate sadness, the horror and shock of the Fischers being taken away, and relief, too, that Opa is still here. The diaphanous curtains tremble. I watch them move, and I don't go back to bed for a long time.

In the morning, we sit together in the kitchen. There's gruel for breakfast, and water to drink. We've eaten through the last of the food Mr. Weissinger brought us—we shared with Esther and Conrad, and the Fischers, too, so the food went quickly, in spite of our rationing. Astra's hand feeds Mitzi little bites of herring that she's saved back from her own portion of dinner last night.

The mood in the kitchen doesn't match the warmth of the morning sun. And I can tell from the particular silence between them that Astra and Marcel have been fighting.

"One of us had to be man enough to say it," Astra says. Mitzi's sharp teeth and little barbed pink tongue take another bit of fish from her fingers.

"'Man enough,'" Marcel repeats with a shake of his head.

I know what they're talking about. But I don't know how to *feel* about it. There was a moment when those men were ready to take Opa away. They would have loaded him into that truck; they would have driven off with him, and not the Fischers.

It isn't *better* that the Fischer family has been taken. There is no *good*, or *better*. Only terrible, or worse.

"Anyway, we don't know that anything happened to them, not really." She's given Mitzi all the food she had left, and now she turns her attention to picking through her coat, looking for fleas. It's a nauseating thing to do, right here at the kitchen table.

"There were other people in that truck," I say, though my whole family saw it, too.

Marcel nods. "The deportations are starting again." He takes the last sip of his coffee—or what we pass as coffee these days, a weak brew of hot water with thrice-used grounds. He stands. "I'll see what I can find out at the hospital. But you all had better pack a rucksack in case they come back tonight, so we're not sent to Transnistria with nothing."

We spend most of the day combing through our meager belongings, finding both our warmest clothing as well as anything that we might be able to trade for food or use for bribes.

Astra is in a truly rotten mood, worrying about what will happen to Mitzi if we're taken away. Finally, she decides to see if Esther and Conrad will take care of the cat if anything happens to us.

She drags me along with her.

Conrad answers the door, and maybe he knows Astra better than I thought he did, because rather than inviting us in, he asks her what she wants.

"Is it that obvious?" Astra asks.

Conrad says nothing, which seems to surprise Astra, an unusual thing. She takes half a step back before she begins to explain what she's come about.

Esther joins her brother at the door; when Astra has finished trying to convince them that they should take Mitzi in if anything happens to us, Esther says, "What would we feed her?"

Conrad is less accommodating. He says bluntly, "We're not taking care of a cat, Astra. You should put her out on the street. She'd have better luck hunting rats in the alleys, anyway. You'd be doing her a favor."

Astra's face tightens. I know Conrad is wasting his breath; there's no way she will throw that cat outside.

There was a time when Conrad would have done anything for Astra, even after she left him on the steps of the concert hall, even after she married Marcel. But Conrad has changed. Astra has run out of favors.

"*Anyway.*" Astra ignores Conrad and speaks only to Esther. "We don't know why they came for the Fischers. But we're packing up in case they return tonight, and you should, too."

Esther's eyes pool with tears. "Thank you, Astra," Conrad says, and then he shuts the door.

I don't think anyone in my family sleeps that night. I lie awake until nearly dawn, staring up at the ceiling and waiting for the sound of a hand on the door.

I wake to full light, and I get dressed quickly—or as quickly as I can, these days. There's nothing for breakfast, but that's all right, as I don't have an appetite. I drink some water and then take myself upstairs, to make sure Esther and Conrad are okay, too.

Conrad cracks the door. "Hey, Rieke. Esther's resting right now. She didn't sleep. Nightmares." He opens it wider. "You can come in, if you want."

The apartment is frigid. Even wood is precious, so when Conrad places some scraps in the fireplace along with strips of newspaper for kindling, I am grateful. They've pulled their worn duvet close to the hearth, and I sit down as Conrad builds the fire. It comes alive with a crackle,

318

orange flames licking the wood.

He sits beside me. I glance over at his profile, and for a moment it's as if we're back at Madame Lucia's studio, him seated at the piano and me at the barre, waiting for the first note. Then he looks at me, his gold-flecked eyes illuminated by the fire. I see that his lips are soft and kind. I see his goodness.

"Do you remember all those days you played for us, while we danced?" I ask.

"Sure," he says. "Of course."

"And then," I continue, "the time you saved my opa and Marcel. Even after the way Astra treated you."

He raises his shoulders, drops them. "None of that matters anymore."

I don't know what he means—if it doesn't matter anymore how he felt about Astra and how she treated him, or if it doesn't matter that he played for us, or that once he saved my family. If he means that nothing matters, anymore, at all.

For once, I allow myself to study his face without glancing quickly away. All the things I felt about him, from another lifetime, spring to life, like the flames in the hearth. Maybe it's the glow of the fire. Maybe it's Astra, or the absence of her. Maybe it's my own desire to know something of love—not what has happened with Mr. Weissinger, for that isn't love—before it's too late.

I don't want to think about Mr. Weissinger. I don't want him here in the room with us. And it's a skill I've begun to develop—to take something ugly, set it behind a door, and close it. I remember the name of Esther's long-ago screenplay, the one she never finished: *The Hatch in the Floor.*

Maybe each of us has a hidden hatch behind which we set our secrets, the things we can't stand to have out in plain sight.

319

Conrad's hand is on the cushion. I look at his long fingers; once, they flew across the keys with such precision, such grace. His nails are dirty now, his fingers stained with soot. Calluses. A scar across the back of one hand. My fingers ache to touch it. And so, I do—I lay my hand, trembling, atop his.

I clear my throat, but I don't know what to say. How is someone who feels the way I feel right now supposed to speak? "We could . . . do something, if you want. I wouldn't mind." I don't have the courage to look up from our hands, mine atop his, on the cushion. Then, he spreads apart his fingers so mine can fit between them. Slowly, my fingers nest into the openings he makes for me. At first his fingers are warm and mine are cold, but soon I can't tell the difference between his flesh and mine.

So much time passes that finally I look at Conrad's face. Tears brim in his eyes, streak his cheeks, yet he cries without making a sound.

At last, he clears his throat. "I'd like to hold you," he says. "If that's all right."

I nod. He opens his arms, and I move close to him, tucking my feet beneath me. I feel the weight of his right arm around my shoulders and the line of his leg against mine. After a moment, I rest my cheek against his chest. His woolen sweater is scratchy, but I don't mind.

His arms circle me. Our bodies fit one against the other. I feel his warmth and his rib cage. I am aware that he is a skeleton inside a sheen of flesh, and that I am, too. I am aware of the sound of each breath he draws, and the rattle in my chest that is always there, keeping me from ever filling my lungs completely.

The fire is so warm, and I allow my eyes to close.

Thump *thump*, goes his heart against my ear. Thump *thump*.

We are two bodies, alive right now, together.

# TWO

# PAYMENT IN ADVANCE

The soldiers return on Saturday.

I don't think any of us slept more than an hour or two at a time all week long. Marcel told us that the night they came for the Fischers, over two thousand people were taken from their homes in the middle of the night. Jews from all over the city—young and old, poor and well-off alike. There were many places where, as in our building, one family was taken while a family just next door was not. There must be a reason for this, but we don't know what it is. Wild rumors fly, but that's all they are . . . rumors.

We've known it could be any of us taken next, at any time. If we've been lulled into a feeling of security over these past months, it's gone now. And anyway, whether consciously or unconsciously, we have been waiting for their return.

So when, on Saturday, in the deep velvet of the midnight hour, there comes the rumble of a truck on the street below, we all come from our rooms to gather together on the sofa.

The moon is gone, and no one moves to light the kerosene lamp. We sit in darkness and wait. When we hear the boots in the hallway, Astra hisses, "We should have gone somewhere. What are we *doing* here?"

Mama and Opa hush her. Likely because they're thinking the same thing I am, that we know why we're still here. It's because of me.

Just moving from one room to another winds me, now. Each time I cough, I feel myself drowning in my own lungs. Often, there is blood. If they come for us tonight, if they find us in our apartment, it will be my fault.

I blink into the darkness, suddenly desperate to see my family's faces. I want to tell them how sorry I am. I want to tell them that they should have left me and gone somewhere, anywhere.

There is the thump of footfalls in the hallway. We hear someone cry out, the sound of a body falling. We sit in the dark and clutch one another's hands, waiting for the pounding on our door that we know will come. All our belongings are lined up near the front door, side by side by side, as we are.

But the knock never comes. The sounds in the hallway die down and fade away; the night grows quiet. Still, we sit on the couch together. Still, we wait.

It's Astra who finally speaks, near sunrise. "They would have come by now if they were coming, and I need to piss." She stands. Mitzi, who has been curled in her lap, gives a meowl of displeasure about being displaced.

"She's probably right." Marcel stands, too, and goes to the window. He lifts the sheet we've hung for a curtain. Pink light filters in, making everything prettier than it has any right to be.

Opa gets up, stiffly. He puts his hand, heavy and warm, on the top of my head.

322

When Astra comes out of the bathroom, I say, "We should check on Conrad and Esther."

"You stay here," she says, heading straight for the front door. "I'll go."

"You're not going anywhere," Marcel says, but Astra just laughs and goes out, as she pleases.

Grumbling, Marcel follows.

In my head, I see Esther's shorn copper hair, the way it's started to curl again. On my cheek, I feel the press of Conrad's sweater. I haven't told anyone about that moment, about how it felt to me. Seconds pass like hours, and it's only by the pressure on my weak lungs that I know that I'm holding my breath.

When Astra and Marcel return, I see the hunch in Astra's shoulders, the hardness in her eyes, and I know immediately what they found. A high, sharp ringing fills my brain and I pull myself to standing. "Don't say it!" I scream the words, trying to hear myself over the ringing in my head. "Don't say it!"

Astra's eyebrows shoot up in surprise. She doesn't spare me, not a moment. "They're gone." She is ruthless. "Both of them."

Then she slumps into the chair by the window. "Gone," she says, again.

The next day, when Marcel comes home from the hospital, he tells us what he's learned about who was selected, and why we were spared. "They took everyone with a permit signed by Mayor Popovici. There's a new mayor now, and the Popovici permits are no longer valid. The government felt that Popovici was too easy on the Jewish people."

"Too easy," Opa says.

Our family's permits were issued by the governor rather than Mayor

Popovici. That's why we're still here, and the Fischers and Esther and Conrad are gone. Just a different signature. That's all that separates us from them.

I hate that word—luck. I hate it.

News trickles in over the next days and weeks: the holders of Popovici permits have been taken to the Maccabi-Platz stadium for processing. Then, to the station. There, they are packed into those train cars meant not for people but for cattle. And then, deportation. Taken farther away even than Transnistria, beyond the Bug River. Over four thousand people.

Forced into slave labor.

Starved.

Frozen.

Shot when they were too weak to work.

Wasted by typhoid fever.

Dead.

Dead.

Dead.

And even though, as summer fades into autumn, I continue to be visited by George Weissinger, and even though, as the sky fills with clouds and rain and sleet as autumn becomes winter, even though my hair begins to fall out—maybe from illness, maybe from despair—even still, I am lucky.

This is what fortune looks like, now. I stand in front of Mama's cracked mirror, my face broken by it, the brush in my hand full of hair. And I remember Esther, how she was cleverer than I at cards, but that what matters more than cleverness, it turns out, is luck. The hand one is dealt, the card, facedown, on the top of the pile, when you happen to be the one reaching for it.

I know how sick I've become when, in early December, Astra starts being nice to me.

"Cut it out," I say when she brings a cup of hot water to my bedside, which makes her laugh.

"I could spill it down your front if you'd prefer," she says.

One morning, I wake to find Opa standing beside my bed, looking down at me. When I open my eyes, he sniffs and looks away, but not before I see the tears he tries to hide.

So when Marcel says that it's time for us to find a way to get me treatment, I agree. I have to live. For Opa.

"Until now," says Marcel, "the risk of taking you to the hospital outweighed the risk of keeping you home. But the scales have tipped. Without treatment, I don't think you will recover."

He turns to Opa. "Heinrich, do you have anything left to sell?"

Opa clears his throat. "We'll manage," he says. But I know that we have practically nothing; we've been living on Marcel's small salary, slashed by the current government to even less than he made under Soviet rule.

I know what a hardship this will be.

Marcel and Opa leave my room, murmuring to each other about finances. It's just me and Astra, then. She stands in the far corner, half in shadow, leaning against the wall. She looks too skinny, of course, but beautiful still. Her slippered feet are angled slightly out, as if she's ready to perform.

"We don't have any money," I whisper, my eyes on her feet.

"But," says Astra, "we know someone who does."

Slowly, I raise my eyes to her long thin legs, draped in the dressing gown we pilfered from the fourth-floor apartment, then across the concavity of her hips, up over the swelling of her breasts, to the sharp ridge of her collarbone, resting, at last, on her face. She's staring right back at me.

I have thought already about what she's suggesting. About the man she wants me to ask.

Astra's face shadows with empathy, and I remember the day I saw her sitting naked in the bathtub, Mama running a washcloth down her back. The soft splash of the washcloth dipping into the water. Astra's broken sobs.

Her face blurs. I blink, and the tears spill, and her face is clear again.

She's rearranging her face, now—the terrible empathy is gone, replaced by cold disaffection. I know she's reshaped her expression as a gift to me. Then: "You've paid in advance for anything Mr. Weissinger gives you. You might not have wanted to, but you paid. That's the truth."

I open and close my mouth. No words come out. Then, I nod.

She nods back, pushes off from the wall, and leaves the room.

The next time Mr. Weissinger visits, I tell him I need to go to the hospital and that we have no money to pay for it.

Gracefully, he insists on covering the bills. Smoothly, he handles the details.

All I have to do is—accept.

That is what Opa must do, as well. He must accept that I have gone behind his back, asking Mr. Weissinger to provide for me when he could not. He must accept the largesse of a man he does not trust. I believe it hurts him as deeply as it hurts me.

"People will wound you. Strangers. Your own family, too."

I have wounded my Opa. But wounding him is better than allowing

326

him to starve, to save my life.

There comes a snowstorm, nearly three days during which there's no chance of taking me to the hospital. I spend them in bed, sleeping as much as possible, trying not to think about what I've accepted.

When the weather breaks, Mr. Weissinger arrives in a car he borrowed from "a friend." Marcel holds my arm and leads me down to the street. Mama follows, carrying my suitcase, and Astra and Opa come down, too.

Mr. Weissinger is wearing a new hat, and he's dressed in a suit and tie. Unlike us, he looks like he's been eating plenty. He has a friend who can loan him a car, he's even wearing a new hat.

Opa takes George Weissinger's hand in both of his. "I owe you a debt I cannot repay," he says. He brings Mr. Weissinger's hand to his face, and kisses it.

Astra catches my eye. She knows what I am thinking—that Opa can never know what Mr. Weissinger has done to me. She nods once quickly, then takes Opa's arm. "Come on," she says to him. "Let's let them get going."

My family loads me into the backseat of the car, and it's decided that Marcel will ride along to help get me settled.

It happens so quickly. Before I know it, I've been passed into the car, my bag has been slammed into the trunk, and Mr. Weissinger and Marcel have climbed into the front.

Mama kisses me, wailing, and then Opa kisses each of my cheeks.

Last of all, Astra leans in to kiss me goodbye. I don't know why, but it's saying farewell to her that breaks me, and I collapse into tears.

"You'll be fine." Astra extracts herself from the tangle of my arms. "Chin up, rat tail." Then she closes the door, and Mr. Weissinger steps on the gas, and we are off.

I twist back to look at the three of them—Opa, Mama, Astra. Then I turn forward again and lean my head against the seat. I shut my eyes, and hot tears leak down my cheeks.

At the hospital, Mr. Weissinger takes charge. He leads me to a wheelchair and sits me in it. He gives instructions to the nurse, who looks about Astra's age, to put me in a private room and to spare no expense in my care. With that, he leaves to park the car.

The nurse waits until he's gone before she laughs. "Private room!" she says, shaking her head, as she wheels me down a hallway. She delivers me into a room with three beds. "This is the TB room."

Two of the beds are occupied: in the far one lies a woman about as old as Mama, asleep with her face turned toward the window; in the near one is a girl about my age, sitting up and thumbing through a magazine.

The nurse who pushed my wheelchair—Nurse Ruby, she tells me—helps me out of my clothes and into a hospital gown, doing up the ties for me. "Do you have any valuables?" she asks.

I shake my head no. The only thing of value I own is my locket, but I've left it at home, rolled into a sock in the back of my dresser drawer. Nurse Ruby tucks me into bed and even brings me an extra blanket when she sees I'm shivering. She's wearing a gold cross on a chain around her neck, though she looks Jewish to me.

Marcel has put on a white coat; he comes into the room with a medical chart and another doctor whom he introduces as Dr. Kessler.

"We'll need to get an X-ray," Marcel says to Dr. Kessler, who nods.

It's interesting to see Marcel transform into a doctor; I've seen him as a playboy at the gambling table and on the dance floor, and I've seen him in pajamas and his robe at home. I've seen him trudging through the ghetto, overburdened by worries and our few possessions. But this is new, to see him here, like this.

"Lean forward, dear." Dr. Kessler fits in the earpieces of a stethoscope. His hands, at least, are warm. "Breathe deeply."

I try, but I can only take half breaths without dissolving into a coughing fit.

Mr. Weissinger has found our room. He stands in the doorway, holding his hat, watching.

"Mm-hm," Dr. Kessler says. Then, to Marcel, "The right lung sounds much worse than the left."

"Do you think an artificial pneumothorax is our best option?"

"Mmm," says Dr. Kessler. "Let's test, and get that X-ray, and then we'll see." He strings the stethoscope around his neck and pats me through the blankets, on my knee. "Get some rest."

Then he leaves, and Marcel follows. Mr. Weissinger crosses the room to stand at the side of my bed. One of his hands reaches out to take mine. His fingers, too, are warm. Everyone is warmer than me.

Still holding my hand, Mr. Weissinger leans down to kiss my forehead. I shiver. "You're so cold," he murmurs into my hair. "I'll see if I can get you another blanket."

I close my eyes, and when Mr. Weissinger returns a few minutes later, I keep them closed, pretending to be asleep, hoping he'll leave. He spreads the blanket across me and tucks it tightly around my legs. Then I feel him sit on the edge of the bed.

I open my eyes. Mr. Weissinger is watching me.

"Listen," he says. "All you need to do is get well, all right? I'm going to go out of town for a while. There's been some trouble with a loan I made—nothing for you to worry about. I don't know how long I'll be gone. But when I return, and you're recovered from all this, then we'll talk about getting married."

I go cold, much colder than I was a moment ago. I open my mouth, but nothing comes out.

"It will have to be a civil ceremony, of course, but that's better than nothing. I don't have a ring for you yet." He leans in close. I'm afraid he's going to kiss me on the mouth, and I brace myself. But instead, he kisses my eyelids—first the right, then the left. "It'll be a long while before I'm back. A year, maybe more, hopefully less. But when I am, we'll set it all to rights."

Still, I am unable to speak, but Mr. Weissinger doesn't seem to need me to say anything at all.

Only then does he kiss me on the mouth, one of his hands cupping the back of my neck, holding me close.

At last, he leaves. I fall back against my pillow. *That didn't happen,* I tell myself.

The girl who has been reading the magazine lowers it and says, "Say, that's the first proposal I've ever seen!"

I'm in no mood to answer, so I don't. I just close my eyes.

In my head are voices. Opa's: *"It's better not to owe anything to a man like George Weissinger. When he collects, he always makes sure to make interest."*

And Astra's: *"You've paid in advance for anything Mr. Weissinger gives you. You might not have wanted to, but you paid."*

330

# THREE

## TREATMENT

Some time later, Nurse Ruby rolls a cart into the room. "Mealtime," she says, taking a tray from the cart and arranging it on a little table with wheels that she pushes to my bed. She does the same for the other two patients.

The woman who was sleeping wakes up now, adjusts herself upright with pillows, and pats her hair. When she notices me, she nods politely and smiles.

"After lunch, we'll go over all the rules and regulations," Nurse Ruby says to me. "For now, the most important things are that you should keep talking to a bare minimum and that you need to try to control your cough." With that, she leaves.

The girl my age, the one who witnessed my "engagement," turns to me. "We're lucky to have Nurse Ruby today. The other nurse is way meaner." She speaks in a stage whisper that seems to require even more effort than a normal voice. "I'm Dotti. What's your name?"

"Frederieke. Nice to meet you."

"That's Mrs. Silver." Dotti nods at the older lady, who raises her fork in greeting. "She's really good about following the rules. You won't get a word out of her. Trust me!"

Dotti seems like a fine girl, but I'm not really in the mood to be friendly, and anyway, I don't want to get in trouble. So I smile, and then busy myself with my lunch tray. It's more food than I've seen in one sitting in I don't even know how long: a small piece of baked chicken, some sliced potatoes, a ramekin of what looks to be lime gelatin. I cut into the chicken and take a small bite. It is warm and moist. I close my eyes and chew.

I must have fallen asleep in the middle of my meal, for when I wake, the light in the room has shifted, and my tray is gone. Mrs. Silver appears to be writing a letter; Dotti is engrossed with her magazine, again. I sit quietly. I have nothing to do and anyway I don't want to do anything.

Soon, a nurse comes in. It isn't Ruby; this nurse, though about the same age, has the pursed, grim expression of someone who's been alive for at least a hundred years.

"Fresh meat," she says when she sees me, smiling. "I'm Nurse Rachel. I'm here to tell you all the rules."

It turns out that Nurse Rachel used to work in a sanatorium in the countryside. That's why she survived the slaughter that happened in her village—her entire family was killed when the Germans trooped through on their way to Czernowitz. "And our neighbors, too, of course, and all the Roma, as well." She reports this flatly in response to my simple question of how long she's worked at this hospital. I resolve not to ask more questions.

"I'm sorry," I say.

She shrugs and hangs a paper bag from a hook on the edge of my bedside tray. "This is for used napkins. No coughing, spitting, or blowing your nose into handkerchiefs, or your sleeve, or the sheets. Only paper napkins."

I nod.

"If this were a proper sanatorium, we'd keep you here for months, or even years," Nurse Rachel says. "As it is, I have no control over what the doctors decide. Patients come and go at an alarming rate." She speaks as if the only thing that matters to her is running a proper ward, as if the fact that we are all Jews living among people who seem to wish us dead is none of her concern, even though she's Jewish, too. I admire her single-mindedness, as crazy as it seems to me.

She sets a small stack of paper napkins on the table, pulled from a supply drawer on the far wall. She also brings over a cup. "Always cover your cough. And this cup is for your sputum. The doctor will test it to confirm a diagnosis of tuberculosis. Tomorrow morning, first thing, you will collect a sample. You'll breathe in deeply, like this—" Nurse Rachel fills her chest with air, her cheeks comically full, then she releases it. "Hold the breath for five seconds or more if you can. Then release. You'll cough, of course, and sputum will be forced up from your lungs. Spit it into this cup and repeat the procedure until you have collected enough to reach this line." She indicates a faint line on the cup.

Her description of the procedure is nauseating, but I listen and nod.

"Don't collect saliva. Saliva is thin and mostly clear, and it's no good for the test. What we want is the thick, sticky stuff from your lungs. Okay?"

"Okay," I say, though my stomach is turning. Absolutely disgusting.

"Other than the sputum collection and remembering to always cover your cough—and also, to try not to cough, in the first place—your main job is to rest. The doctor will order an X-ray, and we will see what happens from there."

That night, I barely sleep. The room echoes with the coughs of my roommates, and mine, too. Is this what it was like for my family, being jolted awake every two minutes? Maybe they are glad to have me gone. Maybe they'll sleep soundly for a change.

I indulge in self-pity for a while. I roll this way and that.

Then: "Lie still, won't you?" calls Mrs. Silver, angrily. It's the first time I've heard her voice.

In the morning, I follow Nurse Rachel's disgusting instructions and fill the cup up as best I can. When Nurse Ruby comes to drop off our breakfast trays, she takes a look at the cup. "Excellent," she says. I feel, ridiculously, proud of myself.

Breakfast is oatmeal with real cream and a little ramekin of brown sugar, a soft-boiled egg, a piece of buttered toast—*butter*, not margarine—and black tea. I try to eat it all, but it's impossible, and I feel ashamed of myself. I lie back against the pillow and try to catch my breath, worn out from the activity of eating. I know how hungry my family must be, and here I am unable to clear my plate.

Then it's time for my X-ray.

"It's just like having your photograph taken," Nurse Ruby assures me when I tell her I've never had an X-ray before. Maybe the photographs she takes are different than the ones I have taken, for I've never stripped naked to the waist to pose for a picture before. Everyone in the room—the nurse and the X-ray technician, a young redheaded man—act like there's nothing out of the ordinary about my bare chest as they help me from the wheelchair and out of the hospital gown, so I try to pretend I feel the same. But truthfully, it is terribly embarrassing.

The X-ray technician stands me in front of a black glass panel, then pushes a smaller frame of whitish glass against my chest. It's cold, and I wince, but no one seems to notice.

Other than that, it is just like a photograph. It doesn't hurt a bit, and as soon as the image is taken, Nurse Rachel helps me back into the top portion of my gown and redoes the ties. Then she sits me in the wheelchair and pushes me into Dr. Kessler's office.

I wait with my hands in my lap. There's a framed photograph on the doctor's desk of a woman with a small child. It looks like it was taken a long time ago.

Finally, Dr. Kessler comes in.

"Hello, Frederieke," he says. Then he proceeds to tell me the results of my sputum test and X-ray.

I had known, surely, exactly what was wrong with me. Still, when he tells me that I've officially been diagnosed with tuberculosis, my heart still beats faster.

He tells me about the treatment he recommends. But though I hear the words, their meaning doesn't seem to sink in, through the panic.

I live in my body. I know how sick I am, how sick I've been for more than a year now. But as soon as Dr. Kessler confirms it, I'm terrified of losing my life. It's a strange thing, the reflex to fight death, or illness. The fear, when a man in a white coat shows you a photograph of the inside of your body, points out the cloudy gray shadow, explains with technical terms the disgusting sticky fluid produced by your own body, collected by your own hand. Well, who can explain such a thing?

When I come back to myself, Dr. Kessler is saying, "We'll begin by giving you an artificial pneumothorax."

"What's that?"

"It is the clinical term for a procedure that will help your lung to rest.

335

We use a needle to penetrate into your chest cavity—not your lung itself—and then we let in air, forcing your lung to collapse."

"How will I breathe, then, if you collapse my lung?"

"You have two lungs, Frederieke. The left is mostly healthy. It's the right that needs the rest. Any other questions?"

He pokes his head into the hallway and calls for Nurse Ruby.

"We'll schedule the first treatment for tomorrow afternoon." And with that, I'm rolled away.


More meals follow—lunch, then dinner. Each time a tray is deposited at my bedside, I continue to feel tremendously guilty. I do my best to eat every bite. My stomach distends like Mitzi's did, after her feast of mice.

When the lights go out and the night nurse has done her last round, Dotti seems in the mood for a chat. Either Mrs. Silver is already asleep, or she's ignoring us, for she doesn't complain.

"That fellow of yours is quite a bit older than you," Dotti says. "I suppose that's not a bad thing. It's better to have an older man who can take care of you than a young one who knows how to sweep you off your feet but not how to bear your weight." She says it like it's something she's heard before rather than like it's an original thought of her own.

"Mm-hm." I have no interest in discussing Mr. Weissinger with Dotti, or anyone else.

"I've never had a boyfriend." Dotti sighs. "You're awfully lucky."

There's that word again. "I suppose we're both lucky, to be getting treatment," I answer.

"Sure, sure," says Dotti. "So lucky."

She's quiet then, and after a minute, I think she must have gone to sleep. I almost have, too, when she speaks again.

"If we're so *lucky*," she says, her voice dripping with bitterness, "then why did we get sick in the first place, hmm? And why were we born in a country that hates us so much? What do you say to that?"

I don't have anything to say to that. Not really. I've thought the same things myself.

"Maybe everyone is both lucky and unlucky," I say, quietly. "Maybe it's like one of those scales, where things have to balance out. Luck on one side. Misfortune on the other. Maybe the best we can hope for is that the scales balance—that the unlucky side doesn't get so heavy that the scales break, and it can't be balanced again."

I can practically hear Dotti thinking this over. At last, she says, "Maybe."

Then she does fall asleep. I lie there for a while longer, wondering if I believe what I said to Dotti, or if I only said it to make her feel better. It's a nice thing to imagine—that there's a big scale somewhere, and that there's someone operating it, like God, keeping an eye on us and trying to help balance things out.

The best I can think, as I lie there in the dark, is that I *want* it to be true.

The next thing I know, it's morning, and Nurse Ruby is there to take me for the procedure Dr. Kessler described.

After helping me go to the bathroom and even running a comb through my hair, she settles me into a wheelchair and tucks a blanket around my legs. The gold cross she wears on a chain is right at my eye level, and I can't help but comment.

"You wear a cross."

She nods. "It was my mother's idea. She took me and my brother to

337

be baptized." Standing, she shrugs. "I don't think it will change anything. A Jew is a Jew, to those who hate us. But it makes our mother feel better."

Then she takes the handles of the wheelchair, and we're off. Truthfully, I am terrified. But Nurse Ruby told me the X-ray would be okay, and it was, so I trust her.

"Will this hurt?"

There's a pause before she answers. "It won't be pleasant. Usually there's anesthetic to numb you for the pain. But it's all been taken for the other hospital."

"The other hospital?"

"The non-Jewish hospital." Though she tries to keep her voice even, I hear the bitterness. But then she says, "Dr. Kessler will be as quick and as gentle with you as possible. And I'll stay with you the whole time."

Then we're at the surgical room. Nurse Ruby wheels me in, helps me unfasten the ties on my gown, and helps me up onto the operating table. The room is exceptionally cold, which sets me to shivering violently. Maybe it's not just the cold.

Nurse Ruby lays me on my left side and lifts my right arm up over my head. Then she takes a small paintbrush and wipes some foul-smelling liquid all over my right side. My nipples pucker with the cold. There's a machine, just near the table I'm on, with two glass canisters, and rubber tubes going in and out of them. At the other end of one of the rubber tubes is a long silver needle, with a plunger. I close my eyes and try to pretend there is nothing there.

Then Dr. Kessler comes in. He's wearing a different white coat than he was yesterday; this one buttons up all the way to his chin, and he has on rubber gloves. And behind him comes another doctor—Marcel.

Before I can think, tears have sprung to my eyes. Who would have thought that I could ever be this glad to see *Marcel*? It hardly even bothers me that he's seeing me without a shirt.

He drops me a little wink when he catches my eye, a half smile. I smile back. No matter how I've felt about him, he is my family. And now I'm not entirely alone.

"All right, my dear," says Dr. Kessler. "I wish I could tell you this will be painless, but the best I can say is that it will help treat your illness, at long last. Dr. Goldmann here tells me you're a brave girl, so that's good. Are you ready?"

Of course I'm not ready. Still, I nod.

"Hold her arm, Nurse." Nurse Ruby takes hold of my wrist, firmly. Then the doctor says, "Scream if you must, but don't squirm. Understood?" He looks very seriously into my eyes. I nod again.

I will not move.

"Dr. Goldmann, her legs." Marcel comes over and puts one hand on my hip, the other on my thigh just above my knee. Between him and Nurse Ruby, I feel pinned, like a moth on a velvet bed.

Dr Kessler takes up the long silver needle. I want to close my eyes, but I feel hypnotized by the sight of the thing he's going to put inside me. I can't look away as he comes nearer, as he puts one rubbery hand on my side and feels around for the spot between my ribs, as he touches the point of the needle to my skin.

I can't see his hands. I stare instead at the hairs sprouting from his nostrils. They're mostly black, but here and there white hairs poke out, too.

The needle goes in with a searing pain. If I hadn't seen the needle sitting on the table before the procedure began, I'd swear it was a poker taken fresh from a flame, it burns so intensely. I pant with the pain, and tears well up, the tears from my right eye dripping across the bridge of my

339

nose, as I'm lying on my side.

"That's the worst of it," Dr. Kessler says, softly. Inside my chest I feel a sharp crackling that reminds me of popping corn. I close my eyes and see flashes of light behind them.

It doesn't take long. Soon Dr. Kessler extracts the needle. He sets it back on the metal table with the apparatus and pulls off his rubber gloves as he heads for the door, pushing it open with his shoulder and then disappearing into the hallway. Marcel pats my leg, then follows Dr. Kessler. I want to call after him, to ask about Mama and Opa and Astra, but I'm afraid to speak, afraid it will hurt or somehow damage the work the doctor just did.

"Just lie still, now." Nurse Ruby takes my wrist and guides my arm back down to my side, then helps me roll over onto my back. There is a sharp pain in my chest. As if she can feel it too, she says, "You'll be tender for a while." She spreads a blanket over me and goes to the head of the table I'm lying on. It's on wheels, I discover as she pushes it toward the doors. They part outward when the foot of the table pushes against them.

I stare at the ceiling tiles as we wheel down the hallway. Here and there a light flashes by. There's nothing I can do but just lie there and let Nurse Ruby push me through the hospital. I tilt my head very slightly back; there is the underside of Nurse Ruby's chin. I don't know why her chin makes me feel so vulnerable. Maybe it's that *she* seems so vulnerable, from this angle. It's a girl's chin, I think to myself. Ruby is just a girl.

Then I close my eyes. The left front wheel is wobbly, I can feel it. After a little while, we take a right turn, and then we're back in my room. Still, I keep my eyes closed.

"We're going to move you, okay?"

I nod. I feel the sheet beneath me go taut as Nurse Ruby grabs the top of it and someone else takes ahold of the foot. "One, two, three," says Nurse Rachel's voice. I am suspended as they lift the sheet and swing me off the table and onto my bed. Then they pull the sheet out from under me, tuck the blankets around me, and that's that.

"Lie still," Nurse Rachel says. "Just rest. You need to be very careful not to move."

I fall asleep. In my dream, I'm in the surgical room. Dr. Kessler has his back to me; he's adjusting the machine. I decide that I'm going to get up and leave. I'm not going to have the surgery, after all. But when I try to get up, I find that I'm already bare-chested, on my side, and Nurse Ruby is holding my wrists. Marcel is there, a hand on my hip and another on my thigh, and there's a third person—Nurse Rachel—holding my feet. My heart begins to pound with panic, and I do my best to twist this way and that, and then Nurse Ruby says, "You can't do anything about it. You might as well just lie still."

"That will make this more pleasant for everyone," agrees Nurse Rachel.

But then I realize that Nurse Ruby is not Nurse Ruby, but rather Astra wearing a nurse uniform, with Nurse Ruby's golden cross dangling from her neck, and Nurse Rachel is actually my mother, firmly grasping my feet.

Marcel is still Marcel, but when Dr. Kessler turns around from the machine and comes toward me with the shining silver probe in his hand, he isn't Dr. Kessler at all, but Mr. Weissinger dressed in a white doctor's coat, his hands disguised in black rubber gloves.

"When this is over," he says, coming with his needle, as he bends to penetrate me, as my family holds me there, captive, still, watching, "When this is all over, we will be married."

A scream gurgles up in my throat.

"Wake up, why don't you, you're having a bad dream."

My eyes flutter open. I try to sit up but there's a sharp pain in my right side. Then I remember what happened, that I'm supposed to lie still.

"You all right?"

It's Dotti, from across the room.

I nod. "Yes," I whisper. "Just a dream."

"More like a nightmare, I'd say, from the way you were thrashing about."

There's a thick lump in my throat, and I try to swallow it down. "It's okay. I can handle it."

"Well, it's just a dream."

My eyes close, and in that moment, I hear Astra, again. She's telling me that I paid in advance for anything Mr. Weissinger gives me. *"You might not have wanted to,"* she says, *"but you paid. That's the truth."*

I have paid. I have paid, already.

I'm not asleep or dreaming, but I'm not quite awake, either. I'm turned upside down, unmoored by the pain and the procedure.

I'm standing on the roof of my long-ago home, looking out at my city, at Czernowitz, spread out below like a beautiful girl on a soft bed. There is her cap, the faraway green dome of the train station. At first, I'm alone, but then pigeons begin to land, one by one, until the roof is dark with them. They peck, step closer, necks bobbing, soulless beady eyes wanting more, more, more, a great gray mass of need and desire and greed. If I don't have bread, my flesh will do. I brace myself, close my eyes, and wait for their beaks to pierce me. It will hurt. It *does* hurt, to be eaten.

But then, something happens; a feeling of peace washes over me like a great warm wave. I don't know why it comes, or where it comes from. Only that it *has* come, unbidden. And with it, this knowledge: I won't let them have me. I won't let them eat me up.

I open my eyes. There they are—sharp-beaked, beady-eyed, greedy little beasts, coming closer, closer, closer, with each neck-jutting step. I stomp my foot, loudly, powerfully, and the flock of pigeons jolts with fear, lifts up into a cloud of feathers and beaks and eyes.

I spread wide my arms, and I yell, "I will never marry George Weissinger! Never!"

The flock of pigeons turns in a mass and flies away, growing smaller and smaller. I strain my eyes to follow them, and as they disappear, I promise: it doesn't matter if he returns tomorrow or in three years. It doesn't matter if he returns with a million dollars or a giant diamond ring. George Weissinger will never be my husband.

Most likely the war will kill me. If not the war, tuberculosis. But if by some bizarre luck—yes, *luck*—I do survive, it will not be to marry that man. I will make sure of it.

The pigeons are gone. I am alone. I am at peace. I am on the roof, and I am here, too, in this hospital room. Slowly, gradually, I'm pulled away from the roof, return fully to this room, this bed, this moment.

If nothing else, I have settled one thing. One important thing. At last, I sleep. And there are no more dreams.

I wake to a gurgling sound. The thud of a palm against sheets. The rustling of legs under covers, kicking frantically. Then a glass shattering on the floor.

My eyes open to stare at the ceiling. I push myself onto my side and then up to sitting. From the hallway, light streams into our room.

In her bed, Mrs. Silver seems to still be sleeping, but Dotti—

It's Dotti who thrashes, who gurgles, whose hand had knocked the glass from her bedside table. Her eyes, wild and wide, lock with mine. Pink foam comes from her lips, and then blood—so much blood.

"Someone, help!" I throw back my covers and put my feet on the cold floor, push myself up onto them unsteadily. Shards of broken glass pierce the bare pads of my feet as I reach for Dotti, who reaches for me. Her hair, down around her face, is laced with foam and blood, the front of her nightgown is soaked with it.

"It's okay," I say, though, of course, it isn't. "It's okay."

Lights flash on as the room fills with nurses. "Back up." Nurse Rachel pushes me aside. I stumble and feel the stab of pain in my right side from the pneumothorax, feel the grinding of glass shards in the bottoms of my feet.

I press myself against the wall to make more room for the nurses.

"Massive hemoptysis," Nurse Rachel calls to another nurse who rushes into the room.

Now there are three nurses in a semicircle around Dotti's bed. It wouldn't have mattered if there were thirty. Dotti's head lolls forward, then snaps back. Blood streams in bright red rivulets down her neck, pools in the sheets, drips to the floor.

My eyes follow the trail of blood from her mouth to the bed to the floor. There, among the blood, among the glass, is Dotti's magazine. One of the nurses steps on it as she runs past, slipping on the pages slick with blood. She recovers her balance and kicks the magazine under Dotti's bed so it will be out of the way.

"It's no good." Nurse Rachel is the one who says it. Her fingers press against the vein in Dotti's neck. Dotti's body has fallen back into the pillows. Her eyes, still open, stare at me, but she can't see anything anymore.

Nurse Rachel removes her fingers from Dotti's neck. Then she turns to me. "Frederieke. You shouldn't be up." She lifts her chin to the nurse beside her. "Clean her up and get her back in bed."

I let myself be led away. I feel Dotti's body behind me. I am covered in her blood.


I spend the next two days lying flat in bed, staring up at the ceiling and thinking about Dotti. I catalogue all the things I know about her. The list is short.

She liked to read magazines.

She had tuberculosis.

She was a romantic.

She is dead.

That is all I know. Now that she's gone, I desperately wish I'd spoken with her more.

I ask Mrs. Silver, who is working on crochet, "What did you know about Dotti?"

She looks up from her work and sighs. "She liked to talk."

"What did she talk about?"

Mrs. Silver purses her lips, then shakes her head. "We're not supposed to talk."

Whatever Mrs. Silver knows about Dotti, I'll never know.

What difference would it make? Dotti is dead.

Ruth is dead.

Esther is dead, or as good as dead.

So many ways to die—tuberculosis, suicide, Nazis.

I count the holes on the ceiling tiles. I count the stars behind my eyes. I count the girls who will never be women.

# FOUR

## THE WHEELBARROW

Days in the hospital all feel the same. It's the nights that are different, each from the next.

I've heard that people tend to be born and to die in the nighttime; Mama told me that I came just after midnight. Astra, of course, made her grand entrance at two o'clock in the afternoon.

Every hospital sound is louder at night: the hum of the electric lights. The footsteps of the medical staff in the hallway. The ticking of Mrs. Silver's watch.

With nothing to do during the long and restless nights, I listen to each passing second, marked by the *tick tick tick* of her watch. And I wonder where she got the watch, if it ever needed repair, and if maybe she took the watch, in better days, to Opa's shop.

I allow myself the pleasure of imagining the scene, playing it out behind my eyes like a movie: Mrs. Silver, dressed in a fur, sweeping into Opa's shop, clutching her beloved, broken watch in one gloved hand.

"I can't believe I was so stupid," Mrs. Silver says. "I forgot about the watch and climbed straight into the bath. Can you believe it?"

"Ladies do this more often than you'd think," Opa says. He waves to her to pass the watch to him and bends his dear head over it. "I'll have it back in tick-tock shape in no time."

I don't know why it gives me pleasure to imagine Opa fixing Mrs. Silver's watch; the woman annoys me. It would make more sense for me to imagine him turning her away, refusing to help.

But that wouldn't be my opa.

As if I've called him up by magic, suddenly, there he is—in the doorway, backlit by the light from the hallway.

"Opa?"

He steps into the room. "Thank Hashem, there you are."

I struggle to sit up, but the pain in my side pins me flat. This is no dream. "What are you doing here?"

"I've come to get you out of here. To take you home."

Behind Opa is the shadow of a man. Panic surges in my chest, but then I see it's Marcel.

"Marcel?" I say. "Is everything all right?"

He grins at the ridiculousness of my question. Of course, nothing is all right. It's been years since things have been all right.

"Sorry to wake you, Rieke," he says, looking up and down the hallway. "You'll need to go with your grandfather."

"In the middle of the night? But . . . why?"

Opa reaches out his hand and takes Marcel's, shakes it. They nod to one another, faces grim. Then Marcel heads up the hallway in a hurry, and Opa comes around to the side of my bed. He finds my shoes, then pushes back the covers, frowns when he sees the bandages. "What happened to your feet, Frederieke?"

347

"Nothing. I stepped on broken glass."

"We sent you to the hospital to get cured, not broken." Leaving the bandages as they are, Opa fits my feet into the shoes. Then he reaches out his hand.

"Opa, I can't go with you. They did a procedure on me. I'm not supposed to even sit up."

"Rieke, we must go. I am sorry, but we must."

His voice is deeply serious. It frightens me. I take his hand. When he pulls me to sitting, I feel a tearing in my side. My vision goes black for a moment, then starry. But I can still breathe, and Opa seems to understand that I need to move very, very slowly.

With his help, I manage to stand. We shuffle together to the door. I'm still wearing the hospital gown. At the door to my room, Opa finds my coat on a hook and helps me into it. He leaves my dress where it hangs; it would be impossible for me to bend my arms to get into it, anyway. Then he takes his scarf from his neck and his hat from his head to bundle me.

"Careful, careful," he says, and we go slowly up the hallway to the main door.

"What about Marcel?" I whisper. "What's going on?"

"We must get you home, Rieke," he whispers back. "They're coming to clear out the hospital."

I remember what Marcel told us about other Jewish hospitals—how Nazis emptied them of their patients and killed every one.

I hurry now, going as fast as I can, but that's not very fast at all. I'm terrified that we're going to be stopped by somebody—a nurse or an orderly. I feel that we're breaking some sort of rule, that Opa and I will both be in terrible trouble if we're caught. But no one stops us. We make it to the door, and then we're outside. For a moment I have this awful fear that an alarm will sound. But nothing happens, nothing at all, except that the air is icy cold, and a wet slap of snow hits me in the face.

I inhale sharply with the shock of it, and the pain that comes with this sudden breath almost knocks me out. Thank God for Opa's arm around my waist, holding me up. It must take us five minutes to make it down the stairs to the street. Each step is a punishment, and more than once my vision tunnels to black. But when we reach the sidewalk, I know that I can go no farther.

"I'm sorry, Opa," I gasp. "I can't make it home."

He nods, leans me against a pillar. Then he clears snow to make a space on a step and lowers me to sitting. "Wait here." He heads off at a near-run.

I don't know if breathing is so painful because of the artificial pneumothorax or the exertion or the frozen air. All I know is that it *is* painful, terribly so. My feet go numb with cold, my rear end goes numb with cold, but my lungs feel full of awful fire.

After a time, I hear a squeaking noise coming from the direction Opa went.

Then, I see the strange shape of Opa bent over, pushing something. It's a wheelbarrow.

"Hashem works in mysterious ways." Opa smiles, pleased with himself. "I passed a construction site on my way here."

If I had unlimited breath, I might tell Opa that if God were working to help us at all, I could think of at least a dozen things he might do differently, things that would be more helpful than a rusty old wheelbarrow. But I don't, so I keep my mouth shut and use what energy I have instead to climb into the wheelbarrow bed. I sit down and grip the siderails; my head is between the handles and my legs swing like a child's over the far edge.

Opa grasps the wooden handles and lifts. There's a moment before he finds his balance when the wheelbarrow tilts back and forth, unsteady on its single wheel, but then he manages to get it under control.

We make a wide turn in the street and head toward home. Snow drifts down, melting on my knees and hands but settling on the cold metal of the wheelbarrow.

Nearly all the windows on both sides of the street are dark. Except for the squeak of the wheelbarrow and the crunch of Opa's footfalls on the newly fallen snow, the world is silent. I can almost pretend that we are alone in the world, the way I did all those years ago in the country.

"Opa. Do you remember that summer? The one after Father left, after we came to live with you? When we took that trip, into the mountains?"

"Oh, yes, of course," he says, panting a little.

I shouldn't make him speak; pushing the wheelbarrow is too difficult for him as it is. And I shouldn't speak either.

"Do you remember the geese? And the dog, Peter?"

"Yes, yes," Opa says, with a small laugh.

"And the bear, Opa. Do you remember the bear?"

"I do. Of course, I do."

"I wasn't scared."

"Not scared of a bear?" Opa says, each word an effort.

Each word costs me, too. "No. I wasn't scared."

It's true. Back then, when I was a child, I believed that Opa could protect me from everything. He saved me and Astra from squalor when Father and Mama abandoned us. That day with the bear, I knew Opa would save me again, and he did.

But that was a long, long time ago. Long enough ago and far enough away to be a fairy story.

"Once," I say aloud, "there was a girl in the forest who walked along a shimmering creek. She picked ripe dark berries and ate until her fingers and her lips were stained purple with their juice, until her stomach felt full and fat with their sweetness. Then, suddenly, a bear appeared. Big and black, the bear had razors for claws and knives for teeth, and it was hungry. To the beast, the girl was just a berry, ripe for the picking. But before the bear could take its taste of her, her grandfather appeared. He put himself in front of the girl, strong as a house, wide as a wall, immovable, impenetrable. Knowing he'd met his match, the bear shook its shaggy head and turned away. Then the girl and her grandfather took each other's hand; together they went out of the forest and down the hill, to live happily forever after."

I fall silent. My chest hurts, from speaking. The only sounds are Opa's labored breaths, the rusty wheel of the wheelbarrow, and the hush of the snow.

Believing that story gave me comfort when I was young. But that was long ago, and I was a different girl. I'm older now and know the truth of things. Still, when I speak next, I say, "I wasn't scared of that bear. Because I knew, Opa—I knew that you would keep me safe from it."

This is what I actually know: the only thing Opa wants in the world is to protect me, to protect us. How can I let him think that he has failed?

"Well," says Opa. The wheelbarrow hits a bump, and I'm thrown in the bed, and there's a moment when I fear I'll find myself on the ground. But once again, Opa manages to keep it upright. "I don't know if I would have been able to save you from that bear, Rieke, if it had decided to eat you for lunch. But I do know that it would have eaten me first. All right?"

This is a gift I can give to Opa: I can let him believe in a story I know isn't true. I reach back. There is Opa's hand, cold on the wooden handle.

"All right," I say.

We are alone. In all the world, in all the stories, in all the time that has been and is to come, right now, with my hand upon Opa's as he pushes me through the snow, there is just us, and this moment. Opa, and me, together. It's cold—desperately cold—and it's dark—terribly dark—and yet, I am shot through with a feeling I have never experienced before. My body comes alive with it. Time disappears, space collapses and expands. It's as if the sky opens and a bolt of lightning reaches down and stretches its finger straight to my heart, filling me with pure electric light.

Opa would say that this is God.

I believe that this is love.

At last, at last, we reach our building. With a grunt, Opa sets down the wheelbarrow. He puts a hand to his back as he comes and pulls me to standing. Clutching each other, we wobble side to side. Then, we find our footing. Still, we hold on to one another.

Up above, in our apartment, the kerosene lamp glows as if to guide us home. Mama and Astra stand in the window, watching for us, and when they see that we've arrived, they disappear from the window to come downstairs.

I'm still wearing Opa's hat, so my head is protected from the falling snow, but Opa's head is bare but for his skullcap. The hair that pokes out around it is the same color as the snow that falls. When did that happen? When had his hair gone completely white? When had the skin around his eyes, behind his glasses, become so deeply webbed with lines?

A snowflake falls on Opa's cheek. I reach and wipe it away, leaving a trail like a tear.

"Opa."

His hand, big and rough like a bear's but with no claws, no malice, only love, comes up to cup mine. "Okay," he says, patting my hand. "Okay."

The building's door bursts open and then Mama and Astra are here, nightgowns underneath their coats. Mama's coat is misbuttoned, and Astra's collar is shoved inside the neck of hers.

"Oh, thank God!" Mama pulls me into her arms.

"Gentle," I say, but she doesn't hear me through the sound of her own cries, and she rocks me back and forth.

"Mama." Astra slaps Mama's hand away from me. "She said 'gentle.' Be careful with her."

Mama lets go as suddenly as she'd grabbed me, and I stumble backward. But even though it hurts, it makes me laugh, for I am so glad to be here, home, with them all.

"Get her upstairs, get her warm," Opa says.

Mama takes my right arm, Astra takes my left, and together we go slowly up the steps.

"I had a procedure," I say to explain my slow, broken pace.

"Oh, we know," Astra says. "Marcel told us all about it."

From the bottom of the steps, Opa says, "Turn on the kettle. I'm going to return the wheelbarrow."

One hand on the door pull, Mama says, "Oh, Papa, just leave it there, for God's sake. Come upstairs before you catch your death."

But Opa waves her off. "A person has to have a moral code. If not, what is a person?"

I turn to Opa and toss his hat down the steps. It hurts to do so, but that doesn't matter. He catches the hat, pulls it firmly onto his head, and smiles at me. Then he lifts the wheelbarrow's handles.

Nothing ever looked more welcoming than our own apartment. Someone has put a log in the fireplace, and it crackles and glows. Mitzi perches on the back of the sofa, slowly blinking her light green eyes. Astra pulls a chair as close to the flames as she can, and Mama helps me out of my coat and lowers me into it. She kneels to take off my shoes and gasps when she sees blood soaking through the bandages.

I don't feel like telling them just then about Dotti and what happened, so instead I say, "It's nothing. It's fine. I just stepped on broken glass, that's all."

"We sent you to the hospital to get better, not worse," she says. Opa said nearly the same thing, which makes me laugh, but I don't have the energy to explain why.

"Oh, Mama, she's fine," says Astra. "Leave her alone."

The kettle screams and Mama goes to quiet it. Astra tucks a blanket around my legs and feet.

"Astra. Opa told me they're going to empty the hospital."

She nods and stands, goes to warm her hands by the fire. "Marcel heard a rumor yesterday morning. We didn't know if it was true or not. But then this evening, Opa's friend Mr. Strasberg broke curfew to come tell us that it's true. The hospital will be emptied tomorrow morning."

I think about Mrs. Silver, the ticking of her watch.

"Marcel took Opa to bring you home and stayed to warn the other doctors, to see how many patients they can get out of there before dawn." Astra's fingers are twitching for a cigarette.

Mama comes in from the kitchen carrying a tray with four cups and a steaming teapot. She stops to look out the window as she crosses the room. "Oh, good, here comes your opa," she says. And she's about to turn from the window when something else catches her eye. "Oh, no," she whispers.

"Mama? What is it?"

She doesn't answer. She stares, face bright with horror. The tray begins to tip, then falls with a terrible crash, cups smashing, teapot bursting apart in shards and steam and boiling water.

"Papa!" She pounds the window with her open palm.

Astra doesn't bother going to the window; she heads straight for the door. I jump up, forgetting my weakness, gasping with pain as my legs tangle in the blanket and I fall to the floor. I stumble to my feet and follow Astra down the stairs, a terrible pain in my chest.

I find her at the bottom, her body blocking the door. She has a hand on the doorframe, the other on the handle. I try to push her hand out of the way, to yank open the door, but she is stronger.

"Don't," she says. "It's too late."

She tries to turn me, to block me from seeing through the window, but I claw at her face and scream, not words, just sounds.

"Please don't look." She wraps me in her arms, pinning my hands to my sides. It hurts, to be held like this. I struggle to get free, but Astra is stronger. Astra has always been stronger. "Opa wouldn't want you to see," she says into my hair.

Even then, I struggle. At last, I break free—I don't know how—and manage to pull open the door. I half stumble, half fall, onto the stoop.

Opa lies in the street, his head on the curb as if it rests on a pillow. Two SS officers in matching uniforms, with matching caps and matching armbands, stand over him.

I cannot describe Opa's face, because it is no longer his face.

Then one of the officers—not men, for no human being would do such a thing—lifts his boot in a marching step above Opa's head. "Fucking kike," he says, and then his boot comes down.

# FIVE

## THE LOCKET

Together, Mama, Astra, and I somehow manage to get Opa upstairs and into our apartment. We lay him on the sofa and sit together, holding his hands, kissing his hands, crying into his hands, as he bleeds into the cushions. His breaths grow fainter and fainter, and by the time the sun rises, filtered gray through the clouds, he has stopped breathing entirely. Astra pulls a blanket over his broken face, and the three of us wail and sob together until I collapse, choking on the blood in my lungs, and have to be helped to bed. I let Astra tuck me in. She pulls an extra blanket from a chair and lays it over me.

I must faint, for suddenly I'm opening my eyes with a gasp. Astra is by the bureau, head down, her back to me. I struggle to get up, but Astra comes and sits beside me. "Shh," she says. She brushes my hair back from my temple. I can't look at her. I can't look at anything. I squeeze shut my eyes and slow my breathing, I pretend to fall asleep, and wait.

At last, Astra leaves the room.

I lie still as long as I can stand to. I hear Astra go through the apartment to rejoin Mama, whose cries echo through our apartment. Then, when I am sure they will not hear me, I sit up, throw back the blanket, and go to the bureau. I feel in the back of the drawer for the sock with the locket.

*"Listen,"* Astra had said. *"If you get in a situation that you can tell is going to be terrible—really terrible, the kind of thing that isn't worth living through—you can take this pill."*

I thought I could survive anything. I thought that I wasn't like Ruth, or her mother—I thought that I would never choose death. But this—this I don't want to survive.

With Opa's murder, the balancing scale has been broken. Any last hope of things cycling back has disappeared. Any belief I had left, in anything good—hope, humanity, God—is gone. In this moment, in my room, I know that things will never be fixed, will never go back to what they once were.

I take the sock back to my bed. I sit. Slowly, I unfold it. There is the necklace. I pour it out into my hand. The chain pools there, cool and soothing against my palm. Fingers steady, I wedge open the locket with my thumbnail.

But save for the photographs, the locket is empty.

All this time, I've had the pill and not wanted it. Now, I need it, and it's gone.

*"You can actually survive a lot worse than you'd think,"* Astra once said.

With the last of my strength, I throw the locket at the wall.

I don't know how many days pass. I lie in bed, at first unable to eat and drink, and later, refusing to.

Far away, I hear Mama, crying; Astra, yelling at Marcel; a door, slamming.

Fever rages in my body. I dream of the pneumothorax machine, of Dr. Kessler and his needle. I dream of Dotti, her mouth foaming blood. I see broken glass—the window of Opa's shop, the purple horse, the cup by Dotti's bed—all shattered—and my finger, and my foot, and my heart, pierced through. I hear Opa patting his pockets, looking for his keys. "Okay," he says. "Okay."

When I peel open my dry eyes, sometimes I am alone; sometimes, Mama is at my bed, or Astra. But I can't manage to keep my eyes open, and I don't want to.

If Astra has taken the pill from me, fine—but still, I will die. I will it to be so.

"Rieke, you must eat," I hear Mama say, and some faraway part of me feels badly for compounding her suffering . . . but not badly enough to obey. The world without Opa is not a world I want to live in. All the questions I had—about fairness, about luck, about God—they have been answered with one stomp of a boot. And I know Mama's pleas won't last much longer. We had little left of the last gift of food George Weissinger brought before I left for the hospital, and with him gone, there won't be more food for her to force on me.

It isn't that hard, to die. My body is ready to let go; it just needs my permission. Time passes; I drift in and out of consciousness. When I wake, I see the boot against Opa's temple, again and again, and so I sleep instead. There, I go further back in time. The hospital, Mr. Weissinger, the ghetto, the war—all of it drifts away. I am a child by the river. Peter is there, his red coat gleaming in sunshine. He pants and grins, and I press my palm into his warm, soft fur. Opa is there, too; his face, unbroken, turns to me and smiles.

Sleep is easy. Death will be, too. It's life—living—that is not.

Not dead yet, part of me is aware of the passage of time. Part of me feels water wetting my lips, part of me feels the weight of people taking turns sitting beside my bed. Part of me hears their prayers, but I no longer wrestle with what praying means, or if someone is listening to the prayers, for I know the answer now.

Death will come soon.

Then one day from my stupor I hear someone marching in. Something is set down with a clatter on the bedside table.

"Enough." It's Astra.

I try to roll over, away from her. But Astra puts a firm hand on my shoulder.

I try to hold myself firm, but Astra is stronger. She rolls me onto my back, and then pulls me up to sitting. I make my body a sack of bones, but still, she moves me.

It hurts, to open my eyes. They are dry and scratchy. Astra props another pillow behind my back for support. That hurts, too. It hurts to be in this body. It hurts to live.

Astra has her hair pulled back tightly at the nape of her neck, the way she used to wear it for dance. Her mouth is pale, and her eyebrows, which she usually darkens with pencil, are light. She brings a chair in from the kitchen and sets it close to my bed, then sits. I notice but do not care that her ring finger is bare.

There is a bowl of soup on the bedside table. It steams, and little pieces of pinkish-gray meat float in the broth. I have no idea where she would have gotten meat.

"I'm not hungry."

But that doesn't matter to Astra. She fills a spoon with broth. I clench my lips tightly, and my teeth behind them. She can't make me eat. I'm

359

done letting Astra push me around.

She jams the spoon against my mouth, and when I don't open it, she lets the burning broth dribble down my chin, down my neck. I gasp, and Astra takes the opportunity to shove in the spoon. It hits my front tooth with a zinging pain, but some of the broth trickles down my throat. I cough and sputter, then swallow.

Astra fills another spoonful. This time, I let her feed it to me, and she rewards my obedience by handing me a napkin. I dry my chin and neck.

The soup is hot and salty. With the fourth spoonful, she feeds me a sliver of the meat. It's oily, rubbery. In spite of myself, my stomach surges with ravenous hunger. I hate my traitorous hunger—yet still, I eat.

"Okay," says Astra when the bowl is scraped empty. She lays her hand over mine. "Okay."

# PART V

# IN THE NAME OF LOVE

### 1945

Eventually, Marcel returns home. Weeks pass before Astra speaks to him. Months pass before I am strong enough to leave my bed. And two more years pass before Romania switches allegiances yet again, this time to unite with the Allied Powers against Hitler. The Soviets have joined the Allies, too, and now their troops flood back across our borders; this time, it's the Russians' turn to chase the Germans out of the city.

Marcel tells us that word has reached him about George Weissinger. Apparently, he found himself on the wrong side of a poorly placed loan, and he was last seen on a transport to Siberia. I am apathetic to the news. It wouldn't matter if George returned; I am keeping my vow. A world away or standing in my doorway, I will never let him touch me again.

When I am finally strong enough to leave my bed, I spend my time sitting by the front window reading Opa's religious books. They are in Hebrew, so I can't understand much, but he taught me the basics of the alphabet when I was young, and if I go slowly enough I can decode a word here, there.

The members of Opa's minyan who are still alive stop by when they can to bring us food, and sometimes one of them will sit with me for a little while, helping me sound out the words. I know it goes against their practice to let a woman do this, but their love for Opa means more than that, I suppose. Anyway, they don't need to worry—I'm not reading the texts to find God. It's Opa I search for.

The closest I come to finding him is in the opening pages of his Bible, each as thin as onion skin. There, written in his own slanted hand, is the record of our family line. His father's name, his mother's name, both accompanied by birth and death dates. Opa's brother's name—Yoachim Fischmann—with a birth date and a death date, as well. Opa's name, Heinrich Fischmann, with the date of his birth, and alongside him, the name of my grandmother, Martha, who died before I was born. Underneath their names is my mother's maiden name, Anna Fischmann, alongside her birthday. Then Astra's, and then mine. Right there with God, for Opa, was us. His family.

I find a pen. Careful not to tear the fragile paper, I record the date of Opa's death. Then I close the Bible, and I feel no desire to open it, again.

In early February 1945, an announcement comes: the Russians, now in charge of our city, declare that any remaining Jews who wish to leave will be granted permits to exit the territory. They want to fill the city with Russians, and the more of us that leave, the more room it makes for them.

In my house, the others argue: should we stay, or should we go? Mama is worried that this might be some sort of trick, a ruse to get us on a train east to Siberia rather than west. Marcel says it will be better for him to stay here for a while; they need doctors badly, and there's hope at last that he might be able to be promoted, if Jews are given back citizenship and all that it entails. Astra says a fresh start is what we need, and that we should go.

They ask what I want. I look out the window down onto the street where Opa was murdered. And beyond, to the familiar view of the only city I've known, the only place I've ever wanted to call home.

"I want to leave," I say.

Still, they argue, every day, until Marcel stops coming home again. Back to Colette he's gone, he's always gone. Astra tosses her head and says that we'll apply for permits.

By April, we have them, and on the fifteenth, we go. Each of us packs just a single suitcase—we've been warned that there won't be room for much. Before we leave, I walk slowly through the apartment, from my little room at the back; through to the kitchen, where we sat as a family so many times; up the hall, past Opa's bedroom door, still shut, and Mama's, and the room Astra and I once shared; the bathroom, permanently smelling of cigarettes; and into the sitting room, the wide window from which I watched the world.

The first night we slept in this apartment, when I was very young, I promised myself that I'd never leave. And since then, I haven't—not willingly. But this does not feel like home, anymore.

Mama locks the door and then, out of habit, I suppose, slips the key into her purse.

We walk to the station, where we will board a train headed for Bucharest. Astra carries my suitcase along with hers. When I try to take it, she says, "It balances me out."

I once said the same thing to Opa. Remembering, I begin to cry. Everything makes me cry these days. For Astra, nothing does. Not even Mitzi's disappearance. When I finally emerged from my room, several months after Opa died, there was no sign of the cat.

"We had no food for her," Astra said when I asked her what had happened. "I figured she'd have a better chance catching mice on her own than being stuck with us."

This, I did not believe—that she would throw Mitzi out, and that Mitzi wouldn't come back. But then, I thought about the soup Astra fed to me. The oily pink-gray meat that floated in it. Could she have done such a thing? Such a terrible thing?

People do things for love. Sometimes, they do great things. Sometimes, terrible. Sometimes, the great and the terrible are one and the same.

We reach the station. There's a tense moment when we show our permits to a guard, but he barely even looks at them, waving us toward a freight train. Better than the cattle cars we'd once seen in this same station, but still, no seats. Astra clambers in first, finding a spot for our suitcases, then helps me and Mama climb aboard.

As morning stretches toward afternoon, we do not move. The cargo container grows more and more full, and warmer, sun pounding down on the metal box. By sunset, the train car is completely packed, yet still people try to board.

"There's no room," Astra shouts irritably at a young woman who's doing her best to clamber up. "Find another car."

"Astra?"

I narrow my eyes, raise a hand to block out the sun, so near the horizon. "Esther?"

It is her. Her hair is shorn again, peppered now with gray. Astra gives her a hand and pulls her up. We take turns embracing. I look behind Esther for Conrad. But there's nothing, no one, not even a shadow. I don't ask what has become of him. She looks at our sad little group and also says nothing.

Sometimes the only gift you can give a person is not to make them answer painful questions. Even nothing can be a gift, sometimes.

When the sun sets on our second night aboard the train, we still haven't left the station. Astra, Mama, and I arrange ourselves for sleep, Esther not far away. We sit, side by side by side, the press of strangers all around. Their bodies stink, but ours must, too. Mama's head is on Astra's shoulder, and Astra's head is on mine. Here we are again—or maybe still—the three of us.

Mama sleeps. Astra sleeps. I do not.

The door to the cargo container is open. Men with machine guns slung over shoulders walk up and down the platform. One runs the mouth of his gun along the side of the train, metal on metal, an assonant cry.

This is what I know:

Anything might happen. One of the men—any one of them—could decide to aim his machine gun into this cargo container. No one would stop him.

A Soviet official could come and revoke all our permits. Why not? Though we have permits to leave the city, we once had permits to stay, as so many did, and many of those had been revoked. Ours could be taken, without cause, without reason.

The train could pull away and take us not to Bucharest, where we want to go, but instead to Siberia, and death.

An illness could sweep through and kill us more slowly, stealing our breath or our ability to control our bowels. I have seen illness. This, too, would be no surprise.

One of the passengers on this very train could lose his marbles and go crazy with a knife. My own people, I know, are capable also of terrible things.

The sun, even—perhaps it might not rise.

But none of these things happen. What happens is this.

The sun rises. The people on the train comport themselves like humans, turning to give each other privacy for bodily functions. A mother who has milk in her breasts helps to feed the baby of another mother, who doesn't.

And then I notice—the uniformed men on the platform perk up, begin to gather in small groups, begin to share a message, one from the next. They start to move with purpose.

Maybe we will leave today, this morning, now.

I feel a sensation in my stomach so unfamiliar that at first I think it's a wave of illness. Then, I realize—it's hope.

And in that moment, there is a desperate cry from the platform: "Astra! Astra!"

My sister looks up like a cat who hears the opening of a can of fish. She pulls herself to standing, out from between Mama and me. Her hand goes to her hair, smooths it back. She is swan-necked and tall, too skinny, but still, she moves like the dancer she is as she pushes through the other passengers to reach the train's open door. She leans out.

"Astra! Astra!" comes Marcel's voice again, and then he must catch sight of her leaning from the train, for the timbre of his voice shifts. "Astra."

Mama and I press forward until we have a front-row view of the spectacle that is Astra and Marcel. There he is, that son of a bitch, his usually neat hair all a mess, his eyes red-rimmed with drink and tears. "Thank God, Astra. I thought I'd lost you."

He reaches for her waist. And Astra—my beautiful, terrible sister—she leans down, puts her hands on his shoulders, lets him take her. Marcel sets her on the platform, and he bends her across his arm, and they kiss.

The train erupts in applause. Everyone desperately needs something to cheer about, and it's as if Astra and Marcel are on a stage and this is the end of some beautiful performance. People whistle and clap and men wave their hats and women laugh and even little children jump up and down, though they have no real sense of what is going on.

"Astra, my wife, my love."

The train screams a whistle—a sharp, high blast.

"Astra," Marcel says, "you can't leave—not now."

"Astra." I stretch my hand down to her, out of the train car. "Come on. The train is going to leave." But even as I say the words, even as I reach my hand, I know what will happen.

Because the thing about Astra, the thing that has always been true about Astra, the thing that makes Astra *Astra*, is that she does exactly as she pleases. And what pleases Astra now is to stay. Is Marcel.

Astra tells Mama, "Hand down our things. We can leave later. Another time."

Mama does as she asks, passing down first Astra's bag, then her own, and then letting Marcel take her out of the train car. He swings her around like she is a young woman, and she even laughs a little.

Then, my mother says, "Rieke, come. We'll go with your sister."

They turn to me and reach for my bag, for my hand.

These three people—life and war have married us, one to the next. But this—this is Astra's life. Must it be mine?

It hurts too much to look at their faces. I let my gaze drift up, soften, see past them. There is the train station. Beyond it is my city. My ruined, broken city.

The train screams again.

I am with Opa. We are by the river, my mouth is full of sweetness.

369

There is no bear; there is just the two of us. Opa turns to me and smiles. And he says, *"We can love more persistently than they can hate."*

Can we? Can *I*?

What is it—love? Does love mean staying, following, obeying? Or is it—could it be—that love might mean accepting when one thing has ended, and allowing something new to begin? Seeing a chance at a life, and taking it?

*"That is what we are here to do, my girl. To build, with love."*

This is what I know to be true: in many ways, the war has broken me. It has filled me full of illness, and hunger, and fear, and death. I have so many reasons to hate. And I *do* hate—I do.

And yet.

One more loud scream, and the screech of metal wheels on metal tracks, and the train begins to roll slowly away from the station. I feel a tearing deep inside.

My sister runs alongside the train. Mama and Marcel stand, frozen, behind.

"Frederieke!" Astra calls, astonished.

I lean out. I raise my hand.

Astra slows, then stops, one hand across her stomach. The other, she raises, a mirror to mine, fingers splayed apart. And then, she waves. She waves, and she smiles, and she laughs, a wide, open-mouthed laugh, the laugh I love her for.

I laugh, too. I laugh, and I cry, and I wave goodbye. To Mama and Marcel, to Astra, to the city I loved. To Opa.

The wind pushes my hair in my eyes, and I let it, and the train goes faster and faster, and the world becomes a blur of green and blue and brown and red.

For a long time, choices were made for me by others. By my family. By the Romanians, the Russians, the Germans. By George Weissinger. By war. Antisemitism. Illness. Hate. My world grew smaller, and darker, until the light almost went out. For a while, I even wanted it to.

I didn't expect to survive any of this. I didn't *deserve* to, more than Ruth, or Conrad, or Dotti, or Opa, or any of the millions of others who did not survive. And yet, here I am—here, in this moment, moving in a direction, for better or worse, of my own choosing.

I turn in that direction, and the wind almost knocks me off my feet. My hair blows back like wings. Behind me lies my city, and my family, and the whole history of my life.

I did not expect to survive any of this. But here I am. Shell-shocked. Traumatized. Empty. Broken, in nearly every way.

But I did survive. I am alive, somehow.

And so, I must live.

# AUTHOR'S NOTE

*Everything has a name . . . And names are very important. Can you think of something that exists that doesn't have a name? And darling, everything has a past. Everything—a person, an object, a word—everything. If you don't know the past, you can't understand the present and plan properly for the future. We are going to build a new world . . . How can we avoid the past?*

*—Chaim Potok, Davita's Harp*

My job, as a writer of fiction, is to tell a good story. But as I set to work crafting *The Blood Years*, I knew that with this book I had the duty and the privilege of telling the emotional truth of a terrible time while honoring and respecting the people who suffered, endured, and often died during the Holocaust. I needed to find a way to not sensationalize real pain in service of my fiction . . . while still crafting a fictional narrative to string together what I knew about the teenage years of the real Frieda Teitler, my grandmother.

Imagine that someone gives you a precious plate, and it shatters. Now imagine dropping that plate into the shards of six million shattered plates, some radically different from your plate, some nearly identical.

Can you ever put the plate you were given together again? Most likely, no. But what you can do is sift gently and delicately and reverently through the shards, finding as many of the pieces of your plate as you can, and collecting other sharp-edged, beautiful, terrible pieces as well. And then you can take all these pieces and sit with them for many years, and then do your very best to make something with them—a mosaic. A piece of art that honors the original plate, even if it cannot be salvaged, that finds a way to make art from so many broken, priceless things.

That's what writing this book felt like. It's my nana's story, but it's not hers alone. It's also a tribute to the other Czernowitzers who endured the Holocaust and the pogroms before—and to all those who perished.

Many of the core events of my grandmother Frieda's young life have been included in *The Blood Years*. Among other truths, my grandmother really was born after her mother was advised to have another child to be a playmate and distraction for her older sister, Astrid. Her father abandoned the family when Frieda was young, and from then on, she, her mother, and sister lived with Heinrich Fischmann, her maternal grandfather. On a summer trip to the Carpathian mountains, Frieda and Astrid were chased by geese, and during their youth, both sisters were avid dancers. When her first period came, my nana did truly believe she was dying, as her mother hadn't prepared her to understand what was happening with her body. Ruth did join the Moiseyev dancers, and she did end her life when her lover returned to his wife and children after the Russians lost their grip on the region.

Antisemitism did cause Heinrich Fischmann to leave his jewelry and repair shop, Frieda's favorite place to spend time; Frieda and her family were forced into a ghetto; she was serially raped by a much older family acquaintance who paid for her tuberculosis treatment; her grandfather truly did cart her home in a wheelbarrow before the hospital was emptied, the patients killed; she witnessed her grandfather's murder at the hands of Nazi soldiers outside their home.

Finally, my nana really did leave on that train, her sister and mother choosing at the last minute to stay behind with Astrid's philandering husband. As for what happened after the train pulled out of the station... well, that's another story.

I could make a much longer list of all the "true" events in *The Blood Years*, but of course, a work of historical fiction includes both history and fiction. When I was filling in gaps, I did my best to lean on accounts from other survivors, though I fictionalized them. It was important to me to honor the real, lived trauma of those who lived through and perished during these terrible years, and so whenever I could, I hewed closely to facts.

The war years in Czernowitz, Romania, and the fate of its Jewish population have not been extensively written about. I read everything I could get my hands on—memoirs of Czernowitzers who made it out alive; fiction and poetry written about the time and place, authored by survivors; doctoral dissertations that focus on this region and time; scholarly texts about the long history of violence against Jews in Romania; and more. Please spend some time with the reading list included after this author's note; it includes the books and websites that formed the backbone of my research.

I'll especially draw your attention to *Ruth's Journey: A Survivor's Memoir* by Ruth Glasberg Gold. After I read this astonishing book, I immediately wrote to its author. To my surprise and eternal gratitude, she responded. When I first heard Ruth's voice, I was overcome. Just like my grandmother, Ruth has a particular accent—different, I believe, from anyone other than Czernowitzers of their generation, who were compelled to learn Romanian, Ruthenian, and Russian in quick succession, layered over their German and Yiddish. Hearing her voice was like reuniting with a part of my beloved nana.

Over the past several years, Ruth has read and critiqued my manuscript, answered hundreds of questions, and has become my dear friend . . . even more than that—found family.

On the topic of family: you will find at the end of this book some photographs of the real people who inspired this story: Frieda, Astrid, Anna, and Alfred Teitler, and Heinrich Fischmann.

*The Blood Years* is a love story to family in all its complexity, and an interrogation into questions around duty and faith. And it's an invitation to *you*, dear reader. A double-pronged invitation. First, look back—at history, at what came before. Some people lie about the Holocaust, downplaying its terrors or even outright denying its existence. Others oversimplify the complex tragedy or couch it in simplistic terms. An example—the Holocaust is often discussed solely through the lens of "religious persecution." This flattens the complexities and misunderstands why Jews were (and often are) the target of so much hate. It wasn't simply that Jews follow a different religious belief than Christians—after all, not all Jews are religious. Believing or non-believing, *all* Jews were marked for persecution and death. Nazi ideology (and the prevailing ideology in Romania even before their collaboration with Nazis) was a continuation of an old and deep antisemitic tradition. Long before Hitler came to power, anti-Jewish rhetoric painted Jews as grasping, greedy, pestilence-spreading, and of a "different race" than non-Jewish people. Jews have been accused of being children of the devil (indeed, several children during my childhood asked if they could see *my* horns); being collectively responsible for the death of Jesus; ritually killing gentiles (non-Jews); being lecherous, greedy, and money-grubbing; poisoning communal wells and purposefully desecrating Christian religious symbols; carrying and spreading disease (the term "dirty Jew" was a favorite slur of a group of boys in my high school); and many other terrible things. For hundreds of years before Hitler's rise to power, the dehumanizing and "othering" of Jews led to many, many organized massacres—called pogroms—across Eastern Europe. Adolf Hitler was not the source of anti-Jewish hate; he channeled it, organized it, and unified it.

Jews were targeted *in part* for their religious beliefs, but to focus only on that persecution denies and erases the larger efforts toward "annihilation of the Jewish *race* in Europe" (Hitler speech in January 1939, italics mine).

So: the first part of my invitation to you is to look back. History is incredibly rich, interesting, distressing, terrible, and wonderful. It's worth your time and attention. Learn about the larger past, and dig into your own family's past, as well. Your elders are full of stories, many of which they would love to share with you if you open the door to them to do so.

The second prong of my invitation is this: Look around. Pay attention. Notice things. Life is beautiful and important and worth living . . . but that doesn't preclude the ugliness, the selfishness, and the hate that exists, too. It's imperative that we don't choose, as Astra says to Rieke, to be "stupid, on purpose." Antisemitism was not defeated in 1945 when Nazi Germany fell. In 2017, white supremacists chanted "Jews will not replace us" as they rallied in Charlottesville, Virginia. Symbols of antisemitism, including a sweatshirt emblazoned with "Camp Auschwitz" and the phrase "work brings freedom" (which was a translation of the Auschwitz motto "Arbeit macht frei") was worn by a rioter who stormed the United States Capitol during the 2021 insurrection; others wore shirts that read "6MWE," which meant to indicate that six million Jews were not enough to die during the Holocaust. In the United States, white supremacists see Jewish people, Black people, Indigenous people, Asian people, Latinx and Hispanic people, Muslim people, LGBTQIA+ people, immigrants, and multiracial people as their enemies. Though *The Blood Years* is a historical novel, antisemitism and hate are not problems relegated to the past. It's imperative that we pay attention and look around. What's happening in your country, your community, your family, *today*? Where do you stand? What do you stand for?

This is what I know: it is easier to destroy than to create. A whole fleet of kids can work for hours to build a castle in the sand, and one bully can destroy their creation with a few swift kicks. It can feel like your heart is being torn out of your body when something like that happens. But does this mean that we should not build, should not dream? No. I tell you—No! You can choose each day—each moment—to soften, to listen, to wonder, and to grow. Your capacity for love—whether or not you are Jewish—can be stronger than their capacity to hate. I truly believe that this is true. There are more of us who want to build than those who wish to destroy. And we are stronger when we are passionate, informed, and united.

Together—let's build the world, with love.

*Anna, Astrid, and Frieda Teitler*

*Heinrich Fischmann*

*Frieda Teitler as a young girl*

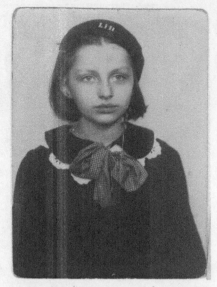

*Astrid Teitler as a young girl*

*Frieda Teitler as a teenager*

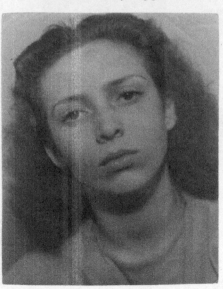

*Astrid Teitler as a teenager*

*Frieda Teitler as a young woman, shortly after the war*

*Astrid Teitler as a young woman, shortly after the war*

# READING LIST

## TEXTS:

Appelfeld, Aharon. *All Whom I Have Loved*. Schocken Books, 2007. (Originally published in Israel as *Kol Asher Ahavti*, Keter Publishing House Ltd., 1999.)

Appelfeld, Aharon. *The Story of A Life*. Schocken Books, 2004. (Originally published in Israel as *Sipur Hayim*, Keter Publishing House Ltd., 1999.)

Ausländer, Rose. *While I Am Drawing Breath*. ARC Publications, 2014.

Bartov, Omer. *Anatomy of a Genocide: The Life and Death of a Town Called Buczacz*. Simon & Schuster, 2019.

Beradt, Charlotte. *The Third Reich of Dreams: The Nightmares of a Nation 1933–1939*. Quadrangle Books, 1968.

Blum, Martha. *The Walnut Tree*. Coteau Books, 1999.

Fichman, Pearl. *Before Memories Fade*. Booksurge, LLC, 1989.

Frunchak, Svetlana. *The Making of Soviet Chernivtsi: National "Reunification," World War II, and the Fate of Jewish Czernowitz in Postwar Ukraine.* A thesis submitted in conformity with the requirements for the degree of Doctor of Philosophy in the Graduate Department of History at the University of Toronto, 2014.

Gold, Ruth Glasberg. *Ruth's Journey: A Survivor's Memoir.* University of Florida Press, 1996.

Hirsch, Marianne & Leo Spitzer. *Ghosts of Home: The Afterlife of Czernowitz in Jewish Memory.* University of California Press, 2010.

Kelso, Michelle L. *Recognizing the Roma: A Study of the Holocaust as Viewed in Romania.* A dissertation submitted in partial fulfillment of the requirements for the degree of Doctor of Philosophy (Sociology) in the University of Michigan, 2010.

Marin, Irina. *Peasant Violence and Antisemitism in Early Twentieth-Century Eastern Europe.* Palgrave Macmillan, 2018.

Ravel, Adit. *A Boy Is Not A Bird.* Groundwood Books/House of Anansi Press, 2019.

Rosenthal, Bianca. *From Czernowitz to the German Order of Merit: A Memoir of Cultural History and Autobiography.* Graphic Communication Institute at Cal Poly, 2015.
Schultz, Bruno. *The Street of Crocodiles.* Walker and Company, 1963. (Originally published in Poland with the title *Cinnamon Shops*, 1934.)

Sebastian, Mihail. *Journal 1935–1944: The Fascist Years.* Rowman & Littlefield, 1998.

Van de Velde, M.D., TH. H. *Ideal Marriage: Its Physiology and Technique.* Random House, 1930.

Wallach, Kerry. *Passing Illusions: Jewish Visibility in Weimar, Germany.* University of Michigan Press, 2017.

# WEBSITES:

History of Jews in Bukowina: https://www.jewishgen.org/yizkor/bukowinabook/buk1_129.html

Interview: International Poetry Festival Capitalizes on the "Secret" of Czernowitz: https://www.rferl.org/a/Interview_Seeing_Czernowitz_As_A_Retrospective_Utopia/2148482.html

Jewish Telegraphic Agency: https://www.jta.org/archive/only-one-third-of-czernowitz-80000-jews-remain-alive-russian-correspondent-reports (copy of original newsprint here: http://pdfs.jta.org/1944/1944-06-21_142.pdf?_ga=2.197417455.1198097131.1665344874-1712152727.1665344874)

Jewish Virtual Library, A Project of AICE: https://www.jewishvirtuallibrary.org/traian-popovici-and-the-jews-of-czernowitz

JGuide Europe: The Cultural Guide to Jewish Europe: https://jguideeurope.org/en/region/ukraine/eastern-galicia-podolia-and-bukovina/chernivtsy-czernowitz/

Joy of Movement, Ballet Class Structure: https://www.joyofmovement.de/2018/03/ballet-class-structure/

Museum of Tolerance, Timeline of the Holocaust: https://www.museumoftolerance.com/education/teacher-resources/holocaust-resources/timeline-of-the-holocaust.html

National Library of Medicine. Tuberculosis sanatorium regimen in the 1940s: a patient's personal diary: https://www.ncbi.nlm.nih.gov/pmc/articles/PMC1079536/

*Tablet* magazine article, "A Last Conversation with Aharon Appelfeld": https://www.tabletmag.com/sections/arts-letters/articles/last-conversation-aharon-appelfeld

*Tablet* magazine article, "Everything is Regurgitated: Living Off Jewish Memory in Old Czernowitz, Once the Jerusalem of Ukraine" by Vladislav Davidzon: https://www.tabletmag.com/sections/arts-letters/articles/everything-is-regurgitated

The Czernowitz-L discussion group: http://czernowitz.ehpes.com/index.html

The Holocaust in Romania: https://roholocaust.com/the-holocaust-in-romania

The Museum of Family History: "Town with a Past": https://www.museumoffamilyhistory.com/czernowitz.htm

The Museum of Family History Interview with Nathan Getzler, "The Jewish Ghetto":
https://www.museumoffamilyhistory.com/ce/ghetto/czernowitz.htm

The Museum of Family History Interview with Rosi Gruber-Feuerstein, "Czernowitz, My Dream": https://www.museumoffamilyhistory.com/czernowitz-home-hb.htm

United States Holocaust Memorial Museum Archives, "Selected Records Related to A.C. Cuza and the National Christian Party": https://docslib.org/doc/371674/selected-records-related-to-a-c-cuza-and-the-national-christian-party-rg-25-059m

United States Holocaust Memorial Museum: www.ushmm.org

United States Holocaust Memorial Museum, Adolf Hitler Issues Comment on the "Jewish Question": https://www.ushmm.org/learn/timeline-of-events/before-1933/adolf-hitler-issues-comment-on-the-jewish-question

USC Shoah Foundation, The Institute for Visual History and Education: https://sfi.usc.edu/collections/holocaust

Yad Vashem, The World Holocaust Remembrance Center: https://
www.yadvashem.org

# ACKNOWLEDGMENTS

First, of course, I am so grateful to Frieda Kuczynski, née Teitler—my nana—for entrusting me with her stories. I'm indebted also to those who have contributed to the collective memory of what happened in Czernowitz, Romania, before and during World War II. Many of their books are shared in the reading list.

I owe a special debt to Ruth Glasberg Gold who, like my nana, is a survivor from Czernowitz. Ruth served as an early reader, correcting many of my historical and cultural errors, though any that persist are entirely my own.

So many dear friends have patiently read many drafts of this book. I'm deeply beholden to: Natalie Blitt; Martha Brockenbrough; Tess Canfield; Sara Crowe; Nina LaCour; Mary Rockcastle; Laura Ruby; Eliot Schrefer; Laurel Snyder; and Francisco X. Stork.

My sisters Mischa and Sasha Kuczynski have also been integral to the creation of *The Blood Years* and they, along with our brother Zak, share the inheritance of Nana's rich love of story, as well as the obligation to keep her memory alive.

Thanks go as well to Rubin Pfeffer for his early belief in this complicated project, and in me. I love you.

Jordan Brown, my editor—how can I thank you for your commitment to this most precious story? You were willing to tell me things that were hard for me to hear, and your stewardship and care show on every page of this book. Truly, I could not have done this without you.

To all the wonderful folks at Balzer & Bray/HarperCollins who've shepherded this book into its final form, including Donna Bray, Alessandra Balzer, Julia Tyler, Jenna Stempel-Lobell, Alison Donalty, Audrey Diestelkamp, Patty Rosati, Mimi Rankin, Lauren Levite, Jessica Berg, Gwen Morton, Josh Weiss, Megan Petitt, Alison Brown, Andrea Pappenheimer, Kerry Moynagh, Kathy Faber, and Suzanne Murphy, as well as Leo Nikkols for his inspired cover art, I tip my hat in gratitude.

And, of course, I must acknowledge my husband Keith, who has listened to me talk about this book for the past ten years, always with a kind and gentle ear.

Last, and most importantly—my children, Max and Davis, and my niece Alice and nephews Sam and Henry: you inherit Nana's story. Please, remember it, and share it.

*Frieda Kuczynski, née Teitler, later in life*